Red and Grey

Red and Grey

Christine Brant

Dark Dragon Publishing
Toronto, Ontario, Canada

Red and Grey

ISBN: 978-0-9879726-6-8
eISBN: 978-0-9879726-7-5

Cover Illustration © by Paula Stirland
http://hatefueled.deviantart.com

Dark Dragon Publishing
313 Mutual Street
Toronto, Ontario
M4Y 1X6
CANADA
www.darkdragonpublishing.com

Printed in the United States of America.

For more information on Christine Brant

www.christinebrant.com

For my two very best friends, Jason and Rachel, I love you both.
I could not have done this without you.

Acknowledgements

I will begin with thanking my husband, Jason, and sister, Rachel. Nothing I write would be as well thought out without their input.

Many thanks to Tyner Gillies, an incredible story-teller, for motivating me through his blogs and his writing. To the author who I look to for continued inspiration, Kelley Armstrong, thank you for taking a few minutes to listen to my story at the SiWC.

I would be remiss without mentioning Peggy King Anderson. During a workshop she asked us to consider Little Red Riding Hood from the wolf's point-of-view and I first began to ponder Grey's story.

I must thank all the people who coordinate and attend the Surrey International Writers Conference each year. I would particularly like to thank, kc dyer, for all her advice and time. It is priceless and helps shape my stories. I would also like to thank Kathy Chung for coordinating such a wonderful conference. Without the SiWC I would not be the writer I am.

I owe a great debt of thanks to David Colbert, my first editor. Without you Red and Grey would never have made it past the vomit on paper stage. Thank you Karen Dales, my amazing editor at Dark Dragon Publishing.

Finally, I would like to thank some of my earliest readers who saw potential and encouraged me to keep going, Mark Scott, Deb Gorski, Michelle Lisenbee, Mary LaCount, Amy Nelsen, and Arlene Vradenburg, your words of support and encouragement were priceless.

To everyone I don't have the space to name here, thank you, it has been said that it takes a village to raise a child. The same can be said for a story raised into a book.

1

Connor

Connor nocked the arrow in his bow. He could see the wolf in front of him. Wet red blood stained its side slick against the beast's black, matted fur. The wound Connor inflicted earlier was not fatal, but it had allowed the hunters to trail the beast throughout the day.

Connor crept closer. His body crouched low under the cover of the bush's new growth. The wolf turned. Connor froze, and wondered what he had done to alert the animal to his presence. He stayed downwind and had made no noise. Despite that, the wolf seemed to have sensed him. Dark gold eyes stared directly into Connor's, holding his gaze.

His fingers ached as his knuckles whitened on the bow. He fought to ignore the surge of energy and emotion that tried to surface. Something in those eyes seemed familiar. Of course that was impossible.

The wolf did not run, did not snarl, and did not move at all. It just stared into his eyes for several heartbeats.

Then, the wolf's whine invaded the woods around him, silencing the other creatures in the forest, its tail swished back and forth once. Connor lifted the bow, taking aim. Why didn't it run? It didn't matter; he would end this hunt.

Connor pulled the string taut and prepared himself. His arm trembled, and the bow slipped in his sweat damp fingers. What was wrong with him? He never reacted to a hunt with this deep sense of dread. Killing this wolf would be a mistake.

The wolf blinked, its ears pivoted forward, and its head tipped to the side. An unexpected intelligence flashed in the animal's golden eyes. All Connor needed to do was let the arrow fly.

He lowered the bow.

He couldn't do it. Every instinct he possessed told him this was wrong.

A noise from the left drew his gaze. Connor's chest tightened. He wanted to shout for the wolf to run. His older brother loosed an arrow. Connor turned back to the wolf. The animal met his look as the arrow embedded itself in its chest.

Connor sucked in a breath as the wolf stumbled sideways and fell to the ground. His lungs aching with the wolf's, he watched it struggle to draw its final breath. The spark faded from the golden gaze.

The unnaturally quiet forest held Connor in its grip, and hot pain spread through his gut. Hearing his brother shout to the other hunters that he had killed the prey, the fear of being found like this forced Connor into action.

Standing on shaky legs, Connor coached his face into a disinterested expression. His brother and cousin emerged from the forest. He clenched his hands into fists to hide any evidence they shook.

"Beat you again, little brother," Daniel said, hitting his shoulder.

Connor ignored his brother and continued toward the wolf.

"What's wrong with Connor?" his father demanded.

Connor squatted near the wolf's body and examined it, keeping his back to the other men. "Nothing. I'm fine, father."

His father grunted in response and the rest of the hunting party arrived.

"He wasn't eating well, looks half starved. That's probably

why he killed Eric," said Connor. He tilted his head, his gaze roving over the animal's thin body. His vision blurred and lost focus as he gazed at its face, its vacant eyes still open. For an instant he saw Eric's brilliant blue eyes looking up at him.

"Don't matter why he did it, boy. Only that he did, and now he's dead."

His father's gruff voice dragged him back to reality and Connor shook his head and ran a hand over his face. He rose and nodded.

By the time Connor arrived home he almost talked himself into forgetting what he felt and what he saw in the woods. He sighed as he entered the house. Minna looked up from the stove.

"Have you washed?" asked his brother's wife.

"Yes, Minna, I washed at the well."

She grunted. "How was the hunt?"

"We killed the wolf," Connor said, unable to force the words 'it went well' from his mouth. "Daniel's arrow took it down."

Minna grunted again and returned to whatever she was doing. Connor moved further into the darkened house, toward his mother's rocking chair. The air inside was too warm, it made him long for the, cool spring breeze of the forest, and the sun against his skin. Connor knelt as he reached his mother's side.

"Hello, mother." He smiled, hoping she would recognize him today, perhaps talk to him for a few minutes.

"Daniel, you're home." She sounded pleased.

"That's Connor, Old Mother, not my Daniel," Minna snapped from the stove.

His mother sat silent for a moment and Connor thought she forgot he was beside her. Then she looked over at him eyes wide and bright. When she spoke, her voice was almost a whisper. "Mr. Grey, no one told me we were having such an important guest. I would have gotten ready."

Reaching up she patted her hair. Connor's chest tightened, he wanted to get up and leave but she was talking to him, and anything was better than nothing.

"No, mother, it's me, your son, Connor."

"Of course you're my son." She smiled a warm smile, the kind she used to give him when she made cookies for him as a child. "Now, you must remember, when they ask you the difficult questions that the correct answer is always love. Your father and Minna wouldn't tell you that. Neither would your brother, even though he's a good boy, but you, Connor Grey, you know the truth."

Connor's fingers flexed on the arm of his mother's chair, changing the pattern of its squeak as the door opened and Daniel and his father entered.

Minna turned toward Connor. "What's wrong with your mother?"

"She's just mumbling nonsense. I think she's about to have a bad spell," Connor said, releasing the chair and straightening from the ground.

He sighed. She was speaking in riddles and calling him the wrong name. Before he could step away from the chair she caught his arm and tugged his sleeve. Connor squatted back next to her chair.

"Don't forget, Connor. I love you." She grasped his hand tight, her eyes dark with concern. "Never forget. Promise me."

"I promise, mother. I love you, too." He leaned forward and kissed her cheek. That at least he could give her.

She smiled, released him and went back to her rocking.

"What happened out there, Connor? You got to the wolf first and far as I can tell, you had a clear shot." Daniel asked.

Connor shrugged. "Not my day I guess."

"When's it going be your day, boy?" his father demanded. "That's the same line you pulled when that little brunette from the other side of town didn't want to marry you."

Connor ran a hand through his hair. "I'll let you know when it happens."

Connor glared at his father, only the sound of the fire cracking and popping dared break the silence that hung thick and tense in the air. Daniel inched toward Connor, and Connor knew his brother would shield him from his father's wrath in any way he could. Even his mother stopped rocking.

To everyone's surprise, his mother broke the silence. "When

Connor's day comes, it will be glorious. But, sadly, we won't be there to see it, Benjamin."

The tension evaporated as Minna snorted. "You're right, Connor, she is about to have a bad spell."

Connor nodded and turned to walk to his room.

2

Connor

Pounding dragged Connor from sleep the next morning. Dark dreams of golden wolf eyes haunted his sleep and woke him often during the previous night.

"Connor, get up," his father demanded from the other side of his door.

Connor stumbled out of his tangled sheets and opened his door.

His father stood tapping his foot. "Your mother is worse. She needs medicine. Go fetch it."

"Of course, Father." Connor tried to ignore the chill that raced up his bare back. He knew it had little to do with the cool spring air. Getting his mother's medicine meant a visit to the witch woman's house.

An adult and an apprentice blacksmith, the witch should not terrify him the way she did. The sun was not yet above the horizon when Connor left the house, but the sky was no longer black. Instead, the air seemed almost grey, shifting into lighter shades while he walked, as if the sunlight filtered through the remaining bits of night.

Leaving the town center, Connor passed more homes with dark windows and doors still closed, no doubt barred. He continued through the cobbled street on his way out of town. The witch lived beyond the town limits. Her house sat back off the dirt road, close to the woods on the mountain side. She was not far from where they had hunted the wolf. People claimed she could bless or curse a person at will and paid her quite well to buy her spells.

Connor remembered hiding behind his mother's skirt the first time he met the witch. Both women had laughed, calling him shy. In his mind, since that day, the town had started to change. It became a darker, heavier place. People stopped trusting each other, helping each other, and caring for each other, unless they had something to gain. More people got sick, more children died. He tried to tell people, but they laughed at his fears, or worse. He learned soon enough to hold his tongue.

Connor tapped on the witch's door.

It opened too quickly, as if she knew someone was coming.

Her face twisted into a smile when she saw him. He clenched his hands and forced himself to stand straighter, meeting her pale green eyes. He hated her eyes and met them only when he had to. They made his head hurt.

"Connor, is your mother having an episode, child?" Her, head tilted to the side and her eyes roamed over his body, the look calculated. "But not so much a child anymore."

"Yes, ma'am." Connor had no idea what to say to the woman. He did not like the way her gaze sized him up.

"Come in, boy. No reason to stand outside." Connor hesitated, but she motioned him in again. "You need to come in. It will take me a few moments to get the herbs together for your mother's medicine."

Connor shuffled inside the doorway, jamming his hands into the pockets of his pants. From here he surveyed the warm and cluttered main room. Herbs hung from the rafters and dried on the walls. Some he recognized; others were foreign. The witch walked over to the burning hearth. Her movements were light and quick. How did she escape the aches of age he saw in so many others? More imagination, more theories his family would no doubt find either amusing, or irritating.

"Well, don't hover in the doorway; come sit down at the table. I'll give you a cup of tea."

"No, thank you, ma'am. I'm fine." He tried to keep his voice polite, but he could hear the rough edge to it.

"Would you refuse my hospitality?" Her tone chilled him. "After all I've done for your mother. Would you truly offend me so?"

Connor walked from the doorway to the table. He could not risk the witch refusing to make more medicine for Mother. He sat on the edge of one of the rough wooden chairs. It wobbled with his weight. Looking down at the grain of the table, he focused his attention there.

"That's better. I thought you must have some manners." She placed a mug of steaming liquid in front of him. "Drink up."

Connor lifted the mug and smelled the brew. The translucent golden brown tea, mixed with honey, met his nostrils. The color and scent seemed harmless. He took a small sip. The taste was as sweet as the smell, different from what he was used to but not unpleasant.

Another smile contorted the witch woman's face, and the look made Connor's stomach cramp in discomfort. He intended to sit the mug back on the table, but the smell rising from the liquid tempted him and he lifted it to take another drink, this one deeper. Maybe it would soothe the strange pain in his abdomen. For a moment it seemed to help.

She nodded, triumphant, and turned away from him, back to the herbs she sorted. Connor's head began to feel light and his vision swam. He blinked several times. What was wrong with his eyes?

Connor's stomach churned and he lifted the mug hoping the tea would calm it. This time the liquid seemed too thick and too sweet. It clung to his mouth and throat as it slid along his back and into his stomach.

A heavy sensation settled over Connor's body and he set the mug down before he spilled it. His head felt odd, his vision thick. With effort, he focused on the witch. A strange aura surrounded her, something he had never seen before. As if feeling his eyes on her, she turned to him, a satisfied smirk on her lips.

"The job's done. There's no going back now."

"Are the herbs ready?" Connor asked, trying to stand. His legs felt weak and he fell. His back scraped the edge of the chair as his knees hit the rough wooden floor. The witch never moved from the fire.

"Oh, your mother's herbs," she waved a dismissive hand, her voice was calm. "I suppose your father will have to send Minna for them later. His youngest can be so unreliable. Such a disappointment, Connor, his hair is too light, his eyes are too blue. Is he really even the miller's son? His brother is so much darker. And the imagination that Connor has."

Connor grasped the table edge and tried to pull himself off the floor shaking his head. "I don't understand."

The pain hit a sharp stab in the chest. Connor gasped, releasing the table, he doubled over, his breath hissed between clenched teeth.

"Yes, you'll do well. Strong, healthy, and young. Everything a protector should be." The witch muttered, turning her back on him again.

Connor fought against the pain, trying to inch his way toward the door. His arms and legs refused to obey the commands he gave them. The harder he fought, the more intense the agony became.

The pain raced from his chest to his back. It snaked up his spine and tightened, squeezing him. Connor fell from his knees onto the floor, his cheek hitting the uneven boards. They felt cool against his burning skin.

Terror followed the course of the pain, wrapping Connor in its fist. Curled in a ball on the floor, he moaned. His arms and legs twisted, joints cracked and popped. He felt fire on his skin. He cried out in panic and did not recognize the sound of his own voice. The cry was too high-pitched, more a whine.

What was happening?

He tried to stretch to ease the pain. Tried to uncurl his limbs, but they would not work the right way.

His legs bent at the wrong angles.

He opened his eyes and grey filled his vision. Trying to lift his head, he found his neck moved wrong.

What had the witch done to him?

He panted for air, past another ripple of searing pain. Yes, panted. He could feel his mouth open, his breath coming in short little gasps. His tongue hung out. Too long, it scraped his teeth, and they were too sharp.

Grey, all he saw was grey. The witch stood above him, her face contorted in a smile. The air around her seemed thick and heavy, it twisted and curled. Evil, the word filled Connor's mind and he knew that was what he saw.

The witch squatted in front of him, before he realized what she was doing, a rope slid around his neck, and she grabbed his jaw. Her fingers bit into his skin, pressing teeth too sharp to be his own painfully into his lower lip. Connor tasted blood. He felt the weight of the rope, but he couldn't feel it rubbing his skin, he should feel the fibers on his flesh.

"You're uglier than the first one, but you're smarter too, aren't you? You figured out a long time ago how things worked in this town and it cost me a great deal of effort to discredit you."

She scowled as she spoke, but then her gaze traveled over his body and her mouth twitched into a smile. "Now I have you exactly where I want you. No one is ever going to feed you but me. You will have to obey me if you want to live." She dropped his jaw and stood back up.

Connor opened his mouth to protest, the sound that emerged from his throat was a low, rough, rumble. A growl? The witch laughed and turned back to her work.

Connor rolled onto his stomach from his side. His legs, all four of them, were under him now. A spell! For a moment Connor could not breathe, could not think. Pushing himself onto his feet—four feet—he stood still. His body felt foreign. He stood too low; his head reached the top of the table. He tried to take a step but his legs did not move the way he expected them to.

Not a spell; a curse.

He needed to get home. His father would know what to do, how to fix this. He took another step, more careful this time, and the rope tightened around his neck and throat. He had forgotten the rope.

"Thinking of home?" The witch's voice cut into his thoughts. "Your family?"

Terror raced along his skin, was she reading his mind?

"Are you thinking of the father who sent you here this morning? Do you wonder why he didn't send Minna? Do you think he will help you now? Perhaps you aren't smarter than the first?"

The first? What first? Why did she keep referring to a first?

She pulled something from a shelf near the fire and tossed it to him. It was a shirt. His eyes only saw grey, but the pattern appeared familiar, it was the one Eric's family said he wore the day he disappeared.

Connor felt the horror start in his stomach and inch its way through his chest. Gold eyes flashed through his mind.

He grew up with Eric, was his friend. The memory of Eric's eyes in the wolf's face came back to him. Everyone assumed the wolf killed Eric. It showed up days after he disappeared and seemed unafraid of humans, not the way a wolf should be.

Revulsion gripped Connor. The wolf's body collapsed onto the floor and the witch laughed.

He heard a whine and realized it came from his throat.

"That's right, boy, learn your place quick. You won't last a week without me."

Connor lay, assessing this body, tensing muscles that felt unfamiliar to him, then relaxing them one by one, learning the feel of this new form. The witch turned her back to him. She walked to the hearth, dumping the rest of the brew from his mug into the fire. Flames flared high and bright. They crawled up the wall in a way he had never seen fire act before.

A wolf.

The words seeped into him. He flexed his unfamiliar leg muscles and then laid his head on the floor. His eyes followed the witch's movements. What could he do? He would not let his father or brother hunt him. Despite everything, he loved them, and they loved him. He could not allow them to kill him.

His lip lifted in a silent snarl. He would not be the witch's slave. There was only one solution.

He had to run.

3

Melody

Melody fought to control her tears. Her fingers brushed the vivid red fabric, pushing the velvet pile in one direction then the other. Unshed tears burned her eyes.

"Your mother and I chose it for you the last time your aunt's caravan passed through. I suggested green, but your mother insisted on red," Nanna said.

The tears escaped, running in slow rivers down her cheeks. Melody continued to move her hand over the fabric, so soft it flowed between her fingers. Fine gold thread ran along the edges and swirled in looping patterns. She could picture Aunt Ellen, or Cousin Tara, placing the stitches in the soft glow of lantern light inside the travel wagon. She would have chosen this exact thick, heavy fabric for herself.

"She said red was the best color for you, better than green. When she realized she was dying, I asked her if she wanted to give it to you herself. Your mother told me... to hold it... she..." Her grandmother's voice broke and she cleared her throat. "Amber said that you deserved something beautiful on your birthday."

Melody stood, the folded fabric flowed from her hands. It hung long enough to touch the floor. She lifted it, swirling the material as she settled the cloak on her shoulders. The clasp glittered gold, a perfect match for the threads decorating the edges. A tiny red gem glittered in the center. Melody lifted the hood over her hair to cover her black bun. She turned to face Nanna and brushed tears from her cheeks.

"What do you think?"

Nanna's eyes widened, shimmering with tears. Her fingers trembled as she reached up and touched the cloak. "Your mother was right, child. You look more beautiful than I imagined."

Melody tried to think of something to say as she slid her hands up and down the cloak's folds. Words eluded her. She met Nanna's eyes and tried to smile, but the gesture caught and instead a sob escaped.

Her grandmother's arms wrapped around her and Nanna's hand stroked her back through the thick material of the cape. The touch, while comforting, felt distant. Melody rubbed her cheek against Nanna's shoulder. The old cotton of her grandmother's dress absorbed her tears exactly the way it did when she was a child with a scraped knee. This felt right. The raw ache in her heart hurt so much worse than a skinned knee and yet her Nanna's arms still gave her a comfort she knew she would never find anywhere else, not now that Momma was dead.

"Why are all these terrible things happening, Nanna? Daddy goes to the mines every day. What if…" She caught her breath, and her body tensed, unable to finish the thought.

Nanna pulled away, sinking into her rocking chair. Melody unclasped the cloak, pulling it off her shoulders, and spread it over her lap as she dropped onto the sofa. She stroked the cloak, and together she and Nanna sat in silence, each lost in their own thoughts.

"Everything's changed since Momma died." Melody broke the silence. How could her entire life have changed in such a few short weeks?

"Yes, everything changed when Amber died."

Melody's head snapped up at Nanna's easy agreement. Fear knotted in her stomach as she studied Nanna's calm face, waiting for her to say more. She expected a lecture on responsibility and adult behavior like the ones her father delivered in recent weeks.

"When your mother died, so did her magic. For a while I stayed in Varin, keeping the village stable, but after I came home …" Nanna's voice trailed off and she shook her head. "The village has no protection now. Life without protective magic is harsh, Melody. This is the first time you've ever experienced that kind of life. "

Melody closed her eyes. The fear receded, replaced by an all too familiar feeling of frustration. She should not have spoken, should have known better than to open up this particular line of conversation. Nanna's easy agreement should not surprise her. Nothing new, nothing different, fairy stories as Mother called them.

"Your own magic is still locked away. I know it feels hard to reach, but you must try—"

"Don't, Nanna. Stop. Please. You know how I feel about fairy stories and such. You know Mother never wanted you to tell me those types of tales."

Melody, eyes still closed, heard Nanna's harsh sigh. "Of course, dear."

Melody knew only the reminder of her mother silenced Nanna. Another quiet extended between them, this one felt heavier and Melody continued to pet the cloak on her lap.

"Your father told me last week, several young men in the village asked to court you." Melody could hear the smile in Nanna's voice.

Melody opened her eyes and forced a smile. Trust Nanna to change the subject to the only thing she wanted to talk about less than magic. "Only two, not several. Danny Miller and Milo Carter both asked Daddy for permission to court me."

"You aren't interested in either of them." It was a statement, not a question, and Melody could not help grinning at Nanna's astute observation.

"Danny is lazy. He wants to marry me for one reason; Daddy's money. Milo …" Melody narrowed her eyes and shook her head, trying to understand it even as she explained, "…well, the man is prudish. He makes it plain he doesn't approve of my dress, my behavior, and more often than not, me in general. So why court me? I mean, you've met Milo, can you imagine life with a man who doesn't know about affection and well…passion? I can't."

Melody felt her face heat as she spoke, but she watched her mother and father touch and kiss too many times. She craved that type of relationship for herself. "I could never love either of them." Melody sighed. "Is it so wrong, Nanna, to want to marry someone I love?"

"Your observations reveal wisdom dear, and no, it's not wrong at all. Love is a magic all on its own, Melody. It is the most wholesome and simplest magic, but don't think that makes it any less powerful than a witch's brew."

Melody gazed down at the crimson of the cloak, and listened to the rough tones of her grandmother's voice. She said she did not want fairy stories, and yet the tone and the words seemed to ease the ache deep inside her.

"Our family has a rich, long history of love matches. Even your parents, though their match seemed so ordinary. Your mother and father loved each other very much and they were so very happy together, but you know that. You witnessed it firsthand." Melody could hear the smile in Nanna's voice.

"Wait, Melody. Wait to marry until you're in love. Where I came from you would still be quite young to be a bride. I know around here this is considered the best age, but don't rush, sweetheart. Love is worth waiting for."

"Thank you, Nanna."

Melody left Rose Cottage, her basket full of dried herbs. The cloak on her shoulders made the spring chill a distant memory. Melody moved through the garden gate onto the tiny forest trail never glancing at the wagon rutted road to her right. She walked to Nanna's cottage through the forest so many times she never even considered the road. From the time Melody could walk, until illness made her mother too weak to make the trip, mother and daughter came together each week down this trail.

A breeze ruffled the leaves above her. It occurred to Melody that this was the first time she walked the path alone. Her fingers tightened on the basket and her gaze swept over the trees. For a second, she stopped. Sounds intensified around her. She heard the birds singing, crickets chirping, and the scratch of tiny feet on the forest floor. Normal, healthy forest sounds.

Spring wrapped her senses in the brilliant greens of new grass, the crisp scent of fresh buds on the trees, and damp earth under her feet. Bright sunlight filtered through branches and created a patchwork of light and dark on the path. Melody relaxed, and smiled to herself. There was no danger here, not in the middle of a bright, clear, spring day.

She resumed her walk, still following the patterns of light on the dirt trail under her feet. The swirling edge of scarlet caught her eye. Why would Momma choose red for her cloak?

It was no secret that Melody loved brilliant colors. The more emerald the green, the deeper the blue, the richer the purple the better, but red though? Red; the color associated with blood and death. Nanna would have chosen green, the color of growth and life. What made her mother choose red?

The question nagged at her until a sudden movement jerked her from her thoughts. Her fingers dug into the handle of the basket so hard her nails left indentations on the wooden handle. Sweat dotted her forehead. Something lurched off to her right. There were too many shadows around her. She was not alone on the trail.

A doe bolted out of the brush a few feet ahead of her. The soft brown of its coat blurred as it leaped across the path.

Her breath caught in a gasp and one hand lifted from the basket to touch her chest. Shaking her head, Melody laughed at her own foolishness. Her heart slowed to a more normal rhythm.

She was being foolish.

In all her years of making this walk nothing threatened her or even frightened her. She knew there was nothing to fear in her forest, except, everything in Varin was changing.

Would the forest change as well?

4

Connor

Connor lay on the floor, his clothing scattered about. The witch moved in and out of the house several times, the first time he lunged to his feet, the rope forgotten. It jerked him off his feet and tightened around his throat. He lay panting on the wood floor.

The witch laughed.

"Hurts doesn't it, wolf?" She watched him from the opened door. "You'll never get out this door. That rope has magic."

She walked through the door and left it open, a dare for him to leave if he could. The growl came out almost against his will. Thick fur rippled over his body as he flexed his muscles. He rose, and walked away from the door. The rope went slack.

If he could find what the rope tied off to perhaps he could chew through it. He followed it to its end only to find that it led to a pile of rope loosely coiled on the floor. The witch did not lie when she said the rope was magic, it tied off to nothing. A new thread of panic rippled through Connor.

There must to be a way out.

The witch returned. At the sight of him inspecting the pile of rope, she chuckled. "Now you understand."

She lifted the coils from the floor and gave it a tug. Connor gazed up at her.

"Do you see these?" She held up two identical packs of herbs.

"One is your Mother's medicine. The other is poison. Which one should I give Minna when she arrives?"

Once again, Connor couldn't stop the growl that seemed to start low in his chest and rumble up and out of his throat. The witch laughed.

She wrapped the rope around her hand and gave it a tug. It tightened the noose around Connors throat. He could not breathe, his mouth fell open and he panted for air. The witch leaned close to his face.

"I'm your mistress now, and you will live to protect and serve me. Do you understand wolf?" She snarled the words.

The noose loosened and Connor felt his tongue scrape over his teeth as he panted, passing in and out of his mouth with each breath. The witch's head snapped up and cocked to the side.

She pointed to the bedroom door. "Get in there."

Connor walked across the room and into the bedroom. The witch stood in the doorway and tossed his clothing, and the rope, onto the floor near him. "You make a sound and I'll send your mother the poison, do you understand?"

A new kind of fear began to creep over Connor. This woman would kill his mother if he did not cooperate. He sat down and hung his head low.

"Good wolf, learn your place and it won't be so bad."

He heard the door slam shut and he lifted his head. He walked to the door, hoping whatever task occupied the witch kept her from hearing his claws click on the wood floor. He lay by the door and tilted his head to the crack by the floor to listen.

Several minutes later a knock sounded on the outside door.

The witch sounded genuine and happy when she opened the door. "Benjamin, what a pleasant surprise."

"Have you seen Connor? I sent him to fetch his mother's medicine earlier this morning and no one's seen him since he left the house." His father sounded less annoyed and more worried than Connor would have expected.

"No, he never arrived. Do you need medicine? I think I might have some made up if you want me to fetch it." The witch sounded so accommodating. Connor wanted to growl, he needed to warn his father that it might be poison.

"Yes, but I'm worried about Connor, you're sure he didn't come here?"

"I'm certain. You know boys, he likely got side tracked, went fishing, or—"

"No, not Connor, not if it involved his mother, that boy may be unreliable about some things but never when it comes to his mother. If he didn't make it, then something happened." His father sounded so certain, so angry, that for a moment Connor felt relived.

The witch spoke again. "Perhaps there is more than one wolf in the area. They do tend to hunt in packs."

His father grunted. "I don't know. We didn't see signs of a pack yesterday."

"Tell me, how bad is your wife's condition this time? I need to know how much medicine to give you."

A finger of fear ran along Connors back. Would the witch try to distract his father by killing his mother?

"It's been a bad episode."

"I'll go ahead and give you some extra medicine."

Connor almost snarled, but he felt the rope move around his neck, even though the witch stood in a different room.

He heard his father thank the witch and the outer door close, but the witch did not release him from the bedroom. She left him there alone, unaware if she sent his mother the medicine or the poison. He wanted to whine and growl, or use his claws to scratch the door. Instinct told him she would enjoy that and he refused to give her the satisfaction. Instead, he turned and inspected the length of rope that hung from his neck.

He glanced around the room. His new body did not move with as much ease as his old one, he still could not figure out how to turn his head and shoulders right. As he tried, he could feel the weight of the rope where it settled above his shoulders.

Perhaps he could use the post of the bed to push off the rope. He rose and walked over to the bed and attempted to position his neck behind the rope against the post. It did not work.

He tried to put his head under the edge of the bed and lift his head up to catch the rope on the lower edge of the wooden bed frame. He slid the rope over the top of his head and off.

Freed from the rope Connor wanted to bolt, but he could not open the door. He lay facing the door and tried to content himself with learning about his new form. He tensed different muscles and felt how they moved under his skin. He felt his fur twitch and undulate over his new shape. He prepared for the witch's return.

He heard her steps as she moved from one end of the small house to the other approaching the bedroom. His ears swiveled toward the sound without his conscious thought. As she stepped through the bedroom door, Connor moved. He pushed himself to his feet and tried to run. The movement felt awkward. Which leg should go first? How did you move two legs together? Half way to the door, he stumbled. Regaining his feet, he forced himself to move forward again. He stumbled through the main room of the house to find the front door opened. Relief coursed through him. Behind him, he heard the witch move after him.

"How did you get that rope off?"

He made it through the front door and into the yard. The ground became uneven and he fell forward, his shoulder scraped the ground. An ache spread from the point of impact. Connor noticed how balance worked at a lower level in this body. He needed to remember that.

The witch called after him. "There may still be time to save your mother, wolf."

Connor stopped and lay still for a moment, trying to forget the pain.

"I could go, tell them I sent the wrong medicine. It might not be too late. All you have to do is come back."

His father's words rang through his mind. An ache began deep in his chest; it was already too late. He knew it in his heart. She would never go to his father and say she made an error. He could hear the lie in her voice. Every instinct screamed it to him. He turned his head and saw her creep closer to him, the rope in her hand.

Connor rose and forced his body to move forward again. This time, considering how wolves ran, he moved with more care. The woods seemed so far from the house, but if he continued to fall, he would never reach his goal. With each faltering step, he began to adjust to the feel of this new shape, and his gait smoothed.

He heard the witch stumble behind him in her attempt to run after him.

As he drew nearer to the woods Connor pushed harder and ran. His speed surprised him. He lost focus on the world around him. Not until his body pushed through brush did he realize he made it to the woods.

"You just killed your mother, boy." The witch's voice sounded out of breath and closer than Connor liked. "You'll die without me. Like the other one. And to think, I considered you smart all these years." She blew out a breath. "If you have any sense you'll come back."

He stumbled a few more steps to a large holly bush. Under the cover of its leaves, he dropped to the ground. She lied. He forced the words through the ache in his chest. She killed his mother. If he chose to stay now he would be her slave, and his mother would never have wanted that.

He needed to focus on escape, take stock of his body, its movements so foreign from his human form. Running took a different set of muscles and skills then walking. Now, weight shifted from his back to his front legs in an almost rocking motion.

Standing again, he walked deeper into the words. Feeling each step, Connor absorbed how when a front leg moved forward so did the opposite rear one. He stretched into a fast walk, and the motion did not change, just extended. Then he ran, focusing on the way his muscles adjusted with the new action.

A scent teased his nostrils. Connor did not recognize it, but the wolf did. Food. Meat. A rabbit. The thought, his thought, yet not; this was the wolf thinking, and he was the wolf.

No, that was wrong. He was a man, not a wolf.

His body tensed, and stopped. His stomach growled at the scent of the rabbit. Dark hot dread seared his nerves. He started to run again. Not caring how he moved, only that he did. He raced southwest, toward the thick woods and the mountains.

He kept running, disregarding the aches in his muscles, as the day progressed. He ignored the nagging thirst that hit him midday, ignored everything except the need to get away. As he ran, he learned how to avoid trees and underbrush and learned how to extend his body to move closer to the ground.

The sun began to sink and Connor's legs collapsed under him. He fell to the forest floor, a soft carpet of leaves and decay mixed with new spring growth caught him. He panted. Chest heaving in rapid short breaths, his tongue lolled out the side of open jaws. He could almost taste the forest around him. Too exhausted for any movement, his eyes closed.

He slept.

He awoke to darkness. Sounds assaulted him. Crickets, an owl, the scurry of a small animal, they surrounded him. The odors that accompanied them were almost overpowering. Scents never before held the intensity they did now. His nose twitched. A bird, a rabbit, decaying leaves, he recognized every scent. How did he know them?

Processing the night sounds, his eyes adjusted to the dark. He began to comprehend his situation, alone in the night forest. Fear shivered over his skin. A wolf growled and the sound left his lips. The noises around him quieted, except the distant hoot of an owl.

Truth dawned on him. He was one of them. A predator in a forest full of prey, and they knew him. The wolf took pleasure in that simple fact and his human fear diminished.

The wolf inside stretched and his body responded in kind. Rising slowly, he lifted his head and smelled with more interest, learning the aroma of the forest around him. The wolf began to take control. Connor fought the sensation. His stomach growled. He needed to eat. He would have to hunt like a wolf to eat. The wolf flexed again and this time he let it.

Instinct—a wolf's instinct—took over his body. Humanity seemed to fade and for a moment that did not bother Connor.

A soft scratching caught his attention and he began to move. Pain lanced from the pads of his front paws up his legs. The joints ached with each step and he whimpered.

His front legs trembled with fatigue, unused to moving on four limbs. The wolf insisted he needed to eat or the pain would get worse. The human demanded rest was essential or the pain would prevent him from sneaking up on his prey. The two compulsions clashed.

In the end, Connor decided he needed both. He lifted his nose to pull in a deep breath. Fragrances of the forest, rich and deep, enticed him. The decay of vegetation on the forest floor blended with the scent of night air. The green of early growth teased him, and while the color evaded his eyes, it seemed to permeate his nose. He could smell the brown musk of a mouse, and the stronger scent of a rabbit. His stomach growled. Ignoring the sensation, he turned slightly and inhaled again.

Then he caught it, the scent he wanted; the cool, clean, pure, blue scent of water. He took another deep breath, focusing on that liquid smell, and moved toward it. Each step became a test of will. Meeting the challenge, he forced his body forward. The bouquet of water grew stronger until he could also hear the bubbling sounds of a stream running over rocks. He broke through a layer of brush and saw it, gleaming brighter in the moonlight.

Connor approached the water and sank down. He lowered his sore front paws into the stream. The water flowed cold and clear off the mountains. It immediately soothed his tender feet. He lapped the water and his burning throat also found relief. Both of his natures accepted this, relief from pain and thirst was almost as good as a meal.

Connor drank until his stomach felt swollen. Turning his head to the side, he let it drop, and for a few moments enjoyed the numbness the water provided. After a short time, the night creatures began to move around him. A frog croaked from the other side of the stream.

The wolf saw it and thought, "*Food.*" Connor recoiled in disgust. His stomach protested with a cramp of hunger. With a quick movement, his teeth closed around the frog. The metallic taste of blood filled his mouth. He felt the frog's body cease moving. The wolf told him to eat but Connor fought the urge. The wolf won. He ate the frog in a single swallow.

Connor felt the truth settle over him with resignation. He was the wolf.

5

Melody

Sweat ran down Melody's back. The cotton nightgown clung to her like a second skin. She shivered. Remnants of emotions from the dream lingered. Yet the details evaded her, fading from her memory the moment her eyes opened. Chilly predawn air caused her to tremble.

She could almost hear Nanna's words, "Life without protective magic is harsh…" Melody shook her head and forced the words away from her mind. Fairy stories.

Goose bumps covered her skin the moment she rose. Grabbing the pile of clothes, she laid out the night before, Melody hurried from her room. Her teeth chattered by the time she reached the bathing chamber downstairs.

The room sat off the kitchen, a fire burned in a metal grate heating a huge pot of water. The warm room chased away the chills and the goose-bumps faded. Blue and white tiles covered the floor in a checked pattern. The tub's drain took the water out of the house.

Melody pulled the cord and tilted hot water into the tub, then pumped in enough cold water to bring the bath the right temperature. Discarding her nightgown, Melody sank into the tub with a sigh.

Clean and relaxed she emerged from the tub, dried off with one of the fluffy towels Nanna Blanch sent them, and dressed. The house stood still and empty, her father already gone, of course. He left for the mine before dawn every day since Mother's death.

Sighing, Melody sat on a stool by the fire grate to brush out her long black hair. Before her mother's death, Daddy stayed and ate breakfast with them each morning. Nothing felt right around her. That must be the explanation for the nightmares that haunted her sleep. She should take her sheets to be washed today. Sweat and tears stained the sheets from night after night of dreams that left her shaking in fear. The idea of sleeping one more night on the dirty bedding made her skin itch.

It would take Widow Cramer two days to finish her wash if she took the woman her sheets as well as the other laundry. She could do it faster herself.

As she debated the idea, a memory crept into her thoughts.

"We always do the wash together on the day after we visit Nanna, Momma."

"Melody." Her mother knelt on one knee and met her gaze. "We have a great deal, and when people are given much they also have responsibility. Widow Cramer and her daughters just arrived here, and they wash clothing in order to make money. We could do the wash ourselves, or we could help provide for another by giving them work."

"Why not just give them money, Momma? Then they could do their own wash."

"Most people don't want charity, love. They want to have a useful job. Widow Cramer wants to be able to take care of her girls without begging for help. We can be part of making sure that happens."

Melody shook off a wave of sadness. All those years ago she did not truly understand her mother, but she trusted her. She bundled the sheets and her clothing together and took her coin pouch with her as she left the house.

It did not take long to reach the Widow Cramer's house. Varin Village was small, and Melody and her father lived near the cobbled square in the middle of the village. Only the square boasted paver stones. The village was too small for the streets to merit such luxury. Dusty passages ran between houses and the odd shop or two. As soon as the spring rain started the streets would turn to mud.

By the time she left the house, the village was awake and busy. Melody smiled to everyone she passed. A few nodded, but many did not return her greeting. No one ever ignored her mother. In fact, the walk would have taken twice as long. Everyone would have stopped to talk to her mother, and she would have given them each a few moments of her time.

It served as a reminder that she would never be the vivacious woman the entire town loved.

At the widow's home, Melody tapped on the door. Jessica, the widow's youngest daughter, who was the same age as Melody, opened it.

"Oh, Melody it's you. Come in." Jessica spoke with cool formality and turned her back on Melody the moment the words were spoken.

"Thank you. I brought some washing. It's more than usual for this time of month, but…" Melody trailed off, unsure what to say to explain her need to have the sheets washed. It seemed silly to have nightmares at her age.

"Melody, welcome. How are you today?" Widow Cramer greeted, as she entered the front room of the small house.

"I'm well, thank you. How are you?"

"We're fine, child. What are you up to today, any exciting plans?"

"I brought the wash. After this, I plan to visit James and Clara. I baked some bread for them."

"Oh, poor James. Such a tragedy." The older woman shook her head and tsked softly.

"Yes, but it would have been so much worse if Trevor wasn't at the mine that day." Jessica said. She smiled as she continued and Melody felt a strange twist in her stomach. "He went to deliver some boards. James would have died if Trevor hadn't pulled him free from the collapsed arch."

"True, dear. There is a silver lining. Losing one's leg is better than losing one's life."

Melody nodded. Neither seemed like good options to her. "I wish the healer had been able to save his leg. It will be difficult for him now."

"Well, we can't all be as fortunate as you, Melody. Some of us must learn to live with life's difficulties." Jessica said with syrup in her voice.

"Jessica, what an awful thing to say, and after Melody lost her lovely mother," the widow scolded.

Melody fought back a wave of bitterness by forcing a smile. "I am very fortunate. I hope I can offer some comfort to James and Clara."

Jessica made a noise and Melody stiffened, ready for another verbal assault. She and Jessica never got along. Even before the other girls stopped talking to Melody, Jessica did not like her. Their relationship never degraded to open hostility, not until Trevor Branch started to show an interest in Jessica. Melody felt another wave of emotion roll through her at the thought of Trevor.

It was not jealousy.

Melody was not jealous of how the tall, handsome woodcutter, with his sandy blond hair and bright blue eyes grinned at Jessica. She was not jealous because he was easy going, always talked to everyone, and yet never seemed aware of Melody. She was not jealous that he took an interest in pretty, blonde Jessica. Most of all she was not jealous of the way Trevor put his arm around Jessica, or touched her cheek or hair as they walked and talked in the market or the town square.

The worst part, Jessica somehow knew how Melody felt and seemed determined to rub in that Trevor belonged to her. Widow Cramer interrupted her thoughts to ask about the sheets.

"Hmm, oh, yes, I know it's a week early, but I needed to get them washed if you have time."

Melody felt a flush creep up her cheeks at the strange look the Widow gave her. "Well, yes, child, I suppose we can do that. It might take me a day longer."

"Of course, I understand." The house seemed to grow smaller and warmer as they spoke and Melody placed the bag of clothing and linens on the floor. She shifted from foot to foot, and tried not to make eye contact with Jessica.

Melody pulled her coin purse from her basket and poured the contents into her palm, handing the correct amount over to the Widow. In her haste to leave, she barely heard the woman's thanks and her promise to have everything ready the day after tomorrow.

Outside, in the spring sun, Melody squinted and took a slow, deep breath. The scent of fresh baking bread filled her nose. The sound of people calling to each other and bartering on the market street on the other side of the house calmed her. Trying hard to forget the way

Jessica smirked at her, she began to walk away from the house toward the home of James and Clara Salter.

She tapped lightly on the door, almost afraid to see it open. How could she face the people on the other side? Clara opened the door and smiled out at her. She used to live in Briar Creek before her marriage to James.

"Melody, how are you today? Do come in." She pulled the door wide and motioned Melody in.

"Hello, Clara," Melody entered the house and returned the woman's smile with a tentative one of her own. How could Clara be smiling?

"You've just missed your father."

"Really, Daddy came here?"

"Well, of course. He's been here every morning since the accident. He comes and sits with James for an hour or so. They discuss what James will do after he recovers enough to work again, among other things."

Melody stood silent, not sure what to say.

"Here, let me take your cloak. How lovely. Is it new?" Clara asked.

"Yes, Nanna gave it to me. A birthday present from her and my mother…" Melody handed her cloak to Clara and shuffled her feet, unsure of how to talk to the other woman. Did others besides Nanna think she could protect them with magic she didn't even believe in?

"They chose a beautiful gift. This color is perfect for you."

"Thank you, Clara. I brought you some fresh bread."

"Thank you so much. You and your mother always baked the best breads."

"I love to bake. It's a small thing, but I hope..." Melody shrugged her shoulders. She forgot that once again she placed her hair up in a bun and reached up to tuck it behind her ear. Not finding the usual strand, she let her hand drop in an awkward motion. What should she say? No words that came to mind felt right. She should have come sooner. Her mother would have. Her father did. What if they expected something she couldn't give?

"I'm sure it will be wonderful." Clara took the basket she held out. Melody nodded and followed Clara into the house. "Let's go sit with

James and have some."

Melody swallowed hard and tried to control her churning stomach. Why was this so hard? The answer her mind supplied left her hands clenched in fists, nails biting into her palms.

What if the town needed her to protect them with magic she didn't believe in? Could she be failing them with her lack of conviction?

6

The Past

Cold steel sliced through the soft, warm, flesh of his body. Pain seared his abdomen, and not just pain of the flesh. A deeper, brighter pain overwhelmed him. Heat raced under his skin, a red-hot fire that glowed through his pours and blazed through his shields.

How did that damned prince acquire a magic blade? Who dared give him such a tool? He growled in his mind. He knew the answer even as he asked the question, a Godmother.

The young woman leaned into the prince's side. She shone a beacon to his dimming vision. Her silver blonde hair shimmered down her back as her body emitted pure, bright power. The power rested so close to him, yet beyond his reach.

Once again, he arrived too late in her life.

In the final seconds of the body's life, he fled. The sword weakened him, but it did not destroy his soul, or end his life. No doubt, whatever Godmother created and gave the blade to the prince, and the prince himself hoped it would.

For long moments, his spirit floated free. He observed the prince withdraw the sword from the now dead flesh. The beautiful woman rested her head on the prince's chest. He leaned down and tilted her face up for a kiss. They stood in each other's embrace, reveling in their victory, unaware the sword failed to eliminate him.

The memory of her body against his ached and he blocked his awareness, but not in time. The prince drew her closer, his hand caressing her back.

He should be the one holding her.

Too late again.

He could not think of that now. He needed to find a new host to give him form and shape. Traveling free of the body caused pain to ripple along pulses of magic in his spirit. He forced his focus as he inched along the terrain. The air pushed him in every direction. He fought to stay on the path he wanted.

If any of his Brothers stumbled upon him now, they would devour his magic and consume his entire being. His existence would end. That could not be permitted. He must find an acceptable form before his weakness drew their attention.

The sword had depleted him more than he liked to admit.

He let the wind carry him away from the ancient stone castle. He did not blame the woman, who would have been his lover, for the loss of his home. The fault lay with the Godmothers, all of them.

He could not feel the chill of the wind, or see the fiery autumn leaves. His spirit could not perceive color until he once again found a host to support him. The wind blew north. A village lay not far ahead. He could sense it with the magic innate to the core of who he was, or who he had been, once. He forced himself to move in that direction despite the pain.

Why would she do this to him? Why bring the prince down on him? He offered her the world. He never hurt her physically, and still she chose some weak prince, a man without a hint of magic.

Every woman he tried to forge a bond with refused him, every woman since *her.* Betrayal burned inside him. He needed the completion of a bond.

He became aware of a sparse village. A man, so thin his ragged clothes hung from his body, shuffled down the dust covered street. A bony dog ran up to the man, moving its tail hopefully. The man yelled and swung at the animal with his cane and it fled. A child sat curled in a ball against the wall of a house. The child shivered from a breeze he could no longer feel against skin he no longer possessed. The frail form looked up, terror painted on its dirty face, this human felt him. This place was too close to his former home. No one here caught his attention.

He stopped forcing himself in a clear direction and let the wind take him. His essence flew north-east, toward the sea.

Instinct dictated he should leave this area. She lived here. Soon her magic would touch the entire land. She might feel him. It was unlikely, very few recognized him from one form to the next, but she might.

How could his timing always be so off?

He floated, and allowed the wind to take him where it would, without a set direction or purpose. If any Brothers lived nearby, he passed them unnoticed. Days and nights blended around him. He no longer kept track of the passage of time. He could not feed and could not gain strength, not without a body.

Eventually, the wind carried him into a large town. People thrived. Red brick houses lined cobblestone roads. Here he managed to generate enough interest to force himself to stop. Here he began to search through each well ordered structure for a sign of turmoil. Pain stirred with hope, desire mixed with need.

In the seventh house, he found what he sought. A boy lay on a cot near the fire. He shivered despite the warmth from the blaze. The thin, young, body fought to support the boy's dying spirit. The boy's need to live warred with the inevitable. It tasted delicious. Even though he could not feed, his essence lapped at the taste. He craved more.

He flowed around the boy, and enjoyed the energy of impending death. Finally, he touched the boy. The thin form jerked in surprise.

"Who's there?" The weak voice pleaded.

I can heal you. Make you strong.

The offer slid into the boy's mind, less a voice than a breath of thought. Nonetheless, the boy heard. He could feel hope flare in the ill boy.

Disgust filled him. So weak he needed to ask, what humiliation.

"I've never been strong."

I can make you stronger, better, than you have ever been. Let me in and I will heal this body.

"How?"

So many questions. Let me in and I will answer. I will make you well.

"How do I let you in?"

So easy, so eager for hope, this body fought so hard to contain the spirit. The flavor of the boy's need enticed him. It gave him the will to surround the boy, to cover him, despite the pain and effort. **Ask me to enter.**

"Will you enter?"

He moved and merged with the form, even as the boy spoke. With its illness, the body made an easy target to inhabit.

"You promised..." A weak protest, as his spirit pushed into the body and forced the boy's out. A heartbeat later, he was in control. The boy no longer existed, his soul freed to go wherever souls go.

"...to make this body strong." His voice spoke now, weak and wispy from the lips of the body that lay dying moments ago. "I will."

A decade ago, he took the body of a sorcerer in his prime. Five hundred years ago, he destroyed a king who ruled five kingdoms with the strength of his magic. He forced those souls out with sheer power. He never asked or begged.

After all he accomplished, one magic sword forced him to seek refuge in a fatally ill boy. Here, bound to the body, he became safe; his strength began to consolidate the moment his spirit settled. His Brothers could not devour him. He used his magic, and skills accumulated over his long life and began to heal the body.

7

Connor

Connor lost track of the days as he journeyed. Time meant less to the wolf. After the first night, his paws no longer ached. The feel of his new form began to seem natural. He moved with ease, and he did move. He could run longer as a wolf, further than he could have as a human. The muscles he built as a human seemed to have shifted into this new form.

It took longer to master hunting.

To begin with, he had to overcome his aversion to eating raw meat. For days he let himself go hungry despite the push of the wolf to make him eat. The hollow ache in his stomach, and the need to stop and rest more often than he wanted, forced him to hunt. He soon discovered his fast, jerky, movements alerted his prey.

Hunger required Connor to learn fast. He cultivated the ability to stay silent. Instead of fighting it, he allowed the wolf's instincts to be a guide. Soon he caught and ate prey with regularity, but he never seemed to get enough. He woke to an empty stomach most mornings craving food he could never find. He could not even be sure what he desired, but he knew he needed something more, something different.

His diet included rabbits, moles, opossums, groundhogs, mice, an occasional beaver and even fish when he encountered a river big enough to support them. Sometimes, he ate berries he recognized. They did not satisfy as much as the meat but they helped keep the hunger at bay. He tried to catch birds but never caught them before they took flight.

Fish surprised Connor. He followed a river one day, his stomach crawling with hunger. He considered the water and thought of the days he spent fishing, to his surprise the wolf's instinct rose. As with every other skill, learning to fish as a wolf took a different set of muscles, and of course teeth. Soon Connor mastered the task.

He still tried not to *think* about what he put in his mouth. He tried to tell himself that he did not enjoy the tang of iron in the blood of his prey, and he fought the surge of excitement and energy the hunt and the kill gave him.

Both instinct and human knowledge told him that now, in spring, game might be plentiful, but he knew this would not last. He needed to improve his skills before winter. His pattern changed as he continued to travel. He slept long portions of the day, and traveled and hunted through much of the night.

He hunted with more ease at night and Connor felt safer under the cover of darkness. He continued to move toward and then into the mountains. He needed to cross the mountains. A deep inner knowledge whispered to him that he could find safety and rest on the other side, and he did not question it. He could feel it.

As a human, he would have ignored this belief, knowing that to admit it, or worse, talk about it, would create humiliation and isolation. As a wolf, he did not need to consider these things so he let his instincts guide him. Human or wolf, if he allowed the question into his mind it would torment him, so he refused to consider it.

Connor stayed in the deep woods, away from the roads and the pass where the traders crossed the mountains. He did not want to be seen.

One night, after losing a rabbit, he realized he could see the pass from the ledge where he stood high above. A caravan crawled through the pass. He heard the whinny of a horse drift up on the breeze. The scent of people and livestock rose to his nose. Did he ever hear or smell as clear as this in the past?

He wanted to be with them. The need to hear voices became a gaping wound in his chest. He did not do it on purpose. His body acted, without any conscious thought on his part. His head went back, his face tilted toward the moon and a terrible, mournful sound left his mouth.

He howled.

The sound that left his body was terrible, beautiful, and perfect. It engulfed the night around him, mourned his former life, his lost mother, his family. At the same time it embraced and celebrated the new shape of his life. He sat, stretching further toward the sky, his left front leg lifted from the ground and he howled again. Below him, he heard horses stamping hooves, people shouting. His eyes closed and his face tipped toward the moon, Connor sang the loss of his humanity.

8

Melody

Melody placed the bread and jams into her basket, and paused beside the door to put her cape around her shoulders.

Outside, the breeze brought the smell of spring rain and new growth to her nose. Inhaling, she stood for a moment on the wooden porch that surrounded the entire front of the house. The village market took place a few streets away. Carrying the basket and a small pouch of coins, she walked in that direction. She wanted to buy Nanna some mint tea.

Mud from the street sucked at her boots and Melody lifted the edge of her cape over the mire.

The sun overhead and the thick feel of the post-rain air made her smile. Today would be perfect conditions for a walk to Nanna's house. Humming, Melody came around a corner and almost collided with Jessica. Her long blond hair braided and looped over her head, Jessica strolled with her hand tucked into Trevor's arm. Melody fought a rush of embarrassment and forced a smile.

"Hello, Jessica. Trevor." Melody nodded to each of them and tried to ignore the blush that began on her cheeks. "How are you today?"

"Melody," Jessica smiled but the gesture never reached her eyes. Melody saw her fingers tighten on Trevor's arm. "Why do you wear that cape? The color is all wrong for spring, and, well, I know your mother chose it, but do you think, perhaps, illness clouded her mind when she chose red? I've heard that in the cities women wear red like that to let men know that they'll... well, you know.... do things."

Melody felt the blush deepen on her cheeks. Her fingers tightened on the handle of the basket and her teeth clenched so hard they hurt. Trevor glared at Jessica, and even Melody could read the reproach in his face. He stepped away from her, and extricated himself from her hand.

"I think that color is very becoming on you," Trevor said in an obvious attempt to amend for Jessica's rudeness.

Jessica glanced up at him, her eyes were narrow and angry when her gaze returned to Melody. This time she did not even try to smile. "Maybe your mother knew something we don't. Tell me, Melody. Why did you need your sheets washed a week early? What did you do in your bed to make them all stiff with sweat?"

Hurt and embarrassment warred with anger so hot it burned her stomach. Despite her best efforts, the anger boiled over into her words as she spoke.

"My mother knew a great deal about me, Jessica, including the fact that I love rich dramatic colors. Personally, I love the color, and apparently," she cut her gaze to Trevor, "it is very becoming on me. Where are your boots, Jessica? It is quite muddy to be out without them." She spoke in a sweet voice, asking even though she knew Jessica could not afford to buy boots.

Jessica's face hardened and she placed her hand back on Trevor's arm. Melody moved to step around the couple and continue to the market. Did she just say those words?

Trevor stopped her with a hand on her arm.

Glancing up, she saw him turn away from Jessica and take a step after her. Jessica made a small noise of hurt or anger, turned her back on the two, and moved away down the street.

"Don't let her words hurt you." Trevor's fingers warmed her skin. "She's jealous of all the men who want to court you. She's always been jealous of what you and your family have."

"I understand that, Trevor, but it isn't my fault. I never asked for any of these things." She gazed into his clear blue eyes and wished he would see her the way she wanted him to. Instead, his smile seemed almost sympathetic.

"Melody, your family has the biggest house, in the best location. Your father pays people to work for him. He owns both the best and the worst farmland between here and the mountains. You have never needed, or wanted for anything. Most people think that, until your mother died, you were ... spoiled."

"Do...does everyone think that I'm spoiled?" Melody stumbled over the words.

"No, Melody. Jessica is very jealous. What you said just now won't help." His face turned rueful. "But not everyone feels that way about you." His fingers tightened a fraction on her arm.

She turned her attention down to his strong, calloused fingers against the soft green fabric of her dress. He followed her gaze and immediately released her arm and took a step back. She missed the sensation of his warmth on her arm and looked up into his eyes confused.

"I didn't..." she stopped and shook her head. She spoke with careful control, not meeting his eyes. "Thank you for your honesty and kindness Trevor. I appreciate both."

He nodded and turned to follow Jessica down the street. Could she be spoiled? Is that why the town did not love her the way they loved her mother? Perhaps their rejection had nothing to do with magic. She walked toward the market. With each step, the cape billowed behind her black boots.

9

Connor

After the night in the pass, Connor turned west. The encounter with the caravan brought too many emotions to the surface. He remained deep in the mountains now, and he stayed near the edge of the snow line, where tiny scrub trees mixed with large fields of rich, green grass.

Eventually he moved south again, following that nebulous pull that guided him. The snow melted a little more each day as the late spring warmth seeped into the ground.

His skills as a hunter improved, his body moved with grace. He knew how to keep his body low to the ground when he ran, and how to lope through fields, curving around rocks and the tiny trees that dotted the meadows. He learned to recognize and avoid the scent of other wolves. Some nights, he heard them, howling their own songs to the moon. On occasion, their songs left him feeling desolate and alone. This terrified him more than the thought of an encounter with a wolf pack.

Late one night he came upon the river. Flowing fast with the spring thaw and rains, life teemed around it. He watched an elk, undisturbed by the scent of a lone wolf, bend and drink from the water. He saw fish jump and glisten in the moonlight, heard the splash of the water against the rocks. A bear, with two cubs fished further down-river. The scent of raccoon drifted down from the tree next to him. Everything alive in this area seemed drawn here.

The pull south felt stronger along the river, and continuing south now would mean he could avoid crossing. He obeyed the urge. After hunting, he turned south, knowing he would leave the mountains behind.

Each night, as he traveled, he saw and felt more evidence supporting this. Trees grew bigger and closer together, creating a canopy that left patches of moonlight speckled over the ground. Flowers bloomed, filling the night air with sweet scents. He paused sometimes, examining the blooms whose color he could only remember. In his mind he tried to blend the smells that were now so sharp with those memories.

Within nights, he left the true mountains and entered the foothills. He stayed close to the river, where it was easier for him to hunt. The ground began to flatten out. Fewer large hills scattered the landscape of long flat stretches. The forest was thick and Connor spent more time dodging trees than loping in long straight lines. One morning, as he drifted to sleep listening to the sound of the river, he realized he no longer felt a pull to move south. He felt comfortable, almost content, where he lay.

The next night he explored the area around the river. A scent caught his interest and he turned away from the river. Soon he found a small cave. His nose indicated another wolf denned here at one time, but all the evidence indicated the previous resident abandoned it some time ago.

He explored further from the river and found his evening meal without difficulty. He dragged it back to the shallow stone cave, and lay down to eat. The warm spring air ruffled his fur and he enjoyed the sound of the river and the feel of the soft dirt and leaves that covered the floor of the little cave. He could live here.

Allowing instinct to guide him, he began to mark the territory he deemed his own. Game in these woods appeared plentiful. Rabbits, mice, even wild turkey. He could supplement his food with fish from the river.

The wolf was content in his new home.

10

MELODY

Melody walked through the market, her hair pulled up off her shoulders in a long ponytail. She wore a sleeveless deep blue dress. She loved the feel of the warm sun on her arms and shoulders. She did not need anything special today. Daddy made sure the household supplies arrived at the kitchen door each week, just as they did before mother died.

Glorious sunshine drew her out of the big empty house. Despite Varin's size, the town supported an active market. Some people came from Briar Creek and several farmers came from the outlying areas of both communities to sell goods. Today, the market bustled with both shoppers and vendors. Melody smiled at several people, she hoped someone would take a moment to talk to her. A pleasant conversation would make her day complete.

In opposition to this desire, she saw Jessica in the distance. Deliberately, she turned to avoid her, and as she did so, she bumped into Milo.

Melody did not find him unattractive. Except when he frowned, which he did far too often, then his brows drew together and lines appeared around his eyes.

"Melody, what are you wearing?"

Melody blinked in confusion. "A dress?"

"Hardly, your neck and arms are completely bare."

Melody laughed, she could not help it. "Milo, it's a beautiful day. The sun is brilliant and the air is light and warm. Why would I want to cover up my arms on a day like today?"

"Propriety."

The single word stung like a slap and Melody took a step back. Words came out of her mouth before she realized what she planned to say. "Yes, well, I never considered my arms my most provocative feature."

She heard someone titter and realized their argument attracted an audience. Several people stopped browsing the stalls to stand and watch them. Melody squared her shoulders, not about to back down. Milo did not have the right to tell her how to dress.

"What are you doing in the market anyway? Your mother paid someone to get your household supplies."

For the same reason she paid someone to do her laundry, Melody thought. However, Melody enjoyed the market, and people did not come to the house for visits the way they did before her mother died. Long hours alone in the house bored Melody.

"I'm not my mother." She heard the mutters, broken words of agreement and disappointment. Head up, she continued. "I enjoy visits to the market. I enjoy the outdoors and the sunshine. I do not enjoy insults from rude men who never learned basic courtesy. Didn't your mother ever tell you what to do if you couldn't say something nice?"

His face reddened and his eyes narrowed, his hands fisted at his sides. Melody wondered if she might have pushed Milo too far. Would he hit her? For a moment he appeared as if he might.

"When I convince your father that I'm the proper man to be your husband, I will not tolerate this type of behavior."

Melody rolled her eyes. Did Milo consider himself some kind of saint? "What exactly will you do Milo, burn my clothes and keep me indoors as your prisoner? Tied to the bed perhaps?"

She heard the soft gasps of shock around her. Color stained her cheeks and her jaw snapped closed. Since childhood, she had possessed the unfathomable ability to appall the adults around her. Melody always assumed she would lose the talent with adulthood. Apparently not.

Milo's fists clenched, his knuckles whitened. She wondered again if he wanted to hit her. Melody pulled the basket from the side of her body to the front, and grasped it like a shield between them.

She noticed the silence around her. Even the vendors had stopped yelling their wares to watch her. She felt shame wash over her. The dress was pretty. She had made it last summer, and her mother had liked it. They did the embroidery work on the bodice together. Melody stood alone, in the middle of the market, her mother gone, her father never around, even Nanna had returned to Rose Cottage and left her to deal with the people of Varin and their whispers alone. She let her shoulders slump, allowed her body to take on the posture of defeat.

Swallowing, she gave Milo a sheepish glance. "I'm sorry, Milo, that was inappropriate, and uncalled for. Please forgive me."

Milo nodded his face regal and Melody felt like a peasant granted a pardon by the king. "Perhaps you should go home. I'll escort you."

Revolted, at Milo, at herself, at the people staring at her like an aberration, Melody kept her eyes lowered as she placed her hand on his arm and allowed him to lead her out of the market street.

They turned right, toward the town square. Normally, Melody liked the sound of her boots clicking across the square. Today they sounded like an accusation. Milo did not speak to her and she felt relieved by the silence.

At the porch steps Milo stopped. He would not come up, the house loomed empty and he would not want to be inappropriate. She pulled her hand off his arm and without a goodbye or a thank you she fled up the stairs into the solitude of the house.

Melody had kept the tears at bay throughout the walk home, alone now they burned an angry path down her cheeks and she knew they were more from frustration and rage than sadness. Clenching and unclenching her hands, she paced in circles around the parlor.

She would not marry Milo, and no one could make her.

11

Connor

Connor crouched in the brush. The sky boiled with dark clouds that shifted and changed constantly in the wind. Dust swirled down the bare road. At any moment, the storm would tear open the sky and rain would drench the forest.

He snarled. It *should* have been an easy meal.

For three days he had watched the nanny goat before he selected his prey. No one came in search of her or the kids. Moments ago, he attempted to separate the smaller of the two kids from its mother in a meadow north of here, but the nanny goat surprised him with her ferocity. A bruise ached on his shoulder from the nanny goat's horns. Her maneuver gave the kid a chance to run.

Frustration swelled inside him.

The kid ran out onto the open track and across into the thick forest on the opposite side of the wheel-rutted road. He did not realize how close they were to the road. His primary goal, to obtain the kid, distracted him. From his position he could see the bridge that spanned the river. Scents from the village carried across on the wind.

He hunched in the bushes and felt the grass rub his stomach. Shifting slightly, he scanned the road in both directions and considered. He did not want to run out in front of anyone and bring hunters down on himself. He had been so careful to stay north of here, away from the road and the village. He almost whined as he moved from paw to paw, glaring at the path.

He smelled the food before he saw her.

Fresh bread, roast beef, and strawberry pie.

His nose identified each scent in turn. They hit him like a physical force. He forgot the kid.

His body yearned toward these smells. He wanted that food with something more than hunger; he needed it with a persistent, deep, ache.

Then he saw her. She wore a simple dress. Even to his limited vision, it stood out dark against her pale skin. Over this, she wore a cape.

It was red. The color of blood. The one color he could still see in all its brilliance.

Scarlet stained the ground or colored the water every time he ate. The hood of the cape hung down; dark hair fell free along her back. The wind whipped several strands out behind her and the edges of the cape swirled around her legs.

Her head tilted back and a bit to one side, a smile curved her lips, it gave the impression she enjoyed the feel of the wind on her skin.

The smells that enticed and drew him came from the basket on her arm. He wanted that basket, needed the food with an intensity that left him burning.

How long had it been since he ate real food?

He evaluated the girl again. The wolf saw her neck arched, unprotected, and vulnerable. She carried no weapon and the angle of her throat beckoned like an invitation. Her skin would tear so easily. She posed no more threat to him than the kid.

She appeared to be light; he could easily overpower her.

An image flashed through his mind. The girl, lay on the ground, throat opened, blood, the same rich color of her cape covered her pale skin, and mixed with the dust of the road. It would be fast, so easy. He could have the basket and the food he had not even realized he needed until this moment.

What would her blood taste like?

Disgust crawled like a living thing under his skin. This was wrong. She was human, not prey.

As he watched, she passed him, her cape billowed in the wind and her hair tangled behind her. Her walk remained unhurried despite the presence of the oncoming storm. He felt sure she would welcome the rain if it caught her. She kept her face tilted into the wind, her eyes half closed and her lips slightly parted. All at once, she turned sharply, off the road and disappeared into the forest.

Where was she going? How could she walk alone into the woods?

The fool.

He scanned the road, and then moved across it without hesitation. He kept his body low to the ground. The girl followed a tiny trail, hardly more than a game path. Thick vegetation encroached on the narrow dirt track. Stalking along beside her took no effort. He moved past her a few paces, and turned to watch her.

Her face captivated him, with long lashes and high cheekbones. Her body was slender, her breasts round and firm, her hips curved in perfect proportion to her waist. She walked with a careless grace, the gentle sway of her hips and arms natural. She was strong, the weight of the basket did not seem to bother her or slow her pace. The wolf saw more, something as a human he could not identify, but instinct called it magic.

A different hunger overwhelmed him.

Hot lust rolled through his body. Connor never looked at a woman the way he watched her. Now, when the wolf could do nothing, this girl enticed him in ways the girls of his hometown never did.

Most days, he no longer felt like Connor, no longer thought of himself as Connor, not since the night in the pass when he mourned his lost humanity. Now he did.

To his surprise, the wolf's instincts approved. The idea that both his natures agreed disturbed Connor.

That did not stop him from enjoying the way her body

moved as he stalked her through the forest. The girl must be a fool to walk alone in the woods full of predators. Yet she walked as if nothing could harm her. He knew none of the other animals would hesitate to hurt her because of her humanity.

She needed protection.

He would make sure she remained safe. He owed her that much after he considered her prey. He ignored the part of him that said he just wanted to watch her body move and argued there was more than protection on his mind.

He stayed with her until he saw the cottage in the distance. He stopped and watched from the safety of the brush as she walked the rest of the way to her destination. In the distance he could hear a soft fluid voice that he knew must be hers.

His stomach growled and for the first time since he saw the girl he thought of the lost kid. Connor turned and retreated into the woods as the sky grew darker. The first fat drops of rain fell and he felt them hit his back. He increased his pace as he loped through the forest toward his den.

12

RED AND GREY

She stood alone. She could feel that her body was upright. The sky above her and around her loomed midnight black, but no stars broke through the void. Blackness swirled around her.

She could not move. Darkness crept up her legs,

around her calf muscles. It twisted making it impossible for her to run. Her arms were crushed against her sides by the blackness creeping up her body. She tried to twist, tried to pull free. The effort left her weak and out of breath, without hope of escape.

Melody needed to scream, call for help, but she could not. The blackness devoured all the air around her. She gasped, tried again to yell. A small sound left her mouth, a whimper, nothing more.

He loped through the woods, trees and scents shifted around him. He felt the ground under his paws. The soft forest floor cushioned his steps.

Light reflected off tree trunks and soaked into the ground. He continued to run. He enjoyed the feel of his muscles and how they moved under his skin. A sound broke the stillness of the night.

A whimper of fear somewhere to his right. Prey?

He changed his direction, changed his gate and kept his body low to the ground.

The clearing opened in front of him, no stars shone here, no moon glow. Only one thing seemed to emit light in this place. A dark malevolent presence lurked without human form.

The girl stood in the center of the clearing. Her skin seemed to glow and it cast off the only light. He knew her immediately. He stalked around the clearing, watching her. Blackness engulfed her legs and swelled around her. He saw her struggling, heard her fight to take a breath. She stood trapped.

He growled.

The deep sound of an animal's growl rippled over Melody like cold water. Melody closed her eyes and tried to draw a deep breath. She opened her eyes and scanned the area she could see. The animal growled again and colored sparks lit the air near the edge of the clearing.

Orange and red seemed to flicker around the beast's face and Melody closed her eyes in hope that when she opened them it would be gone.

The wolf watched her struggle. She remained immobile, easy prey and he was hungry. He could have killed her earlier but let her walk away. He could have her now, and eat his fill. Her skin would be so soft, so easy to tear.

No. This was wrong.

Disgust rolled through him.

She was not prey.

Her eyes were closed. Long, dark lashes lay against her cheeks, standing out against the paleness of her skin. The other hunger she awakened in him surged past the inhibitions and instincts of the wolf. He slid into the clearing. His feet hardly touched the earth; they seemed to hover on top of the blackness. He moved close and sniffed the air.

Her clean scent felt like water to his senses. She opened her eyes and saw him. She didn't scream, just watched, eyes wide, as he approached.

Her gaze found the wolf, it moved closer. Sweat mixed with tears ran down her cheeks. She swallowed back a sob, choking on the effort.

She was going to die. If the blackness did not consume her, the wolf would. Terror clutched her stomach and she fought the urge to try again to yell, knowing the effort to be useless.

The wolf moved forward and the tip of its nose touched one of her fingers. Stars exploded into the sky, the blackness in the clearing fled. Flowers in every color of the rainbow sprang into life around her. Trees appeared around the clearing, crisp green leaves covering brown branches. The sky above transformed into the darkest shade of blue she had ever seen, and in middle of it all stood a huge grey wolf.

She drew a long deep breath. The wolf stared up at her.

13

Melody

Melody sat up in bed, sweat ran down her back and her nightgown clung to her. She fought to suck in a breath.

The dream.

It changed.

She remembered. Her breath came in short, hard gasps. The dreams from the past weeks began to clarify in her mind.

The blackness, it choked her nightly, sucking everything out of her. For hours she fought the void and struggled to breathe under the weight of the blackness.

The wolf, though, was new. Somehow, his presence chased away the blackness. When he touched her, the stars came back and she could breathe.

Wonderful, a wolf lurked in her nightmares now. She could trade one death for another? She felt wetness on her cheeks and knew it came from tears, not sweat.

The wolf stood to her hip. She saw his teeth flash and felt a growl rumble through her body with his touch. If her dreams forced her to fight the wolf and the void, she held no hope.

"Stop it," she hissed the words into the semi-darkness of her room. "A dream. Nothing but a stupid, scary dream." Except today she remembered the dreams and in the past they always eluded her. Why could she remember the wolf?

She rose, shivering from the sweat drying on her skin. She

snatched the clothes she laid out for herself the night before, and crept to the washroom. She did not know why she worked to be quiet. Her father may have spent the night at the cabin near the mine. Either that or he had already left. Still, she tried to keep her footsteps light and to remain quiet as she bathed and dressed.

Melody entered the kitchen, surprised to see her father seated at the table. Timothy Saltman sipped coffee from his favorite mug and peered out the back window. Melody grinned as she caught his eye. Maybe he overslept this morning and ran late on his way out to the mines.

"You're up early, Melody." He sounded surprised.

Perhaps it was earlier than she thought. "Bad dream," she explained with a shrug.

"I'm sorry to hear that." He looked back out the window. Mother would have asked to hear about the dream.

Melody watched her father as she moved to sit at the table across from him. More grey peppered his hair than a few months ago. Her mother's death and trouble at the mines had taken a physical toll on him. Her hand traced the grain of the wood in the table as she considered how to open a conversation. A problem she never struggled with until a few months ago. Maybe today he would spend a few minutes with her before he left for the mine, the way he used to.

"Do you want me to make you breakfast?" She wondered if he heard the hopeful tone in her voice.

"No, I'm on my way out." He pushed back from the table and stood his motions a bit stiff.

"Daddy-" Melody paused, he arched an eyebrow at her and she gave him a weak smile. "Have a good day today."

After he left, Melody sat in silence in the huge empty house.

14

Connor

He called her Red.

He returned to the path the next day, and the next he waited for her. The first day he tried to track the kid as an excuse for his actions. He never found the kid, yet he continued to return day after day. On the seventh day, he saw her again.

This time the sun gleamed high and bright. She walked alone again. No red cape swayed around her ankles. The dress she wore left her arms bare. Without the wind of the storm, her hair hung against her back, dark and heavy.

Once again, the scents from the basket enticed him as much as the girl. He could smell chicken, roasted with potatoes and onions, fresh yeast rolls and another pie. His stomach growled even though Connor made sure he ate before he came to the path each day. Every fiber of him longed to taste the food in her basket.

He tried to forget the food. Instead, he inspected the girl. She hummed to herself. The dress she wore clung to her chest, revealing the swell of her breasts over the top of the fabric. It flared from her hips and hung to her ankles in a gentle wave of fabric. Connor wondered how thick the dress was, how easy would it be to tear? What would the skin under the dress feel like?

Her voice sounded soft, sweet, and fluid. As she began to sing quietly, he found his ears swiveled to catch the words. He did not recognize the song, but the tune flowed simple and sweet, like a lullaby. Her hips swayed with the tune and she walked, almost as if her body wanted to dance.

What would her skin feel like? How would it taste if he licked her?

No, her skin would feel like nothing because he would never feel it. She would never touch a wolf. Even if somehow she would, or could touch him, his coarse grey hair would keep her fingers from his flesh. He would never feel her body against his the way he wanted to.

He growled low in his throat. Her head snapped around, the song died on her lips, and she stopped in her tracks. Her eyes scanned the brush. He stayed still and her gaze passed over where he hunched. She scanned the other side of the road, he knew from his past her limited human ears would be unable to determine where the sound came from.

She walked again, her steps slow, careful.

Red appeared nervous.

She should be. There were bears, wild boars, and snakes in the forest that would not hesitate to hurt her. Maybe fear would make her more cautious. She turned off the road onto the tiny forest path, as she had before, and continued to walk. He crossed the road with barely a glance to make sure it was safe. Once across he moved swiftly to keep pace with her. She remained more alert than usual, with each step surveying the scrub along the path. At one point, her eyes rested on the spot Connor occupied and her step faltered.

He thought for a moment that she saw him but then she looked away and continued to walk. Her pace stayed fast and her gaze continued to dart around her. She did not sing again and Connor felt disappointed. When the cottage came into sight he stopped and watched her until she reached her destination.

Connor laid waiting.

Red would still need to walk back.

15

Melody

Melody sat hunched over Nanna's table and traced the grain of the wood. She considered the sound on the path. Melody thought she heard a growl, but nothing attacked. However, after that she noticed that no birds sang. No squirrels darted across her path and no chipmunks scolded her from forest floor. These were all signs of a predator nearby.

"What's troubling you child?" Nanna asked.

"If..." Melody hesitated. Instead of asking about wild animals, she broached a different subject. "If I could somehow do magic, how would it work? How did Momma use it?"

"Ah, well, those are two different questions, love. From childhood, your mother's magic flowed out of her and around her like mine does. It attracted people to her; even here, so far from town, it pulls at people. There isn't a week that goes by I don't have visitors from Briar Creek and Varin."

"Maybe people like you." Melody grinned and wiggled her eyebrows.

"I'm sure they do, but it's more than that. It's the magic. It touched everyone and everything your mother did. Her love for your father strengthened the magic. She could almost focus it, but for her the magic just existed." Nanna's eyes took on a faraway look and a faint smile tugged at her lips.

Melody did not argue or joke. She stared down at the table and continued to trace patterns in the wood. Why couldn't it be that easy for her? What would it feel like to have everyone love her simply because she *was*, not because she had something they wanted?

"For you." Her grandmother placed a cup of herbal tea in front of Melody on the table and took the seat opposite her. Nanna fidgeted with her own cup, she turned it in a circle on the table, and then reversed the direction and turned it the other way. Melody watched, fascinated. Nanna never fidgeted. "Well, it never worked that way for you. You *used* magic, almost as if you could see it. Then, well, something happened that no one could have expected and the magic was...gone. Like you could no longer reach it, or see it, or even feel it. You still have it, but, you've stopped believing and you don't use it anymore."

The words slid into her chest like a knife. So, magic became this thing she could not see or feel, yet somehow hoarded to herself, to the detriment of all the people around her. It hurt to draw breath. How could she be so incredibly selfish? She didn't mean to be, but did that matter?

She yawned. Maybe it would be easier if she were not always so tired.

The idea of telling Nanna about her dreams, about the darkness that surrounded her and tried to suffocate her moved like a whisper through her mind.

She rejected it.

Just like magic.

She would never refuse to help or do good if she could, so the answer must be she could not. The magic Nanna seemed so sure of was nothing but a fairy tale. Instead of talking, she took her mug and moved to the little sofa by the fireplace. She curled her legs under her and stared into the fire. Melody sipped her tea and let the quiet settle around her.

Nanna came and sat in the rocking chair. After Melody swallowed the last of her tea, she put her mug on the floor and snuggled onto the sofa under a soft brown and green blanket.

"Tell me a story, Nanna, please."

"Well, now, there is a request I haven't heard for years."

Melody closed her eyes, her head rested on a cushion on the sofa.

"Did you know you are a princess, Melody?" Melody felt a smile tug at her lips she begged for this story over and over as a small child. "It's distant now. My mother's, mother's grandmother was a princess in a court far from here, across a great ocean. Her name was Adele, and she had six sisters, three older and three younger.

"When Adele was a young woman–younger than you are now–a wizard came to the kingdom. Everyone loved the king because he treated them with kindness and did his best to rule with fairness, but the wizard began making demands of the king and his people. The king fought him and the wizard became enraged. As punishment, he turned the king's daughters into swans. For years the wizard kept the princesses trapped at his home and forced the king to meet his demands, threatening the lives of his daughters should he disobey. The daughters could only become human one night a month, under the light of the full moon.

"Each month the wizard brought the daughters to their father to visit him on this night and each month the girls saw the kingdom and the home they loved become a bit darker and more dangerous. They mourned for the place where they grew up and for the changes they saw in their father and the people.

"After almost three years, the sisters plotted together to escape the wizard. If he no longer held them captive, their father could not be forced to meet his demands. They'd tried before and always failed. This time, though, they were all a bit older and a bit wiser. Instead of trying to go home to their father, the girls decided they would have to vanish into the wilderness.

"They put their plan in motion and the night before the full moon the seven swans escaped the estate of the wizard. Over the years, the man became overconfident in his ability to hold them. As the sisters hoped, he didn't search for them right away, because he assumed they would return to their father's court and he would gather them the next night.

"To the wizard's shock and dismay, the girls were not where

he expected them to be. The loss of his daughters enraged the king; he believed the wizard destroyed his beloved children. His fears forgotten, he killed the man where he stood."

Melody relaxed and let the soft rasp of Nanna's voice sooth her. The gentle cadence of the words wrapped around her like a blanket. She remembered as a child she used to beg for stories every time she saw Nanna and Pop Pop. She felt young and safe now, as she lay warm and quiet in the house as familiar to her as her own.

"The king mourned. He believed his daughters were lost forever. Meanwhile, his daughters fled into the deep forests far from their father's kingdom. They didn't know about the wizard's destruction or their father's grief.

"For a time the sisters lived as all animals must, they ate, they slept, and they protected one another, and one night every month they enjoyed a few short hours of humanity.

"One evening a young hunter, possessed of great skill, came to the lake the swans called home. He had left his village on an extended trip in an attempt to find something spectacular and make a great name for himself.

"When he saw the lake and the seven beautiful, perfect swans gliding on it he was overjoyed. The feathers from one of those birds, perfect and silvery white, would bring him a bag full of gold. He chose a target, careful to select neither the largest nor the smallest bird, but rather the one in the middle. He sighted down the arrow and took aim. Before he could loose the arrow, the largest bird lifted its wings and trumpeted, at its signal all the others swam toward the shore.

"The hunter lowered his bow confused by this. Swans usually prefer to sleep on the water, safe from predators like foxes and raccoons. Could all these birds be nesting? The sun sank as he watched the birds leave the safety of the water to walk on the land. Curiosity overcame his desire to take home a trophy. He put his bow and arrow away and crept closer to where the birds left the water.

"As the suns last rays disappeared and night was truly upon them, something stirred in the bushes. The hunter watched in awe as not a swan but a woman rose from the brush and stood naked in front of him."

"What, naked, you never told me that part of the story before." Melody opened her eyes and shot Nanna an accusatory glare.

"Before I told you the children's version of the story, now you're an adult. I'm telling you the adult version. Do you want to hear it?" Melody nodded. "Then hush and listen.

"A lovely woman, with hair the color of sunshine on a summer day and eyes that sparkled green stood before him. Flawless ivory skin covered her perfect body in moonlight. The woman turned her head toward the water and the other bushes and laughed. To the hunter it sounded like music. He couldn't drag his eyes away from her.

"She reached into the brush and pulled out a simple white gown and dropped it over her head, as she continued to laugh. 'Who would see us Odette? The wise old owls or a wolf, perhaps? Should I care about the sensibilities of a wolf?'

"'Modesty, sister, even if we are alone in the woods we should maintain modesty.' Another beautiful girl rose from the brush, her hair darker, and her face as lovely although clearly she was the older of the two. A gown already covered her body. 'How would Father want you to act?'

"The first sister dropped her head and her cheeks flushed pink. She didn't answer. Instead, she left the brush and came to sit on a rock only a few feet from where the hunter hid in the woods. As he continued to watch, five more young women emerged, two were hardly more than girls.

"He watched them all take seats together. 'Perhaps it's time we went home. Perhaps Father has defeated the wizard?' The first girl said.

"The one she called Odette shook her head. 'Adele, why would we return? What can we bring our Father but grief and pain? We're swans more than we're human. What if the wizard remains? What if he traps us again?'

"'We can't know unless we try.'

"The sisters overruled Adele. She became silent and stared up at the moon. She appeared so sad that the hunter could no longer stay hidden. He stepped out of the woods and cleared his throat. The women jumped in shock. All of them fled except Adele, who stood up and faced him. He saw her hands tremble and knew she was afraid. He handed her his bow, as a gesture of good faith, and told them not to be afraid. He would not harm them.

"He offered them his protection as an escort home to their father. He told them of the rumors he'd heard of a kingdom far away where a king killed a wizard and saw the hope flare in the swan princess's eyes. The girls spoke to each other and they decided that they would allow Adele to make the dangerous trip back to their father's kingdom with the hunter. The others would stay hidden in the woods and wait for her return with news of their father.

"The hunter introduced himself to Adele. His name was Matthew, and for the rest of the night they talked together of their trip back to the princesses home. In the morning, he watched her change back into a swan as the sun's first light brightened the sky. Together they began the trip to her home.

"That first night, as they slept, the hunter had the most interesting dreams. He dreamt of Adele. In the dream, they walked and talked together and he found her intelligent, understanding and a wonderful conversationalist. He woke in the morning eager to continue the discussion they began the night before. He talked to Adele throughout the day, and though she could not respond, he felt certain she listened.

"In the evening, as they drifted into sleep, Adele found herself once again in the hunter's dreams. This frightened her, so she didn't tell the hunter that she heard everything he said. Instead, she pretended to be only a dream. With each night that passed, keeping the secret became more of a challenge, and with each night, Adele fell a little more in the love with Matthew.

"Through all this Matthew began to wonder if the dreams could be real. At times Adele would say something that he felt certain he told her during the day, and not at night in his dreams. How could she know those things if the dreams were not real?

"One evening, shortly after they slipped into their dreams, she blurted out that she loved him. She prepared herself for his rejection, instead he told her he loved her too and kissed her.

"In the next night's dream she ran into his arms and held him, Matthew held her and promised he loved her. That night, in their dreams, the two made love. He wondered at her sudden need to be close to him.

"The next morning they reached her father's kingdom, and he understood. Matthew requested an audience with the king. When Adele saw her father for the first time, she tried to rush to him. A guard blocked her path and swung a sword at the swan.

"Matthew blocked the blow. In the process, he received severe injuries. He told the king that the swan was his daughter Adele, who left her sisters and came to make sure they could return in safety. He described to the king how and where he had found the man's daughters.

"The king and his men left immediately. The swan Adele acted as guide, although her true desire was to remain with Matthew. The young man was forced to stay behind to recover from the wound he received. The family reunited at the lake on the night of the next full moon and the sisters were overjoyed to be back with their father. He took them home and planned a Ball to be held in their honor on the next full moon. The king also announced that he intended to give Matthew Odette's hand in marriage as a reward for his service to the kingdom."

"Odette seemed to accept this decision, even though she hardly knew Matthew. Adele, however, was crushed. Throughout her journey, she continued to dream about Matthew. At first she spent her nights nursing him back to health from the wound he received protecting her. Later, as he recovered, they talked, kissed and loved each other. Upon their arrival home, Adele became afraid to sleep. For days before the Ball she refused to close her eyes. The king must have told Matthew. He never once protested the match."

Melody never heard the story quite this way before. Certain details were omitted from the version she listened to so often as a child. Melody felt a blush stain her cheeks and felt a moment's relief that her face pressed into the sofa cushion.

"Adele loved Matthew so much she believed he deserved to

marry Odette and become king. In her heart she knew he would be a good and fair king like her father. Besides, everyone said Odette was the most beautiful, the most graceful, and the wisest of the sisters. How could Matthew not want to marry her? Adele refused to sleep, not wanting to fall more in love with Matthew, or have to face him in her dreams, but she knew her heart would never recover.

"The night of the Full Moon Ball arrived. It began an hour after the sunset, to give all the swans a chance to dress in their royal gowns. Each princess looked beautiful in her finery. However, everyone agreed that Odette, with her soft brown hair and deep brown eyes, was the loveliest of the sisters.

"Adele tried to stay at the back of the party that was to continue until daybreak at which time the girls would once again become swans. She danced only when someone insisted and kept far away from Matthew, who danced with each of her sisters and twice with Odette.

"At midnight the King honored Matthew, praising him for rescuing his daughters and offered him Odette's hand in marriage. To the shock of everyone gathered, Matthew refused. He politely asked the king if he could instead marry Adele, and there, in front of all her father's guests, he declared his love for her.

"The king looked at his younger daughter. Tears filled her eyes.

"'Do you love him as well?' he asked.

"Adele nodded.

"'Then I give you both my blessing and I praise you again, young Matthew, for your wisdom and knowledge that love is a far greater gift then money and power could ever be.'

"All the people cheered, and Adele and Matthew kissed for the first time outside their dreams. Everyone danced and celebrated until dawn light started to spread through the room. People watched in wonder to see the magic everyone in the kingdom knew happened each morning after the full moon, but nothing happened.

"Matthew and Adele's kiss, a kiss of true love, broke the spell. The entire kingdom rejoiced. Within the month Adele and Mathew married and lived happily ever after."

Melody did not move, or open her eyes. What would it be like to be loved by someone so much he would give up a kingdom and riches to be with you? How would it feel to love that deeply?

16

The Past

The woman smiled, a small hopeful smile, when her son sat up and ate. She openly wept when he stood and walked across the room. She bled when he killed her, her death feeding him.

The young body became strong fast. Magic healed the illness with ease.

In a matter of days, he walked the cobbled street. He allowed his power flow unchecked in a way he never permitted in the past. Pain seeped from every home. Doubt and fear flowed from each individual. He drew it to himself and drank it in. Within weeks of his inhabitation, the town verged on collapse. Murder, theft and distrust now ruled. They fed him and he took them in with a hunger that could not be quenched.

He heard a sound, a whimper. He turned and saw them. A young woman clutched a child. The little girl's thin arms wrapped tight around the woman's neck. Blonde hair, beautiful platinum blonde with soft rings of curls, tickled the back of the child's tiny neck.

He could hear that neck snap, almost feel the bones under his fingers.

She turned crystal blue eyes toward him. Her mother made a small noise, moved back into the shadow of a building, as if she could sense danger.

The sounds of the mob broke into his contemplation. The woman paled and tried to make herself small. The mob yelled. Words like witch and whore reached his ears. The child continued to watch him. Her eyes clear as the sky.

Something tugged inside him, a feeling he hardly understood. Her face, her eyes, they pulled at some emotions inside him he did not understand. Could this be pity? Had he not learned to expunge pity years ago in the Ancients prison?

The mob moved closer. The woman whimpered.

He could feel the chaos, the fear, the anger...it could feed him. He should step back, watch, and absorb the power this would give him. They would beat her to death and destroy the child.

The emotion, the undefined something, revolted him. An image of the small face bruised and bloody, her tiny arms broken, her eyes losing their light, staring blank in death imposed itself on his mind.

He could help her. He could save the woman and her child. He should move off the path, step aside, watch, and take the power. Instead, he stood still, turned his back to the woman and the child, and faced the oncoming mob.

They came and he feasted. He drank in every drop of their energy, their anger, their life. They could not fight him because they never even came near him. He pulled everything from them before they rounded the corner.

A few died, the life drawn completely out of them. Power surged inside him. He could have gleaned more from the death of the woman and girl, but it was still a glut of magic. The mob turned away. Fear and death tainted the air and made him stronger. He turned back.

The woman cowered; she hid the child behind her. Fear of the mob morphed into fear of him. He crouched in front of her.

"I can help you, make you safe."

He held out his hand. After a long moment, the woman

placed her fingers on his palm. He lifted her to her feet. He could taste her fear and the urge to devour her poured through him. The little girl gazed up into his eyes. The child had no fear, only trust... and hope.

He chose to let them live.

He took them safely through the town. He could feel the soft glow of magic to the north. There the woman would be given help and a place to heal. He provided her food and money and sent her north. The child kissed his cheek.

Warmth filled his chest. He felt...good.

As he turned back toward the devastated town, another emotion filled him. He almost felt sadness for the lost lives. The feeling filled him with terror and he pushed it away.

Brothers felt no regret.

17

Connor

After a few weeks he knew Red took the path every seventh day, although, he could no longer remember the name of that day. He accompanied her each time he traveled as her silent, invisible, guardian. He began to anticipate this time each week with excitement.

The late summer weather felt perfect this close to the mountains. Game remained plentiful. One afternoon, as he loped through the woods, he smelled something. The scent made the hair on the back of his neck stand up. He recognized it immediately. Wolf.

A male, not yet fully adult, was in his territory. Connor growled and followed the scent. The puppy sniffed at the base of a tree, one Connor had marked last week. The puppy did not seem aware of his approach.

He snarled, not a soft sound. A deep, angry rumble moved through his chest and out his mouth, curling his lips. The young wolf whipped around, but did not challenge. Instead, he fell onto the ground and whined. His body prostrate, tail hitting the ground in a rough rhythm. The animal looked up into Connor's face, its eyes wide and mouth gaping in a lupine smile.

He reminded Connor of a puppy he knew as a child. It lay on the floor in this same pose when it wanted to play. Connor's growl faded and the wolf pup flopped his tail back and forth and yipped a sharp, high bark. It was smaller than he was, and thinner. This puppy could be a potential pack mate.

The puppy's fur was a darker color than Connor's, so he called him Black.

Connor sniffed his muzzle in a gesture of greeting and Black leapt to his feet and cavorted around him. Had he been human, Connor would have raised an eyebrow and laughed. As a wolf, he snorted and nipped at the puppy's shoulder.

Black flopped onto the ground again, and rolled onto his back to paw at the air. His ribs showed under his coat.

Black needed to eat. Connor shook his head and turned back toward his den. Black leapt to his feet and followed at his heels. As always, Connor heard the rush of the water before he saw the river. Black, hearing the sound, leapt ahead and ran into the water up to the first joint of his legs. He plunged his nose into the cold water, then pulled it up and sneezed.

Sinking onto his haunches, Connor watched him, intrigued. The puppy played happily in the water for a moment. To get Black's attention Connor did something he avoided until this moment, he barked a single sharp yip that vibrated off the trees. The sound surprised him as much as it did the younger animal. It also terrified him. In his mind, it was the last step to becoming an animal, to completely losing his humanity.

Nothing changed. No sudden shift occurred inside him, no loss or pain. Everything remained the same, and he relaxed.

Black jumped from the water and came to stand before Connor, his tail wagging. Connor turned and led the way deeper into the forest. He picked up the trail of a wild turkey and led Black on a hunt.

Black's mother must have taught him silence well. He crept close to Connor and moved through the brush without a sound. Connor broke from the bush and rushed the bird. As if reading his mind, or following some instinct, Black moved further ahead and cut the bird off.

Connor watched Black's fangs flash as he caught the bird's neck. Suddenly, he no longer seemed like a puppy. This was a hunting partner, dangerous and vicious. Together their abilities would allow them to bring down bigger game, the type Grey avoided alone.

With a snarl, he shouldered Black away from the fresh kill. The puppy submitted, dropping to the ground to lay his head on his paws. As Connor tore into the bird and ate, Black watched. For a moment, Connor felt guilt but the human emotion passed. This was how a pack behaved. The strongest, the dominant, ate first. Allowing Black to eat with him would be giving him too much status in their newly formed pack.

So he ate until his stomach was almost full, then he left the carcass. Black leapt onto the bird's remains.

Connor turned and sank to the ground, his head on his paws. His eyes averted, but Connor could not close his ears to the sounds behind him. Connor's gut twisted as he heard the wet tear of Black's teeth in the birds flesh. He tried not to think about what he had become.

18

Red and Grey

Darkness snaked up her legs. From her calves, it crept onto her thighs. Blackness wrapped her hands and twisted around her fingers, it held them trapped. She moaned and fought to breathe against the void surrounding her. It sucked the air away from her. Her chest felt too heavy and her head felt too light. She desperately hoped the wolf would come. Maybe somehow he would help her again.

She struggled to see the sky. There was no moon, no stars, only blackness. It loomed thicker tonight, heavier. It seemed to grow every night. She could just make out the outline of a few trees. The blackness burned with cold as it pulled her into its depths.

She gasped in another breath, whimpered and tried in vain to struggle free. Sparks flared and she heard a growl. She felt him, the wolf, as he approached.

She fought and gasped for breath as he watched and the wolf knew he would help her. This was Red, who walked alone in the woods and sang to the forest. As he approached, the blackness shrank away from him. Grass appeared under his paws and tickled his feet as he strode closer to her.

"Wolf," she begged, drawing his gaze to her face. Her eyes

were wide, full of fear and a plea he could not ignore. He moved close, and stretched his neck so his nose touched her hand.

Darkness evaporated around them. He felt it dissolve, as if a weight lifted from the air. Bright light flooded the clearing. The smell of wild flowers and forest rushed in to fill the void.

Red stared down, eyes wide, her hand still touching his nose. He could feel her fear, smelled it. She took a cautious step back. He hoped, for her sake, she did not run. He could not guarantee what he would do if she ran. The instinct to chase ran deep.

She gazed down at the huge animal, Melody felt small and weak. He destroyed the blackness, allowed her to breathe. She owed him. His coat appeared dark grey, and his eyes bright amber.

"Thank you, Grey." She whispered the words as she caught her breath. The soft orange and pink sky seemed to surround them. The air swirled with colors so thick she felt certain she could reach out and touch them, hold them in her hand.

The urge to run assailed her and she took another careful step back, and broke contact with the wolf.

Darkness rushed toward her.

Without thinking she dropped onto her knees and grabbed at the wolf, he moved close. Fear forgotten, she dug her fingers into his fur, pulling her entire upper body against him. His growl vibrated through her. He stretched his head over her shoulder, leaning into her. She clutched him as close as she could.

Grey snarled and his entire body shook with the sound. Her arms squeezed his shoulder and she buried her face in his back. He faced the forest, and growled at the invisible threat.

"Thank you, Grey, thank you," she murmured the words into his coat. Finally, he stepped back and lay down on the ground, careful not to break contact with her. She stretched out next to him, her fingers curled into the fur on his back and her head on his chest. Within minutes, they both slept.

19

Grey

Grey, the name fit. From the moment Red spoke the word it felt right.

Five days after Black's arrival, it was time to watch Red on her regular route. Grey did not want Black to know about Red. Instinct warned that it was not a good idea. Grey left the den early to go watch for her. Black stood to follow, but Grey spun and snarled. Black wagged his tail and took another tentative step. Grey growled again. He snapped at the puppy's shoulder and Black dropped to the ground.

Grey began to walk again. Again, Black tried to follow. They repeated the ritual three times before Black understood. He laid down, front paws extended toward Grey and muzzle on his paws, just outside the den, and watched him leave. Black, no doubt, thought he would not return. Grey felt sorry for the younger animal and wished that he could explain to him. Grey shoved the human desire aside. Black did not understand human emotion.

Grey forgot about Black as soon as he arrived at the trail. He sat in the brush to wait for Red and wondered what smells would drift from her basket today. The scents always left him craving what he knew he could never have. Despite that, he enjoyed identifying the different foods she carried. Sometimes the smells brought back memories from the time before he became a wolf, a time that seemed so distant now. Other times unique scents drifted and he wondered at the flavors of the food she carried.

She never left the cottage empty handed. Often, he could smell herbs, flowers and, sometimes, he saw fabric spilling over the edge of the basket. Whom did she visit? A sister? An aunt? He hoped she did not visit her mother each week. That would mean Red was married. That idea brought with it a wave of anger Grey knew he had no right to feel.

The moment she appeared, he knew something was not right. She shuffled along, her eyes swollen and her shoulders slumped.

She wiped her eyes with the back of her hand and alternated between focusing on the ground and searching the canopy of branches above her, almost as if she needed answers she could not find.

As he watched, he could almost feel the grief pour off her. At one point, she stopped and sank down onto the forest floor, and wept. The basket sat beside her, forgotten. A fleeting thought of stealing the basket whispered through Grey's mind, and then his attention turned back to Red.

"Why is this happening?" she yelled the words up at the trees. Birds took flight. "Is this my fault? Did I kill him? Is it my fault they died? What's wrong with me? Where is this magic that's supposed to protect us?"

Her voice shook with fear and grief. Grey wanted to go to her. He wanted to lick the salt tears from her cheeks and find a way to soothe the anger and the sorrow that flowed from her. He wanted to feel her arms wrap around him the way they did in his dream. He wanted to understand who she believed she killed and how it was possible she could blame herself for anyone's death.

The desire twisted into a fierce knot inside him and he took a step forward, but he forced his body to stop, forced himself to watch her cry.

20

Melody

James is dead. An infection set in." Melody spoke with a calm voice and dry eyes. She cried her tears alone in the forest, away from watchful eyes. "He died in his sleep. Clara found out she was pregnant three days ago. They were so excited about the baby. She plans to leave Varin and return to her family in Briar Creek. I have to admit, I'm glad. Nothing good seems to happen in Varin right now. At least in Briar Creek she'll have a chance to be happy."

For a long time, Melody sat in silence, and let the misery flow out of her. Nanna stood behind her and ran her hand over Melody's hair in long slow strokes.

"Tell me, Nanna, please. If this magic is real, how do I use it? How do I make all these terrible things stop? Just being there isn't working. What do I do?" Melody knew she was begging, but she didn't care. She would accept magic; even embrace it, if she could make the pain stop. She wanted the world to make sense again.

"I don't know, love. I'm so sorry but I don't know. I wish I did. I wish I could tell you all the answers, but..."

"I hate this. I hate it all. I want all this pain and death to stop, Nanna."

"You seem so tired, love." Nanna said gently. "Why don't you lie down in your room and take a rest? If you sleep too long I'll send a dove to your father that you plan to spend the night."

Fear raced along Melody's nerves and her fingers clenched around the warm mug of tea on the table in front of her. She shook her head. "I can't, Nanna. I can't sleep."

"Why, Melody, what do you mean?"

"I never sleep through the night anymore. I–I just can't. I try. It gets worse every night though." Melody struggled with whether or not to share the dreams with Nanna.

"Oh, sweetheart, I didn't know. Why can't you sleep, Melody?"

She shrugged and struggled to find the right words. "Every time I sleep I wake up wet with sweat. I cry in my sleep." Melody could not make herself tell Nanna about the dreams. Something held her back.

"Try to sleep here, love. Maybe my magic can protect you a little. Maybe it can let you rest at least."

Without much hope, Melody allowed herself to be led to the guest bedroom that had always been hers. Nanna tucked her into bed and slipped out of the room. Melody closed her eyes and immediately sleep overtook her.

21

Red and Grey

The warm breeze carried swirls of color around the meadow. Melody spread her cloak out on the grass, shades of green rolled around her as she sank down. Bright sun shimmered on the warm light air that flowed around her. She inspected the clearing. No hint of darkness lingered. At the edge of the woods, her eyes caught a shape. Grey moved in the shadows of the trees.

She watched him walk toward her and nerves tensed her stomach, but not the terror that came with the dreams of darkness. He walked straight up to her. She met his gaze. Her breath caught.

His eyes drew her attention, so much emotion reflected in those eyes. Hope, mixed with longing and desire, emotions a wolf should not know. He moved a step closer and his nose touched her cheek. He could kill her, right now. She knew that with absolute certainty. His breath flowed hot over her cheek, neck, and shoulder. If he opened his jaw, he could crush her throat. She waited.

His tongue swiped the flesh of her cheek.

She laughed aloud, all her nervous fear forgotten. Grey sank back onto his haunches and gave her a look she could only define as offended. She stretched out to touch him and he lifted his head out of her reach.

"I'm sorry, Grey," she said, dropping her hand. "I'm not laughing at you. Honest, I'm laughing at me. I was thinking you could kill me, and instead you gave me a kiss." She reached out and took the wolf's face in her hands. He did not move this time. She leaned forward and touched her forehead to his. "Thank you, Grey. Thank you for making the darkness go away."

Grey turned his head and licked the inside of her wrist. She tasted good, tasted right. Her fingers were buried in his fur and he liked the feel of it. She leaned her head against him, her arm wound around his body and her fingers stroked his neck and chest. The desire he felt as he watched her walk amplified a hundred times with her touch.

She yawned and Grey could feel her weariness in the way she leaned on him. He shifted his weight and lay down. She followed his lead and stretched out with her head on his body. Her fingers curled in the fur of his shoulder. He closed his eyes and tried to sleep.

Grey's eyes opened as he cradled Red's head on his chest, her arm draped over his stomach. His skin felt warm and it took a moment for him to understand the sensations that cascaded along his nerves. His body had changed while he slept. He lay holding Red as a human. She curled against his side. Her soft curves pressed into his bare body and one of her long legs lay over his.

She stirred. Her leg moved up his a fraction. His body was instantly ready to take hers. Grey fought back the urge. Purple air swirled around them and settled into the minute area between their bodies.

"Red, wake up," his voice sounded gruff, harsh. He did not even recognize it as his own.

She moved again to his relief. She pushed away from him slightly, looked up at him and her eyes widened. She stared, for a long time, at his face. She seemed unaware of his nudity, or his arousal. He read confusion in her wide green eyes. "Grey?"

"Yes, Red." Her eyes were green. He could see the color. He looked up into the sky and saw blue and purple swirl into soft golden clouds. Around him the grass and flowers twisted together into a riot of colors and smells.

"Oh." She pulled away. Her eyes got so huge they seemed to engulf her face. Now she knew he was naked. He watched the flush turn her face scarlet. She rose and turned her back to him. Now she would run. His mind raced trying to think of some way to distract her and keep her with him. He remembered the tears from earlier on the path.

"Why did you cry, Red? Tell me."

"A man died today." She did not turn, but the air around her stained pale yellow and sickly green. He heard the defeat in her voice. "His injuries came from my father's mine several weeks ago. The wound became infected and he died."

She rubbed at her eyes; she did not want to cry anymore. "I feel like it was my fault. Nanna said I should protect people, protect the town, but I couldn't do anything. I don't know how."

"How could it be your fault?"

"I'm supposed to have magic, to be magic." She glanced over her shoulder at him. Clothing had appeared on his body from the waist down. Red relaxed, she turned to face him. "I don't, or if I do, I can't find it, can't use it."

"You do." He stood up and moved from the grass to the place where she spread her cloak on the ground. He sat back down on the cloak, and looked up at her. "I can feel it on you."

Red felt foolish standing while he sat. She walked back to where he rested and sank down onto the edge of the cloak. She stayed far enough away that she did not touch him.

"So I have magic. It's useless. I'm useless. I can't help anyone." Her eyes ran over his chest. She could not stop them. Muscles moved under his tanned skin. She dragged her gaze back up to his face. His amber eyes sparkled and his lips twitched. Was he laughing at her? She bit her lower lip so she would not say something foolish.

"Not useless, Red. Maybe you can't use the magic now, but that doesn't make you useless. You're a lot more than *just* magic." He moved, his body came closer to hers. She tensed. Would he touch her? Did she want him to?

"You're a lot more than *just* a wolf," she countered and raised her eyebrows at him.

He grinned, the gesture very wolfish.

"Apparently, *here* I am." He tilted his head and evaluated her with his gaze. "If you want magic, if you really think you need it, you'll find it, Red."

The way he said it, with such confidence that an answer existed and she would find it relaxed her. He lay down, stretching out to cover most of her cloak. He tucked one of his arms behind his head. The other he extended in invitation.

He liked the way she watched him. He stretched his arm and raised an eyebrow she looked nervous. She licked her lips and he followed the motion with his eyes. She hesitated. Finally, she moved toward him.

With her head resting on his shoulder, and one of her hands on his ribs, he relaxed. He looked up into the purple-blue sky and watched the golden clouds drift on a blue-green wind.

22

Grey

Black made an ideal hunting companion. Sometimes Grey thought the smaller wolf could read his mind. On a deeper level, he recognized instinct. Wolves were built to hunt together, and they knew how it worked. It frightened Grey that he never sought out those instincts. They just happened. He and Black never went to sleep with empty bellies.

The air turned chill and the scents of fall inundated the forest. They hunted a yearling buck with an injured foreleg. Black took the most dangerous position; behind the buck's rear haunches. The animal's injury lowered the risk of a kick. Still, if he did kick, Black could be hurt.

He harried the deer to tire it. Grey loped along and herded the deer to keep the animal out of the deep woods. He waited for the critical moment to leap in and take the buck down. The prey stumbled and Grey moved. His body seemed to fly. He caught the deer's neck and his teeth sank in. The animal thrashed as it attempted to regain its equilibrium and dislodge Grey. Grey held the neck, keeping the prey off balance. The buck stumbled. Black hit the buck's hindquarters, and tore into his flank.

The prey fell hard to the side. Grey moved, loosened his grip only to sink his fangs further up the buck's neck. Black attacked the exposed belly and narrowly missed a flying hoof. Grey clenched harder and the prey jerked in his jaws. The taste of blood and the heat of the animal's flesh filled his mouth. His heart pounded and his blood pumped hard through his veins. The hunt was good. The kill was better.

The buck relaxed in his jaw and the fight left its body. Black whined with excitement and anticipation.

Grey released his hold. He licked the blood from his lips. The taste excited him. Black scurried back from the prey, his tail wagging. Grey moved in and pulled a mouthful of flesh from the carcass. Black whined again and Grey snarled, not moving from where he ate. After another two mouthfuls, Grey looked up at Black and the puppy charged in and ripped through the hide to reach the meat underneath.

For a time all that mattered was the kill and the food that it afforded them. They would spend the night here and eat off this kill tomorrow as well. Grey ate his fill and continued to eat until he felt stuffed. Extra weight could only help in the winter when food would be harder to come by. Black ate his fill as well. Both wolves lay down near the carcass, and Black fell right asleep.

Grey stayed awake longer. He did not dream of Red every night. Most nights he dreamt of the hunt, like any other wolf. He did not know what triggered the dreams, but every time he lay down, he craved them.

His eyes drifted closed and his body relaxed.

He raced through the woods; his paws flew over the ground. Light snow drifted from the sky and covered the ground. The trees glowed with moonlight. Grey could smell the doe, the scent of her blood. He spilled that blood. Now she ran. Grey pursued.

His prey suffered an injury from his teeth, and he would finish the hunt. He dodged around a tree and saw her ahead of him. She moved fast in an attempt to reach the thickest part of the woods. He charged toward her, pushing through the underbrush.

The light around him shifted and seemed to radiate up from

the ground. He lunged forward and his teeth sank into the flesh at the back of her neck. The doe made a sound and threw her head back in an attempt to free herself.

He felt his body jar, but ignored the sensation. Instead, he ground his teeth deeper. The metallic flavor of her blood flooded his mouth. The blood flowed into his throat, over his lower jaw and down the doe's neck. She dropped to her knees. Grey released her neck and spun his body to latch his jaw onto her throat.

She struggled and pushed at him, her breath came in short gasps. He tightened his jaw, heard tendons tear, and warm blood soaked the front of his chest. She stopped moving, stopped pushing and fighting.

He let his body relax, let his muscles still, and dropped to the ground, mouth still locked on her throat. Grey ripped flesh from her and began to eat. He tore into the skin of her throat and her chest.

He devoured her arm, grasping it in his hands and tearing the flesh from the bone.

How long had he been sitting here, as a human, covered in blood, eating a human arm?

He looked over at the doe. Not a doe, but Red, lying on the ground, her green eyes staring lifelessly out of her face. She lay still and cold. Her chest ripped open to expose ribs and organs, her throat gone. One of her arms was torn off at the shoulder. Blood covered the ground around her and splattered over her face.

Grey started to shake. His entire body seemed to vibrate. He dropped the arm and tried to stand, but his body shook too hard to let him gain his feet. Instead, he turned away from the body on hands and knees and vomited. He had killed her, ripped her open, and eaten her flesh.

Still shaking and gagging, he tried to crawl away from the body. As he moved toward the darker woods, he felt wetness on his cheeks and realized it came from his tears. He fell to the forest floor, his body trembling. He retched again as the tears became harsh sobs. He grabbed handfuls of the snow that covered him and began to scrub at the blood on his chest.

Sweat ran down his body despite the snow. He scrubbed and scrubbed at his chest using huge handfuls of snow. Nothing happened, the dry blood stayed caked to his skin. He wanted to howl in frustration and grief, but his human body would not allow him to make the sounds necessary. Finally, he collapsed in exhaustion, letting the sobs rip through his chest, the snow covering him in a heavy blanket.

23

Melody

Melody grinned across the square at Nanna while she arranged the pies on the table. Over a half dozen pies, apple, cherry, wild berry and custard, decorated the table, ready for the guests to arrive. Around the pies, she organized the breads and cakes she made.

Nanna walked over and smiled at her. "Well, dear, it isn't what your mother used to do, but it is very impressive."

Melody smiled again. No, her mother coordinated the event each year. She flitted from person to person, and place to place, to make sure everything ran smoothly for the harvest celebration. She became the center of motion, the center of celebration, and the center of socialization. To her relief, no one asked Melody to take on that role. Instead, Mrs. Hartman took over the position as organizer.

Melody did what she was best at; she stayed out of the way and baked. As a result, enough desserts to feed the entire village filled the table in front of her. The entire town, and several families from Briar Creek, would gather tonight to celebrate the harvest. There would be music and dancing, and her father would give every family in Varin a bag of salt. They could use it to trade with the last of the caravans that came through in the fall or sell it to the traders and use the gold in Briar Creek.

Nanna smiled. "You should go get dressed for the party, dear."

Melody glanced down at herself and laughed. Her dark blue dress was covered with a dusting of flour. Her apron hung crooked, her fingernails were caked with dough. She suspected her hair was a mess with flour and knots. She nodded. "Of course, I'll be back before the music starts."

Melody smiled. For the first time in months, she felt like part of the community. She gave a tiny leap as she walked, landed on her toes, and spun around once. With the exception of a few odd looks from her neighbors life had begun to make sense again. She felt the stares and heard them whisper, but she could ignore those things tonight since most people spoke to her and treated her like a friend.

As she approached the edge of the celebration area, Melody crossed paths with Jessica. She hung on Trevor's arm as they approached the square.

"Oh, Melody, that flour really...highlights your hair. Tell me, is that the way Danny or Milo prefers you?"

Melody forced a smile. "This is the 'I've been baking all day style.' I am not sure either of them would say they preferred it. Although I am sure they both enjoy the result." Melody snapped her mouth closed at the expression on Jessica's face and felt her cheeks turn pink. "Not that I'm concerned with what they think... I mean..."

"Can't decide which one you want?" Jessica sneered at her. "Tell me, does Milo know what you've been doing with Danny? If he did, I'm sure you wouldn't have to worry about his offer."

"What are you talking about Jessica?" Melody felt bewildered by the turn in the conversation.

"Oh, please. You can't keep secrets from me. I do your laundry. I've seen the condition of your sheets these past weeks. It's obvious you've been doing something on them besides sleeping. Maybe it isn't Danny, though. Maybe it's one of the mine workers. Who sneaks into your room at night while your father is off at the cabin?"

As quickly as it rushed to her face, the blood drained. Melody felt cold all over. Jessica thought that she – her stomach churned. She flashed a glance at Trevor and saw disapproval written on his face. Her gaze dropped and she shook her head. Her fingers clenched and unclenched and she ground her teeth together. Rage pumped through her body with each heartbeat. What would happen if she hit Jessica?

"I have nightmares, Jessica." She forced the words out, emotion coloring her words. She struggled not to react physically to Jessica's verbal assault. How difficult would it be to hit her? "Now, if you'll excuse me."

Melody pushed past them and walked the short distance to her house. As soon she arrived, Melody felt her body slump. Now she understood the stares and the whispered words.

People didn't believe it, did they? It was just gossip. People couldn't believe that, about me?

Her stomach churned as she went through the motions of getting ready. Her movements came without thought. She washed and brushed her hair, changed into the dress she worked all summer to make, and finished by putting her red cape on her shoulders. Through all this, her mind stayed focused on what she knew everyone must believe about her. Her father stood waiting for her inside the door.

"Melody, you look beautiful."

"Thank you, Daddy." Melody blushed. Either her father did not know the rumors or he chose to ignore them. Whatever the case, she was grateful.

"You look so much like your mother when she was your age."

Melody smiled up at her father as he tucked her hand into his arm. "Tell me, Melody, have you made a decision yet about whom you want to marry?"

Melody gritted her teeth and fought the urge to stiffen her shoulders. "No, Daddy. I can tell you I don't want to marry

Danny or Milo. Since they are the only men who have expressed interest–"

"Not the only ones," her father interrupted her. He led her through the front door as they continued to speak.

"Who else?" Melody stopped and turned to stare at her father eyes wide.

"Trevor Branch has asked about the status of your courtship several times over the past few weeks. I think he intends to speak to you about it soon."

"Really?" Melody heard the excitement in her voice and tried to make her tone more even. "I expected him to announce his engagement to Jessica any day now."

"He's given me the impression that they might not be as compatible as he originally believed."

"That is a surprise." Melody fought the urge to smile and lost.

They began to walk again, and moved toward the glow and noise coming from the square.

"So, if he asks my permission I should tell him you're not interested?" Melody could hear the grin in her father's voice. He was teasing her like he used to before Mother died.

Melody put her hand over her stomach, as if she could hold in the butterflies. "Please tell him yes, Daddy," she whispered as they arrived at the square.

Almost everyone was there. Food, drink and laugher all filled the square. Melody spotted Nanna by the huge fire where venison and lamb roasted. Nanna waved. Her father leaned down and kissed her head, released her arm and moved off into the crowd.

Melody barely moved into the press of people before Danny appeared by her side. He reached for her arm but she sidestepped away from him.

"Melody, you look stunning tonight," he smiled, the expression almost tentative.

"Thank you, Danny." It took a great deal of effort to keep her voice civil.

"Your dress is beautiful. Is this the one you've been working on?"

"Yes." Melody kept her answer short, wishing he would understand her lack of interest. Off to her right she heard the musicians start to tune their instruments.

"Your embroidery work is very skilled."

"Thank you."

"Do you want to dance?" She heard the hopeful note in his voice.

Melody loved to dance. It was her favorite part of the festivals and feasts. She sighed and turned to face him.

"Yes, Danny, we can dance."

He smiled as he took her arm and led her to the dancing area. Danny was not a wonderful dancer but he wasn't terrible either. By the end of the dance, Melody felt warm and she took off her cape and handed it to Nanna who took it with a wide smile.

"You seem so happy tonight, love," Nanna said.

"I am. The weather is perfect, the music is playing, there was enough salt for Daddy to give gifts, and...well, I feel hopeful tonight." Thoughts of Trevor played through her mind.

"Good. Hope is a powerful thing, Melody. Hold onto that."

Melody grinned. With a pivot and a bounce, she headed toward the dancers. Halfway across the square a thought occurred to her. What if Trevor just heard the rumors a few moments ago from Jessica? What if, right now, he sat listening to terrible lies about her?

Worse, what if it he already knew the stories and those lies caused his sudden interest. Her gait slowed. Within another handful of steps, Milo approached her. He caught her arm and turned her to face him. As his eyes scanned her, his brows drew together and his mouth narrowed into a frown.

"Hello, Melody. You are aware of the rumors, are you not?"

For a moment, she was too shocked to reply. When she did her words came out in stutter, "I...I have some idea."

"Are they true?"

"How dare you ask me that?" Melody felt a wild fierce anger build inside her. "How dare you–"

"I will assume that means no." Milo's grip tightened on her arm, he held her when she would have run away. "Given your knowledge, that is an interesting choice of dress for this evening.

Have you considered that if you didn't wear such revealing clothing, or that red cape, maybe the gossip mongers would have less reason to center their attention on you?"

She gaped at him in amazement. He somehow made the word 'red' sound dirty. "My mother chose my cape for me, Milo." She held her neck and face so stiff Melody thought she might crack. "As for this dress, my father and grandmother both approve. You have no right to criticize."

As she finished speaking, she jerked her arm out of his hand and pushed past him into the crowd. She could almost feel him following her. Melody stiffened her back and refused to slow down or glance back.

Then Trevor stood in front of her.

"Melody, what's wrong?"

She gazed up into his kind blue eyes. She clenched her jaw and fought back tears of anger and embarrassment. Did he believe the rumors too? Did he want to see if he could get into her bed?

"What's wrong is that everyone seems to think I'm someone I'm not. Or else they want me to be someone I'm not. I am not my mother and I am not a...a slut," she hissed out the last word in a low voice.

Trevor smiled a bit, but his eyes were full of pity and compassion. "I'm sorry you're hurting, Melody. I know what it's like when people want you to be something you cannot be. Would you dance with me, Melody?"

Melody bit into her lower lip to keep herself from breaking down at his sympathy and nodded her head. He felt sorry for her. She did not want his pity, but she would prefer that to his belief in the rumors Jessica spread. Trevor took her arm and led her to the dancing area.

Trevor took her in his arms and Melody felt engulfed, covered, and hidden from all the problems around her. She glanced up at him with a tentative smile. He grinned down at her and her heart beat a little faster.

"Melody, I believe I made a mistake about who I have been spending my time with of late."

"Trevor, if this is about the rumors, they aren't true." She cut him off, not wanting him to continue if his only intentions were to get her in bed. "I'm not going to, I mean I don't-"

"What?" For a moment, he appeared genuinely confused. Then he shook his head and beamed at her. "Oh, that. I know the rumors aren't true. Men talk, Melody, and you are a beautiful woman. If anyone visited your bed, they wouldn't keep quiet about it. They would want everyone to know they touched you. I know it's a vicious rumor started by someone jealous of who and what you are."

"Oh."

"I wanted to tell you, I think that Jessica has stepped across a line with her lies and it's not a line I plan to walk across with her."

"Thank you, Trevor. That is the kindest thing anyone has said to me in...well, in a long time." *Anyone human, anyway.* Thoughts of Grey and his trust in her ability to find her magic, and his assurance that she possessed value simply by existing, came to her mind, making her smile.

"You've been so sad, Melody. I don't like to see you hurting."

"I...I just don't know how to be my mother."

He stayed quiet as they continued to move together to the music. Their bodies seemed to fit and Melody relaxed in his arms. They flowed together around the dance floor. For a man of his size he moved with surprising grace. After a few moments, he spoke again.

"I would like to call on you Melody, if that meets with your approval. I think... I hope that maybe you and I can..."

Melody looked up and met his eyes again. Could this be real? After everything that went wrong in the past months, Trevor Branch was interested in her instead of beautiful, blonde Jessica. Warmth spread inside her. She could not hide her grin.

"Could you pinch me, maybe?" she asked, her voice more breathless than she expected. It must be from her heart trying to pound its way out of her chest.

"Why would I do that?" The slow smile that stretched across Trevor's face made her think he did not really need an answer.

"Trevor, I would be honored if you wanted to spend time

with me."

"I'll get permission from your father tonight."

As the song ended, Trevor disappeared into the crowd and Melody floated over to the food table. She filled a plate and almost danced to where Nanna sat with her cloak.

"Nanna, Trevor wants to call on me," she whispered as she sat down next to her.

"Oh, is that a good thing?" Nanna's eyes twinkled with laughter in the firelight.

"No, Nanna, this is a wonderful thing!"

24

Melody

Thick, heavy blackness coiled over Melody. It spiraled around her and encased everything.

Unable to stand, she struggled on her hands and knees. The weight of the void pressed on her back, pulling her toward the abyss. She could see it snake up her arms. Her flesh disappeared and she realized she could no longer move her hands, no longer feel her fingers.

She tried to scream, but the void sucked the breath from her lungs. She fought to stand. The effort proved futile. The air hung too heavy and the blackness too strong. It was impossible to move. She lifted her head. She could feel the darkness crawl up her neck. At the moment her face remained free. She squinted in the direction she knew the woods should be. She could no longer make out trees through the thick black curtain. She attempted to move her legs, tried to push herself toward the trees, or where they should have been.

Memories of earlier this evening filtered into her mind. She felt protected in Trevor's arms. Could he help her?

"Trevor," she tried to call out the name. Her voice dissolved into the void.

Nothing changed. She wrestled in another breath against the pain in her chest.

Trevor was not here. Trevor never appeared in her dreams.

She needed Grey. He could save her.

"Grey." His name was more a whimper than a word.

Her wolf did not appear.

A sob tried to rise in her throat, but unable to draw enough breath it choked her. The blackness climbed up her throat toward her face. Soon it would cover her and suffocate her.

Melody continued to fight.

25

GREY

He struggled with the decision. The dream after the buck made him wary. Sometimes dreams could act as a warning.

He used to dream of the witch woman, that she stood and laughed over his mother's dead body. Eventually, he had forced the dreams from his mind, not allowing them to affect him. He would not make that mistake again. Odd that he forgot his mother and the witch for so long, neither had entered his mind in months, not until he started spending time with Red.

He needed to see her. She strengthened his fragile humanity.

He would not kill her, Grey promised himself. He had developed more control than that over the past months.

Still, as he loped through the woods, he debated the wisdom of his decision, and even as he reached the road, he hesitated. His eyes scanned up and down the rutted path. He inhaled the scents drifting across the river from the village.

Nothing stirred. He crouched close to the ground and crept across the road. The branches on many bushes were bare and scratched at his fur. He found a thick area of evergreen growth low to the ground. A small clear patch of ground awaited him where he lay each week to watch for Red. Patches of his fur mixed with leaves, needles, and other debris.

He heard her before he saw her. Her footsteps were light, but a heavier tread accompanied hers. His head snapped up, ears pivoted to catch the sound. They entered the forest trail off the road.

The man next to her stood tall and broad, carrying an axe over his shoulder as if it weighed nothing. The stranger wore heavy boots, and his dress and tool reminded Grey of the woodcutter from his old town. The man's free hand entwined Red's.

Grey wanted to growl. He wanted to show his teeth and snarl. He needed to challenge this male who touched his Red. She belonged to him. For weeks, he had followed and protected her. This male was in *his* territory. He held back the anger.

He rose and moved through the brush on the tiny trail he was creating parallel to the path Red followed. He listened to them talk.

"I've tried, Trevor. I did what Nanna asked. I've gone to births, I've visited the sick, I've done what I can, but I'm not my mother. I offered Sarah to go to the birth of her baby, but she cringed and told me she'd rather I not."

The unknown male laughed. Grey saw Red's body stiffen and he felt relieved. The woodcutter continued to hold her hand and

Red did not pull away despite her tense shoulders.

"Melody, I know what it's like to try to fit a mold someone else makes for you. It can be very difficult, but sometimes people have good reasons for wanting you to act a certain way. Sometimes the mold is there to protect the people around you."

"So you think I should try harder?"

Grey heard the pain in her voice, she was not happy with this strange male. Some of his anger alleviated.

"Not necessarily." He paused and lifted their entwined hands in front of them.

Grey's hackles rose. The man studied their hands and grinned at Red.

"Everyone has to find their place and everyone makes mistakes on the way. Maybe you haven't found your place yet, Melody."

Red's eyes locked on their hands. She nodded her head. The hood of her cape hung down and a breeze teased her hair. Grey watched and ached. He wanted to be the one touching her; the one walking beside her. He could smell the scent of her as the breeze shifted, warm, clean, and female. The scent of apple pie and chicken from the basket assaulted him. The hunger that never eased gripped his belly.

"Thank you for walking me today," said Red. Their hands dropped between them and they continued along the path.

"I'm amazed you come this way every week. Doesn't it frighten you to walk alone through the forest?"

"Oh, no. I love the walk. Sometimes I sing and there is no one around to complain." The man chuckled and Red grinned. "Besides I adore the colors. The forest is so rich with color, especially in the fall and spring."

"You don't get lonely?"

"No." She laughed aloud. "Why would I? The walk isn't that long."

The male grinned again and shook his head. "You truly are unique, Melody. I can see why you don't fit in Varin. Maybe the village is too small for you. You need somewhere bigger, like this forest. Have you ever considered that the problem isn't you, but the village?"

Red halted, her fingers fell from his and she turned to stare up at the male. Grey shifted his position to see her face. She appeared surprised, almost frightened.

"I've never been further from Varin than Briar Creek. I wouldn't know what to do outside of Varin."

The male smiled. He caught her hand again and tugged her forward. "I have no doubt you would figure out what to do with the world, Melody."

Grey fought the growl of challenge. This male wanted to take his Red. Grey wanted to fight, to rip and tear, to kill. His dream flooded his mind. No, he would not hurt Red, but the male...

They were close to the cottage. The male released her hand. Grey watched the male lean in and press his lips to her cheek, and molten anger threatened to engulf him. He struggled with the need to attack. The prey turned his back to Grey.

What if Red stepped in? He might unintentionally hurt her. He forced his body to the ground, forced his lip to relax down over his teeth.

Red moved toward the cottage and the male moved back down the trail the way they came. Grey ignored the retreating form of his prey. Instead, he found his usual spot under the cover of some bushes. Another patch of ground cleared by continued use. He lay down to wait. Red still needed to walk home.

26

THE PAST

The decision to cross the sea came at a great price. The Western Continent was home, the land of his birth, yet the new world to the east held the enticement of people who would not remember who and what the Brotherhood used to be.

Magic could not cross moving water. It was one of the few laws he could not break. For him to cast a spell across a river or the ocean would be impossible, but magic could be carried across water.

There was, however, a price.

Any magical creature, even one in a human body, understood that a sea crossing would be dangerous, and could turn deadly. Few Brothers dared make the voyage. There would be less competition on the other side of the ocean. He felt certain that few Godmothers braved the journey.

Despite his knowledge and preparation, he did not expect to spend so much of his time vomiting over the side of the boat. He felt worse with every day that passed.

An older woman with grey hair she kept in a tight bun and wrinkles covering every exposed surface of her skin took pity on him, and began to care for him.

She came to his cabin every morning with a brew she mixed to settle his stomach. What amazed him was that despite her total lack of magic, the brew seemed to help.

"Why are you helping me?" he demanded on the tenth day of the three-week trip.

"Because you need help," she smiled. Her wrinkly cheeks pulled up and the lines around her eyes creased deeper. "You're suffering and when a person can relieve the suffering of another they should. To withhold goodness is wrong."

Her words tugged at memories he thought long dead. "But you don't know me."

"That doesn't change the fact that I should be kind to you."

"What if I'm an evil man? What if the world is trying to eliminate me so that I will no longer plague it with my malicious ways?" He sat forward to grab her arm. His grip firm, but not tight enough to hurt or frighten her.

The woman smiled and shook her head. "That's not for me to judge." She reached out and wiped his forehead with a damp cloth. "Besides, if that were true, why would those same forces have seen fit to make sure you and I arrived on this boat together?"

He could think of no way to argue with her words, and they reminded him too much of the words of another for his comfort, so he stayed silent.

Midway through the voyage hunger plagued him. His magic was starving with the need for violence, tragedy, and death. It withered inside him and burned off his life force from a lack of other fuel. However, everything ran smooth and easy, from the weather to how the crew got along. He might be able to generate something, some rage or pain, but his body became so weak and ill he could not act as a vessel for the magic. Instead, he grew weaker with each day. The loss of physical nourishment and the loss of pain around him made him frail and fragile. Every movement threatened to break him.

The elderly woman brought him broth, tea, and water. She bathed him, washed his clothing, and aired his room. She spoke to him as well, and he often found himself listening to her for hours on end. Though, sometimes he could not remember what she talked about.

As soon as the boat docked, he dragged himself down the ramp to dry land. The moment his feet touched the shore, temptation to use his power flooded him. He was weak, but it would take so little, just a hint of rage to push the people on the dock, cause a fight, and see blood spilled. Then he could feed the gnawing hunger that never let up.

A familiar voice made him glance back and he saw his caretaker making her way off the boat. She waved to a family on the dock. They called to her. Two small children jumped up and down yelling the word grandma. A woman and a young man held them back with smiles and laughter.

If he started a fight what would happen to them?

He should not care.

He did.

These people belonged to her. He could see the affection in her face, in theirs. He did not want to hurt her.

He held the magic, held the power, refused to hurt the family of the woman who helped him, who had done good for him. What would it be like to see that expression in someone's eyes as he approached them?

How would it feel to be the object of open honest affection again? Like he had been with...

Terror followed the thought. What was he becoming?

This would be the last time. He swore to himself that this would be the last time. He walked away, leaving the family and all those around them untouched.

27

Melody

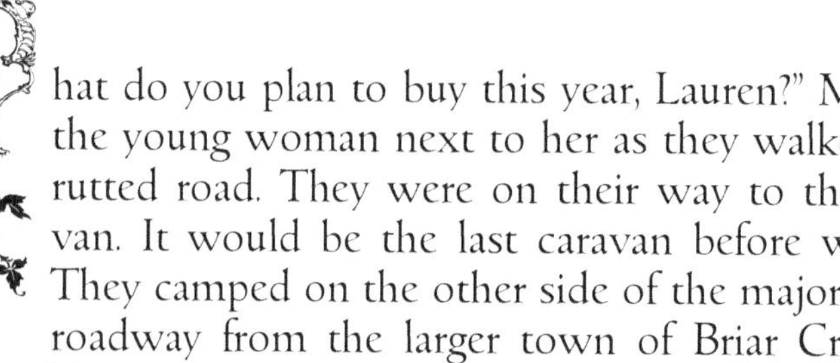

"What do you plan to buy this year, Lauren?" Melody asked the young woman next to her as they walked down the rutted road. They were on their way to the trade caravan. It would be the last caravan before winter set in. They camped on the other side of the major north-south roadway from the larger town of Briar Creek. Melody increased her pace to stay next to Lauren, brown leaves crunched under her boots and her red cloak swirled around her ankles in the cold fall breeze.

"Oh, well, not much. I have the salt your father gave us, and some blankets I made over the summer to trade. I need fabric to make new clothes for Jamie. He grows so fast, and I hoped to find a book for him. He loves stories and we only have the one book that belonged to Jonathan as a child." Silence lingered between them. After a time, Lauren asked "What about you?"

"I'm not sure. There isn't anything we need. Mostly, I want to go to visit with my relations since this is my Aunt Ellen's caravan." Melody admitted. Nanna would be there as well. Aunt Ellen always brought news from the far North Country where Nanna's sister Blanche lived, and from the rest of the family scattered around the continent.

"Oh yes, I always forget that your grandmother's people are nomads."

"Only some of them." Melody felt the implied insult and reacted to it. "Nanna's sister is married to a very wealthy man." Melody did not say a king, no one would believe her, she wasn't even sure if she believed it. "They have eight children. Three of those children started this trade caravan. Aunt Ellen, and many of the children and grandchildren, still travel with it."

Lauren nodded, her smile tight. "Your family is very lucky. With your connections to the caravan you must get the best deals, and you don't even need them."

As soon as she finished speaking, Lauren lengthened her stride to pull ahead of Melody. Melody slowed and felt a flush creep up her cheeks. She had not meant to brag, had she? She could not deny the urge to hurt Lauren when she felt insulted. Melody did not like that idea. Who else would she hurt because of her own pain? Who had she already hurt?

Besides, Lauren did not lie. Aunt Ellen and her relations always brought gifts for the family. They also gave them the best deals and held out special items they believed their family would enjoy.

Melody owned dozens of books. One that stood out in her mind was a fairy tale book from the old country across the sea; tales of magic and enchantment with beautiful, colorful pictures. She had spent hours gazing at the delightful illustrations as a child. Jamie would love it.

Melody walked, lost in her thoughts, the rest of the way to town.

As they entered Briar Creek, a much larger town than Varin, Melody could not help but notice the wider cobbled streets and regular rows of homes that the village lacked. Briar Creek sat on the major roadway from North to South that crossed the mountains. A fair amount of farmland and pasture lay stretched around the town and kept the forest at bay in a way Varin did not.

Melody took in the differences between Varin and Briar Creek as she walked. In Briar Creek, people did not know all their neighbors names. The larger population supported several shops including a small general store that did trade with all the caravans for specialty items and sold the farmers' goods to the townspeople so that farmers did not have to maintain stalls in the market street, although many still did.

What would a city be like? Trevor said he thought she would fit into a city and the idea tempted Melody. Would it be so hard to leave with Aunt Ellen and the caravan? She could travel north and meet Nanna Blanche. Find out if she really was a queen and see her kingdom.

That would mean saying goodbye to Daddy, Nanna, and Trevor. And Grey?

The road lay on the far side of Briar Creek. Across the wide path, one large enough for four wagons to move side-by-side or two-by-two and pass each other, was an open field where the trade Caravans camped. Caravans came almost every other week from early spring to late fall. Briar Creek was not big enough to be a winter home to a caravan, but it did warrant a stop from each for a least a few days of trade.

Melody ignored the area where the vendors shouted their wares. People milled around trading or buying. She saw several cousins and an uncle with displays of merchandise from the north. Passing all this, she walked toward a circle of huge caravan wagons. Here, only a few people moved around, they seemed casual enough, but Melody knew they guarded the wagons. She recognized a cousin and approached him with a smile.

"Brandon," she called out, and smiled as he turned toward her.

"Hey, Melody, how've you been this year?" He hugged her.

"It's been a rough year, can I go in?" Melody nodded toward the circle of wagons. She would find her Aunt Ellen in there.

The woman wasn't really her aunt. She was her grandmother's sister's daughter. That relationship proved far too complicated though, and since she was around the same age as her own mother, she had always been Aunt Ellen.

"Of course. Nanna Rose is already here."

As Melody stepped between two of the wagons she felt as if the air around her hung too thick and heavy, and as suddenly it thinned out again. The sensation surprised her. She reached the edge of the wagon and heard voices.

"Was there no other way?" Nanna's voice sounded desperate

for reassurance.

"No," came a sharp reply. "I'm telling you, there were no options. It was a matter of survival-" The unfamiliar male voice stopped. "Someone's coming."

Melody glanced behind her to see who might be approaching before she realized that the man referred to her. Nerves twisted her stomach. She took a deep breath to fight the strange fear that twisted her stomach, and stepped around the corner of the wagon.

The man standing near Nanna was tall and dark. His black hair hung a little longer than most of the men she knew and curled a bit at his neck. His skin was a much darker bronze than her pale white coloring. His eyes flashed copper. He was without question handsome, but in a wild way. None of this was responsible for the way Melody's heart started to pound as their gaze locked.

His eyes held violence, an almost feral element that seemed vaguely familiar. The way he held his body made her think of an animal preparing to attack. Melody felt cornered by his glare, and her mouth went dry and her fingers curled into fists.

"Who are you?" He growled the words, eyes narrow, nostrils flared almost as if he could smell her.

"My name is Melody." She glanced at Nanna, who seemed calm, but Melody noticed the surprise in her eyes.

"My granddaughter," Nanna said. Her voice soothed; the same tone Melody heard her use with birds who broke a wing, or children with scraped knees. "Melody, this is one of your cousins. His name is Andrew."

Melody forced her fingers to unclench and ran her hand down the side of her cape to make sure it was not sweaty before she held it out for him to shake. Nanna followed the nervous motion with her eyes.

"It's a pleasure to meet you," she lied.

He did not take her hand. Instead, his gaze ran over her and he scowled. "She doesn't smell right."

Nanna's head snapped up, her eyes narrowed and her gaze sharp on Andrews face. A moment of tense silence followed.

Melody dropped her hand to her side and shook her head, trying to free herself from his gaze. "Well, I came to see Aunt Ellen. Perhaps I'll talk to you later, Andrew."

She did not feel comfortable with her back to this man. She continued to move forward, pausing to hug Nanna, but her gaze never left Andrew and her back stayed stiff. Andrew moved aside so she did not have to touch him as she passed.

She didn't smell right? What did that mean? Melody gave a sharp little laugh. She smelled fine; she bathed this morning. He was obviously disturbed.

She found the largest caravan wagon and approached the back to knock on the door. It opened a second later and Tara, her cousin and Aunt Ellen's daughter, poked her head out. Her face broke into a huge grin when she saw Melody.

She and Tara looked a great deal alike, with the same long, straight, black hair and green eyes, but Tara's skin was darker than Melody's. Several times, as young children, Aunt Ellen left Tara with her mother over the summer months. The two girls were as close as cousins could be. In fact, Tara was one of the few people Melody considered a good friend.

"Melody, it is so good to see you. I've been waiting for you to get here."

For the first time in the months since her mother died, Melody felt completely safe and relaxed. She smiled, a real smile, and threw her arms around her cousin. Tara returned the embrace and hugged her hard.

"I'm so sorry about your mother. I wish we could have been here sooner." Melody felt as if someone pulled the plug on a drain and all the pain building in her began to spin and spiral. Instead of letting go, Tara pulled her into the wagon, as if she could sense the storm about to break. The door was not closed before Melody began to sob, feeling as if the tears would rend her in half.

Her cousin's arms surrounded her and she felt Aunt Ellen engulf them both in her embrace. They hugged her close, safe, and anchored, as she sobbed out the grief and pain of the past months. She tried to talk, tried to explain, but the words came out broken and confused. She could not be sure they made any sense at all.

She did not know how long she cried before the tears stopped and Aunt Ellen tucked her into one of the wagon's beds. Melody drifted into sleep before she realized she was tired.

28

GREY

Black smelled less like puppy now and more like wolf, though smaller than Grey, in height and breadth. They hunted well together and kept themselves fed without a problem, but Grey worried about the upcoming winter months. They lived close to two human towns and game would be scarce, especially when the humans started to hunt as well.

Black splashed in the river, playing in the shallow water in an attempt to catch a fish. Grey had no trouble fishing, but aquatic hunting seemed to elude Black. Stretched out on the bank, Grey relaxed in the pale autumn sun and watched Black. The sun warmed his back enough that he did not notice the breeze.

He let his head rest on his paws and continued to watch the monochrome world around him. He could still remember colors; remember how leaves changed before they fell from the trees. Now he could smell the leaves like never before. He could smell new growth, young leaves, mature leaves slick with rain or changing color as they released their hold on life, and the decay as the leaves turned into earth after they fell from the trees. Today Grey could feel them crunch under his paws. From the scent that emerged, he could even tell which tree shed the leaf.

Despite this extraordinary sense of smell, he missed the colors. He missed the yellows, oranges, and browns. He missed Red. He chose not to follow her for the past two weeks. He left her alone after he saw the woodcutter touch her. Between that, and his dream, he decided to stay away.

Still, he missed her. He could picture the way her hair moved in the wind, hear her voice singing softly as she walked, and see her body sway to music only she could hear. Grey closed his eyes. Somehow, he even kept the dreams at bay and she eluded his dreams since the night he hunted her in his sleep.

With thoughts of Red in his head and the sun warming his fur, he slipped into sleep.

29

Red and Grey

She opened her eyes in the middle of the soft green meadow, safe, the sun warming her skin. The air swirled in golden waves, safe, and protective. She closed her eyes and let the feel of the soft grass. and the weight of the air, relax her.

She did not hear him approach. She felt a sudden cold wetness against her cheek. Her eyes flew open and she sat up in a single motion. The wolf did not move, he stood there and stared at her.

"Grey, you're here." It should not have surprised her. No trace of blackness marred the meadow. He had to be here. "Where have you been? I needed you. I called you. You never came." As soon as the words were out Red slapped her hand over her mouth and felt blood rush to her face. "I'm sorry, Grey. I shouldn't have said that. That was incredibly selfish of me. You don't owe me anything, and I don't own you. There's no reason you had to come and help me. Please forgive me."

His bright intelligent gaze met hers. His eyes reflected so much more emotion and thoughtfulness than a typical animal's. The air shifted and she smelled roses on the breeze. She closed her eyes and inhaled. When she opened them again Grey the man sat where the wolf had been.

"Oh!" Her eyes widened as her gaze took him in.

Grey saw the way she watched him, as if trying not to see him before she turned her back to him, her face flushed.

He remained silent for a minute then cleared his throat. "It's safe."

Red turned, the heavy golden air moved with her and the scent of roses drifted around her again on swirls of golden pink. He was dressed, although he had not moved.

"The dreams, Red. Tell me."

She gazed up into his eyes. "The blackness, it gets worse every night. The void sucks the air away. I can't breathe, can't fight, soon it's going to kill me, suffocate me. What happens if you die in a dream?"

"Nothing. Dreams are just dreams, Red." Grey hoped the words were true even as he spoke them. Obviously, he did not kill her in his dream. Still, he had not ignored the warning either.

He inspected the meadow around him. The grass grew in deep green tracks and the sun hung golden yellow in air that swirled the same color as the sunshine. Trees, brown, green and flaming orange surrounded the small clearing. He took the colors in and drew a deep breath, trying to remember how every color smelled.

"What are you looking for?" Red asked.

"Not for. At. The colors; the wolf's eyes can't see color like the human eyes."

"But your eyes stay the same. I mean, they seem the same, whether you're human or wolf."

He looked back at her. Her eyes were so vividly green and her skin so pale and white against her black hair. He wanted to touch her, feel her skin. Could it possibly feel as smooth as it looked? He moved so close to her he could smell the scent of her skin.

She smelled so human, like fresh baked bread and flowers all twisted together with her unique female aroma. He closed his eyes and absorbed the scent.

He opened his eyes and found Red gazing at him, her head tilted to the side and her eyes narrowed. She bit her lip and shook her head.

"I was wrong, they do change. Right now they appear more wolf than human."

He smiled at her, then reached up and touched her cheek. He ran his fingers over the curve of her cheek to the skin of her throat. She did not move. The desire to touch her smooth warm flesh became more intense. He needed more of Red.

His fingers slid around her throat and he felt her tense.

He realized he held her entire throat in his hand. She was very soft and delicate. She met his gaze.

"I would be more comfortable if you moved your hand." She spoke quietly and he felt her swallow against his palm.

Grey grinned and flexed his fingers once before dropping his hand. Red smoothed her skirts around her, not willing to meet his gaze. The gesture appeared regal but the pink stain of her cheeks ruined the effort. The color seemed to radiate into the air around her. He chuckled and she shot him an offended look.

"The blackness wasn't here this time," he said.

"No, you're right, only the golden air." Red reached her hand out and cupped a handful of the air in her palm. She pulled it toward her and swirled a finger through it making it a tiny whirlwind of color.

Grey sat in silence, transfixed. He knew he could not touch

the color the way she did, even though he could feel it brush against his skin and tease his hair.

"I shouldn't have yelled at you. I'm very sorry," Melody said, not glancing up from the colors she twisted in her palm. "Are you alright? Did you stay away because you were hurt, or in danger?"

"I'm fine, Red. You didn't upset me. I'm not hurt, or in any danger." More likely she was the one in danger from him, but she seemed unconcerned with that.

She looked up from her handful of air as if to evaluate his truthfulness. She turned back to the air and continued to play with the colors. "Did you know I'm rich, Grey?"

"Wolves don't care about money."

"I wish people didn't either." She sighed and opened her hand to let the air flow out of her palm. Watching the colors swirl back into the air around her, she noticed they seemed deeper and richer than when she first grabbed them. "I want to be able to help the people in the village. I can't use magic like my mother, and she always said people hate charity."

Grey stayed silent and she reached out and picked a pale yellow flower. She stroked each petal in turn, her fingers leaving a bright path of orange behind.

"The people in my village don't like me. I try hard to be what I should, what they want me to be, but I keep failing."

"Why do you care if they like you?" Grey asked. He scrutinized the flower in her hand.

Feeling guilty about picking it, she put it back into the grass and swirled a finger around the dirt at the stem. Roots sprang out and buried themselves in the rich, brown earth.

"Because I live with them, we're all part of the same community."

"Have you ever been yourself? Maybe they don't like you trying to be someone else. Who says they won't like you if you allow yourself to be you?" Grey watched the power flow off her and around her with no effort on her part. It did her will as if it loved her, but she said she could not reach it. Perhaps her magic and his humanity could only be touched here in the dream world they created together.

"How do I know who I am?" Red asked. She looked up at Grey and wondered if he could answer the question she herself could not seem to grasp. All she seemed to figure out about herself was who she could not be.

He did not answer. He still gazed at the flower. The orange remained on the petals and half dozen flowers just like it sprang up around the one she put in the earth. She had created a new type of flower in the meadow.

"Do you..." She trailed off and looked down at her skirt. She smoothed out an imagined wrinkle and bit her lip.

Grey watched the gesture and almost smiled, once again she ruined her attempt at being proper by being herself. "Do you like me, Grey?"

"Why else would I come here, Red? You don't own me." He tossed her words back at her.

"I'm glad you like me." She looked away, up. He followed her gaze, taking in the pink orange sky where blue clouds made wispy shapes. "I like you, too."

30

Melody

Melody opened her eyes to warm semidarkness. It took a moment for her to remember she lay inside the caravan wagon. She felt as safe and comfortable as she had been in the meadow. She rolled over, and half expected to see Grey sitting next to her. Instead, she saw her aunt.

"Hello, Melody." The woman smiled and Melody felt warmth fill her. She adored Aunt Ellen.

"Hello. I'm sorry about earlier. I've tried so hard not to cry, I guess it kind of exploded."

"There's no need to apologize. I understand," her aunt said, turning back to the sewing in her hands. "Your grandmother said you wanted to talk to me. I sent a dove to your father with a note that you plan spend a day or two here with us."

"Thank you. I left a note at home, but he might not get it and I don't want him to worry. I don't know what to say though, I... it's all...what can I say, or ask to make everything make sense?"

"I suppose that depends on what you want to make sense." Aunt Ellen smiled and raised an inquisitive eyebrow.

"Life, pain, death, magic...all of it, everything."

Aunt Ellen set her sewing down and gazed into Melody's eyes. Her eyes were a deep soft blue, similar in color to Melody's mother's. "Sweetheart, people have tried to understand those things for thousands of years. Most think we're no closer now than a thousand years ago."

Melody laughed a little and nodded. "Alright, I'll settle for understanding me. Who am I supposed to be, Aunt Ellen? What does magic have to do with me and who I'm supposed to be?"

"Two very different questions. The first one, only you can answer. You need to find out for yourself who you are, but I would ask you this, who do you want to be, Melody? The second question I might be able to help with. First though, tell me about the dreams."

Melody looked at her surprised. How did Aunt Ellen know about the dreams?

"You mentioned them while you cried," Aunt Ellen said with a grin.

"Oh," Melody paused. "There's blackness in my dreams and a wolf."

"A wolf?" The words were sharp, surprised. As she spoke the wagon door opened allowing a breeze and a strip of bright daylight to slip through.

Tara poked her head in and smiled. "Oh, good! You're awake. Did you sleep well?" She climbed into the wagon as she spoke.

"Actually, yes. It's one of the few times I've slept without nightmares since my mother died."

Aunt Ellen watched Melody with eyes narrowed. "Go back to the dreams, Melody. Tell me about the wolf."

"Well, sometimes he's a wolf. He was a wolf the first time I saw him and he's usually a wolf when he arrives. Sometimes he's a man, but, Aunt Ellen, he isn't the problem. Grey doesn't scare me...well most of the time," she added, as she thought about the moment when Grey's fingers wrapped around her throat. "It's the blackness. It traps me and it sucks the air out of my lungs. It's a void that sucks in everything, the sky and the trees, the air and the colors. It's going to kill me, consume me. Grey makes the void leave."

There was silence in the wagon. Tara sat next to her on the bed and broke the silence. "Here, eat." She pulled several rolls out of her apron pocket and handed one to her mother and another to Melody. For a few minutes, they ate in silence. Safe and comfortable in the wagon with her family around her Melody ate the warm yeasty rolls with cheese and meat baked into them. Rested and full, she built her courage to ask the question she needed to have answered.

"Aunt Ellen, terrible things have happened in Varin. Nanna said I'm supposed to protect the village and I know recently I've developed a mean streak. I don't intend to... but... could all these horrible things be my fault? Is there something wrong with me? I've begun to realize that I am a selfish person. Could I be holding back my magic? I'm not sure who exactly I want to be, but I know I don't want to be the kind of person who would withhold good, a person who would keep magic to themselves when it could help other people."

"Oh, sweetheart," Aunt Ellen sighed and smiled. "Everyone can be selfish sometime, Melody," she spoke in a reassuring gentle voice. "Don't allow the action to define you. Don't allow it to become a habit or a lifestyle. Make sure it's a mistake, an error in judgment when it happens. Now, the magic; let's start at the beginning. Magic runs in our family. It's in your blood. However, not everyone's magic manifests in the same way." Softer and smoother than Nanna's, with none of the rough edges of age, Aunt Ellen's voice provided the same soothing effect.

"Everyone interacts with magic in a unique way. For example, your grandmother and I both manifest a kind of luck magic. All the people around us benefit from that magic. Health, good fortune, wealth, but Tara's magic is much more tangible. Can you show her, Tara?"

Tara grinned and lifted her hand. Melody watched in fascination as a small glow of light appeared above her palm. It floated up to the top of the wagon and hung there, casting a soft, warm light over the whole wagon. "It lasts for hours, or until I call it back. I can also weave shields into fabric that make them impenetrable to swords or arrows. Your cloak has a shield like that. I recently learned to put shields around objects and people. Those I have to hold up, though. There's a shield around the caravan wagons right now. I can feel someone pass through it and I can tell if they intend to do harm, if so, I can keep them out." Tara flushed. "I can do a few other things, too."

Melody knew her mouth hung opened. She sat too amazed to speak. How long did they know, and why hadn't anyone told her? Why lie for all these years? She forced her mouth to close and swallowed. Did her father know? Was he in on the family secret no one thought to share with her? Only Nanna tried to tell her the truth, and Melody accused her of telling fairy tales.

Aunt Ellen spoke again. "I don't know what your gift is, Melody. Nanna Blanche could tell you, but you would have to come back with us to let her see you and touch you. That's part of her magic, to understand other people's gifts.

"No matter what your gift is, the things happening in Varin are *not* your fault. Listen to me carefully, Melody. This is important. Death is a natural part of life. A sad and difficult part, but also a natural and normal part, death is not your fault. The child, the one who drowned, well, magic cannot cross moving water, so even your mother couldn't have saved her. Your mother's luck might have led someone to the girl while she still lived, but there is no guarantee.

"However, I agree with you. There has been too much death in Varin in a very short time, including your mother. All these things, combined with your dreams, make me wonder if there isn't something else happening in Varin, something that thrives on death and destruction."

"Are there really things like that?" Melody asked.

"Of course," said Tara, nodding her head. "Evil exists."

Melody shook her head and ran a hand through her hair. "Why didn't anyone ever tell me? Why the big secret? Why keep all this from me?" Now the warmth seemed too hot and the cozy light in the wagon made too many shadows. The silence in the wagon felt like a weight around her shoulders. Melody wondered what caused her aunt and cousins stress. What were they trying to hide from her, and why?

"Tell me why I've never known this before. Tell me what everyone's hiding? Please, Aunt Ellen. How can I deal with this if everyone keeps lying to me?"

Tara looked up and met her eyes. She shrugged. "I would if I knew. All I can tell you is that Mom always told us never to talk about magic with you. Personally, I always thought it was stupid."

Aunt Ellen shot her daughter a rueful smile. "Yes, well, Melody, Amber asked–no, more *told* us–that she wanted you to know nothing about magic. She begged the family to keep it a secret from you. It became so important to her, we all agreed."

"She always told me magic was nothing but fairy tales. Why would she do that? Why would she lie?" The deception seemed so out of character, her mother had always been honest, except it seemed, about this. Melody chewed her lip, struggling to figure out why her mother lied.

Aunt Ellen sighed and nodded. "Your mother is dead and you're grown, it's time for you to know the truth. I'll tell you the story the way I know it.

"When you were about five years old, a troll came to your village. It searched for you, found you and took you away with him. Your grandfather, mother and father, distraught, followed him into the mountains. Nanna Rose summoned a stronger magic, a being called a Godmother to assist with the search and rescue. Godmothers are powerful and few. Nanna Rose knew one so she called and the Godmother came.

"In the mountains, your mother tried to talk the troll into giving you back. She offered to go with the troll herself if he would return you to your father. The troll possessed a great deal of magic. He didn't want your mother. He made it very clear that he wanted you. I've always suspected that he knew something about your magic that we don't.

"Nanna and the Godmother arrived moments before the troll and your grandfather began to fight. The troll held you in one of his arms so your grandfather would have been at a huge disadvantage. He couldn't engage with his teeth and claws the way he wanted to, or even use his weight against the troll.

"The Godmother called a halt to everything by freezing everyone in place where they stood. She spoke to the troll privately. No one knows what she said or did, but somehow she persuaded the toll to give you to her without a fight. He said, 'Keep your word, Godmother.' And that was the end of it, in a way.

"The Godmother picked you up and carried you back to your parents. She kissed your head and handed you into your mother's arms. The Godmother told your parents and grandparents that as long as your mother lived there was no reason for you to be burdened by magic. After that, she pulled your mother aside and she told her something more, something different. No one knows what she said.

"Your mother took every word very seriously. The words 'not being burdened' became like a mantra to her. She insisted that no one discuss magic with you. Your grandmother, of course, told her stories, but your mother made certain you never thought of them as more than stories. They all agreed to keep your grandfather's dual nature from you."

Melody felt numb. She tried to remember a troll, tried to remember why her grandfather would have claws to use, tried to remember anything about that incident, but she could find nothing, not even a hint of a memory. She shivered despite the warmth around her. "What dual nature?"

Tara answered. "Perhaps it's best if Nanna Rose tells you that story."

Melody nodded, unable to think of a good reason why they should have to tell her now. "Why did the troll want me?"

"It's hard to know for sure. Sometimes trolls can see things, about the future, things that might happen. I always suspected that was why the troll wanted you. Perhaps he saw something and he thought you could make it happen. I suspect that the Godmother promised to make sure what he wanted came about without you involved. Really, no one but the troll and the Godmother know for sure." Aunt Ellen tilted her head her face speculative. "And perhaps you, Melody."

Melody shook her head and searched her memory. The harder she tried to remember the harder she hit a solid block wall in her mind that held nothing.

31

Melody

Melody's mind buzzed with information she did not know how to process as she walked away from the caravan the next afternoon. She had always accepted healing, it was a known fact, but this was unreal. She had watched Tara work all sorts of magic, seen Brandon move boxes without lifting a hand, and felt the shield around the caravan. A few weeks ago the idea of magic seemed like a child's fairy tale, now a completely new world had been revealed to her.

Aunt Ellen said that magic often ran in families, the way it did in theirs, but sometimes it appeared in a person with no magical history. Either way you were born with magic. Melody felt relieved to know other people struggled with the same trials she did. For some people it must be even harder. For those that heard voices, all their life they walked the edge of sanity until someone found them, told them about the magic and taught them how to control it.

Melody considered herself fortunate not to hear voices, she only had to endure what people said out loud. She could also count herself lucky to be part of a family who were able to help her through this. But how could she ever expect the people of Varin to accept her if she could manipulate magic, they already saw her as too different.

One part of the conversation continued to haunt Melody. Eventually, the conversation turned back to her dreams. Aunt

Ellen tried to warn her about Grey.

"This wolf may seem safe, Melody, but evil is often seductive. Have you considered that he might be manufacturing the darkness and then arrive at random times to give the appearance of saving you?"

"They're only dreams, Aunt Ellen." Melody tried to laugh the topic off, but Aunt Ellen frowned and shook her head.

"I think they might be more than that. Perhaps someone is interfering in your sleep, or perhaps your mind or some manifestation of your magic is trying to tell you something. Don't write off dreams. They can be very powerful."

Later in the evening, as Melody and Tara curled up together in the wagons bunk beds, her cousin offered a possible alternative. Her voice sounded almost wistful when she spoke. "What if Grey is a human, trapped like the princess in the story of the swans?"

Melody giggled. "Tara, that's a story."

"Have you been listening at all, Melody?" Tara said. She leaned over the bunk and watched her cousin eyes wide. "The stories are true. The swans were real."

"Okay, fine. The swans were real, but Grey isn't. I mean he's not a real wolf. I've never seen him in reality, only in my dreams." She frowned and bit her lip. "Unfortunately, I think Aunt Ellen's explanation of my magic trying to tell me something is more probable." She could not consider the idea that Grey could be evil. Grey saved her, listened to her, held her and let her sleep. She could not, would not, accept that he was evil.

To her relief, no one brought the subject up again, and Melody slept that night in blissful oblivion without a single dream. Aunt Ellen offered to take Melody with them to see Nanna Blanche and find out more about her gift, and even to meet people whose job it was to teach others with magical gifts. The caravan would be here another few days and much of the family would be through Nanna's house before they left. Melody promised to consider the offer and give her answer to someone at Rose Cottage.

In her heart, she already knew the answer. She could not walk away from Varin, not yet. Things seemed to be improving, and there was Trevor. She felt her face break into a smile. Trevor wanted to court her. She would do what she promised, and think about the offer, but not for too long.

"You seem happy." Trevor's deep gentle voice broke into her thoughts.

"Trevor, where did you come from?" Melody turned to see Trevor approaching from the side of the road. She lifted her hand to her chest and shook her head. "You startled me." Her fluttering heart settled back to a normal pace, glad to see him.

"I had some work in Briar Creek and saw you walking home from the caravan. Since I finished, and needed to come this way, too, I thought I might say hello. I called out, but you appeared deep in thought and didn't hear me till I was right next to you."

"I have been deep in thought, and I am happy." Melody laughed as she spoke. "Especially, now that you're here. Will you walk me home?"

Trevor appeared pleased. "Of course." He smiled and taking her free hand, he tucked it into his arm. "Did you enjoy your visit with your family?"

"I did. We caught up a lot and I enjoyed the visit with my cousin." She bit her lip.

"You have deep thoughts on your mind again."

"Do you believe in magic?" His arm tensed under her hand and she felt him pause to gaze down at her. She did not glance up at him, afraid of what she would see if she did.

"I guess I haven't thought about it too much. Why? Do you?" A mocking tone colored his voice.

Melody felt a shiver run down her spine. Did he think her a fool?

"I didn't," she spoke slowly, in an attempt to evaluate his reaction. "But now I think I do."

He chuckled. "You sound so certain of yourself." He put his hand over hers and squeezed her fingers. "If you want to believe in magic, I'm willing to accept the possibility as well."

Melody felt relief wash over her. She suspected that he was humoring her. Still, his willingness to play along seemed better than him saying she was crazy. "Thank you, Trevor."

For a few moments, she remained silent, but Melody felt braver with his acceptance. "My aunt offered to take me with her to the far north, there's a big city, the kind you said I would fit into."

"Really?"

Once again, he tensed and this time Melody did look up to watch his face to see what he might think.

"Do you think you'll go with her?" He sounded nervous.

Melody stared into his blue eyes and realized they had stopped walking. "No, I think that there is something...someone, here that I would like to stay for."

He continued to hold her gaze for a long moment before a slow smile spread across his face. "It's good of you to stay and care for your grandmother."

Melody knew from the twinkle in his eyes and the slight tilt of his mouth that he was teasing her. She felt her cheeks flush a bit. "Why, yes. I am a very good person."

He chuckled, the sound rich and happy. Melody liked to make him laugh. They walked the rest of the way to her house in silence. There he released her hand at the foot of the stairs and promised to call on her one evening soon.

Inside, Melody looked around the empty house. Her note lay undisturbed on the table by the door. Of course, Daddy would have gotten the dove from Aunt Ellen and would not have felt the need to come home to an empty house.

Melody let her eyes scan the room again. Her mother's shawl still hung on the back of a chair in the sitting room, the large brick fireplace in the same room sat empty and clean. All the furniture in the room sat covered in a layer of dust and if she walked across the floor, she knew her feet would leave prints on the dirty floor. A fine layer of dust had settled on a shelf of books lining the far wall of the room. Everywhere she looked, there were things she did not use, things she did not need. Who did she want to be? Did the person she wanted to be live in this home?

32

Grey

Early winter moonlight, bright and clear, filtered through the stripped forest canopy overhead as Grey and Black hunted big game. Both ate their fill. Grey's body felt swollen as he curled up to sleep. Cool wind swept through the trees.

The breeze brought scents. One smell stood out to Grey. His head jerked up and he whined. Beside him, Black woke immediately. The scent on the wind grew stronger and Grey rose, allowing a long, low growl to escape his throat. He shifted toward the wind, trying to find the source. The hair along the back of his neck rose and his lips lifted in a snarl. Black growled next to him as the smaller wolf caught the scent as well.

Grey took off knowing Black would follow. They raced through the woods. Bodies curved around trees, feet crunched over leaves on the ground. He let the smell guide him, moving fast and silent. Within moments, he approached his goal.

He stopped. Black skidded to a halt beside him.

Mere feet from them stood the intruding wolf. Grey shifted his body, dropping his head, tucking his tail, and snarled. As large as Grey, this adult male trespassed on their territory. Black growled behind him.

The new wolf took a step back, a rabbit hung limp from his jaws. He eyed them but did not drop his kill. Grey growled and moved forward a step. The other wolf met his eyes, and for the briefest heartbeat, Grey saw something he recognized. He stopped moving, stopped growling, meeting the other wolf's gaze.

Memory tugged at him. Something faded, old and half forgotten, something seen through human eyes tried to force its way into his mind. The experience of looking into a wolf's eyes and seeing more than he should was familiar. Could this be the same *more* that reflected from his eyes?

Grey understood. Still, he could not let this wolf hunt on his territory. He growled again and began to advance.

The strange animal seemed to understand. It turned and ran. Grey chased, but never extended himself, never moved so fast he actually caught the stranger. Black stayed by his shoulder, always allowing him to set the pace and lead.

The moment the stranger crossed out of his territory, Grey stopped. He stood still as Black panted at his side and watched the new wolf disappear over the rise of a small hill. For a long time he could not force himself to turn around. While the wolf's instinct demanded he not turn his back on an enemy Grey knew it ran deeper. The part of him that was still human watched intrigued. Another like him existed.

Could that wolf be someone he knew, someone else who escaped the same witch?

Grey tried to pull up memories of the mill or the town and people he knew before he became a wolf. They felt like another life. So distant they were almost unreal.

Grey felt certain he did not know this wolf.

He turned and loped back to his den. Black kept pace with him and they both collapsed onto the ground in the den. Grey felt Black's warm body pressed into his back. He curled his tail close around him, feeling warm and safe. Lying still, he listened to Black breathe.

He was not alone in this new life.

33

Red and Grey

Trapped and unable to move, her breath came in short sharp gasps. She could see nothing, only blackness. No sky, no trees, no ground, the blackness was everywhere and everything. The void sucked away the air around her. She forced her body to fight the blackness and pull in air. She could no longer feel the tears on her cheeks. She could not even attempt to call for help. There was too little air and too much pressure. She no longer felt her fingers or her toes. The only light radiated from the skin of her face.

A rip and the blackness tore open in front of her. Light and color exploded through the fissure that followed the course of the wolf's body. The sound, color, and life of the forest flooded into the meadow with him.

He snarled, a vicious angry sound that would have made her shiver except she knew the growl was to protect her, felt it in the pit of her stomach and with every beat of her heart. Grey had come to save her. He would never hurt her. She fought to breathe. He stalked toward her. Where his paws left the ground, a spot of vivid color, grass and flowers, remained behind and spread in ever-growing circles.

He halted in front of her, his head level with her stomach. She felt the warmth of his breath over her body and the darkness began to loosen its hold.

"Grey," she whispered the word as she drew in a deep breath, lungs desperate for air. The next came even easier. Still held in place by the blackness, she waited for him to touch her, to save her.

Grey watched her, unable to move, or escape. He could feel a presence in the darkness, but no one appeared except for Red. He should hunt for the other that held her. Her whimper drew his gaze back to her face. The memory of her blood, the taste of her flesh in his mouth made him want to run. So vulnerable, it would be easy to hurt her and he would never forgive himself if he did.

She said his name, a plea for help he could not ignore. He shoved his head into her hand, the blackness around her vanished. She collapsed onto the ground and her arms wound around his neck before he knew what she planned to do.

"Thank you, Grey. Thank you." She kissed his head, ran her hands through his fur. It felt like heaven when she touched him. She pulled her tearstained face off his shoulder and met his eyes. He licked her cheek and tasted the salt of her tears. "If you were human, Grey, I would kiss you for real."

She leaned on him, her body liquid against his. He lay on the ground and she tucked her head into the curve between his shoulder and neck. He wrapped his arm around her. Her body fit perfectly against his side and her weight was a welcome blanket.

"Do you believe in magic, Grey?"

"Yes." There was no hesitation as he answered and she relaxed ever further into his embrace.

Blues and greens swirled around them and Melody was content. When did he become human? She could not remember. "I do, too. It scares me."

There was a moment of silence and she wondered what Grey thought of her admission. "It would scare me too, Red, if I wasn't a wolf. Wolves have little use for magic. The animals we hunt don't threaten us with spells. We have teeth and claws."

"Yes, I suppose those do help." His hand stroked her hair, his body warm and hard under her head and fingers. Purple and red joined the colors around them and caressed her skin.

Grey drew in a deep breath and let the scent of Red flood him. He loved her scent. He loved the texture of her hair under his fingers. He watched the rainbow around them. The colors whispered across his skin. They tangled and slid between their bodies, twining and binding them together with tender gentle touch. He loved that she put color in his life.

"What frightens you, Red? Tell me," he asked after several minutes of her silence.

"They say I'm supposed to be magic, but I don't know how. I accept that it's true, and I want to help the people around me but...what if I can't?" She bit her lower lip and waited. Stands of pale yellow and black curled away from her and she did not meet his gaze as she spoke. Her fingers curled and her shoulders stiffened, she drew her body away from his a bit.

"You help me," said Grey.

"Really, how?" Red asked in surprise.

She pushed up on his chest, her head tilted to one side as she gazed down at him. He lay still to absorb the feel of her hand on his chest, her fingers spread on his bare skin to give her balance and he felt the way her body changed as he spoke. Did she realize the tension slid off her or the lines on her face relaxed? The scent of her fear evaporated, only her wide green eyes and open curiosity remained.

She remained unaware of his nudity. He hoped she would not choose this moment to notice this fact.

"You let me see colors, and you make me feel human," he said. Grey reached up and touched her cheek, unable to resist the contact. "You said if I was human..."

She watched a slow, dangerous smile spread across his face. She felt suddenly wary and nervous. Despite that, her face turned into his caress, enjoying the touch. A breath caught in her chest. She said she would kiss him. She swallowed hard. "Do wolves like to be kissed?"

He shifted and she felt the soft grass on her back. He was above her now. The smile vanished, his face serious. His fingers traced the curve of her cheekbone.

"Yes." It sounded more like a growl than a word.

She lay under him, one of his legs covered hers, but he did not move any closer and she did not feel afraid. If she pushed him, he would move. She did not want to, that knowledge came out of nowhere, and surprised her with how right it felt. She swallowed and watched his face, inches above her own.

"Well, than I suppose I owe you, since I said..." She licked her lips. His gaze followed the action and he wanted to copy it. She moved fast and closed the distance between them. Her hand touched his bare chest again. Red leaned up and brushed her lips across his.

The touch felt so soft, so light, and so gentle. Perfect, and yet not enough.

She pulled back and Grey snarled. He lowered his head. Grey moved slowly to give her time to push him away. She did not. His mouth touched hers again and this time he led, devouring her in a hot, forceful kiss. She did not fight.

For a moment she stayed stiff and still, then her body relaxed. Her lips parted and her tongue touched his mouth. Her fingers spread on his chest. He growled against her mouth and nipped at her lower lip, applying enough pressure to make her gasp in surprise. Her fingers flexed against his skin. She tasted good, perfect, her unique flavor seemed to invade his body.

He needed to stop. She tasted too good. He jerked his head away from her.

One of her hands curved around his neck, the other grasped his shoulder and she pulled herself up to close the space between them. There was no reluctance in her body or lips when she kissed him again. Her mouth caressed his; her tongue stroked his lips. It was too much, if she kept this up...he needed...he had to make her stop.

Melody felt his hand tangle in her hair, and she licked at his bottom lip. Instead of stroking her hair, he tugged, not hard enough to hurt, but enough to let him pull away from her. She leaned back and broke the contact. Confused, she watched him. What did she do wrong? Why did he pull away, make her stop?

She watched him, trying to understand what he could be thinking. Grey's eyes blazed and his gaze fixated on her lips. He did not meet her eyes. Was he angry?

Grey forced himself to move off her body to lie on his back to stare up at a dark violet blue sky. The soft grass did not scratch his bare skin. The way her supple curves pressed against him made him feel human, long to be human.

"You are magic, Red. I can see it on you, taste it when I kiss you." He stopped and glanced over at her.

She appeared upset, confused, and ashamed? She had kissed, and been kissed, by a wolf. Why would she not be upset? Suddenly, she leapt to her feet and raced away from him.

His body shifted, crouching into position to chase and hunt. Grey forced himself to stop. He would not chase her. It was too dangerous. Desire shifted into rage in a heartbeat, he snarled. He wanted to hunt, chase, and God help him, he wanted to kill. Instead, he forced himself to pace around the meadow. His claws dug into the earth and ripped clumps of grass from the ground.

34

MELODY

The basket hung heavier than usual this week. Melody baked an extra pie as Nanna would have lots of company for the next few days. The two apple pies and two loaves of walnut bread accompanied a roasted chicken. Melody left a note for her father to let him know she planned to stay at least one night with Nanna.

Not that he would get it, but it remained the right thing to do. She rarely saw her father since the harvest celebration; he more or less lived in the small cabin near the mines now. Perhaps, for him, it seemed easier to sleep there than face the memories of her mother.

With thoughts of sleep, the dream from the night before stole into her mind. Aunt Ellen said evil could be seductive. Her face burned to associate that word with Grey. In reality, to her mind, he defined the word. The way his body felt against hers, the way he held her and stroked her hair, the way he kissed her, even the way he watched her, she felt it all over her body.

Melody admitted the truth. She would do whatever Grey wanted. Her body craved his touch and she knew herself to be seduced. He stopped though.

Grey did not allow anything to happen. Could this be another argument in favor of the dreams as a warning? What could they warn against?

The wind whipped through the trees and a cold drizzle fell from the sky, yanking her mind back to the present. She appreciated the thick warmth of her cape more than ever. It kept the worst of the drizzle off her skin. The edges of the cape hung damp with mud. She would wash it at Nanna's. She would not let Jessica touch her cape.

She turned onto the forest path and felt a ripple of tension run over her skin. She searched the path as far as she could to make sure there was nothing, and listened; no birds, not surprising given the wind. The forest felt muted. The only colors that met her gaze were the browns and drab greens of the pines.

She listened to the wind for another minute. A rush of air whistled through the branches above her. She closed her eyes and tried to feel whatever it was that made her shiver. Grey said he believed in magic. He said he could feel it and taste it on her. Maybe it was only fear that kept her locked away from her gift.

Stupid to rely on what Grey said. He wasn't real. Of course, he agreed with her, she made him up. Imaginary friends were not supposed to disagree with you. What if he was a manifestation of her power, trying to help her reach her gift? Or, could he be evil?

Still, she stood with her eyes closed and tried to feel whatever lingered out there. Something...she felt something. Her eyes flew open. Colors exploded everywhere. They burst from the bushes and trees, seeped out of the ground and dropped from the sky with the rain. Bright and vivid, she felt like she could reach out and touch them, play with them, and manipulate them the way she did with the colors in her dreams. She scanned the bushes around her, amazed at what had not existed a moment before, and saw an area of grey. Her stomach clenched and her hands tightened on the basket.

It lay partly hidden behind the forest green, and yet pulsed stronger and brighter. She felt pulled toward the color, despite the knot in her stomach. She took a step closer. A rumbling growl filled the air over the quiet splash of the rain on the forest floor. Sweat trickled down her spine and the air became too humid, her cape felt too heavy. She had heard that growl before, in her dreams.

A wolf hid in the woods. The colors swirled and danced with a rhythm that echoed her heart. Pain built behind her eyes.

Did that branch just move? Was it the wind or something else? She closed her eyes and forced herself to swallow her fear. Would the colors be gone when she opened her eyes? Could the wind and rain be making her this jumpy? She opened her eyes and took in the world around her, still bright with unnatural colors. She took another step on the trail, but she could not help but be cautious as she scanned everything around her. The pain continued to throb behind her eyes. It intensified every time she focused on a specific color.

The colors stormed around her. They moved with the wind, in the trees, everywhere. A slash of grey moved along the trail to her right, behind her, it teased her peripheral vision. Something stalked her through the forest.

35

Grey

How could she stand there in the middle of the forest with her eyes closed and let the rain fall on her face? When her eyes opened, she looked at the forest as if it was a new thing she had never seen before. She took several distracted steps toward him. The scents from the basket got stronger and stronger. The needs he fought tore at him. He could not help but growl.

He woke up aware that today Red would walk through his

forest. Waves of human emotion threatened to overwhelm him. He would see her today, with the taste of her lips still fresh in his mind.

As he hid in the wood and waited for her to arrive, cold rain drenched him and he thought about the dream. If Red possessed magic, could she help him? Stories always said that a kiss could break a curse, but he was still a wolf. Of course, they were just dreams, but maybe they tried to tell him something. Maybe he could kill her, or maybe she could save him. Maybe it was his choice and the dreams were his warning.

Now she stood there and the smells from her basket maddened him. He could almost taste the walnut bread.

His mother made that for him when he was a little boy. Before she became ill, before the witch poisoned her, they would sit and eat the warm bread together with butter one of the farms traded for mill services. She listened to him when he told her the things that scared him, like the witch woman who cursed the town. Or, the things that delighted him, like the first time he had caught a fish in the lake.

He remembered her last words to him, that she loved him, and her reminder that love was always the answer.

This close to Red, he could remember things about being human that seemed distant when he ran and hunted as a wolf. Not just those memories, but more recent ones, the taste of her mouth and the feel of her skin.

Red stood and held the food his body craved, the food his memory pleaded for. She took steps toward him with the body he longed to touch and taste, completely oblivious to the danger she approached. So he growled.

He saw shock and fear cross her face. Watched the way she scanned the woods. She heard him.

He waited and kept his body still. When she continued on the forest trail, surprise and anger warred inside him. The scent of the bread grew stronger and his stomach rumbled with need.

She looked toward where he hunched in the bushes. She could not have heard that sound. Her ears were not strong enough, yet she gazed in his direction.

Once again, she started forward. Grey waited until she walked ahead, and then he moved forward toward her, staying low and silent. Leaves littered the ground, the wet scent of their decay prevailed in the forest and the empty branches provided scarce cover compared to the summer months. She did not look back again, though she glanced to her right several times.

The rain continued to soak him and the scent of the bread teased his nostrils. He knew from the scent that it was still warm, and his mouth watered.

How easy it would be to take it from her. He would not have to hurt her. He could frighten her. Make her drop the basket.

What would he do when she ran? In the dream, he fought not to chase her. Could he stop himself in reality?

Halfway down the trail he caught a new scent, one that raised his hackles. The strange wolf moved through these woods in the past few hours. Something cold and hard settled in his chest. First, the male invaded his territory and now it dared approach his mate.

The word overwhelmed his mind with a fierce heat.

No, that was wrong.

She was human.

Grey was an animal.

He rejected the word, slashed at it with his mind. Not possible, not something he would consider.

The smell bothered him. That wolf should not be here. He growled again without meaning to and her head shot around. She stared into the bushes with eyes he knew to be a brilliant green. The red cloak flowed around her body as she spun; even wet with rain it moved in a graceful swirl.

She looked at him. He met her eyes not knowing if she could see him or if she only imagined him. Either way, her gaze locked with his. For a long time she did not move. He could see the rain hitting her face; drops of water clung to her eyelashes and ran down her cheeks.

Another gust of wind pushed her hood back further away from her face and she shivered. Desire rippled through him. He wanted to lick the drops of water from her face, taste her wet skin, and her mouth. He needed to see her eyes get dark with desire the way they did in his dreams. The wind shifted and again he smelled the strange male.

Rage boiled through him. How dare another male invade his territory and put Red in danger? Red–his Red–who tasted perfect, even the sight of her shivering in the rain seemed to be too much for him. These emotions did not belong together. She did not move, did not adjust her hood, only stared.

After several long minutes, she shivered again and turned. She moved further down the path into the woods, closer to the cottage. He followed.

She walked faster now. Grey needed to stand straight to keep up with her, no longer able to slink in the undergrowth, but risking her seeing a glimpse of him. He ignored the danger driven by emotions too human to belong to this body.

The smell became stronger as they approached the cottage and Grey felt the hair on his neck stand up. She walked into danger and he could do nothing to stop her.

36

MELODY

Melody rushed through the garden gate at Rose Cottage. She could feel the wolf behind her. She heard it. She refused to run, not until she made it through the gate. At the cottage door she paused, hand on the latch. A deep male voice came through the wood.

She recognized Andrew's voice. Another shiver whispered over her skin. She glanced behind her at the woods and bit her lip. The wolf might be safer than the man inside the cabin. The wolf had not attacked her. The idea of retreating teased at her thoughts. The colors, and the headache, faded around her, the day returned to dull rain and muted tones. Could this be magic? If so, why did it come and go?

"Are you going to help me?" The voice demanded, sounding clear even through the closed door.

"... I will, but Andrew, understand... I cannot ...stay..."

"I know that, no one can," he snapped, his tone angry and almost desperate. Were they fighting? Did Nanna need help? Thoughts of returning to the forest vanished. "You have the most potential, the most knowledge and skill"

"That was different." Nanna's voice rose, her frustration carrying through the door.

Melody took a deep breath and knocked on the door. A long pause followed before Nanna opened the door. "Melody, you're earlier than I expected."

"I rushed the rain and there may be a wolf..."

"Oh dear, sweetheart, come inside." Nanna's hand fell on her arm, pulling her into the cottage. Warm, dry air engulfed Melody as she stepped over the threshold and wiped her cold, wet face with her free hand.

She glanced across the room and locked eyes with Andrew. She shivered. His face set in a hard scowl, his eyes narrowed as he assessed her. The low, angry sound that came from his throat made her step back out into the rain.

"Maybe I should go home, Nanna. I'll leave the basket. I made you an extra pie."

"What? Melody, don't be foolish. If there is a wolf out there you can't walk home now."

"I..." Melody shrugged in an attempt to explain it to herself as much as Nanna. "I never actually saw anything, I thought I heard something. It might have been the wind or my imagination."

"Either way, I don't want you to leave yet." Nanna pulled her back through the door. She turned to look into the room.

"Andrew, don't scowl at my granddaughter."

His glare did not soften. Instead, he turned his back on her. Once his eyes left her, Melody stepped further into the room and placed the basket on the table. Still shivering, she worked at the clasp of the cape. Nanna's hands gently pushed hers away and undid the clasp.

"I'll hang this by the fire, love. Come and sit. You need to dry off, too."

Very cold, Melody obeyed without hesitation. Andrew angled his body as she moved past so that no part of him touched her. Despite that, she could almost feel the low growl that came from his throat. It sounded so familiar that she turned to stare into his eyes and forgot for a minute to be afraid. She searched for something she did not understand.

He met her gaze, eyes narrow and assessing. Still, she stared. Something struck her with a hint of familiar and yet not. "You...." she hesitated, unable to figure out the connection she felt. She shook her head in an attempt to clear it and figure out what she could be missing.

"I'm leaving," Andrew growled.

"Be careful, Andrew. If there is an animal out there, it might be dangerous, even for you," Nanna said. Andrew made a strange noise, not a laugh, not a growl, but something in between. "I'll be here when you return."

"Thank you, Rose." He glanced at Melody again and then turned and left the cottage.

"What does he want from you, Nanna?" Melody asked as she turned and sat on the chair closest to the fire. The warmth sunk into her, past her wet clothes and skin to heat her heart.

"Nothing right now, we probably won't see him again until close to the end of winter, possibly even spring."

"That's fine with me, but what does he want?"

"Nothing I'm not willing to give." Nanna grinned at her and sat down on the sofa. "You don't need to protect me, love. He doesn't mean any harm."

"Maybe not to you, but he doesn't like me."

"Andrew has been through a great deal and he, mistakenly in

my opinion, thinks that you are somehow tainted."

Melody nodded. She figured that much out on her own. "Do you think it's because of the troll?"

The popping and crackling of the fire filled the silence between them before Nanna sighed. As she spoke, a sense of relief colored her tone. "Ellen told you."

Melody nodded. "Will you tell me about it? I can't remember anything. Not about that and not before that."

"I've tried to tell you before. I wanted to tell you, Melody. You should have known all this years ago. You never wanted to listen and your mother didn't want you to know."

"I'm sorry, Nanna, but Momma's gone and I'm here. I'm ready to listen and I need to know."

Nanna shook her head and gazed down at her folded hands. She appeared close to tears, and for a moment Melody wondered if she should not have asked. "Amber and I didn't fight about much, except your magic. Before the troll came and the Godmother took your magic you were a different child. You didn't have to be gifted in seeing or interpreting magic to feel your magic. It was amazing. You would put a seed in the ground and sing a little song as you planted and the next day a flower would bloom. Not a stalk or a sprout, Melody, but a flower, more vivid and lovely than any other around it, do you understand?

"You would mix the bread for your mother, humming and pretending to pull things out of the air and put them into the bread. Everyone who ate it felt stronger, healthier, better. Sometimes you would stop in front of a particular house and insist to your mother that it needed a specific color then ask to go home and make bread, just for them. Your mother always humored you and took them the bread you helped make them. So many people told your mother stories of how they struggled in one way or another, until Amber showed up with bread and within hours, their situation improved.

"Then the troll came, and I called the Godmother. After that, you were safe, but you were different. Taking your magic damaged you and I have never forgiven the Godmother for that. I never spoke to her again after I realized the change it made in you."

Tears rolled down Nanna's cheeks and Melody stared at her in wonder.

"Nanna, I never knew what I lost. It didn't hurt me." Melody tried to reassure her grandmother.

"It did hurt you. Perhaps you don't remember the way I do. The loss of your magic forced you to relearn everything. You would plant seeds and watch them for days. You sobbed when they didn't grow. You brought me injured rabbits and wept if you could not save their lives the way you could before. Sometimes you would stop and gaze at something or someone and if we asked you what was wrong you would start to cry. You told us that you should see something, but you couldn't. You didn't know what you missed but you knew you were missing something. You couldn't remember magic but you felt its loss."

Indistinct memories of that time as a child came to mind, the other children often did not want to play with her. They called her crybaby. Did the people's dislike and mistrust of her start because she lost her magic? She shook her head. She did not want to think about that.

"But Nanna, all those things you mentioned, couldn't that have been my mother's magic? I mean, the people who got stronger and healthier, that was her, not me."

Nanna shook her head. "Her gift could protect, help, give luck, and maybe, in part, the time she spent with people helped them, but she couldn't bake her magic into food. You did that, Melody. The Godmother told us not to speak to you about it. She told your mother something that terrified her so much she refused to let you even believe in magic. Everything you were able to do stopped. So I let it go, and for years there was nothing."

"So maybe Andrew's right. Perhaps I am tainted. Maybe something happened that day. Was I hurt? Maybe that's why my magic left. Maybe the Godmother took it because it wasn't good. Maybe I'm not good."

Her mind leapt to the dreams and how much she craved Grey's kiss, his touch, and how he pulled away from her and made her stop. Her cheeks flushed.

"But it isn't gone, Melody." Nanna's voice was harsh and she shook her head as she spoke. She wiped the last few tears from her cheeks. "Part of my gift is the ability to see magic, although I can't interpret it the way my sister can. Your magic did stay hidden and dormant, for years until almost the exact day your mother knew she was dying, and then it flared, just a bit. You don't use it. I don't even think you can feel it or are aware of it, but it is there."

The other part of Melody's dreams, the blackness that clutched and choked her , came to mind. "What if the magic itself is tainted, Nanna? Could it want to hurt me or use me to hurt others? Perhaps Momma's magic protected me from my own magic until she became too sick. Maybe that's what the troll saw; evil magic."

"What do you mean?" Nanna tilted her head in interest.

"In my dreams there's something trying to kill me, it chokes me and clings all over my body, all over everything near me." She paused and looked up from the fire to meet Nanna's eyes again. "Maybe Andrew's right. Nanna, maybe I am tainted."

37

Grey

unched low to the forest floor he moved with slow deliberation, his paws silent on the fall of leaves dampened by the autumn rain. He crept closer, enjoying the hunt. Three days ago, he had left Red at the cottage.

The scent of the strange wolf faded. Whoever or whatever he appeared to be was gone now.

Today, Grey could enjoy the hunt.

He sprang, pushing with his powerful hind legs. Grey moved lightning fast across the small space that separated him from his prey. Black spun, not fast enough. Grey hit his shoulder and they both rolled onto the damp earth. For a moment they battled together; a mess of paws and teeth as they wrestled and nipped. Black sprang back, his tail wagged and mouth open in a wolf grin.

Grey knew his own face mimicked the expression, his tail moved back and forth. A cool breeze played across his back, Grey lifted his head and smelled the rain-wet trees. Black ran again and Grey chased him. Both full from the last nights kill. His muscles felt strong as he ran, his longer, more powerful legs made it easy to catch Black. He overtook the younger wolf and knocked him over, again they wrestled.

Black lay panting in the underbrush as Grey stood nearby and surveyed the forest and open ground around them. He drew in a deep breath of the crisp fall air and enjoyed the feel of the sun on his coat. This was his territory, his home, his world, more so than his father's mill had ever been. The knowledge that his territory lay safe again gave him a deep sense of contentment.

Trust in himself rooted Grey's contentment. He knew the truth. Even as a human, instinct, not imagination, guided him. He had been right about the witch. She was evil. She killed his friend, poisoned his mother and cursed him.

Yet, to be honest with himself, at this moment he could think of nowhere else he wanted to be. As a wolf, he learned to be strong, to trust himself, to lead. As a wolf, he learned to survive without his father or brother.

If Grey hunted the wolf-Eric today, the outcome would be different. He would stop his brother, and protect the wolf.

It felt odd to think of his family, his past, of Connor and who he used to be. The edges of what once contained Connor and where the wolf resided blurred and meshed. He became more Grey every day. He tried hard to cling to the last bits of his humanity, but at times, it felt like a foolish thing. Grey was a wolf and content to be a wolf, especially on days like today.

It was the perfect day to be a wolf.

Except for Red.

Seeing her, in life and in his dreams, kept him tied to humanity in a tangible way. The image of the chase superimposed itself over the image of Red. It would be fun to chase Red. Would she play with him the way Black did or would she be afraid? It would be a dangerous game, one he could not guarantee the outcome of. If he were human he would not hurt her, but the idea of it made his body burn and Grey needed to move. He shifted on his paws, nipped at Black's shoulder and took off.

He ran, and ran, reveling in the feel of his body stretching low along the ground. Wind stung his eyes and his tail plumed out behind him.

Black tried to keep up, but Grey eventually lost the smaller animal. He ran toward the mountains, past the edges of the territory he marked and into the open woods. The last time he left Red at the cabin, he watched a human male leave, not a wolf. Yet the smell remained that of the strange male wolf who invaded his territory.

What did that mean? Could he be human again? Would he want to? If it meant he could touch Red, and taste her, yes, but could he give up the wolf? He could not imagine that fate.

He turned and began to race back. He met Black at the edge of their territory and threw his body against the younger wolf. They wrestled and rolled.

It was the perfect day to be a wolf.

38

Melody

H*er mother was dead, but she was here.* She said those words to Nanna. Grey told her to be herself. He asked her why she cared if the people liked her. He was right. She wasted too much time trying to be her mother. The time had come to be herself.

She walked across the square and down the muddy street. Ice crystals outlined the edges of a few muddy tracks, a sure sign of winters approach. Her goal, a small, neat house sat not far from the village square. Window boxes hung empty now, but she remembered that last spring little blue flowers filled them. The house was smaller than her father's was. It stood one story tall, but it was a good size and well maintained. She took a deep breath and knocked on the door.

Lauren opened the door a moment later.

"Melody? What are you doing here?" The woman flushed at her words but did not apologize or retract them.

"Hello, Lauren. I'm sorry to bother you and I won't keep you long. I thought about what you said on the way to the caravan the other day."

"What did I say?" The other woman appeared nervous and her eyes darted up and down the street. "Do you want to come in?"

"No, that's alright. I have several errands to run today. You mentioned a book for Jamie. I'm not sure if you found one, but here." Melody pulled three children's books from her basket and handed them to Lauren. Melody almost laughed at the way Lauren's mouth gaped as she took them in her hand. "They're all children's stories, with lots of pictures. I hope Jamie will like them."

"I don't understand."

"They're a gift for Jamie. I don't use them anymore. I want him to have them." Melody smiled and took a step back. "Have a nice day, Lauren."

"Wait, Melody. I can't accept these. They must cost a fortune, I can't pay you–"

"Stop, Lauren," Melody interrupted. "First off, they aren't a gift for you, they're for Jamie, and I doubt he's worried about paying for them. If it truly bothers you to keep them, you are free to give them away, but I won't accept them back. Give them to someone else who wants or needs them."

Lauren's eyes narrowed and her mouth set in a thin line. "I don't owe you anything, Melody."

"Of course not." Melody watched the way Lauren's arms wrapped around the books. She knew the woman wanted them for her son. "You owe me nothing."

Without a word, she turned and walked away, leaving Lauren open-mouthed and confused. It was not what her mother would have done.

From there she took a right and headed toward the edges of the village. Widow Cramer's house perched on a side street even smaller than Lauren's. It was not as tidy, but there was something about it that felt comfy and Melody imagined that the widow was happy here, even if Jessica was not.

Thoughts of Jessica made her frown. The girl had become sullen and withdrawn since Trevor's affection shifted. She seemed almost sad sometimes and Melody felt a stab of guilt, thinking of the look in her eyes. Since the day Trevor started paying attention to Jessica, Melody wanted him for herself. Now Trevor courted her and all she thought about was Grey.

In a way, Melody felt responsible for Jessica's pain. Melody wished she could ease it somehow. Still, she could do nothing to change that today. Melody knocked on the door of the tiny house and Widow Cramer opened the door almost immediately.

"Melody, do you have wash?" The woman glanced from Melody's face to the bag she carried over her shoulder.

"No, actually this is all clean." Melody smiled at the widow's relieved sigh. "These items belonged to my mother and some were mine; things I no longer need. I know a great deal of people in the town bring you their wash. I thought you might know better who needs new items and whose clothes are most worn. I wanted to give these to you so you can give them out to the rest of the village, or keep them for yourself, as you see need. Most of the fabric is gently used – it could be turned into children's clothes if it's cut up and remade. Whatever works best." Melody finished her speech with a shrug and waited for the inevitable rejection. It did not come.

No trace of shock or offense filled the old woman's voice as she spoke. "A clothing exchange? What a splendid idea, Melody. I've heard of things like this in the large cities to prevent waste. Yes, it could work just as well here, I imagine. What a lovely thought, and you're right, I'm the perfect person to coordinate it. My girls and I see practically everyone's clothes."

"Thank you, Widow Cramer. I appreciate your willingness to help with this."

"Certainly child, I'm embarrassed I never thought of it myself. I wonder why no one ever tried it in the village before."

Melody hesitated, and then spoke, her voice low. "It wasn't something my mother would have done."

To her surprise the widow nodded, she reached up and touched her cheek. "I understand, Melody."

Melody suspected she might. "Oh and here. I have some bread for you. It's the last of the walnut breads. I made a loaf for Nanna and thought you might like some."

The widow took the gift without hesitation and Melody felt her spirits lift. Two more loaves of bread and a peach pie waited in her basket to be delivered to families in the Varin. She might not be able to give her neighbors magic, but she could bake for them. She left the widow's house with lightness in her step.

39

Red and Grey

Sunlight reflected off the warm orange air and filled the meadow. No trace of the void marred the perfect brightness around her. Grey was here. If he was not, the void would be crawling over her. She walked around the edge of the meadow and searched for him. "Grey, where are you?"

She ran from him the last time he came to her dreams. Since that night, she had not seen him. She avoided sleep and allowed herself to nap for a few minutes at a time throughout the night in an attempt to escape the suffocating void. She perfected waking herself the minute she felt dreams starting, to avoid the blackness. A few times, she let the dream take over, but when Grey did not appear, she woke herself. Tonight was different. Tonight she knew she was too exhausted to make herself wake from the dream. Catching sight of the meadow, Red allowed her body to sink into the deep sleep it so desperately needed.

She heard a growl, a soft, warning sound, but it did not frighten her. Instead, she waited. What did Grey want? She looked toward the sound and saw him hunched in the grass. His tail fanned back and forth and his eyes shone bright amber. She understood without words, she had seen puppies in the same pose doing battle with each other. Grey wanted to play.

Red grinned and Grey knew she was not afraid. He flipped his tail back and forth. He crouched low and launched himself. He would be careful to make sure the game ended the way he wanted it to.

She darted to the side, away from him and started to run. As soon as she began to move Grey knew he could outpace her but he stayed behind and allowed her think she could escape him.

Red glanced over her shoulder. She stopped abruptly and Grey wondered what she planned. She turned and moved back toward him. The move startled him enough he let her pass. Clever girl, she managed to surprise him. Grey spun and followed.

Her clothing changed on her body, the skirt wrapped around her legs and twisted into pants that clung to her legs rather than tangling with limbs. She moved faster without the skirt.

She felt the air move around her, and loved the feel of her body moving. She never ran as an adult and it felt good. Her muscles felt warm and strong. She found herself laughing and glanced over her shoulder to make sure Grey still followed.

He was on her in an instant. She felt the weight of his body hit her back. For a heartbeat she worried, but no claws dug into her skin, instead arms wrapped around her. They rolled in the soft orange air. Rather than land on the ground, she landed on top of Grey.

"No fair," she gasped the words as she caught her breath, smacking her hand against his shoulder gently. "You have four feet and I only have two."

"Wanna try again, I promise to use two legs." His eyes flashed bright and playful. Red suspected that even with two legs the outcome would be the same. The idea tempted her, running felt good. Why didn't adults run and play? However, she needed to talk to him. She shook her head and pushed herself off his body, onto the grass next to him.

"Actually, I want to ask you for a favor," she asked.

She bit her lower lip. Grey remembered tasting her lips the last time they were together. He needed to know the answer to a question. Even though he knew, he would do whatever she asked, no matter what she answered.

"Why did you run when I kissed you, Red?"

Her cheeks flushed so deep a red they would have matched her cape if she had worn it. He watched her clench and unclench her hands.

"I didn't run when you kissed me Grey. I ran when you didn't kiss me. I'm not a slut. I'm not. I don't want to be the woman they think I am, but when you kissed me I wanted more. I didn't care what names people called me. I just wanted more. But you... you didn't. I tried to make you want more, want me, but..." She trailed off and refused to meet his gaze.

Grey almost smiled. Could she be that naïve? Did she honestly believe he stopped because he did not want her? Did she think enjoying a kiss made her a slut? He had been right; he would do whatever she asked.

"What do you need Red?"

"I want to learn to defend myself. There's someone who frightens me and I don't like to feel helpless."

"That sounds wise."

She seemed relieved and he wondered who else she asked and who said no.

"Who frightens you?"

"A man. He visited my grandmother and he's coming back. I doubt he would hurt me, but he doesn't like me."

Grey nodded, thinking of the man he saw leaving the cottage. "Of course I'll help you. That's why wolves play, you know, to learn to fight and hunt."

"Yeah, but you cheat." Red accused, rolling toward him and pushing his shoulder again. He caught her hand and rose, holding her hand. Clothes poured onto his body as he stood.

Melody let him pull her to her feet. Grey would teach her to protect herself. She would not let anyone hurt her, or Nanna.

40

Melody

Melody hummed as she walked through the first snowfall of the season. She felt rested for the first time in months. The past week play and laughter filled her dreams as Grey taught her to defend herself with wolf games. She enjoyed every minute of it. Probably too much, but dreams were meant to be appreciated. She woke up each morning body refreshed and ready for the day.

During the days, she baked and took her offerings to different people around the village. She went through her house, surprised that each day revealed something else she did not need. She gave away everything from pieces of furniture to blankets they had left forgotten in storage for years. People accepted her gifts, some grudgingly, some with thanks. It surprised her how little her neighbors reactions mattered. This felt right.

She hummed, spun on her toes, and enjoyed the feel of the skirt and cape as it swished around her ankles. Death no longer seemed to haunt Varin's streets. She felt like she could breathe again. Maybe, even if she never found her magic her life could fall into a settled and peaceful routine.

As she left the cleared streets and entered the forest path Melody admitted to herself that she chose to push aside all of life's complications to try to make the world fit into a neat tidy box. The stresses that continued to creep into her days darkened her mind like the shadows of the trees. Andrew would return soon and Nanna seemed to be preparing for him to have a prolonged stay. Melody found it difficult to accept that a man who hated her would soon occupy the bedroom at Nanna's that used to be hers. Despite what Grey taught her, she did not feel any more confident about dealing with Andrew. Something about him terrified her.

Another thought led to Jessica. Furious with Melody for stealing Trevor, Jessica continued to spread vicious rumors. Melody wondered how Jessica could have become so hard and mean with a mother as sweet as the Widow. Widow Cramer helped Melody decide whom her gifts should go to each day and always offered a word of encouragement to Melody. As for the rumors, it appeared no one believed them, but Melody started to fear the gossip held some underlying truth.

Did the way she feel about Grey, the way she craved his touch, reveal a character flaw? Thoughts of Grey made her chest ache. It took physical effort to pretend she did not feel anything for him.

Trevor came to her house once a week. Her father always made it home for dinner the night Trevor paid his visit. The two men got along wonderfully. If she married Trevor, she might see her father more. The three of them would talk and laugh. Trevor was sweet and thoughtful. Once, he even brought her chocolate he had purchased from the caravan. Trevor proved to be a perfect gentleman and an ideal match.

But she was in love with Grey.

She fell in love with a wolf that existed solely in her mind. Trevor humored Melody, while Grey listened and accepted everything she told him. Trevor teased her when she tried to share her fear about Andrew. Grey taught her to defend herself with lupine ferocity. Trevor hardly touched her, but Grey gave her physical affection. Sometimes, with Trevor, she felt like a child. With

Grey, she felt like an equal, a partner.

After one of their games, Grey kissed her again. With his hands on her waist, he brushed his lips over hers, just once. She felt as if someone placed a warm light inside her and it glowed, heating her straight to her soul. Her body moved toward his and her hands touched his shoulders. She felt him smile, the warm colors around them tickled her skin, and then he really kissed her, the way he had that first time.

The memory of it warmed her inside. She would have smiled except she was in love with an imaginary wolf. Trevor was real, human, and wanting her to love him. Maybe, if Trevor kissed her, she would feel the same way she felt when Grey kissed her.

Melody ran a hand through her hair and pushed her hood off in the process. Bright winter sun reflected off the thin layer of snow that covered the forest in white. She came around the curve in the trail and halted.

41

Grey

Grey heard the boar getting closer.

Unaware of the danger, Red left him no options. If she walked across the boar's path, it would charge. He moved ahead of her and onto the tiny open path. She walked around the corner and saw him, her eyes widening. Her jaw dropped and he saw the basket slip in her hands before she tightened her hold on it.

He snarled, showing his teeth. He hunched his shoulders and lowered his head in an attempt to force her back. She did not move. Instead she spoke. "Yes, I see what big teeth you have."

If he were human, he would have rolled his eyes. Instead, he took a step toward her and growled from deep in his chest, the sound as fierce as he could make it. She did not move.

Red was too brave for her own good. He listened for the boar as it came closer, making angry sounds. Grey suspected another animal injured the boar and now anger and pain drove it. Distracted, Red still stared at him, unaware of the boar. Grey advanced another step and snapped at the air, lips curled, his low growl rumble a constant volume.

Her face paled against the red of her cape. A breeze lifted her dark hair off her neck.

As the boar charged, Grey lunged; his full weight hit her body and knocked her to the ground. The boar tore across the path straight toward them. Grey stood over Red, his legs braced on either side of her body. He snarled at the boar and it hesitated, as if to decide if it should challenge a wolf.

Grey growled, revealing his teeth, snapping at the other animal. It took a step back, and then turned away from Red. At least the animal showed enough sense to be afraid of a wolf. He caught the scent of blood and saw a splash of red on its shoulder as it ran past.

Red held still. Grey inspected her, had he hurt her? Her body stretched out in the snow, the red cape spread around her. The scent of cooked beef and the pie she carried mixed with her scent. She stared up at him, her eyes wide and vivid green. He knew the color so well he could almost see it now as he watched her. She breathed. He did not smell blood. She was not hurt. Relief flooded him.

"You're real." She moved her hand and Grey held his body stiff and still. He let her fingers touch the fur of his neck. Her skin felt perfect, smelled delicious, the food enticed him. The two scents blended. She would taste good. The meat would taste good. The sight of Red beneath him overwhelmed Grey. The dual temptations warred within him. He needed to run.

Despite her fingers curled deep in his fur he bolted. His body jerked away and left clumps of his hair behind. He leapt over her supine form and raced into the woods, following the path of the boar. Grey raced after the injured animal. He needed to eat, his jaw ached with the need to rip and tear. He wanted to kill.

She tasted so good when he kissed her. Grey forced his mind to focus on the hunt.

42

MELODY

Melody paced back and forth across her room, she glared at her bed. "Traitor," she hissed under her breath. If she lay down she would fall asleep and she would dream. Would it be Grey or the void?

He was real.

He felt the same.

He looked the same.

His eyes, his growl, the intelligence and emotions were all the same.

Grey was real.

Melody clenched her fingers so hard her nails cut into her palm. She whimpered. How could he be real?

She had arrived at the cottage covered in the berry pie and beef stew she had been carrying. She told Nanna she fell, slipped in the freshly fallen snow. She lied to hide the terrifying truth. Grey, the wolf from her dreams, stalked her in reality, too. Why?

Obviously, he did not want to hurt her. He could have killed her today. How often did he follow her?

She thought about the day in the rain. It had been Grey she heard in the woods. He watched her the same way he did in her dreams. The moment she recognized his eyes she knew he would not hurt her.

Because he was real.

She stopped pacing and stood in the middle of her room, eyes closed, fists clenched. She could not start that spiral of thought again. She needed to think about this, not react. Melody opened her eyes, walked to the table and sat down.

So there was a real wolf. What did that mean? She knew she had heard a wolf in the woods before. Maybe she even saw a glimpse of him in the past. Maybe her mind turned the glimpse of wolf she saw in the woods into a protector and companion because she felt so lonely. Just because a real wolf existed, that did not mean a real man existed, or that the dreams were real.

He was an animal...who felt the strange urge to protect her from fierce wild boars?

Or, maybe her magic caused that. Worse, what if Aunt Ellen was right? Could Grey be an evil that hunted her in dreams and tried to make her trust him? Did he manufacture ways to protect her?

A sound from the lower floor caught her attention. The front door opened and closed. Heavy footsteps in the entry hall; her father had come home. Leaping up, Melody grabbed the robe off her bed and pulled it on as she dashed down the stairs.

She met her father before he reached the kitchen. "Daddy, you're home! Are you hungry?"

"Hello, Melody, I am a bit. Do you have any food in the house?"

"Of course, I made beef stew and it's in the cold box. I'll heat it for you. I have bread and a cherry pie I made this afternoon, too."

"Yes, I've heard how you've been baking for the whole village. The men at the mine can't stop talking about your breads."

"Oh, well. It gives me something to do." Melody felt her face flush. She busied herself at the stove.

"Of course, I have no complaints, love. Part of the reason I came home tonight is that I needed to talk to you. I figured I would catch you in the morning, but this works better."

Melody stayed quiet. She warmed the stew she was too upset to eat earlier and got out two bowls. She sliced bread, spread it with butter, and then set it on the back of the stove to warm. Her father would tell her whatever troubled him when he was ready.

As if reading her mind, he started to talk as she placed the two bowls, now full of steaming soup, on the table with the thick slabs of bread.

"Trevor came to me today and asked for my permission to pursue your hand in marriage."

Melody's hand froze in the act of lifting a piece of bread to her mouth. She stared at her father. "He what?"

"He came to ask my blessing. I wanted to talk to you first. Who you marry isn't really my decision. It's yours. I mean, I want to see you married, and happy, the way your mother and I were, but who you choose has never been my decision."

The bread slipped from Melody's fingers and into her bowl. She gazed down at it unconvinced she understood her father's words. "He wants to marry me?"

"Yes."

"Why?"

Her father chuckled and took a mouthful of his soup. Melody followed his lead. With her spoon she lifted the bread she had dropped and ate the bite.

"Well, dear, you're a lovely young woman and you're a wonderful cook." He gestured to the bowl with his spoon. "You have money. Why would he not want to marry you?"

Melody felt a strange lump in her stomach at his words. "Is that why you wanted to marry Momma?"

He glanced up and she saw surprise in his eyes. His lips twitched in a tiny smile. "No. I was so in love with your mother I wouldn't have cared if she could cook, or if she looked like a horse."

"He doesn't love me. I mean, he's never said he loves me." Melody studied her soup as she stirred the vegetables and beef with her spoon. She looked up into her father's eyes again and tried to smile. "Do you remember when I was a kid?"

He laughed aloud this time. "Yes, honey, I'm not that old."

Melody smiled and stuck her tongue out. She had missed her father's laugh. "Aunt Ellen told me a story, and I realized I don't remember...well anything, from before I was five."

The laughter died and his face turned serious. "She told you about the troll who took you."

"Yeah."

Her father ran a hand over his face and blew out a breath. He gazed into her eyes and forced a smile. When he spoke again, strain colored his voice. "Melody, that was the most frightening day of my life. I've never forgotten how grateful I felt the moment the Godmother put you into your mother's arms. I never want to face losing you like that again."

"Nanna says I changed after that day."

He stared down at the table and remained silent for a moment before he turned his face up to meet her gaze. When he did he smiled, Melody heard pride and affection in his voice when he spoke. "You have always been my beautiful, intelligent, loving girl. Before that day you could do things, yes, but you have always been who you are. Personally, I think Trevor has overlooked some of your best qualities. However, given your options, he may also be the best possible choice."

Melody felt tears build in her eyes. She nodded and looked back at her soup. "I'm not ready to marry him."

"I understand." He sounded like he did. "Now eat your dinner, you've lost weight in the past few weeks."

43

Red and Grey

The blackness encased her. Tendrils curled up her cheeks. It crept into her nose and mouth. The void froze her skin and crawled inside her, turning her heart and lungs to ice. Grey was not here. She fought alone for hours. The blackness twisted higher and higher. She could hardly breathe past the cold snakes of the void. Tears streamed down her face. They dropped onto the blackness and shone there like diamonds.

She gagged. The void engulfed the sound.

Still Grey did not appear. In her heart, she knew he would not come. Not now, not since she had seen him and knew he existed.

His body ripped through the blackness. The void evaporated into golden sunshine and soft, warm air filled the clearing. She fell to the ground. The air burned her throat after the blackness. Grey loped to her side, nose touching her cheek. Shivers ran through her body, raced down her limbs. Grey pressed against her, stretching his body along hers.

"You came, Grey. I didn't think you would." Her fingers sank deep into his fur.

He licked her shoulder, bare except for the thin strap of a nightdress.

He rested his chin against her shoulder. He shifted and his

arms came around her, he pulled her into his arms, stroking her hair. Her skin felt icy against his, but warmed quickly as his hands ran over her arms and back. He waited until her breathing became even.

"Why wouldn't I come?" he asked.

She heard the deep timbre of his voice as she felt him speak. She pressed her face into his shoulder and wondered if she could disappear into him.

"Because I love you and you're real, but not real. I'm in love with my imagination." His arms tightened around her and she drew in a deep breath. She could smell him, feel him. She turned her face and kissed his shoulder, opened her lips to lick his skin. The flavor of wild green and gold light, sunshine wind and forest filled her mouth.

He tasted like Grey.

He made a noise she did not understand, or maybe she did not care. She moved her mouth off his shoulder and stretched to place her lips against the hollow of his throat.

Red wore next to nothing. The curves of her body felt soft against his chest. She sat cradled in his arm and she loved him.

His fingers flexed against the thin fabric of the nightgown she wore. His free hand ran down her leg to touch bare flesh. If he moved his hand back up...he wanted to, needed to keep exploring the feel of her skin. She moved against him, her lips skimming along his neck.

"Red, you need to stop."

She did not want to stop. She kissed up his throat, her hands spread over his chest. She felt his fingers on her leg, touching her calf, running up over her knee to caress the inside of her thigh. She gasped. Her mouth opened more against the skin under his ear, she felt him growl, the sound made his chest move against hers.

"Stop, Red." The words sounded harsh, an order, not a request.

"Don't want to."

Her breath fanned his ear. Her lips teased at his skin as she spoke. His fingers tightened in the fabric at the back of her nightgown, he heard it rip, and his fingers on her inner thigh curved around her leg, pulling it further up his body.

"Red, if you don't stop I'm going to forget I'm supposed to be a human and not a wolf."

"I love you the way you are."

It was too much. He snarled and shifted so she lay on the ground, his body over hers. Her hands trailed from his shoulders down his chest. He looked into wide, dark, liquid green eyes that were full of desire. He wanted her.

He leaned down and his lips caressed hers. His fingers rose higher on her hip, bunching the fabric of her nightgown. Red let her fingers explore his chest

"God, you're soft," he whispered. His lips trailed along her cheek toward her ear.

Her heart pounded. He could feel it pulse under her skin. His fingers slid behind her to stroke the small of her back and then slid lower.

His mouth moved to her throat and she closed her eyes and tilted her chin. She felt him smile, heard the sound he made that she recognized as approval.

"Grey," she moaned his name.

Grey thought it might kill him to stop touching her. He would have to stop. He felt the air, warm and heavy on his back and her body felt soft and welcoming underneath him. He forced himself to raise his head. Taking a deep breath, he captured all the scents around them, grass, flowers, the forest, Red, her arousal. He opened his eyes and stared back into hers."Did you really think I wouldn't help you?"

She nodded.

"I always will, Red as long as you want me, as long as I can."

"But you're real." She touched him as she spoke, moved her hand to his cheek and stroked it. "I saw you. I felt you."

"How does that change this?" He motioned to the purple air around them that clung to their skin.

She fell silent for a minute and he could almost see her trying to decide the answer to that question. "I don't know," she said at last, "but it feels like it should."

She pushed at him and he immediately rolled off her. Her eyes followed the movement, took in the state of his body. She dragged her gaze back to his face, her cheeks scarlet. He watched her, eyebrow arched.

"I...uhm...I'm sorry."

She did not wait for him to reply, but stood and turned her back.

He made a noise behind her. "You're almost as bad."

She glanced down at the tear along the side of her nightgown that exposed her hip and upper thigh.

"Oh." She closed her eyes and felt it change. The air around her swirled and she felt the purple and blue of the clothes she wanted.

When she opened her eyes again, she wore pants and a shirt. She turned and found Grey dressed, watching her with a wary look in his eyes.

"Tell me."

She answered without thought, telling him the truth, because it was Grey and he never laughed or minimized what she said. "I don't understand what it means that you're real. It scares me. My father came home tonight, that scares me a little too. Plus someone asked to marry me and I feel like I should say yes."

His hands were on her arms. She had not seen him move. Maybe he had not. The air around them grew darker. Black swirled with violent browns and she shivered.

"I thought you said you loved me," Grey accused.

"I do, but, you're not real. I mean, you're real but you're a wolf.

This," -she motioned in the tiny space between them- "this isn't real. Unless," she paused as she remembered the swans, "the wolf is real. Are you real, Grey? Is the human you real?"

Hope filled her voice as she begged him to be human. He dropped her arm.

Humanity felt like such a foreign... *thing*, one Grey was unsure he wanted most days. Even if he did, he knew of no way to reclaim what the witch stole from him. He refused to give Red false hope.

"No, Red. I'm just a wolf."

44

Melody

Melody sat straight up in bed. Her heart pounded against her ribs as she scanned her room in search of danger. The blackness inspired this kind of terror, but this fear came from outside her dreams. She felt safe with Grey in the meadow. He taught her to fight, to escape if someone grabbed her from behind.

Things had changed between them. He stayed a wolf more often than not. If he became human, he touched her only to teach her to defend herself.

The bell rang again and yanked Melody from her thoughts.

Fire!

That is what tore her from the dream and what caused the terror to race in her blood.

In a heartbeat, she leapt out of bed and grabbed pants and a shirt from where they lay discarded on the floor. She dressed as she ran from the room, buttoning her shirt over her nightgown. Melody ignored her cape as she raced out the front door and into the street.

Scanning the area, her body stiffened and she froze for a second. "No, please, no."

People moved all around her. A bucket brigade had already formed from the well and they moved buckets back and forth. One of the storage buildings, where the town stored supplies and food to get them through the winter, blazed red with flames. Heat radiated off the building and swept through the cold night in waves.

She ran to where another line formed from the river to the fire. She grabbed a bucket and plunged into the ice-cold water up to her knees. Filling the bucket, she half threw it at the man who stood at the edge of the water. No one else dared set foot in the frigid water.

The man grabbed the bucket and someone placed an empty one in her hands before she could blink. The cold hit her like a hammer, but she refused to let herself feel it. Instead, she filled the bucket and passed it back. The line moved. People tossed water onto the fire. Shouts filled the air around her, but the people in line ignored it. Buckets continued to move in a steady rhythm.

As she filled bucket after bucket, she longed for magic. She desperately craved what her family possessed. Her body moved without the need to see the water or the buckets. It felt as if some other sense took over. Melody let it, let the instinct or the magic, or whatever it was, move her body.

Closing her eyes, she searched for something, anything that might hold more and suddenly vivid and spectacular colors exploded behind her lids. They tugged at her and Melody wanted to dissolve into the brilliant colors surrounding her.

Fire!

Turning her mind away from the colors ached like an open

wound. Water, she needed water. Water was a moving flowing blue. In her mind, she grabbed the blue and gathered it to her. Every ribbon and band of blue rushed toward her. She held it all in her mind. She turned her mind in the direction of the heat and blaze and hurled the blue toward it, pushing the color with as much violence and strength as she could find in her body. Her mind saw the blue cover and suffocate the reds, oranges and yellows she knew to be the fire.

Throughout this, her body continued to work, filling buckets, passing buckets, and taking empty ones in a mindless cycle.

Until no empty bucket replaced the full one she handed off.

Her eyes flew open but the colors remained, they clung to everything and everyone she could see. They swirled in the air around her and the need to touch them competed with Melody's need to draw breath. She forced herself to focus and stared at the building that burned moments ago. The flames were completely gone. Mist from evaporating water filled the air around the half-crumbled building. One side of the building steamed. A charred, blackened skeleton in the moonlight, the other side remained untouched.

Everyone stared at the building. They gazed at where fire flamed only seconds ago. Melody swallowed hard. She did this. Her body shook, pain lanced through her head cutting off the joy she wanted to indulge.

She did not feel the biting chill of the water, did not understand that her soaked clothes clung to her body, or that she shook with cold, her teeth chattering. The man on the shore ignored her and ran toward the remains of the storehouse with the other town's people.

The bucket slid from limp fingers and her legs shook with the effort to hold her upright. Ice flowed over her skin and into her body. Her head felt too light and her body too heavy. She no longer heard the voices of the people on the riverbank. Darkness crept into the edges of her vision. Some part of her mind told her to move but she could not seem to obey. A deep growl cut through the fog of her senses. Her gaze shifted to the far bank of the river and she saw Grey. He stood at the edge, his head down, body rigid, lips drawn back in a snarl. Something dark lingered behind him.

As she watched, Melody saw his body move back and forth. He crouched and prepared to leap into the water, to her. She could feel it.

"No," she cried and threw her arm up palm out to stop him. "I'm okay."

She lied, and he would hear that in her voice.

"Melody!" cried her father.

She turned at the same moment Grey moved. She took a step toward the riverbank and stumbled. The colors began to fade and with them the last of her strength. Pain crashed through her skull.

"Melody, you're soaked." Trevor's voice. "What were you thinking?"

Someone's arms closed around her and lifted her. She could not see what was happening around her, could not feel anything. Her body shook and her mind felt fogged and distant. She whimpered.

Fire flared, her heart raced. What might burn this time? Warmth started to thaw her frozen skin. Maybe she should let this fire burn. Except it felt so hot, the orange and red scorched her eyes.

She felt it, saw the brightness through her lids. The light was too bright for her eyes and she tried to close them, but they were already closed. She heard a woman's voice, but did not understand the words. They soothed and she tried to take comfort and relax.

Everything faded.

45

Red and Grey

"What were you thinking?" The hands shaking her squeezed too tight. She flinched and opened her eyes to face her assailant. Grey's amber gaze narrowed on her face. "Do you have any idea how cold that water is? You could have drowned! What if you have frostbite?"

"Please stop shaking me, Grey, my head hurts." In her dreams, the pain faded faster than it did in life. He released her arms and turned to stalk away from her. She watched bright reds and black swirled thick in the air around them, angry colors. "I needed to help, Grey, before the supplies burned."

Colors hung in the air around them. They swirled into the grass and earth and moved on the wind. They were everywhere she looked, in the forest, the sky, the clouds; they whispered against her skin, danced around in patterns and moving with a life of their own.

"Not black." Her mind whirled around with the colors and something became clear to her as she watched them, reached out and traced the seam of black and red. "It isn't blackness that suffocates me. Black is a color. The void is the absence of color. You bring me color, Grey."

He snorted and turned to watch her, anger flashed in his eyes. Despite his human form, he seemed like a wolf. "I don't give a damn about colors. Why didn't you stand on the bank and use magic, Red? You didn't have to go into the water."

"I didn't think to use magic until after I stood in the water. Even then, I didn't know if it would work. I felt so desperate and then the magic appeared all around me. I could see it and feel it Grey." Her breath came fast as she spoke, and she could not keep the smile from her face.

She gazed at the clearing around her, looked down at the green grass. She reached out, without moving, and gathered some of the green and tried to push it into the air. She watched it drift and swirl with the red and black. They did not mix, but they moved together. The colors danced and the edges of each softened.

She glanced up and Grey watched her, his face less wolf now.

"I can do magic, Grey!" She grinned as she spoke, the smile refusing to stay inside.

She spun on her toes and threw herself into Grey's arms. He caught her, held her close, and spun her around once. Her arms wound around his neck, his around her waist.

"I did magic," she cried, breathless.

"Yes, you did, Red," he whispered his head close to hers. She leaned up and pressed her lips to his before he could pull away, a brief contact.

"Thank you for coming. If you hadn't been there, I might have slipped into the water before anyone found me," she admitted.

Grey sighed and leaned his forehead against hers.

They had been sharing a dream together. He held her, trying not to touch her any more than necessary while he taught her how to escape from an aggressor. Then Red disappeared, gone without explanation or farewell. He had woken immediately and took off for the village without a second thought. Black followed. Grey did not care. He needed to make sure Red was safe. Finding Red in the river it took every ounce of control he possessed not to charge into the water and drag her out.

"I told you I'd help when I could," Grey whispered the words close to her ear.

"I know," sighed Red.

For a long time he stood holding her, the colors swirling around them. He could feel them, the angry red and the soothing green. As they relaxed, the colors settled into a rainbow haze around them.

"My aunt told me magic can't cross moving water, so how did I do that?"

"I don't know, Red, but I watched you use magic. You pulled it from the air, the river, the town, everything around you. It rushed to you."

"You could see it?" Red asked.

"I can feel it. I felt you use it on me a moment ago." He arched an eyebrow daring her to deny it.

Red bit her lip, shrugged, and then gave him a small smile. "You were angry, and I wanted to see if it would work."

"I don't mind, but I'm still not happy." He pressed his lips to her forehead. She could have died tonight. He could have lost her forever. "I don't want you to get hurt. Please don't scare me like that again."

"I'll *try* not to."

46

MELODY

"Wake up, Melody. Come on."

Melody dragged her eyes open. Pain flooded her at the brightness of the room. The voice sounded familiar.

Nanna sat at her side and patted her hand.

"Nanna?" The sun shone in the window past Nanna's shoulder. Melody closed her eyes and covered them with one bandaged hand. When did that happened?

"Welcome back, love. I heard you had an exciting night."

"I did it, Nanna. I used magic. Now my head hurts like a horse kicked it." Melody kept her voice low, a hushed whisper. Even that seemed to make the hammering in her skull worse. For a moment, the room hung silent.

"Are you sure?" Nanna's voice sounded uncomfortable and hesitant.

"Yes," Melody smiled despite the pain. "I could smell the smoke and feel the heat from the fire even in the river. I knew the buckets would never be enough even while I filled them. I knew if we didn't put the fire out all the stores would be lost and people would starve. So, I closed my eyes and tried to find the magic. I saw colors, all bright and rich and everywhere and I *knew* that the blue could be water so I grabbed it and threw it at the fire. I did it, Nanna, and when I opened my eyes, the blaze was out."

Again, a long moment of silence spread around them. Melody moved her hand and studied Nanna's face. At first, she did not understand the look in Nanna's eyes.

"Nanna, you...you don't believe me." Doubt crept into her voice.

"Melody, no that isn't it. I've never heard of magic working that way before, not in the water, Melody. Magic isn't supposed to work in water. I know you helped put out the fire, I know you did more than anyone could have asked. No one else in the village had enough courage to go into the river, but the rest...magic doesn't work that way. Are you sure?"

Was she? No colors lay over the everyday world now. Melody closed her eyes and searched for the colors. They were gone, only throbbing pain remained. She could not find a trace of the magic that seemed so vivid the night before.

Grey believed her. She groaned. Of course, Grey believed her. What reason did he have to doubt? He was not human and did not understand human magic.

"No, I'm not sure. I thought... I believed... it felt like magic."

"Maybe you did, perhaps it was magic that allowed the fire to be put out so quickly, and allowed you to not suffer any permanent harm from the cold water. It's amazing you didn't end up with frostbite, or worse."

"Maybe." Melody heard the disappointment in her own voice. "What happened to the stores, how much did the town lose?"

"Some, but enough was saved that people shouldn't starve this winter. Mostly, the salt was destroyed. It will affect you and your father more than many, but there were other things lost: flour, sugar, and some of the salted meat. There will have to be more hunting parties out this winter."

"What will they hunt?" Melody sat up, ignoring the pain. Her fingers gripped the blanket draped over her body. "There are wolves in the woods, Nanna. They won't hunt them, will they?"

"Wolves? What are you talking about, Melody?"

Melody rose and the pain in her head intensified. She twisted her hands together. What would happen to Grey if there were more hunters in the woods? She sank back onto the bed, feeling weak and lightheaded.

"Melody, what's the matter?" Nanna asked.

Melody wanted to tell her. She considered it for a long moment. Aunt Ellen's warning and her own need to protect Grey won out over her need to talk to Nanna.

"Nothing, Nanna. Never mind. It was just a dream. There was no magic. It was all part of the dream."

"Melody, please dear, that isn't what I meant."

"No, it's okay, Nanna. My head hurts so much, though. I need to close my eyes, to rest a little longer."

"Of course." Nanna stood and took a step toward the door, but stopped and turned back to the bed. "You know you can tell me anything, Melody. I'm always on your side."

Melody nodded, but could not bring herself to speak. Nanna might always be on her side, but she did not always believe her. Not like Grey. Besides, Nanna might not always be on Grey's side. Not if she thought he could be a threat to Melody.

Once she heard the door click closed, Melody rose. She crept across the room and pressed her face against the cool smooth wood.

It felt like magic.

She sank onto the floor, cradling her head in her hands. She could hear voices and footsteps below her but she could not make out the words. No one came to her room. No one called out for her.

She was alone.

Time stopped having meaning. She never left the door, never moved further into the room. Light faded and the sounds of people downstairs came and went. Doors opened and closed. Her father's voice, and her Nanna's, carried up the stairs. Her body shifted and she lay on the floor. Her head rested on the back of her hand, her hair spread over her face and back.

Finally, the thing she waited for all day, the reason she needed to be alone, the one thing she craved came and she slipped into sleep.

47

The Past

For a while, he lived in various places, feeding for a while here and there while he regained his strength. Careful not to take too much from a single place, he built back his losses slowly, convincing himself not to attract attention. He knew it was a lie.

He felt the familiar presence of a Brother to the south and, he moved north. He traveled from nation to nation, town to town, never establishing roots in any one place. The north loomed prosperous ahead of him. Towns and cities flourished everywhere he went, and he still stayed south of the great mountain range that divided this continent.

After some time, he decided to start the search for a companion again. The decision both exhilarated and terrified him. It would be different this time. He would make sure that they were well and truly bonded. There would be no forced bond, no attempts to woo her away from another. To do this, he needed magic, more than enough to simply stay alive and young, he needed fuel that would keep him strong for years.

He chose a good sized town. Several people here possessed real magic, both a bonus and a risk. If they discovered what was happening, they could fight him. On the other hand, they would give him the kind of edge ungifted humans could not.

He found work at a local Cartwright took a room at the town inn, and made sure his intent to winter at the village and move on in the spring became local gossip before anything started to happen that might seem amiss. Nothing about his plans or actions raised suspicion. The trap stretched out perfectly around the town.

Chaos began as it always did; a word here, a lie there, and rumors no one could credit. His name never became associated with any of the gossip, but he knew the truth.

He chose an illness, magic twisted to infect. He made a cough that wasted the body and ended with blood in the lungs. The healer was unable to stop it, but she did not contract the illness herself, despite her hours spent with the sick and dying. People talked. He fed.

The town grew angry. So many died and yet the healer and her people stayed well. What did she know? Why did she not save them? The murmurs and the planning became an open secret, enough that the healer took precautions. She sent her children away.

He should not have cared. They were not his concern. He felt relief the day they left. Despite that, he did not stop. He needed this. The anger and resentment in the town thrived. He grew stronger.

They attacked her house, killed her husband outright, then dragged her to the center of the town and burned her. He devoured the energy of the emotion and the magic released at her death. Still, there was more power to feed on in this place.

The illnesses spread. People realized they had killed their healer for no reason; that they murdered an innocent woman.

They mourned.

He feasted.

Spring came and he left. The village lay in ruins, the houses still stood but the survivors carried scars on their bodies and souls that would never heal. He walked away. Complete and powerful, he continued to travel north.

48

Grey

Their paws left perfect imprints in the blanket of snow that covered the ground with each step. They ate a small deer, not even a year old, seven days ago, before that it had been four days between meals.

The humans hunted in his territory. Their supplies burned the night Red stood in the river, so they needed the meat. His mind appreciated their needs, but his instincts refused to accept that they invaded his territory and stole his prey.

He tried to take Black further into the mountain's foothills but trappers were active. Even there game was scarce and with the added danger of trappers hunting for wolf pelts he didn't like the risk.

This territory was not big enough to support both towns and two wolves during the harsh winter months, especially with game being rare. He should have realized that before he chose his den. The humans even hunted the rabbits and squirrels.

Grey and Black tracked a turkey today, only to lose it to a party of human hunters. He and Black needed to eat soon. Black whimpered beside him and yelped.

They crouched at the edge of the forest, east of Red's village, on their side of the river. He watched the sheep out on the hills. Timing was essential. Once it became dark enough, they could separate one of the animals from the rest of the herd. Then they could eat. Humans would not hunt the wolves over a single sheep. He remembered enough from the time he lived on two legs to know that no one hunted a wolf over a single sheep. Not unless the animal came and hunted again did they begin to care.

He snapped at Black's shoulder, silencing the younger wolf. He allowed himself to sleep for brief periods each night, careful to stay out of Red's dreams. He was too hungry to dream with her. How long had it been since they were together? A week? Two? In that time, he had not seen her stroll the woods.

He had not seen Red for two weeks.

The sun dipped below the horizon and he crept closer to the sheep. A sound from the barn swiveled his ears in that direction and the sheep began to head back to the enclosure for the night. He and Black needed to act now or they would be forced to hunt again tonight.

He broke cover and began to run toward the sheep. Halfway there he saw the boy. Young, small, he approached the sheep from the barn. Grey slowed.

Black passed him, moving toward the sheep. He would not stop, no human conscious held him back, he was hungry and prey stood in front of him.

The child saw the wolves. He began to run, too, but not in

the right direction. Instead of turning back toward the barn, the boy ran toward the danger, yelling for the wolves to get away from his sheep. Grey felt his body tremble. Black veered, changed direction and headed for the boy. So small, no weapons, an easy kill, Black would have no trouble.

Grey moved. He flew over the snow. His body hit Black's with enough force to throw the smaller wolf to the ground. Black whined and the boy stopped. Grey stood still for a moment, his lips pulled back as he growled at both foolish children-wolf and human.

A single sheep was all he wanted. He took off, nipping at Black as he passed and the young wolf followed him back toward the trees.

He could have killed the boy.

Black would have killed the boy.

The younger wolf snarled at his side as they ran. Grey did not glance at Black, ears flat against his head. His feet left troughs in the snow as he jogged along beside Black. They made it to the edge of the woods, but with an abrupt shift in weight Black changed directions. He turned back toward the sheep, toward the boy. Grey barked. Black ignored him. Grey knew what he must do. He showed Black this place. He led Black to Red's village familiarized the younger animal with a new kind of prey. He made him less afraid of humans.

Grey turned and raced over the snow and caught up to Black with ease, and then attacked. He did not hold back and he did not show mercy. He ripped into the smaller, younger wolf, and tore open his shoulder. Black fell into the snow and snarled a challenge. Grey growled back. Black leaped at him and they met in the air. Black was not as strong and Grey caught the smaller wolf by the neck. He ripped into his neck and heard Black whine. He dug his teeth in deep. Grey wanted to kill him fast. He felt the muscles and tendons tear. They hit the ground and he shook Black's body hard, heard a snap and the puppy ceased moving.

He noticed the blood, hot and wet in his mouth, on his fur. Black's blood. He let the puppy's still body drop from his mouth. He gazed back. The boy stood mere feet away, staring at him, a slingshot hung from his hand. Grey ran.

He did not stop until he reached his den. There he stood outside his home and howled. Head thrown back, he poured everything inside of him through the sound until he felt like he would collapse. Crawling into the den, he did not move. For days he lay there, waiting, hoping he would die, but he did not.

The day came Grey knew Red would walk her path and he began to stir. The idea of staying here, allowing himself to disappear, appealed to him, but the idea of Red in danger when he might be able to protect her motivated him. Stiff and sore, his stomach gnawed at him demanding attention. Grey willed himself to stand and move. The idea that Red might not walk today filtered through his mind and he rejected it. She had to walk. Grey didn't want to die without seeing her again.

He waited at the beginning of the forest path for her. As always he smelled her basket before he saw her. The pain in his stomach fisted and clenched. It took every ounce of control not to growl, not to step forward and demand, with his teeth, that she give him the bread he could smell.

Then he saw her, heard her voice, and thoughts of food vanished.

She scanned the brush along the side of the path, and she said his name. She searched for him. Concern etched her face. Grey heard the pleading in her voice.

She called to him even though no danger lurked in the woods. She called him because she wanted him, not for protection, or comfort. A deep wish to be with her and a longing to go to her spread through Grey. He ached to touch her and hold her.

In spite of all his good intentions, even though he knew he remained a wolf and she needed a human Grey felt drawn by her voice. Red belonged to him and, despite what he told himself, he belonged to her.

49

Melody

Melody walked through the snow with careful steps. After the fire Nanna spent several weeks in Varin where they both hoped that Nanna's magic would aid the town's repair efforts and morale. A few days ago father took Nanna home. To her immense relief, Melody once again walked through the forest trail. Snow lay in thick drifts along the trail and her boot snagged on hidden roots as she shuffled along, inspecting every inch of brush along the path.

Grey was gone. He no longer appeared in her dreams and she suspected he would not appear today either. At first, Melody was afraid for his life, and then she heard the story of the Sheppard boy to the north-east of Briar Creek. A story of two wolves: one black and one grey. The black wolf tried to attack young Sheppard, but the grey wolf intervened, saving his life. The body of the black wolf lay in the snow for anyone to see. Grey saved the Sheppard boy five days ago.

Where had Grey gone? What if he had received an injury? Fear created a dull, hollow ache in her chest. Now, as she walked, she searched for any sign of him.

"Please, Grey, if you're here, I need to see you," she begged, voice loud enough to send a nearby jay scolding into flight.

She saw the brush move on her right, rich bright colors began to seep up out of the earth, and Grey stepped out.

She could see his ribs under his coat. Dark brown areas spattered his muzzle and shoulder and caused his fur to clump together and stand out at awkward, unnatural, angles. Dried blood? More colors, dull and slow, circled around him, spreading into the air in waves between them. His head hung low between his shoulders and he lifted vacant eyes to meet her gaze. Red pulled in a sharp breath and moved toward him.

He growled, not even bothering to lift his lip.

"Yes, Grey, you're a big bad wolf," she said, acknowledging the growl with her words as she continued to move forward. "One who watches out for young women and little boys. I understand. But, I owe you, wolf. You've saved me, and I want to save you."

She continued to walk toward him as she spoke until she stood inches from him. She lifted the front of her cape enough so that the snow did not melt onto her pants as she knelt.

Setting the basket on the ground, Melody grabbed a handful of snow and reached toward him. His eyes locked on her hand. She moved slowly to make sure he could see her. With her mind, she examined the colors around her. Pain throbbed behind her eyes, but she ignored it, this felt too important.

White? No. Grey did not need white, a pale grey, so much lighter than his fur, but dark enough not to be white. She grabbed it and blended it with the snow.

Melody rubbed the snow into the spot where blood caked his fur. She scrubbed him with snow and magic.

He stood, legs locked, and head low and allowed her to care for him.

She moved to his muzzle with a fresh handful of magic-mixed snow, cleaning the dried blood from his face.

"You saved his life, you know? The little boy, he was sure that the black wolf was going to kill him, twice, and you saved me. The boar would have killed me that day if I'd been in its path, but you protected me. Then again, in the river, I slipped into some kind of trance and I might have drowned, but you woke me. You have a good soul, Grey."

He whined under her hands and she peered into his eyes.

"You need to eat, Grey. I need you to eat." She opened the

basket and took out two freshly killed rabbits. Once again, she reached for the colors in her mind. Pain stabbed from her eye to the back of her skull, and Melody fought the urge to flinch, she did not want Grey to know it hurt. She chose grey, blue, green, and dark brown strong forest colors and wrapped them around the carcasses, and watched the magic absorb into the meat. Dropping them into the snow at his feet, she stood. "Please, Grey. I don't want to lose you. You mean too much to me."

She watched as he leaned down and snatched the rabbits. Gripping the fresh meat in his jaws, Grey turned and disappeared into the woods.

50

Red and Grey

The warm purple air that swirled around Red felt so soft that for a moment she did not open her eyes. She enjoyed the feel of the color as it caressed her arms and cheeks. Green grass tickled her toes and its rich scent teased her nose. She drew in a deep breath and opened her eyes to allow her gaze to slide over the purple air and around the empty clearing. She searched for the one person she knew could bring the colors that surrounded her. Grey.

She began to walk the meadow in a slow circle and tried to be patient, even though he did not appear. He must be here. Without him, she would be fighting the void, losing to the void. Brush moved to her left and a figure emerged, Grey, but the change in him startled a gasp from her lips.

Somehow, she had not expected the dream to be so affected by reality. He stopped a few feet away, shoulders hunched; his ribs visibly lined his chest. "Grey..." She reached out to him and he flinched away. "You haven't been eating."

He shrugged. "What do you want, Red? Why did you call me today?" A snarl filled his voice.

Seeing him like this after finding him on the path earlier, Red felt with certainty that her Grey was exactly what he said he was. Not a dream, and yet not human. Here in their dreams, he found a way to be human for her, but he was still a wolf, still Grey.

It did not matter. She did not care what he was; only who he was. He had a good soul and he remained her Grey.

"Because, I love you. I don't want you to hurt. I saw the black wolf with you that night at the river. I know he was your friend. I know you made a difficult choice. I don't want you to hurt, but if you have to, and I understand sometimes you do have to hurt, I don't want you to do it alone. You never make me hurt alone."

Grey closed the distance between them even though Red never saw him move. He reached toward her, but dropped his hand without making contact. She did not move, but the colors around her reached out and stroked his skin, purples, blues, greens, reds, browns, greys, they swirled between them and around them through the air. They reached from Red to Grey and touched his arms. He reached for her again, she held her breath, and this time his fingers touched her. Her body relaxed with a shiver. The colors around her settled over both of them in a warm blanket. He trailed his fingers down her cheek, neck and then around up into her hair. He pulled her close. She put her arms around his waist and leaned her head on his shoulder.

He felt the magic swirl around him, felt it cling to his skin, but he did not fight it. He stroked her hair and held her close. He let her do what she could to heal him.

She chose gold and brown, with threads of amber and green and braided the colors into a thick rope of magic. Looping the autumn-hued rope around them, she pulled it as tight as she could, tying them together in hopes that her strength would be shared with Grey. Colors pulsed and flowed from their heads to their feet, a cocoon that bound them together and held them up.

He hugged her close, stroked her hair and let the magic sink into them.

51

Melody

It took asking six different people to figure out where Trevor cut trees in the forest. She wandered a bit and listened for the sound of his axe on the wood. Could Grey be around? Would he see her?

Thoughts of Grey made a dangerous game; they pulled her hopes and dreams into the waking world. In her dreams, it did not matter that he existed as a huge, grey wolf with soft, thick fur. Here though, in the real world, it did. As much as she loved him, her dreams and reality did not work the same way.

Tara's reminder of the swan princess, her aunt's warning about evil, none of those things mattered, because Grey remained a wolf.

The rhythmic crack of the axe against wood pulled her from her thoughts.

Trevor swung the axe in an effortless arch, bringing it down over and over on the huge tree that lay in front of him. Melody stood and watched his progress for a few moments, every stroke precise and with each bite of the axe the notch in the tree grew deeper. Trevor's body rippled with muscle as he applied his strength to the task. He stood broader than Grey. Of course, Grey did not lack muscles.

No. This was not the time to think about Grey.

She had come here on a quest. She needed to know the truth. Closing her eyes, Melody tried to prepare herself for what she must do and for the possible outcomes. She drew a deep breath, opened her eyes, and stepped into Trevor's line of vision. The axe stopped midway through its arch and Trevor lowered it to the ground.

"Melody, what are you doing here?" His deep blue eyes widened in surprise and, she thought, pleasure. She smiled, uneasy.

"I came, well, to see you." She felt the color creep up her cheeks.

Trevor lifted one blond eyebrow, and then a slow smile crept over his face. His eyes lit.

"Do you mind? Am I interrupting?" From the smile on Trevor's face Melody could tell he did not mind but she wanted to hear his response.

"Of course not. I'll always have time for you." He meant it. She could feel the truth in his words.

"Thank you, Trevor. I appreciate that." She gazed at him. Despite the cold, his shirt hung partially opened. He was handsome, fairer than Grey, with his blond hair and blue eyes. Trevor's body would never be able to stalk the way Grey's did. He loomed too large and too fair to disappear into shadows. Where Grey was stealth, Trevor was brute strength.

What would it be like to kiss him? He had not tried, not once. Would his kiss feel as right as Grey's? Her father had not given Trevor his blessing yet. Instead, he told Trevor, after the fire, that he was not yet ready to give Melody up, but welcomed him to continue the courtship.

They continued to see each other once or twice a week. In that time, Trevor never tried to kiss her or touch her in any intimate or passionate way. Not at all like Grey. She needed to know if she could feel passion with Trevor. She felt passion with Grey.

What if she only reacted to Grey? What if she did react to Trevor? She rubbed her sweating palms along her cape and tried not to think about what that might make her. She loved Grey. Did she love Trevor? She knew the answer to that question in her heart, but was afraid to let her mind examine it. Trevor was human. Grey was a wolf.

"Did you need something specific?" enquired Trevor.

The question made Melody flush. What would he say if he knew the thoughts in her mind? He lifted an eyebrow. Melody felt her face flush further and she clenched her hands in front of her.

With her gaze locked on Trevor's face, Melody asked, "If I asked you, would you kiss me?"

His eyes narrowed and the corners of his mouth lifted just a hint. "I have to admit that is not what I expected."

Melody looked away she focused on the forest floor. She swallowed hard and twisted her hands together in front of her. She spoke without lifting her gaze. "I'm not what the rumors say I am, but, I'm not a prude either, Trevor. I know that if a man and woman marry there should be some attraction and affection between them, and I enjoy being touched but, if you don't want to you don't have to, I just..."

She heard him chuckle, felt his big hand, rough with calluses, touch her hand. He lifted her fingers and kissed the back of each.

"I never said I did not want to, I am simply surprised you asked."

The fingers of his free hand touched her chin. He ran a thumb over her cheek, and gently tilted her face up. She looked into his eyes. He leaned close. Melody felt the warmth of his breath on her face, smelled the woods on his body and the scent reminded her of Grey.

No! She would not think of Grey.

His lips brushed hers, a soft, tender, encounter of flesh. The gentle tenderness of the kiss surprised Melody. He did not touch her body, only the fingers of one hand on her face.

So different from the way Grey kissed her. Trevor did not pull her against him and caress her mouth with his. Trevor did not involve his whole body in the kiss.

Sometimes Grey felt playful, sometimes he seemed almost rough, but there was always passion when Grey kissed her. She remembered the first time Grey nipped her lower lip, and the day he held her in his lap and she kissed his neck.

Trevor pulled back and Melody let her eyelids drop, not wanting to give him any hint of her thoughts. Trevor was a gentleman. He treated her as a fragile lady should want to be treated.

"Thank you, Trevor," she whispered.

"My pleasure, Melody. If I'd known you wanted a kiss I would have offered." His voice teased.

Melody smiled and opened her eyes. He still held one of her hands. "Can you find your way back to town from here? I still have some work to do, but I could walk you if you like."

"No, I'm fine. I don't want to take you from your work."

He released her hand, turning back to pick up his axe he whistled.

Melody thought he seemed pleased with the encounter. She tried to ignore the ache in her chest. She never once thought of Trevor when Grey kissed her.

Now she knew the answer.

52

Melody

Grey did not even try to hide. Melody grinned as she stepped onto the forest trail. Her heart felt light at the sight of the huge grey wolf. His head tilted to one side and his ears swiveled in her direction. Bright amber eyes watched her as she moved toward him and she wished he could talk to her.

"Hello, Grey. I see you aren't hiding anymore." She walked up to him. He stood and fell in step beside her. "I brought you a couple of rabbits. You can have them while I visit with Nanna."

He snorted and she glanced down at him, receiving impression she had offended him. "I'm sorry. I thought it would be helpful. It's not as if I cooked them." She paused and stared down at him for a moment "You would roll your eyes at me if you could, wouldn't you?" Grey stared up at her and she wished again that he could talk to her. She laughed and began to walk again. "Oh well, you can't."

Melody let one hand rest on his shoulder as they walked. Her fingers moved in his fur. It felt better, softer, and thicker than last week.

"I kissed Trevor." He stopped moving this time and growled, his lip lifted with the sound. She did not meet his eyes, but stared at the top of his head instead. "I know, but don't worry. He doesn't kiss as well as you."

Grey blew out a breath and began to walk again.

"I guess I need to get used to it, though, if I'm going to marry him." Her fingers curled into Grey's fur as she spoke and she clutched it in a tight fist. She planned to marry a man she did not love because the man she did love was a wolf.

They were almost to Rose Cottage. Melody stopped and knelt to peer into Grey's eyes. "Will you still come see me after I'm married?"

He did not answer, of course. She sighed and pulled the two rabbits out of the basket. She held them in her hands, and once again ignored the pain behind her eyes, twined deep vivid colors and around them. She did not even have to search for them today. They hung there, hovering in the air around her and Grey; powerful magic, to make Grey strong.

Holding them out, she waited. Grey stared at the rabbits, he did not take them from her hands and Melody wondered if she should drop them. Before she got a chance, Grey reached out and took them from her hand in his mouth. He turned and disappeared into the brush beside the trail. Melody smiled and stood to walk the rest of the way to the cottage.

Nanna met her at the door. "I'm not sure I can get used to you wearing these pants all the time." Her tone sounded light and teasing, and Melody smiled.

"They're much warmer in the winter, and more practical for walking through the snow."

"I'm sure they are, love. Come in and warm up." Nanna moved into the kitchen and Melody followed, undoing the clasp of her cloak. "I received a dove yesterday and your cousins are on their way back. It will be soon, but it takes time to get here over the mountains."

"Cousins? Who besides Andrew is coming?" asked Melody, confused.

"Tara is coming along with Andrew's sister, Anna. There will also be some others who are not related."

"Tara's coming. That's wonderful!" Melody grinned and felt a rush of excitement. "She'll be here for my wedding."

Nanna's head shot up in an abrupt gesture and her eyes

narrowed. "You've accepted someone's offer?"

"Not exactly, not yet, but I've decided that I'm going to accept someone's offer. Trevor's."

Nanna nodded thoughtfully. "You love him?"

"I like him, and he likes me too. We get along well, and he's a good man."

"Those things aren't love, Melody."

Melody closed her eyes and fought the urge to scream. Despite her best efforts, when she spoke her voice came out harsh. "Nanna, is there anything I can do that will please you? You wanted me to be magic, and I tried, but the magic I found wasn't right. Everyone says it's time to marry. My options are in front of me so I made a choice. But it isn't good enough.Who would you have me marry? Milo?"

"Melody, I've never heard you speak that way before."

"Well, Nanna, I'm tired of being told I'm wrong, or bad, or not enough. Not good enough at magic. Not in love enough to marry. Not kind enough to fill my mother's shoes. Not special enough for my father to stay in the house with me. The only person I'm ever good enough for is Grey–" She choked on the name.

"That isn't true, Melody, no one expected you to be your mother. No one wants you to be more than you are. Your father's grief is not your fault or your responsibility."

"Really, you could have fooled me. It's all I've heard since Momma died. What my responsibilities are and how I need to be more, better." Melody rose and grabbed her cloak. "I'm done with that, Nanna. Trevor might not be what *you* think I should choose but what other choice do I have?"

"Melody, don't leave. Please. We can discuss something else, love. Just stay a few more minutes."

Melody paused with her hand on the door. She had never yelled at Nanna. She turned and, leaving the cape around her shoulders, sat back down in the chair.

"Tell me what you want your wedding to be like," Nanna said gently.

"I want to marry in the late spring, when the flowers are blooming. I want wildflowers and lilies at my wedding, and I want to wear the purple dress I saw Aunt Ellen making in the fall. I suppose I should send a dove to her and ask her to bring it."

"That sounds lovely. I'll send a dove for you this week. Maybe Ellen will come, I'm certain that she will be missing Tara by springtime. Purple will be a good color on you."

Melody tried to picture the wedding in her mind. She could see the dress, the flowers, even the village priestess waiting to perform the ceremony, but when she saw the groom, her breath caught in her chest. She closed her eyes and tried not to see Grey's face swimming behind her lids.

"Yes, I'll have to talk to Trevor of course and make sure that's what he wants." She muttered, trying to turn her thoughts away from Grey.

"Of course, just one more question." Nanna asked, her voice calm, but full of curiosity. "Who is Grey?"

Melody opened her eyes and met Nanna's level gaze. She tried not to show any emotion. "He's no one, Nanna."

53

RED AND GREY

Grey crouched inside the tree line and stalked along the underbrush as he pursued his prey around the clearing. Red walked in slow circles, searching for him. Her red cape billowed out behind her. White snow reflected the moonlight and stars. The trees shifted position around him as he watched so he never lost sight of her. Purple, blue and a hint of red twisted in the air around her. She reached out and dragged a thread of silver through the other colors.

They should be dark brown, black, angry orange. They were the colors he wanted to see around her. Those colors would reflect the emotion that churned inside of him tonight.

She dared to tell him how she kissed her woodcutter. That she planned to marry this other man. She said these things hours after being with him, after they talked, laughed and touched. She told him she loved him, while she made plans to marry the woodcutter. Did she tell the woodcutter she loved him too?

The urge to hurt her pulsed in his blood. The moonlight vanished and bright sunshine filled the clearing, the snow lay pristine on the meadow, her feet left no tracks. The memory of her blood on snow made him want to growl. He held it back. He did not want to harm her physically, but he wanted to hurt her.

Clothes flowed onto his body as he moved. He entered the clearing and she glanced up at him, a smile on her face. Something changed on her face. She took a step back, away from him. He could smell her fear. For months, she refused to be frightened of him, even when he wanted her to be. Now the scent of her fear flavored the air. A hint of black and pale yellow-orange colored the air around her.

"Grey, what's wrong?"

"Nothing, Red. Why would anything be wrong?" He continued to advance and she backed up further. "Running, Red?" He arched an eyebrow.

"No, but, something's wrong. Why are you looking at me that way?"

He moved forward, forcing her to back up further. The blues and greens swirled in the air around her. They reached out to touch him but he brushed them away. He could not do that a few months ago. Her eyes widened and the red and pale orange stained the air and forced away the blue, green, and purple. He glanced behind her and the trees shifted again. One more step and her back hit a tree trunk.

"How am I looking at you, Red? Like a wolf?"

"Yes." She tried to move to the side, but he blocked her,

anticipating her attempt to dodge. After all, he taught her that maneuver. He growled, using his arm to trap her and positioning his body so she remained pinned against the tree trunk.

"Stop, Grey. Please."

"If you want me to stop, make me. I showed you how."

His voice challenged her, but more than that, it threatened her. Melody pressed her back harder into the tree. This felt wrong. He appeared angry and hungry. The combination scared her. She watched as he leaned in toward her. Was this some kind of test? He did teach her how to stop a man.

She lifted her foot and stamped on his toes hard. He growled again and leaned closer, his mouth near her ear.

"Ouch." His breath moved across her ear as he spoke and she shivered. "Is that the best you can do, Red?"

She felt his lips touch her ear and she tried not to think about it. She put her hands against his shoulders and pushed, at the same time she tried to shift her leg, he caught her hands and lifted them, pinning them above her head with one of his. Rough bark scratched at the skin of her arms.

"Try harder, unless you don't want me to stop?"

"I want you to stop." Her chest rose and fell with hard, fast breaths, despite that, she kept a note of steel in her voice. She tried to twist and he tightened his grip on her hands moving his leg to pin hers against the tree. "Stop. Please. Grey, please stop."

His lips trailed along her neck and the sensation made her skin hot. She did not want him to stop, but she did not want him to do this because he was angry. She never felt threatened with Grey. She knew if she asked him he would stop, but tonight felt different and she did not want him to touch her when they might regret it later. There had to be a way to stop him.

His body pressed against hers, his shirt dissolved from his skin. An idea formed in her mind and she leaned forward. She put her face against his shoulder and opened her mouth. She bit down hard on his shoulder, her teeth leaving a mark on his skin.

He jolted back and stared down at her. She met his gaze. Her eyes shimmered, snapping green fire, and anger burned her skin. Grey laughed. "That won't convince me you want me to stop. Wolves like to bite when we play, and when we do other things."

"What is wrong with you, Grey?" She jerked her head away from him as he tried to lower his mouth to hers. His fingers tightened on her wrists, they became almost painful for a heartbeat, and then he dropped them. He stepped away and turned his back on her. Melody watched as he began to walk away. She felt the void behind her. With each step he took away from her the darkness came closer she could feel it on her skin, in her lungs with each breath she took.

"The answer is no, Red," Grey said, without even a glance in her direction.

For a second she could not move, could not breathe. What answer? Then she remembered the question she asked earlier. No, he would not come to visit her after she married, not in the woods and not in her dreams. She would lose Grey forever when she married Trevor.

She pushed away from the tree and ran after him. He was further away than she thought and no matter how fast she ran she could not catch him. The void swirled around her feet as she ran. It slowed her steps. She dodged around trees and ducked under low-hanging branches but no matter how hard she tried, she kept losing sight of Grey.

"Grey, please don't leave me." The void snagged her foot and she tripped. "I'm sorry, Grey. I didn't mean to hurt you. Please, don't hate me." The colors around her began to dim and the void flowed up into the sky and twisted around her arms on the ground.

She pulled free by sheer force of will and got to her feet. She tried to run again. She dragged one foot free from the void.

Grey was gone and she was alone. The void began to block out the trees.

"I'm sorry, Grey," she whispered the words, knowing he could not hear her. The void wrapped around her legs. She fought and kicked as it crept up her stomach. Her tears dropped soundlessly into the nothingness.

54

Melody

It hurt to get up each morning. The sun shone too bright and the cold wood floor bruised her feet. Every night she fought the void for hours. Desperate to free her arms or legs, she would free one limb only to lose another. It was always the same fight, the same struggle; every day the same pattern. She used every bit of extra she owned and made food for the families in the village. Every evening her father arrived, staying for a few hours while Trevor came and sat with her, officially courting her. After Trevor left, her father returned to the tiny cottage near the salt mines.

Alone, she would spend hours putting off bed and sleep. She would sort through old household items, or sew new blankets or dresses. In bed, Melody spent more time rousing herself the instant the dream began. In the end, she would lose the battle with her own body. Then she fought the void.

She never opened her eyes in the clearing anymore. She was always in the woods. She could sense the trees around her even when she could not see them. She tried to find Grey even as she fought the void. She called to him. Begged him to find her and help her.

He never came.

Every morning her head ached and her eyes burned. Grey was gone. He had left her and she understood why. He left because of

Trevor. She could not have everything, could not have both men.

Trevor was here, available, willing.

She wanted Grey.

She sat at the small wooden table in her room and brushed her hair. She tied it with a blue ribbon and braided it, staring at herself in the mirror. Dark circles bruised the skin under her eyes and her prominent cheekbones outlined a face that grew thinner and paler each day.

Today she carried a single loaf of bread to Nanna's. She knew she would leave with more than she had arrived with. Melody sighed. Since their fight last week she and Nanna had not spoken.

She heard from her father that Nanna was paying workers from Briar Creek and Varin to come and build onto the cottage. They were adding another room, a large room with a fireplace and an exit door. Curious to see the renovations, Melody wanted to ask Nanna why she needed all this extra space. She suspected it involved the impending arrival of her cousins, but Tara could always stay here in Varin with her, so the addition seemed excessive.

Would Grey walk with her today?

She doubted it. He said he would not come, and for a week, he kept his word. No matter how much she searched and begged in her dreams, he never appeared. She had hurt him. That knowledge made her ache. "I'm so sorry, Grey. I just don't see any other way. I can't marry a wolf," she whispered to the mirror.

There was less snow on the ground, this week, and the winter sun shone brilliantly on the ground, melting any snow that dared lie outside the shadows.

She did not call for him when she entered the forest path and he was not sitting and waiting for her. She did not want to think about whether or not he lurked in the bushes. She just walked. She tried not to wonder if he was lonely without the black wolf, and tried not to worry about whether he had enough to eat. Melody refused to let her eyes wander to the sides of the path.

Rose Cottage appeared different this week. Activity buzzed

around it. People worked and shouted to each other. Melody heard the pounding of hammers and the rhythmic *wush* of a saw. For a while, she stood watching the workers, amazed at the changes in front of her. She saw Trevor cutting boards and recognized several other people from Varin and Briar Creek. With a sigh, she walked out from the cover of the trees and approached the cottage.

As she opened the gate to Rose Cottage garden one of the workers waved hello. She waved back. Trevor looked up from his work, grinned and waved to her. Melody waved back. She tried to smile but it felt painted on her face, she approached the door to the cottage. Nanna opened the door for her before she could knock.

Inside it felt cool, barely warmer than outside. She went into the small living room and sat near the fire. One of the workers called to Nanna and she went to answer his question. After a few moments, Nanna came and sat beside her.

"Melody, you look terrible. What's wrong?" She sounded sad and worried.

"Bad dreams." Melody shrugged a shoulder.

"Tell me about them."

"Why, Nanna? So you can tell me how foolish I am? Or that I'm wrong? A failure?" Melody pleaded for an answer.

"Melody, everyone makes mistakes, including me. I'm sorry I hurt you. I want to help you. I love you, and I hate seeing you so sad."

Melody looked up, her eyes burning with unshed tears. She bit her lower lip and realized that right now the thing she wanted most in the world was to tell Nanna everything. She could no longer fight alone. She needed help, Grey had left and Nanna was the last person who might be able to help her. She ran her hands over her face; would Nanna believe her?

As a child Nanna never let her down, her mother lied to her, but Nanna told her the truth about magic in the best way she knew how. Maybe Nanna could help her find a way out of this mess. She closed her eyes again and decided to trust the one person who tried to tell her the truth.

"It's a wolf, Nanna. His name is Grey and he showed up in my dreams months ago. I've been having nightmares ever since mother died, and Grey chased them away. He kept visiting my dreams and, I fell in love with him. How foolish is that? To fall in love with a dream? I didn't think he was real." Tears leaked from her closed eyes as she confessed her own folly. Her voice broke and she needed to stop. The sound of saws and hammers filled the house and she wiped her eyes with the back of her hand and drew a deep shaky breath before she continued.

"One day, I was walking in the wood on the way to your cottage and suddenly there he was. He saved my life when a boar charged me. I couldn't believe it. He was real! I remembered the swans, and the next time I saw him in a dream I asked him if he could become human, but he said no, he's just a wolf. Except, of course, he's not. Not in my dreams. There, he's human, too. He's so real in my dreams. I wish...I wanted him to be more. And now, I hurt him, so he left, and the nightmares have returned." Melody shivered despite the fire and used the back of her hand to wipe another tear from her cheek. She waited, hands clenched in her lap, to hear if her grandmother would accept her story or reject it the way she rejected her attempt to find magic.

As the moment stretched and the sounds of hammers and saws filled the silence between them her stomach began to twist in fear. She made another mistake confiding in Nanna. Would she doubt her again? When Nanna spoke, the words came as a complete shock. "Do you remember your grandfather at all?"

For a moment, Melody wondered if Nanna heard her story. She gave a nervous laugh, "Of course, Nanna. He was wonderful. I remember we used to play hide and seek, he gave me rides on his back and taught me to fish."

"Yes, I adored that man. But I have to admit, the day I met him he terrified me."

"Pop Pop? Why?"

"Melody, when I first met your grandfather he wasn't human. He was a bear."

For a second Melody sat in stunned silence and stared. "Pop Pop was a bear?" She repeated the words back to Nanna slowly to make sure she heard them right.

"Close your mouth, love," Nanna chuckled. "You remember the story of the hunter and the swan. Well, for me it was a bear and a poor widow's daughter."

"But, Nanna, Grey would know if he was more than a wolf. Wouldn't he?"

"He should, but, sometimes things are more complicated than we want them to be. For example, if he's been a wolf for a long time, he might not remember being human. Or if he was cursed, part of the curse might have taken his memory."

"You heard the story from Briar Creek about the Sheppard boy?" Melody asked.

"Of course! That was your Grey!" Nanna sounded proud.

"Yes." Melody nodded and chewed her lip in thought. "He says he's just a wolf, but he acts like more. How would I know for sure?"

"I don't know." Nanna paused and gazed thoughtfully into the fire. "For your grandfather, that wasn't a problem. He knew he had been a human before. He knew a curse turned him into a bear. There is another, less pleasant, possibility."

"What's that, Nanna?" Melody tried to keep the fear out of her voice but she heard it despite her efforts.

"The story of the swan princess ends well for Adelle, and even Odette, who eventually found her true love. However, there is another part of the tale, though one much less frequently told. It's the story of the youngest sister, Illene. She was a young child when the sorcerer cast the spell.

"Illene spent her formative years as a swan, able to fly and swim. When the sisters returned to their human form, after the hunter's kiss at the ball, she seemed happy for a time. Eventually, she became distraught. She couldn't eat, couldn't sleep. For hours, she would sit by the king's swan pond and sob.

"The king and her sisters did everything they could think of to help her, but nothing worked. So the king searched throughout his country and others until he found a trustworthy witch of great power. By the time she arrived, Illene lay weak and sick.

"The witch listened to the story with great distress. She

explained to the king that because of the way the spell was cast she could not turn one sister into a swan again without turning the rest into birds with her. The king was forced to choose. Lose one daughter, or lose them all while they still lived. He ordered the entire country into mourning for his youngest daughter.

"The witch, however, came up with another idea. She offered it to the king and his youngest daughter. She could give just Illene another nature. She could make the girl a goose, not as beautiful or graceful as a swan, but still able to fly and swim. She could even craft the spell to allow the girl to change forms at will.

"Illene accepted the offer. She remained at the palace for months changing form from goose to girl and back. She grew strong and healthy. In truth though, she still wasn't happy. The time she spent as a human she felt trapped and confined.

"Her father and sisters grieved for her, and for the person they wanted her to be. She began to feel guilty because she chose the animal over the human. After she grew healthy again, Illene flew away. She disappeared from the castle and the kingdom. Her father and her sisters never saw her again. No one knows what became of the youngest swan."

"So even after everything they did they couldn't save her." Melody said sadly.

"No, you don't understand, love. She didn't want to be saved. Maybe your Grey feels the same way. Maybe he doesn't want to be human again."

Melody shivered and she knew it wasn't from the cold.

Could that be possible? What if Grey knew how to be a human but wanted to stay wolf? Because she loved him did not mean he loved her. He had never said he loved her.

"Your grandfather could change to a bear at will, but it took a kiss to turn him into a human. He was able to be both, unlike the swans."

"For both the swans and Pop Pop a kiss changed them. I've kissed Grey, in my dreams." Melody admitted her face flushing.

"Yes, but it has to be in reality, Melody, dreams don't work the same way reality works."

"I've noticed."

Nanna chuckled again.

Melody nodded her head. "I don't want to force him into anything, but, if he doesn't remember or, if he needs help... alright, I'll try it, but first I have to find him."

Nanna smiled. "I'm sure you won't have any trouble. Now, I have a whole basket full of food for you to take home. I want you to promise me you will eat at least some of it."

"Okay, but first, tell me why the extra room."

Nanna gazed toward the sound of the construction and smiled. "I would prefer to wait until your cousins arrive, if you can wait another week or so."

"Uh oh, Nanna. You're being all secretive. I think I should worry." Melody raised an eyebrow and grinned.

Melody left, after saying hello to Trevor, and walked slowly. This time she scanned the woods for Grey. She did not see any sign of him, but then she never had until he chose to let her see him.

"Grey, are you here? I need to see you, in reality. Please." She continued at her slow pace, and every few feet she called him in a whisper, but he never appeared.

55

Grey

Grey hunched in the snow and listened to her call. The sound of her voice pulled at him but he ignored the tug. He watched from the forest as she left the cottage and went to the woodcutter, letting the man touch her, and kiss her.

He would not let her know he broke his word. Grey said he would not come again. He lied. He could not stay away from her for long. He would take whatever he could get. He needed her.

He waited for her today, the way he did every week. As she walked, he crept along in the brush beside her. Now, as she left the forest trail to walk along the main road back into her village, her absence left a deep hollow ache in his chest. Maybe he should have gone to her.

Anger burned out the need.

Why go to her? So she could tell him she kissed the woodcutter? That she planned to marry the woodcutter? He ran across the road and deep into the forest on the other side. He kept running, without a backwards glance. He let his body carry him without purpose, and thought perhaps it would be better to leave this place, maybe he should run forever.

Black was gone. Red was going to marry. Nothing held him here.

Memory of the strange instinct that once called him here across the mountains flooded him. Perhaps, if he left, he could find another place, a better place.

Except he did not want to leave, did not want to run. There could be no better place than with Red. Why else would he have been drawn here?

No, that was wrong. He was not with Red. Being a wolf trapped him on the outside. He could only watch as she prepared to marry her woodcutter. Watching her kiss him, live with him, carry his child. The thought made him shudder and snarl. He would leave, but this time he would not run. He would say goodbye.

56

RED AND GREY

Melody relaxed into the grass. She was safe. Grey came tonight. She did not search for him. If she did, he might run and that thought terrified her more than fighting the void. Instead, she lay back and inspected the peach fuzz sky. Swirls of red and yellow mixed into the clouds and changed tone and hue as they moved on the breeze.

"Hello, Red." His voice washed over her and she smiled, closing her eyes to absorb the sound.

"You came back." Relief ran so thick in her voice it turned the air around her a light golden red. She felt the color spill over her skin as she spoke.

"To tell you goodbye."

Her eyes flew open and she stood at his side.

He refused to look at her, did not want to see her eyes. He could feel the heat from her body but he focused his gaze above her head. "I wanted to apologize for last time, for the way I treated you and the way I left. It was wrong of me."

"I forgive you. I'm the one who needs to apologize. I'm so sorry Grey. I hurt you and I'm sorry. Please forgive me. What I did, what I'm doing, it's wrong."

"I'm an animal, Red. People use animals all the time. It's what you do."

"You're more than that to me. I love you and–"

"People love their dogs, too, Red. I'm not your pet and I'm not your lover. I'm a wolf you used to help chase away the nightmares." Dark brown and black crept into the air with his words and twisted around them.

"No," she said.

He heard the way her voice trembled, felt the colors shift around him.

"That's not true. I might have used you, and if I did I'm sorry. I do love you, Grey. Not like a pet. I'll do my best not to hurt you again. I'm not going to marry Trevor. I don't love him. I understand now, I can't have everything. I love you, Grey, who you are, not what you are. I don't care if you're a wolf. Please, Grey, don't leave me."

Grey fought the urge to touch her, the need to pull her against his body. Could he believe she loved him? Would she prefer him to the woodcutter? His skin burned where she rested her hand on his arm. He looked at the place their flesh touched.

Her fingers looked pale against his darker skin. Her touch felt like silk against his roughness. She moved closer, her body brushing his. He waited, not wanting to move away and lose the feel of her. She leaned close and placed her face against his shoulder. She turned her head and bit him gently.

He did not move and Melody felt panic well up inside her. He said wolves like to bite. She felt his body tighten under her hand and she stiffened, prepared to fight if he tried to leave. This time she would not let him run away. Her fingers flexed on his arm.

"You should be careful, Red. I'm going to forget I'm supposed to be a man."

Relief at his tone and the familiar words washed over her.

"You said that before, but you never followed up on it." She took a step back from him and ran a hand through her hair. She ran her hands up her arms and over her shoulders to the neck of her shirt where a line of buttons ran down the front. She fingered the first button and freed it. "I don't even think you're interested."

She heard him growl, felt him grab her. She found herself lying on the ground and it felt softer than the clouds above them. His hand ran through her hair, holding her head as his lips danced with hers. She relaxed and ran a hand down his back, muscles flexed and bunched under her fingers.

His mouth moved from hers, along her jaw and down her throat. "I love you, Grey."

He continued to kiss his way down her body. His mouth teased her collarbone and his fingers ripped open her shirt. Some small part of her brain thought this might be a bad idea. She needed to talk to him, find out if he wanted to be human, but she wanted his touch, his kiss. She loved him and she needed him to hold her. Maybe if she could not make him stay with words she could make him stay with her body.

"I want you, Red." The words came out more a snarl than the request he had intended.

"I want you, too." Her voice purred against his chest. "Make love to me, Grey. Please."

He felt clouds encase them and they floated. Grey ran his fingers down her chest, over the curve of her breasts. She moaned his name, not the woodcutter's.

"You taste good." He licked her and she arched toward him.

Clothes melted, his hands caressed her skin and her body moved under his fingers. She stretched toward him and moved against his hand.

Her fingers dug into his shoulders and her lips explored his arm as his mouth continued to taste her body. He let his teeth close gently on her nipple and heard her suck in a breath. Releasing her, he moved up her body. "I warned you, wolves like to bite."

She could not think of a way to respond.

His mouth covered hers in a lingering kiss. He pulled back and she leaned up to catch his lower lip with hers and nipped before she let her head drop back to the ground. For a moment, they held each other's gaze before his leaned down and caught her lips in another long, hot kiss.

Her hips rocked up and his body slid into hers and joined them together. The air cushioned them and swirled around them. Melody felt safe and whole. She clung to Grey as his hands and body caressed her.

She could feel him moving, and the colors swirled faster, brighter. Gold, red, purple, every color she could imagine. The colors wrapped around them, a blanket, and held them so close they breathed together. No space existed between them. The colors bound them together and she was complete.

57

Melody

Melody stretched, eyes still closed. She did not feel any different. Her body felt relaxed and rested with no lurking evidence that she spent the night making love with Grey. Was the town right about her? She sighed and ran a hand over her face, forcing herself to open her eyes. Her gaze went to the window and she imagined the people beyond.

No, they were wrong. She loved Grey. She could not regret her decision. Despite that, a thread of fear weaved its way around her mind. What if it did not work? What if he left anyway? They still had not talked. He might not want to be human, even if she could find a way to change him.

She needed to see him. The more she thought about Nanna's theory the more it made sense. Grey always became a human in their dreams. She never became a wolf. Grey knew how to talk. He knew how to wear clothes. He acted human. Well, sometimes. Even those times she encountered him in the woods bright intelligent eyes gazed at her from his wolf features, not the eyes of an animal.

She sat up, still staring out the window. She would talk to Trevor today and tell him the truth. She would let him know she was sorry, but that she did not love him. She pulled her knees up to her chest under the covers and dropped her forehead onto them. How could she have been so sure she wanted Trevor? Why did she not let him be happy with Jessica? What made her want him for herself? Through her actions, she hurt Grey, Trevor, and Jessica.

The weight of her mistake lay across her shoulders as she drew a deep breath. She would be more careful, less selfish in the future. Maybe one day she would even find a way to make things up to Jessica and Trevor.

She dragged herself out of bed and dressed, careful to select a modest dress, and pulled her hair into a tight bun. She threw her cloak across her shoulders before she left the house. She stepped onto her front porch, back stiff and head up. Her hands shook as she locked the door. She dropped the key as she tried to slip it into the bag on her belt. As she bent to retrieve it she hit her shoulder on the door jam.

With a sigh, she began her walk out of Varin. It would be easy to find Trevor this time; she knew where he worked today.

She walked the familiar forest path to Rose Cottage. She knew Grey would not be there, since this was not her normal day to visit Nanna. The walk did not take long enough. Instead of entering the cottage, she walked around it to the area where the sound of saws and hammers dominated. Trevor stood sawing boards and Melody waited until he paused to approach him.

"Melody, what are you doing here?" Trevor asked when he spotted her.

"I wondered if we could take a little walk. I wanted to talk to you about an important matter." She twisted her hands into the fabric of her cape.

Trevor grinned down at her. A current of nerves shot through her stomach as Melody remembered the last time she sought him out. Melody felt the color creep up her face as she began to realize how difficult it would be to explain this situation to Trevor.

They walked around the house and Melody led him to a small bench in Nanna's dormant flower garden. She sat down and he sat next to her.

"What can I do for you, Melody?"

His voice was kind and gentle. In all the years she knew him, Trevor never treated her with anything but kindness. She swallowed hard and refused to let herself be distracted by her guilt.

"Trevor, I...I'm sorry. I want to say this fast and get it over with. I can't marry you. I'm sorry." Melody dared a quick glance at him.

Wide blue eyes stared at her and his mouth hung open. His hands lay limp in his lap. "What, why not?" He sounded as lost and confused as he looked.

"I can't...I'm not in love with you the way I should be, and I think, if you're honest with yourself, you'll admit you aren't in love with me either. Not the way we should love each other to marry."

"Love? This is about love?" Melody dared to look up and saw him watching her with amused disbelief. He shook his head and smiled. "Melody, listen to me. I have waited all my life for you. You're everything I could imagine and more. What I feel for you is much more than love, I *need* you."

Melody bit her lip and dropped her gaze from Trevor's face to shake her head.

"I'm sorry, Trevor, I don't love you. Not like a wife should love a husband. I can't marry a man I don't love." They sat close enough that she felt his body tense as she spoke. When she looked up again the amusement was gone. His eyes had hardened with anger. She crossed her arms over her stomach and dug her fingers into her sides. Maybe she should tell him that in her dreams she had sex with another man. Perhaps if he knew the rumors about her told part of the truth then he would not be so eager to have her for a wife.

"Please forgive me." Melody begged. Melody hoped her eyes reflected her remorse. She knew that words fell short. She saw the calm expression wash over his features. His lips twitched up in an almost smile.

"Melody, I understand you think I don't love you and that you are still reeling from your mother's death and all the changes in the village since then. I won't push you, but I do need you."

"Trevor, I'm so sorry."

"Don't be, Melody. This will all work out. Trust me. I've waited so long for you. I know that we're meant for each other, even if you can't see it yet. I can be patient a little longer."

Melody let him tug one arm free from her side and lift her hand. She hardly noticed the way he kissed the back of her fingers. He rose and she stood with him. When he walked around to the other side of the house she entered the forest path and began her walk home. Her mind seemed sluggish and her feet felt heavy.

He did not believe her, did not accept their relationship was over. He was not going to let her go, but she could not marry him. She did not love him and he did not love her. She knew what it felt like to be in love.

She loved Grey, not Trevor.

Somehow, she needed to convince him their relationship had ended. Next time her father came home, she would explain her decision. He would be disappointed, but he would accept the truth. She could ask him to help her make Trevor understand. Until he chose to visit her again, she would have to avoid Trevor.

There was another person she needed to talk to as well. Without any doubt, this would be the more difficult of the two encounters. She went to her house and took off her cape. The bright red garment seemed like an added taunt.

Instead, she wore her mother's favorite shawl. Melody chose it from the caravan and gave it to her mother one midwinter feast years ago. Once, wool of dark blue, royal purple, deep grey, and even a few strands of black mixed in a brilliant pattern, but over time, the colors faded and muted. While cleaning out the house, Melody had pulled this garment from her mother's closet and found herself unable to give it away.

Now as she put it around her shoulders she caught of hint of a smell. The image of her mother wearing the shawl washed over her and she fought back a wave of unexpected tears. She swallowed back grief that never seemed to completely fade, as she left her house.

Arriving at the Widow Cramer's door, Melody was surprised to find her hands shook. She clenched her hands and used her knuckles to tap on the door. The Widow opened the door.

"Melody, welcome. It's lovely to see you today. Do you have

more clothing for me to share?" The Widow greeted her warmly.

"No, Widow Cramer." Her voice cracked and she swallowed and forced a smile. "I hoped to talk to Jessica, if she's in?"

The older woman's face darkened and Melody saw worry in her eyes. Instead of stepping back to invite Melody in, she came outside and pulled the door closed behind her.

"Melody, I'm not sure that's a good idea. I've been quite concerned about my youngest daughter. She's changed in the past years, and especially over the past few months."

"I'm sorry, Widow, I don't want to upset her. I just want to talk to her for a few moments."

The Widow nodded but did not move. "Melody, she hates you."

She spoke with a calm bluntness that belied the emotion of her words. Melody felt a dull ache in her stomach, and a strange hollow sensation seemed to creep over her. It should not surprise her, and yet to hear that someone hated her hurt.

Once again, Melody swallowed back emotion. It took several deep breaths before she could speak, her voice sounded thick to her own ears. "I understand. She has good reason to hate me. I came in hopes of apologizing and attempting to make amends."

"I suppose you can try if you wish. However, consider this, I can see in your face that you feel guilty, but if Trevor truly loved Jessica you would never have turned his head."

Melody and the Widow stood together in silence for a long moment before the older woman stepped away from the door and opened it for Melody. With her fingers twisted into the fabric of her dress, Melody searched her mind for the best words, the right words, to show Jessica how sorry she felt.

"Jessica, can you come to the front room for a moment? We have a visitor," the Widow called as she led Melody into the family's sitting room. Sparsely furnished with older pieces, it appeared so different from the almost cluttered sitting room in her home.

Jessica entered the room, her face set in a scowl before she even looked up and met Melody's gaze. Melody felt the cold hatred radiate out from the other girl and her stomach twisted.

"Why is she here?" Jessica demanded.

"Jessica, Melody wanted to speak to you for a few moments." The Widow said her voice reminded Melody of the tone one might use to coax an injured animal into your home so you could help it.

Is that what Jessica was? Injured and hurt so bad she could not bear to trust even when someone tried to help her? Worse, Melody caused the injuries, all that pain and bitterness were a result of Melody's bad decisions.

"Jessica," Melody took a step toward Jessica, extending a hand to the petite blonde girl. "I came here to say that I've wronged you and I'm very sorry."

"You bitch." Jessica's words entered the room with a force of cold behind them that felt tangible. She did not step away from Melody but her stance changed, to shift her weight away from the extended hand.

Melody let her arm drop.

"How dare you think you can come here and say a few words to make everything better?"

"No, that's not what I meant."

"What did you mean? Tell me. Did you come here to try to help me or to make yourself feel better? What exactly are you sorry for? Are you sorry you slept with the man I planned to marry? Or are you sorry that you always had everything I ever wanted and you couldn't stand to see me with the one thing you wanted?"

"I never slept with Trevor." Melody protested.

"Please, we both know that's why he chose you instead of me. You gave him what I wouldn't."

"Jessica, stop this instant," the Widow demanded.

"No, Mother, I won't stop." Jessica stalked toward Melody.

Melody stood her ground and refused to back away despite a ripple of cold and the expression of pure hatred in Jessica's eyes.

"I never slept with him, Jessica, and I told Trevor I cannot marry him."

"You're a lying, whoring, bitch. So what? You decided you were too good for him after all? Maybe you took him because you wanted to make sure I didn't have him. Do you expect me to be grateful, to go back to him now that you're done with him?"

"I thought I loved him," she pleaded, begging for understanding. "I used to daydream about him when I was younger, but he never saw me because you were always prettier. I thought I wanted to spend my life with him, but the more we got to know one another the more I realized I didn't love him and he doesn't love me. He humors me, tolerates me, but he doesn't love me. I am so sorry, Jessica. I hurt you, and you're right, my words will never be enough."

"No, they won't."

For a moment, silence filled the room.

"I will hate you until the day I die, Melody Saltman," Jessica said, her face twisted into a sneer.

"I understand," Melody whispered.

Melody saw her pull back her hand but she did not try to dodge the way Grey had taught her. She simply stood still and let Jessica hit her. The Widow gasped in shock and yelled for her daughter to stop.

Melody's cheek stung and she pressed her hand to the burning flesh of her cheek, covering it to protect it from further harm. With her back straight, Melody met Jessica's gaze. It was no more than she deserved.

"I'm still sorry, Jessica, and if there is ever anything I can do to make this right between us I will make every effort to do it." Melody turned and did not wait for the Widow to show her out of the small house.

Could Jessica be right, did she apologize for herself more than for Jessica?

No, when you hurt someone you apologized. Every village child learned this lesson before they began their first day of school. She hurt Jessica, so she had apologized. Even if the apology meant nothing, she had done the right thing.

A wave of exhaustion washed over Melody. Hours remained before nightfall, but all she wanted to do was crawl into bed and sleep. Tomorrow, or the next day she would need to go into Briar Creek to buy more flour, her supplies were running low. She gave most of the flour away, or baked it into the breads she distributed among the families in Varin.

Still she looked forward to nightfall and the chance to lie down and sleep, the opportunity to be with Grey.

Tonight she would tell Grey she had ended things with Trevor. She would talk to him about being human. Tonight she would make sure he knew she loved him and wanted to spend her life with him.

58

Grey

Grey paced the woods near the cottage. Game remained scarce and because of that, he traveled south to hunt. It had been three nights since he made love to Red. Three days since he watched her sit with the woodcutter, witnessed the woodcutters lips touch her hand just hours after she lay naked with him. She said she would not marry the woodcutter.

Had she lied? Did she believe he would not find out the truth because he was a wolf? A low growl tore from his throat. Birds took flight from a nearby bush.

He avoided sleeping at night now. He did not want to be drawn into another dream with her. Not if she ran to her woodcutter as soon as she woke. He had all but abandoned his den. Instead, he stayed on this side of the road, hunting further south, away from the village. The idea of traveling away tempted him. Still, he came back to the cottage, again and again. All the people around it made him nervous.

Something here felt wrong, dark, off somehow. Red spent so much time here and a darkness he could not identify lingered around this place. Maybe it was his imagination, his own jealousy, which made him feel this way.

No, he knew better than that. He had learned to trust himself more than that. Something felt wrong here.

He knew he should leave but the need to stay and protect Red, the compulsion to make sure she stayed safe, was too strong. There was also the nagging hope that she meant what she said, perhaps she would leave her woodcutter for him.

That was not fair to her though. She needed reality, not dreams.

Grey yawned, pale winter sun shone down, fatigue and hunger competed for attention as his stomach growled. Instead of hunting, he began to search for a spot that felt safe. He found a place in a blackberry bush that some other animal had hollowed out and crawled in. He lay down and tucked his nose under the tip of his tail. Daytime had become the safest time to sleep while Red, occupied with the tasks humans did, could not draw him into her dreams.

Lying there, with eyes closed, an image of Red invaded his mind. The way her skin felt under his hands, soft and smooth. The way she moved while his hands skimmed over her body. He could almost taste Red's skin and her magic the way he did when he kissed her. He heard her voice say she loved him, she called his name in passion, he heard her laugh. Why should he let the woodcutter have her if she loved him?

He forced his eyes opened and stared at the dead brambles around him. He needed to get away from here. He would never get her out of his head if he stayed in this place. He would only be able to stay out of her dreams for a time before he hunted her down and tried to drag her away from the woodcutter, the human, the reality she needed.

She would walk in a few days. He would follow her, one last time, to prove to himself that she was safe. After that, he would leave, he promised himself.

He would find a new place, maybe new wolves to be his pack. He would stay away from people this time. So far, away they would never tempt him again. He was a wolf. He would go and live like a wolf.

59

Melody

Melody's body ached, every movement came with pain, and she shifted the basket from one arm to the other. Her shoulders hunched over the basket and used the back of one hand to stifle a yawn. The basket felt heavy, filled with a large pot of beef stew. One of the farmers to the north of Varin slaughtered a bull and all of the town's people were given a piece of the animal. She made stew, left enough at home for her father and now carried the rest to Nanna. She also made corn muffins. None of that explained her exhaustion.

Once again, her sleep became a battleground. The void fought her and each night it became harder to resist. Grey never came. Despite making love with him, begging him with her words and body not to go, he left her alone to fight the void.

He kept his word.

She fought every night.

Melody bolted upright in the middle of most nights, wide awake, drenched in sweat, her muscles contorted with spasms. She would lie in bed and quiver as she fought to stay awake until the sky turned pink. Her chest ached more each day and even breathing in the daytime became a challenge. She feared an illness had set in.

Her feet dragged along the muddy path as she trudged through the woods. Her head lifted at a noise and motion from the left side of the path. A flash of hope hit her with the force of lightning. Grey was here! He had not left her! There was still a chance.

Trevor stepped out of the woods.

Her hope faded and she knew her face fell.

"Did you expect someone else?" His voice sounded wrong.

"No, not really." She tried to force a smile. It fell flat. "I'm sorry, Trevor. I'm not in the best mood today."

"I can see that. What's wrong, Melody?" He sounded concerned.

"It's been weeks since I slept well. I'm tired. Are you going to Nanna's today, too?"

"No, the work there is done. I came to find you. I know you come this way every week. I hoped to talk to you for a few moments alone." Melody nodded. "I understand you plan to say no to all the offers you have received for marriage. However, I want you to reconsider mine."

"I can't Trevor. I don't love you. I'm sorry that I misled you, and that I hurt you, but I can't marry a man I don't love."

He ran a hand over his face and nodded his head. His grip on the axe tightened and Melody's stomach twisted in an odd cramp. His thoughts or feelings seemed to be oozing from him into the air and she did not like it. She could almost see colors around him–but not quite.

"I tried to do this the right way." She could hear the pain that laced his voice and as she watched him, he ran his free hand over his face again, sighed, and shook his head. "I tried to be everything you could want. It was working, too. I could feel it, the bond slipping into place. Now it's so faint, but there is still hope. I can still make this happen. Just tell me, what did I do wrong, Melody?"

"Nothing. It isn't you, Trevor. I swear. I'm sorry I made you leave Jessica..."

"Jessica means nothing to me. She never did. She provided a distraction, a useful tool while I waited for you. Do you have any idea how badly I need you? I do not want to do this. Part of me has changed and I do not want to be this anymore. Maybe I never did. Still, you cannot change who and what you are. You understand that better than anyone, Melody. You tried too, worked so hard to be someone you aren't. You know what it feels like. Can you not see how perfect we are for each other? Neither of us fits the mold they want for us. Together we could change things, force them to accept us for who we are, be better than anyone expected us to be." His voice sounded desperate, and he leaned forward as he spoke and took her hand in his.

"Trevor, stop, you aren't making sense. I don't know how to make you understand. I will not marry you." She pulled her hand away and took a step back, away from him.

He sighed and nodded, his voice took on a calm certainty. "Yes, you will, Melody. With the rumors Jessica has spread, when I tell your father about you and me, he is going to believe me. In part, at least it will be true." He paused and shook his head; he seemed almost regretful. "It will not always be this way. I will be good to you, I swear. After today, you will never have a reason to hate or fear me. We will be bound together and I will make you so much more, but this is the only choice you have left me." He swung the axe down off his shoulder and dropped it to the ground. Melody tensed and tried to figure out what his plan might be. "Your father will insist you marry me."

"Trevor," Melody took another step back and shook her head. She understood now and fear raced along her nerves. She lifted the basket up a fraction in front of her body. She would plead, and she would fight, but she would not allow him to touch her.

"I really am sorry, Melody." He shook his head, sadness in his tone.

"If you're sorry then don't do this, Trevor. Please, don't touch me." He ignored her words, and moved toward her. Melody could not see the trees around his bulk. She remembered the ease with which he swung his axe and her fingers clenched around the handle of her basket. Melody took another step back. Trevor moved in fast, his hand caught her upper arm in a grip that bruised. Melody jerked her arm and the weight of the basket shifted in her grip. Time slowed and all the things Grey taught her in her dreams poured through her head.

She was not helpless.

She swung the basket with the heavy black pot hard against Trevor's side. She felt and heard the sharp exhale of breath as it hit him, but his grip stayed firm. Hot liquid spilled over them both and she let go of the basket in reaction to the heat on her hands.

His fingers dug deeper into her arm. She kicked out at his leg, but he sidestepped and his free hand made a sharp cracking sound as it hit the side of her face. Pain spread across her cheek in a blow that landed harder and more painful than Jessica's. She tasted blood on her lip.

"If you do not fight, Melody, I will not have to hurt you."

"No, you will not do this to me," Melody screamed, but she knew Trevor chose this spot well. Her voice would not carry to the road or Rose cottage, no matter how loud she screamed. The skirt she wore made it difficult to kick, but that did not stop her from trying. His fingers dug at the neckline of her blouse leaving deep open scratches on her chest. Blood welled in them. Her attempts to kick failed so she lifted her leg and stomped hard on his foot, the heel of her boot grinding into his toe.

She desperately searched for the colors, hoping for a hint of magic to help her. She could almost feel them, almost see them, but the void from her dreams seemed to fill the air around her. It sucked at her chest and dragged the feel of the colors away before she could reach them.

Trevor hissed in pain and swung her body around against a tree. Pain flashed down her back and the air left her lungs. His hand pulled the front of her shirt opened and his fingers pawed at her breast.

"Stop!" She tried to yell as she pushed at his hands, trying to escape, but the sound came out more a whimper then a command.

Suddenly the air around her shifted.

A sound, not human, filled the forest and she felt the impact of a body against Trevor's, it rippled through him and into her. Without further warning, Trevor was gone.

She forced her eyes to focus. Color exploded around her and she saw Grey.

60

Grey

Grey forced himself to stay still and wait as he listened to them speak. Smaller and lighter than the woodcutter, Grey's only advantage was surprise.

Red told him the truth. She had refused to marry the woodcutter. He should have trusted her. He would be relieved about that later, and regretted that he had left her alone in her dreams for a week. For now, he would not let this male hurt his mate. He watched Red fight, proud of how she defended herself. Rage coiled in his gut at the sight of blood welling on her lip and the male's hands touching her body. He saw his opening and moved.

His body hit the woodcutter's and for a fraction of a second, he held the upper hand. He sank his teeth into the man's arm, unable to reach his throat. Hot, foul blood filled his mouth; it tasted wrong. He released the arm and pulled, twisting away. Surprise and speed allowed him to knock the man off Red.

The woodcutter snarled. The sound felt less human to Grey than his own growls. The man spun off the ground and his fist slammed into Grey's chest. Grey whined and took a single step back. He stopped and growled low and loud, angling his body between the woodcutter and Red.

This man, who tasted wrong, would not touch his mate again.

"I'll kill you, filthy wolf. You think your magic is strong enough to take me, foolish animal."

Grey snarled and showed his teeth. His back low, he stood ready to strike again as soon as he found an opening. The man's axe lay out of reach and Grey knew he needed to keep it that way. He tried to stay between the woodcutter and his weapon while remaining between the man and his prey.

Red needed to run. If he could hold the woodcutter long enough she could get to the cottage and be safe.

He cast a glance over his shoulder at her. She stood, her back still pressed against the tree, and stared at him. Grey growled again, hoping to break through her shock. She did not move.

He heard movement and spun to see the woodcutter lunge for his axe. Grey attacked without hesitation. He hit the woodcutter mid-chest, using every ounce of his weight against the man and closed his teeth over the woodcutter's shoulder.

Blood oozed from the newly opened wound. He clung to the flesh, ignoring the foul taste, and dug his claws into the woodcutter's chest. The man grabbed at his neck and throat with large hands. Grey felt fingers find purchase and fought the man's attempt to pull him off. He failed, but as the woodcutter ripped him free, he tore off a chunk of the enemy's shoulder. Grey felt the ground against his side like a stone wall.

The woodcutter cursed in pain and kicked, landing the blow on Grey's rear flank. An ache spread through his body as he pulled himself to his feet. The woodcutter moved faster now, toward his lost weapon. Grey saw the man's fingers wrap around his axe and he knew his life was over.

It did not matter, not if Red made it to safety.

Grey charged again. He saw the blow aimed for his head, and he threw his weight, trying to avoid it. Red screamed his name. He felt something fly past him; it felt like Red, like her magic. The woodcutter looked at her as whatever force she threw hit his chest. Grey saw the arc of the axe falter and he shifted again to avoid the blade of the axe in its aborted swing. The flat of the weapon hit his shoulder, but without the force of the woodcutter behind it. The blow that should have killed him did not.

Pain blinded him, burned through his shoulder, and rippled along every nerve of his body. He lay on the ground unable to move, and saw the woodcutter raise the axe over his head. He lifted his head and snarled, searching for Red.

He could not see her. Maybe, she ran.

61

Melody

"No! Grey!" Melody screamed the words as the axe hit his shoulder. She moved without thinking, her eyes scanning the ground.

"*Use what you have,*" Grey's words echoed in her head. The pot, thick and black, lay on its side, half the soup spilled out. She saw the colors around her and she grabbed a strand of dark amber and added a black cord. White-hot pain behind her eyes threatened to blind her, but she fought it back. She snatched the pot up and twisted the power around it as she raced to where Trevor lifted the axe over Grey's motionless body.

She heard Grey snarl and knew he was still alive. Relief and terror mixed in her blood and she felt the surge of energy Grey told her he experienced during a hunt. She swung the pot up, throwing all her weight behind it and used a current of blue air to push it harder. A dull hollow bang rang through the woods as the pot hit Trevor's head. The vibration shook her fingers so hard it hurt.

Trevor crumpled to the ground, unconscious. The axe fell harmlessly from his limp hands.

Melody dropped to her knees at Grey's head. Blood stained his shoulder. He panted hard. He looked up into her eyes. She swore she could read the thoughts running through his head.

"I know," she said, as she wiped tears from her cheek. When had she started to cry? "I didn't run."

She caressed his head and neck, she tried to find the colors, pain crashed through her head. The colors around her seemed dull and hovered out of reach. Trevor made a noise behind her. Sweat beaded on her forehead and she drew a sharp breath.

"Get up. Grey, you have to get up." She pushed at his side. He growled, a sharp sound, but weaker than it should be. "Get up."

She felt his muscles bunch, and then relax. His head dropped to the ground. "Please, Grey. You have to get up."

He whined, but did not move. He was not even trying. Anger mixed with her fear. "Damn you, Grey. Get up. I am not leaving here without you. If you die so will I."

His head lifted. His amber eyes bore into hers. She could feel him weighing her words. Sparks of red and black danced in her vision. She grabbed them and twisted them into her words so he would feel them.

"I mean it, Grey. I will not leave without you." He lifted his lip, but no sound came with the motion. The red faded, replaced with pale yellow-fear. "Please, Grey, get up. I love you and I won't leave you here."

He rolled onto his stomach. A whimper came from his mouth. His lips lifted in another silent growl, and in her mind, Melody saw the Grey from her dreams gritting his teeth against pain.

She ran a hand down his back. She needed magic now and all she found was pain, frustration, and tiny sparks of emotion. She examined the air around her and searched for her magic. Grey struggled to stand and she saw colors, weak and pale swirl in the air around him. She pulled at the green and grey and tried to wrap it around him and blend it into him. It seemed to help.

"Please, Grey. Keep going, you can do it." She continued to coax him with her hands and voice.

A moan came from behind her. Her fingers flexed in Grey's fur and she pulled. He moved his legs under him and pushed, Melody leaned away from him. She did not want her weight or position to prevent him from rising. He braced his legs and Melody watched as his body trembled. He lifted his head and gazed at her. She could almost see his human face, eyebrow arched as if to ask, "Well?"

"Come on, come with me." For the first time, Melody felt cold. She shivered and glowered down at her torn clothes and the red lines of blood on her chest. Pulling the cape close to her body to cover her torn shirt, she began to walk down the path to Nanna's house, one hand twisted into Grey's fur. Grey limped beside her, putting almost no weight on his left front leg.

She wanted to stop, let him rest, help him somehow, but she could not. Trevor would wake up any second, and if he caught them, with Grey hurt, and with the limited magic she could use, there was no hope. Desperately, she grabbed for more colors from the air. She twined deep earth brown and dark forest green, with grey the exact color of Grey's coat, she braided the three strands, weak as they were, around them both, pulling them together as tight as she could. Her body swayed with pain from the effort, and for a moment, she closed her eyes to regain her balance. Pain cut through her with a knife sharp blade, but she gladly paid the price to help Grey.

"We have to keep moving, Grey," she said, as she let the colors go and opened her eyes. "Nanna can help us. We just have to get to her."

She wanted to run, but she would not leave Grey. Fear, desperation, and horror all churned through her stomach. Grey stumbled. Melody leaned down and wrapped her arm around his chest. She tugged him forward.

A noise, like a cracking branch sounded. Did it come from behind them? Grey did not turn. Had he heard it? Maybe she imagined it? Grey continued to move forward. Melody ignored the sound behind her and tried to support Grey's weight as they moved forward.

How many more steps until they reached Rose Cottage? Ten, fifty, a hundred? Another sound came from behind them. Grey's ears twitched. He heard it too.

"We have to run, Grey," Melody gasped the words. She stood straighter and released Grey's chest, but left her hand in the thick fur of his shoulder continuing to tug at him. Melody moved a bit faster and watched as Grey struggled to stay with her. She heard a whimper and realized it came from her own throat. Grey peered up at her face and pushed his nose against her leg.

"No, I won't leave you. You have to come with me." She dug her fingers into the fur at the ruff of his neck and pulled hard. She felt the growl in his chest, heard it as he curled his lips. She hurt him, but it did not matter. If he did not run, they would die. "If you don't like it, run." She heard a growl in her own voice.

Grey pushed forward in a limping run. Melody moved with him. She tugged his fur whenever he started to slow. She cried, but she could not feel individual tears on her skin, did not feel them in her eyes.

Time slowed and Melody would have sworn hours passed before she saw Rose Cottage. Relief pumped through her body as the cottage seemed to grow and fill her vision the closer they came. She must have yelled, called for help, something, because suddenly Nanna appeared, her arm warm around Melody's shoulder, supporting her.

"Come on, dear. A bit further, that's it. Just a few more steps."

The soft voice urged her on and Melody let her fingers slip from Grey's coat. With Grey gone, Melody realized how much she depended on him to bolster her as she dragged him through the forest toward safety. Her body shook and her knees seemed to melt. Nanna held her up as she stumbled into the house.

"Grey?" she saw him limp in behind her and she relaxed. "Clo-clo-close the door Nanna, pl-please." Her teeth chattered as she tried to speak. Her hands shook and she felt shivers race along her nerves.

"I will, love, let me get the fire burning." Nanna's voice soothed. "What happened?"

Melody sank into a chair and Grey moved to stand with his body pressed against her legs. She dug her fingers into his fur, his warmth seeping into her skin. She would apologize later for hurting him. He would understand and forgive her. Now all that mattered was they were safe and together. "He–he tried to rape me."

Nanna spun from where she stoked the fire. Her eyes narrowed and she strode to the door, snapping the lock in place. She returned to the fire and added more wood. Despite her actions, her voice remained calm and firm as she spoke. "Who?"

"Trevor. Trevor tried to rape me, Nanna, Grey saved me."

62

Grey

Grey let his head rest on Red's thigh. Every part of his body hurt, every movement caused further pain. He refused to lie down. The woodcutter might still be out there and he could not leave Red unprotected. She shivered. He could feel each quiver ripple through his own body. Pain followed.

Black spots danced in front of his eyes and he closed them.

"You and your wolf need to get closer to the fire, love. His wounds need to be cleaned and you need the warmth."

He heard the older woman's voice, but ignored her words. Red's hands flexed in his fur, his mate had dragged him, hurt him, and forced him to come with her when he would have stayed behind. He should be furious, but he knew she did it to save him. He only realized she needed his help when she released him and he was free from her weight as well as her hands.

"Grey, let's move to the fire," Red whispered, her voice still shaking. Her fingers left his back and she lifted his face. He did not open his eyes. "Grey?"

The fear in her voice enticed a reaction from him. He opened his eyes and considered the swollen bruise on her face.

"I'm so sorry it hurts, Grey, so sorry I hurt you. Forgive me, please," she begged. "Please come close to the fire with me. Nanna and I will help you, Grey."

Grey took a step toward the warmth, his eyes never leaving Red. She rose once his weight left her legs and she moved with him. They traveled slowly, each movement painful. Grey refused to whine.

At the hearth, Red sat on the rug. Grey let his body collapse, careful to fall on the side of his body not hit by the woodcutters axe. He heard Red gasp, felt her sharp indrawn breath as he rested his head on her lap. Her fingers ran toward his side and stopped short.

"Nanna, we have to help him." Her hand lifted, he felt her fingers even though they did not touch him, and they hovered over the raw, bloody, flesh of his shoulder.

"We will love, I'm heating water now. I have herbs..."

"Maybe I can help him too." He watched her close her eyes. Her lips curved into a smile. Even though Grey could not see what she saw he felt the magic, it flowed off her hand, warm and soothing, the way it had the day she washed Black's blood off his matted coat. The pain on his shoulder changed and the sharp, fierce, fire cooled. He saw her jaw clench as her body tensed and her eyes squeezed together. He could see the pain healing him brought her. He growled. She opened her eyes and smiled at him. She seemed to understand. The magic stopped.

He closed his eyes, his head relaxed against her lap. She did not shake as much now. Heat from the fire blanketed them. How long had it been since he laid near a fire? How long since he rested inside a house? The scent of food cooking invaded his nose. Desire overwhelmed him. How long since he tasted human food?

He fought the urge to whine.

Red's fingers stroked his head, comforting him.

"Here. Grey, is it?" The old woman asked. Grey did not open his eyes. "This may sting, Grey, but it will help. Melody, love, it might be best to move away from his head."

"Grey won't hurt me, Nanna. Grey would never hurt me." Confidence flowed through her voice and into Grey.

"Animals react badly to pain sometimes–"

"He won't, not Grey." She spoke with a certainty Grey did not always feel. At the moment, though, he knew he would not hurt her, not out of his own pain.

Red ran a hand over his face and neck. He felt the water wash his shoulder and the sharp sting of whatever herbs the old woman boiled in it. He growled, showing his teeth, but did not open his eyes or lift his head. Red's fingers continued to move over his head. She touched his ears and her voice caressed him.

He smelled something in the water, a scent foreign, yet familiar. Her hand hit a particularly sensitive place and Grey growled again, his head came off Red's lap and he jerked around to examine the old woman.

He saw the magic swirling around her. It rippled and pulsed from her entire body. He watched in awe and wonder as she touched his shoulder, the magic running from her hands along his skin. He could not feel it the way he felt Red's magic, but he could see it.

Grey did not move, even as the pain lanced through him. Magic curled over his skin then settled onto his body in a soft haze. He still felt nothing–so unlike Red's magic–and once again the pain lessened, the sharp edges dulled, and the searing feel of the wound cooled.

She rinsed the cloth in water laced with herbs and moved it to the wound again. The magic came with her hands and Grey watched it in fascination. It seemed to settle into his flesh around the wound. Her magic did not soothe the other aches and bruises the way Red's did, but the magic worked wherever her hands touched. The pain lessened, the bleeding slowed. Grey contemplated the old woman's face. She met his gaze.

She saw him. He could feel it deep in his soul. She saw past the wolf who lay on her rug and she saw him, Grey, who he had been, who he was, what he wished he could be.

"Well, Grey. I see now, yes." She nodded her head and smiled. Her gaze dropped and she went back to work cleaning the wound. With the pain gone, he relaxed and dropped his head into Red's lap, closing his eyes and slept.

63

Melody

Melody trembled again. Not as bad as before, but she could not seem to control the tremors that rolled down her back and vibrated her limbs. Nanna finished cleaning Grey's shoulder as he slept. Melody chose green to heal him and it seemed to help. Nanna's combination of herbs and magic worked better.

"Have you kissed him?" Nanna asked as she stood with the basin full of bloody water.

"No, should I try? I mean, what if he isn't human? Or what if he wants to stay a wolf?"

"Melody, slow down," Nanna interrupted. "We don't even

know if a kiss will change anything."

Biting her lip, Melody nodded. "I don't want to do anything else that might hurt him."

"I understand, but I think this is worth the risk, love."

Melody chewed her lower lip and studied the wolf asleep in her lap. What would it be like to have Grey, her Grey, here in Nanna's house? What would he say? Would he love her the way she loved him? There was one way to find out. Melody leaned over and lifted Grey's head off her lap. She kissed the tip of his nose gently and waited.

Nothing happened.

Sharp pain ripped into her chest. This truth cut so much deeper than any wound Trevor inflicted. The hope she cherished since Nanna told her about Pop Pop died. She fought the hollow sensation that began to fill her chest and make it hard to draw breath.

At least she did not turn Grey human against his will. Still, it would be so much easier if he were a man, but no, she fell in love with a wolf, a real wolf. She glanced up. Nanna seemed surprised, but not disappointed.

Melody shivered again. She wanted to stay near Grey, touch him, but she also needed to lie down, find a way to get warm. She unclasped her cape and stretched out with her body close to Grey's, with her face inches from his, and covered them both with her cloak. Reaching out, she wrapped her fingers around his paw. Nanna came close a few minutes later and she felt the weight of another blanket settle over them.

The gentle sounds of Nanna's tuneless hum as she prepared dinner filled the cottage. She felt the warmth of the fire from one side of her and of Grey's body, from the other. The tremors in her body stilled. Despite her fear and disappointment, she began to relax. Her body felt heavy and her eyelids drooped.

She slept.

64

Grey

Wood smoke, fresh bread, roasted chicken, Red; the scents filled Grey's nostrils. His eyes flew open. How long had he slept? Where was Red? Was she safe? Had the woodcutter returned?

Body tensing, he lifted his head. Red slept beside him, stretched out on the hearthrug, a blanket covering them both. Her eyes were closed, her face was relaxed. He felt her hand flex on his paw when he moved his leg. Her fingers wrapped around his paw as if she held a human hand.

He glanced around the small cottage. The old woman stood near the stove at the other side of the room, cooking. Tugging his paw free as gently as he could, Grey shifted and rose. His legs felt weak and stiff, but no sharp pain greeted the movement. He took a careful step and found that he only limped a bit on his injured shoulder. Nothing else appeared badly injured. He felt certain he could thank Red's magic for that. Red stirred and he turned to watch her. She sat up and rubbed her eyes.

She reached out and touched his head.

"You saved me, Grey. Again. Thank you so much. I'm so glad you were there, so glad you didn't leave. But I'm sorry you got hurt, and so sorry I hurt you."

She stood and her ripped shirt gaped open. Long welts marred the skin of her neck and chest. Dried blood crusted over angry red scratches. A dark bruise stained her cheek. While he could not see the color of the bruise, he could see the area of darkness on her otherwise fair face. Her lip swelled from where the woodcutter hit her. Grey suspected dark bruises covered her back as well. He felt his lift lip in a silent snarl. She tried to smile but the gesture caught. "It's alright, Grey."

"No, it most certainly isn't," the old woman said, an echo of his thoughts. "That man had no right to touch you, much less hurt you. I've sent a dove to your father. He'll be on his way here, no doubt with a half dozen men. We should get you changed and hide your wolf before they arrive."

"Yes, we have to keep Grey safe. Is your shoulder okay?" She directed the question at him, as she always did. Her eyes moved to the wound. "Oh, it's healing so fast, it looks much better."

"Magic dear. Why don't you put him in my room and we'll give him some food. He must be hungry after an injury and healing like that. I'll make him a plate while you change. You still have clothes in the guest room."

The old woman went to the stove and Red disappeared into another room of the cottage. Grey watched. His mouth watered as she put bread and chicken onto a plate. She carried it to another room and he followed. He watched her lean down to place the plate on the floor and fought to keep from attacking the food.

Chicken, bread, how long? He needed that food with an intensity so strong it made him ache. He whined. The old woman patted his head and left the room. The minute he heard the door latch, Grey devoured the food. He ate it in huge mouthfuls that he hardly chewed and licked every crumb from the plate. He felt full and soothed in a way that he had never been able to achieve as a wolf. The taste was marginal compared to the feel of human food in his mouth and stomach.

His nerves seemed to shiver and pain rippled along his body. It started at his head and poured down the length of his spine.

He dropped to the floor, his body curled. The pain passed as quickly as it came except in his shoulder and hip, which continued to ache. He moaned, creating a sound different from anything he had ever heard from his own throat. He opened his eyes.

Color hit him in a riot of shades and hues, so bright and clear they made his eyes burn. He closed his eyes. He put a hand up over his face.

A hand.

His hand.

His human hand.

He opened his eyes again, slowly this time. The rug under his body was green, blue and yellow. He felt his lips twitch, a smile. He could smile. Rolling to his back, he held his hand over his head and watched his fingers bend and straighten.

He moved each muscle, flexing, relaxing, and testing, reminding himself how a human body worked, how it moved, how it stretched. Grey rose to stand on two legs. This must be a dream!

However, he never needed to remind himself how to walk in a dream. Straightening his back, Grey stretched his arms over his head, and then dropped them, one shoulder burned. He looked down to examine the ugly cut that ran along his shoulder and chest.

He smiled. The pain, the movement, the sight of his own tan flesh, free of wolf fur, all blended in his mind. It all felt so real. It never hurt to become human in his dreams and the pain he felt a few moments ago as he changed had been all too real.

What if it was real?

Red.

He could see her, touch her, taste her. He stood here human and she could be his; his mate, his partner, his wife. Desire surged through him and his body responded in a very human way. This was a dangerous line of thinking. He turned in a slow circle and examined the room. A mirror hung on one wall and he moved to look at himself.

He almost did not recognize the man who stared back at him. His hair hung darker, brown rather than the dark blonde it had been in his human life. His eyes were no longer blue but deep amber. His face appeared more mature and his body was lean and solid with muscle. His skin was darker then he remembered it, tanned even through his wolf's fur.

Connor's father and brother would not know him if they saw

him.

Grey flinched at the thought. It had been a very long time since he had been Connor. Connor was dead. No, not dead, but gone. A memory. He was Grey now.

The changes seemed appropriate to him. This was not Connor's body. This was his body. A sound made him drop, and he crouched behind the bed as the door opened. Red entered the room.

Her long black hair hung loose down her back and over her shoulders. Her vivid green eyes scanned the room. The dark brown of her dress appeared soft against her pale skin. Mate. This time he did not argue with the word, it fit. She belonged to him, everything he ever wanted and needed. His.

65

Melody

Melody scanned the room. Grey had vanished. Fear twisted her stomach. Where did he go? Why would he leave?

"Grey?" She glanced down at the plate, now empty on the rug. Her eyes flew to the windows. Nana always kept them locked in the winter. The blinds remained drawn and did not stir as if recently disturbed. What happened to make him leave her?

Did Trevor return? Had Nanna let him out? She turned and put her hand on the door knob. She felt a subtle change in the air behind her, not a sound, more of a feeling. She spun around at the same moment a man's body pinned hers to the door. His hands landed on either side of her head, his body touching hers. She pressed her back hard against the door despite the ache it caused her bruised skin. She needed to scream, call for Grey, or Nanna, but there did not seem to be any air in the room.

Fear crawled up her spine and she tried to be as small as possible. Everything Grey taught her, everything she knew to do to defend herself flew out of her mind. The man's head was turned and she could not see his face. This was not Trevor. She knew that. His body was too narrow and too lean. He moved and she flinched away from him, and sucked in a breath.

The man put his face near her neck, not quite close enough to touch, and drew in a long deep breath, smelling her? She opened her mouth to scream at the same moment he lifted his head and peered into her eyes.

Amber eyes.

"No." The word came out a whisper, not a yell. Her gaze roamed over his face, she felt his stare, so familiar on her skin. She knew this face; she had touched it, kissed it. "No." She shook her head, careful to keep the movement small so as not to touch his arms braced on either side of her head. "I tried, it didn't work."

He did not move, but she saw the muscles in his arms tense from the corner of her eye. He was naked–of course, he was naked. Grey did not own any clothes. Her gaze scanned down his body, pausing at the wound on his shoulder. Just like Grey, her Grey. She continued her perusal of the rest of his body. It was the same as in her dreams. She forced her gaze back up and met his eyes.

Was he laughing at her?

Melody scowled, anger replacing fear. "Move," she snapped. "Before I kick you somewhere uncomfortable."

"You tried that earlier, Red, with your woodcutter. Doesn't work as well in a skirt." Despite his words, he pushed off the door and turned his back to her. His voice cut through all remaining confusion.

"Grey?" Her voice shook. Melody sucked in a breath. Grey's voice, his body, his face.

He glanced at her over his shoulder and lifted an eyebrow, exactly the way she pictured in her mind earlier. Exactly the way he did in her dreams.

Grey, her Grey, was human.

She did not stop to consider how it happened, and in a heartbeat, she was across the room. He turned to catch her and she pressed herself into his arms, reveling in the feel of him. With her hands on his shoulder, she pulled herself up to crush her lips against his.

He jolted back and made a sharp hissing sound, and she realized her hand clutched his wounded shoulder.

"Oh, Grey." She pulled away and dropped her hands. "I'm sorry." She tried to back away but he caught her before she could move more than a step.

"I'm fine, Red." His hands held her arms, his grip relaxed, but she suspected that if she tried to pull away he would stop her. His gaze wandered over her face, her body. His eyes seemed to become darker as he watched her and she felt warm under his careful examination. He did not pull her closer, did not try to kiss her or touch her. Could her kiss have upset him? She chewed her lower lip, his eyes following the gesture. She felt her cheeks heat.

"I can't believe you're human." The words came out breathless.

He stood silently, his hands slid up her arms, curved over her shoulders and his fingers stroked her unbruised cheek. "You should leave." The words seemed at odds with the tender gesture, but he did not release her.

Melody felt liquid heat flow through her body as his fingers traced her cheek and slid into her hair. "This isn't real, I fell asleep." She let her eyes drift shut.

"It's real." One of his hands stayed in her hair, the other drifted down her back. "You need to go, Red. One man trying to rape you is enough in a day."

Her eyes flew opened. "You would never do that. You would never hurt me."

"You don't know how badly I want you. How long I've watched you and imagined touching you." His hand slid lower to the small of her back and she moved closer to his body.

"You never forced me in our dreams, even the night you were angry." She put her hands on his waist and tilted her face up toward his. .

His body tensed and she felt his fingers flex in the fabric of her dress.

Licking her lips, she focused on the wound on his shoulder. In their dreams, she seduced him, told him she loved him, and practically begged him to love her.

"In our dreams..." She could not think of words to express the chaos of feelings that whipped through her body. Fear, love, relief, and desire all seemed to churn in her blood. She wanted to tell him she loved him, did he want to hear that? She lifted her hand to touch his cheek but his gaze shifted from her to the door behind her.

His hands dropped from her body. He grabbed her arm and yanked her behind him. He stood in front of her as the door swung opened. Nanna stepped into the room.

Melody peeked around him. Nanna considered the two of them calmly.

"Well, now, how did that happen?"

66

GREY

Silent for a moment, Grey considered the question and the events of the day.

"The food," he said at last.

The old woman nodded. "I'll get you some clothes. I have some that should fit you. They belong to Melody's cousin."

The old woman turned and left the room but she left the door open. Red moved out from behind him.

"The food made you human?" she asked. She kept her gaze fixed on the floor. Her unbruised cheek flushed pink, the other a pale shade of green.

"Yes," he started to explain, but before he could finish, the old woman appeared again with the promised clothes. Red ducked out of the room and into the main part of the house.

"After you dress you can join us for a real meal. I expect Melody's father to arrive any minute now." The old woman cocked her head and assessed his face. "Are you ready to meet her father?"

Grey considered the question for a moment. "Is any man ever ready to meet the father?"

The old woman chuckled. "Well put, Grey. I look forward to getting to know you more."

"Thank you."

She left the room and pulled the door closed behind her. Grey dressed. The clothes felt wrong against his skin. They rubbed at his waist and shoulders. The pants were the right length but a bit large around the waist, the belt fixed that. The shirt fit fine, but his fingers fumbled with the buttons. His thumbs felt like foreign tools that he might never learn how to use.

He entered the main room at the same time someone pounded against the cottage door. A male voice thundered through the wood and demanded entry. Grey moved instinctively, he crossed the room and grabbed Red, tugging her toward the bedroom, keeping his body between hers and the door.

"Grey, stop. It's my father," Red said. She pulled against his grip on her arm.

Grey dropped her arm. He turned toward the door, not allowing her to step around him. He watched the old woman open the door. As it opened, the scent of a half dozen men hit Grey's nostrils. His sense of smell remained as strong and accurate in this human body as it had been in his wolf form. The need to growl and show his teeth rippled through him. He pushed it away.

That was not the way to demonstrate strength, not to these men, not in this body. Instead, he straightened his shoulders and moved forward a step. He remembered how to do this, remembered what people expected from ordinary men, even if his father never expected it of him.

"Where is Melody?" The older man in the front of the group demanded as he charged into the house.

"She's okay, Timothy. She's here." The old woman said as she placed a hand on the man's arm.

The man's eyes swept the room, his fingers flexed on the handle of the knife he carried in his right hand. When he saw Grey, his face darkened, his fingers tightened, and he scowled. The emotion elicited a reaction deep in Grey, again he felt the urge to growl, show his teeth, and fight. Human, he must act human.

"Who the hell is he? Why is he near my daughter?"

"Hello, sir." Grey stepped forward and extended his right hand to show it was empty of weapons. "My name is Connor Grey. I've had the privilege of getting to know your daughter over the past few months. Today I helped her escape from her attacker in the forest."

He could feel Red's gaze on his back. He hoped her face did not reflect her shock, but he smiled, imagining her wide eyes and parted lips. He had seen that expression on her face in their dreams.

Her grandmother turned to him and beamed. He saw pride reflect in her eyes. Was she proud? Of him?

"Yes, Timothy, this is Mr. Grey. He's a friend of mine. He often escorts Melody through the woods to make sure she arrives safely."

Mr. Grey. The name struck a memory long buried. An image of his mother in her rocker clouded his eyes for a moment.

The older man started to relax. He stepped into the room and, sheathing the knife, took Grey's hand. Grey kept his grip firm but not tight enough to hurt or demonstrate the dominance he longed to project. Red stepped around him and placed a hand on his arm as she did. The touch relaxed him.

"I'm alright, Daddy." Her voice sounded steady but Grey heard the pain she tried to cover.

The older man pulled Red into his arms. "Baby," he whispered and kissed her head.

Grey forced himself to remember this was her father, not a competing male. The man released her and took her chin in his hand, tilting her head to examine the bruise on her face. Grey noted the bruise looked larger and darker. Dried blood still marred Red's swollen lip. Her father forced her to turn her head the other way and examine the scratches that disappeared into the bodice of her dress. Her face flushed under the bruise and Grey saw her try to move her head, but her father still held her chin. Grey moved forward a step.

The man noticed and turned and looked at him, their gazes locked. He released Red's chin and without looking back at his daughter asked. "Is there more?" Grey respected the edge of hardness in his voice.

"My back, I imagine, it's bruised. Trevor shoved me against a tree. It knocked the breath out of me and it's sore, but then, Gr–Mr. Grey arrived and he saved me. His injuries are worse. He and Trevor fought. Grey was hit with the axe."

"A minor blow," Grey said, trying to dismiss the incident.

The older man's eyes changed, his gaze became more assessing, less harsh. "Were you harmed? Can I compensate you for the aid you gave my daughter?"

Compensate him for protecting his mate? Grey needed to growl, to show this man who Red belonged to. Once again, Red touched his arm. Her skin felt smooth against his arm. Human, he must be human if there was any hope of keeping Red.

"Knowing she's safe is the only compensation I desire, sir." Grey forced a neutral tone.

"Then know you have my gratitude and any help I can give you in the future is yours for the asking."

Red shivered again, her fingers trembled against his arm. Grey slid his arm over her shoulder and she turned in to his embrace. She slipped her arms around his waist and hid her face against his chest. She fit perfectly against his body. A murmur went through the crowd at the door. Her father looked at them and raised a speculative eyebrow.

"How well do you know my daughter, Mr. Grey?"

Grey felt Red stiffen in his arms a second before she pulled back, her face flushed with embarrassment. He wanted to pull her back against his side, keep her safe. He wanted to growl at the people staring at her. He wanted to take her away from here, some place private. He wanted to tend her wounds. He wanted to make sure she understood that he belonged to her and she belonged to him. Instead, he let his arm drop. Let her move away from him.

It was the human thing to do.

67

Melody

What was she doing? Unmarried women did not touch men the way she touched Grey. Especially not men they only met moments ago, but she knew Grey for months before today's events turned him human. She loved him. He was the only person she wanted to touch, the only one she wanted to touch her. It did not seem to bother him.

He had not scolded her or pulled back, just held her as if she belonged there. Maybe he did not mind. Her touch never bothered him in their dreams. This was not a dream though. Here, holding her in such an intimate way could have consequences he did not want. He might not understand that but she did. She would be more careful.

"We've become friends in the past months," she answered her father. "I'm very grateful to him for his help today."

"Why did Trevor attack you?" asked an older man with the group, he was an advisor to the town elder.

"I told him I wouldn't marry him, almost a week ago. I thought he'd accepted my decision." Melody faltered. She turned to watch her father when she spoke again. "He said that if he told you he and I... that you would force us to get married. Daddy, it isn't true, the rumors. They aren't..."

"I know that, Melody. I never believed the rumors." His voice was harsh, almost angry, but Melody heard love and trust in his words. It almost made up for the whispers from the people behind him.

"...might not have been a bad thing to see her married..."

"...heard she tried to seduce Milo..."

"No surprise, really...."

Grey turned toward the people at the door. His body tensed and Melody knew he heard them, too. Her face paled. She had no idea how to stop a confrontation. He would not hesitate to fight and he would get hurt. More pain because of stupid words. Her father intervened. He moved between Grey and the group at the door.

"Trevor wasn't around when I gathered the other townsfolk. Not surprising given what he did, but we'll need to find him. He will answer for hurting you," her father said. "I want you to stay here, Melody. Keep the door locked. You should be safe here. Mr. Grey, since you are injured, could I ask that you stay behind from the search and remain here with Melody to ensure her safety?"

"I would be honored, sir." Grey's voice was so calm and neutral, she was impressed but it also made her nervous. She could not tell what he was thinking.

The group at the door continued to mutter. Melody turned her back to them and moved to the fire, hoping that the warmth would help her stop shaking the way Grey's arms had moments ago.

Her father dropped a light kiss on her head as she passed him. She heard him move to the door. She ignored the sofa and Nanna's rocking chair and chose instead to kneel close to the fire, trying to ignore the sounds of the voices, the feel of the eyes. Grey was human, none of these people mattered, not if Grey loved her.

She heard Nanna speaking as she gave out mugs of warm cider and smelled the buttered bread she knew was still warm from the oven. She felt Grey come to stand near her.

"You should drink this, Red." His voice was pitched so only she would hear him. Looking up, she saw a mug of steaming cider in his hands. She took it and held the mug to her nose. The sharp scent of apples, cinnamon, and spice teased her senses and her stomach growled.

Grey did not sit down next to her the way she expected him to, the way she hoped he would. Instead, he turned and left her line of vision. Melody stared at the flames leaping in front of her. Red and orange curled with hotter blue. She reached out, with her mind and tried to pull some of the warm colors into her. She felt gentle heat burn inside her for a moment.

The voices she tried so hard to tune out cut into her.

"...Can't believe this of Trevor, he's such a kind steady man."

"Only a matter of time before Melody pushed some poor man too far."

She shivered again, the warmth forgotten. Her hands shook around the mug, hot liquid splashed over her fingers. The heated liquid made her flinch. She should drink the cider. She lifted the mug to her lips and took a small sip. The liquid flowed in a hot trail down her throat. Her chest burned, but she suspected that had more to do with embarrassment over what the people were saying about her than the cider.

What would Grey think?

The door closed and the voices disappeared. She heard the lock slip into place. Melody felt Nanna's hand on her head.

"Come to the table and eat, love."

Melody rose. Grey stood at the window and watched the searchers move off into the afternoon forest.

"You would make the search go more quickly. You know the forest better than any of them," Melody said.

He turned and looked at her, his amber gaze roaming over her face and down to the scratches on her neck. "If he comes here you need someone to protect you. Even your father understood that."

"Of course." Melody sat at the table and Grey came to sit next to her. Nanna brought food to the table and sat down with them.

Melody watched as Grey moved with careful precision. He served food to both her and Nanna first before taking his own. How did he know what to do? He was a wolf. How did he know how to sit at a table and serve a meal?

"How long were you a wolf, Grey? Or would you prefer Connor?" Nanna asked.

"Grey is fine. Connor has been gone a long time." He hesitated, looking at the plate in front of him. "A year, I think. Time means less to wolves."

"Certainly. Would you like to share how it happened?"

"A witch; some kind of magical brew." His tone became distracted and his eyes fixed on the food in front of him. He picked up a fork and took a bite of chicken to his mouth. Melody could not take her eyes off his face as he ate the first bite. His eyes lit and a small smile curved his lips. For a second he looked as if everything was right with the world. His gaze caught hers as he spoke. "It's been so long."

68

GREY

Throughout the meal, Grey glanced at Red. For the first few bites, she watched him, her green eyes wide and fascinated. Then she turned away and became careful not to meet his gaze. He felt awkward. Each careful cut of his food assumed the form of an exercise in patience. He banished the growls that tried to manifest in his chest as he forced himself to chew each bite and not remind the strange female openly that as pack leader the food belonged to him and his mate.

He would share of course. Red's grandmother needed to eat

and she belonged to his pack, he decided, but instinct drove him to assert his dominance.

No, none of this was right.

He was a man.

A human.

He made the words a silent mantra, and employed them to suppress the wolfish urges in his body. Red spoke to her grandmother. The words did not register over the hum of his thoughts. Men made conversation.

He tried to listen.

"So after everything, I guess the dreams were real." Red dropped her head. "I should have told you sooner, tried harder..."

"Sometimes things happen the way they do for a reason, love."

Grey watched Red. Tears stained her cheeks and she pushed the food around her plate without eating more than a bite or two. She glanced up at him. Her cheeks flushed and she returned her gaze to her plate. She acted meek, and afraid. Not like the Red of his dreams who played, and fought, and loved him.

"Eat," he growled the word at her, hoping to make her respond. Her head snapped up and her eyes narrowed, anger flashed green fire. For a heartbeat, he thought his strategy worked, until Red sighed, lifted her fork and took a bite of chicken, the anger gone.

Why was she acting like this? What was wrong with her?

He wanted to run, to breathe open air. This house felt too small and too closed and he could not think with such limited space. Red was upset and here, as a human, he could offer her no comfort. He rose, shoving the chair back hard enough to knock it over and paced to the fireplace.

"Peace, wolf," the old woman said.

"Why call me wolf, old woman? Do I look like a wolf?" Grey demanded as he stalked back to the table. He grabbed his chair, clutched it with both hands so tight his fingers ached. He blew out a deep breath and forcing his hands to relax, he placed it back at the table with great care.

"My name is Rose, and no, at the moment you don't look like a wolf, but you are one nonetheless. That's the blessing and the curse of the dual nature."

Grey's fingers flexed on the back of the chair, and closing his eyes, he drew in a deep breath and held it for a moment before letting it out slowly. "Can you explain this to me, Rose, please?" Despite his efforts, he could still hear a snarl in his voice as he spoke.

"Of course. Sit and eat, Grey. Food will help you heal, and wolves are, I'm sure, much happier when they stay well fed. I know bears are." Rose smiled and somehow, despite the words themselves, Grey did not feel as if he had been given an order.

Grey sat down in his chair and lifted his fork to take another bite. Rose beamed at him across the small table and began to speak as he chewed. He would find out later what Red should have tried harder to do, and why she was acting so out of character.

"Those who are dual-natured retain the nature of the beast all of their lives. Some choose it. Most often, they choose to be a cat, or a dog, sometimes a wolf or lion, or even a bird of some type. Different people choose different animals to suit their needs or personalities. They gain the instincts and skills of the beast they choose. Others end up with dual natures as a result of a curse, or spell, or even a magical accident. They become a beast not of their own free will. Curses often take the form of snakes, frogs, bears, wolves, or swans, but anything can work. These people also gain the instincts and nature of the beast, but not by their choice."

"Is there always a way to change back?" Grey asked, curious about the magic.

"Always, but it differs depending on the spell, the strength of the magic, and the person wielding it. If the caster is powerful enough, if it is, say a Godmother, they can create the spell in such a way to allow the person to change at will. Generally, a person who sets the spell but isn't strong enough to make the trigger their own will chooses a trigger like salt, sugar, or some other common herb or spice. They may leave small piles of it around their home and property so they can change back to human form whenever they need to. For a curse, it is often a kiss. Apparently in your case, the trigger is human food."

Grey nodded and took another bite, the woman's voice, or perhaps her words soothed him. Perhaps the magic he could see as a wolf but not as a human caused this. Maybe it soothed him the way it healed him, gliding off her and onto those around her.

"The witch who did this to me intended me to be her protector, to travel with her, keep her safe."

"Food would be a good trigger than. A kiss would be too intimate. Human food would be difficult for a wolf to obtain alone and I'm certain you craved it," Rose said.

"Yes, the scent of the foods that drifted from Red's basket is what first drew me to her. That and the cape."

"The cape?" Red asked, as she studied his face.

"Yes."

"Why the cape?" Red said, eyes wide.

"Because I could see the color. Red is the only color the wolf could see. Everything else is black, white, and shades of grey. But red, like prey's blood, like your cape, that I could see."

Her face paled and Grey wondered what about his statement upset her. Red turned to Rose, her eyes bright with suppressed tears.

"My mother," she said the words in a low almost reverent whisper. "She said it had to be red. Somehow she knew, Nanna."

"Intuition is a powerful gift, love." Rose gave Grey a weak smile, her own eyes shimmering with suppressed tears. "The cape was my daughter's last gift to Melody before she passed away. She insisted that it be red."

Grey watched as an understanding smile touched Red's lips. He wanted to touch them. Desire rippled through him. He needed to touch her. Soon.

69

Melody

Before Grey ran as a wolf, he walked as a human. To hear him say the words somehow made them more real. He knew how humans were supposed to behave, how men expected women to behave. God, what must he think of her? In her dreams, she acted and spoke in ways that no proper lady should. In their dreams, she told him she loved him, but he never said he loved her. He said he wanted her. Even today, in the real world, he said he wanted her, not loved her. On top of that, he heard what the people from Varin said about her.

Humiliation and fear cramped her stomach and she could not sit at the table anymore. She rose and glanced at Nanna. "May I go see the new room?"

"Yes, of course you can. Your cousins should arrive soon. To think, I thought that life would get interesting when they arrived," Nanna chuckled. She was taking this quite well, in Melody's opinion. "I suppose this development will make things more fun."

"You have an odd sense of humor, Nanna."

"At my age one must, child," Nanna replied, still grinning. "Well, go and see."

Melody stepped through the newly framed doorway and onto the cold wood floor to take in the new space. She crossed her arms and rubbed them with her hands to stave off the chill. No fire burned in the central pit that the room seemed built around. She took another step and her bare feet sank into a plush rug. She leaned down and ran her fingers through the dark green and blue checks of the thick pile. Continuing into the room, she found brightly colored curtains hung from the ceiling to separate beds already made with thick quilts and ready for guests. Melody sat on the edge of the closest bed and ran a hand over the quilt, she recognized the design from her childhood, Nanna stored it years ago when she made Melody a new one.

"Beds?" Melody called out. She rose and turned in a slow circle to see all the beds that lined the walls except for where a door led to the outside.

"Yes, for the children," Nanna called back.

"What children, Nanna?"

"It would take too long to explain tonight."

Melody shrugged and turned to reenter the main area of the house. Grey stood in the doorway and watched her with his arms crossed over his chest, one shoulder resting against the doorframe. He looked so handsome and so very human. Why keep that a secret?

Anger flared.

"You lied to me," she accused. To her surprise, he did not get angry. In fact, his lips twitched in an almost smile and he tilted his head in a way she recognized from their dreams. He arched an eyebrow but did not speak.

Frustrated, she scowled and continued, "I asked you if you could become human. You said no. You always told me you were 'just a wolf'. Why did you lie?"

"I didn't think I could be human again. I believed what I told you." He tilted his head further to the side and watched her. "Does it matter?"

"Yes, it matters. If I knew, I would have tried to help you be human again. I would have brought you to Nanna. I would have done whatever I could to help you. I wouldn't have–" Stopping half way through the thought, Melody bit her lip and fought the blush that crept up her cheeks and broke eye contact.

"Tell me, Red."

"The way I acted, the things I said and did." She kept her voice low in hopes Nanna would not hear. The words seemed to tumble out of her, mixed up and jumbled in her rush to explain. "I never behave like that, but I never behave the way I should either. I'm not ... well, you heard what the men gossip about me, what they think of me, but I'm not... I've never.., except with you Grey."

His fingers touched her cheek. When did he walk over to her? She gazed up into his eyes. They seemed so familiar, and yet so new.

"I'm not a slut," she hissed.

"I know that, Red. I never believed you were." His thumb traced her jaw from her ear to her chin. She wanted to tilt her head into the caress.

"But in our dreams, I did things and I let you... I wanted you..."

He cut her off with a shake of his head. "You were perfect in our dreams."

The words should have comforted her, but for some reason they terrified her. Her stomach clenched and she pulled away from him. Perfect. He would be disappointed by reality. "This is the real world, Grey. I'm far from perfect here."

She brushed past him and walked back into the main room of the cottage. She went to the sofa and sat down. Grey came and sat next to her, his body large and warm touching hers. Nanna took the rocking chair across from them.

"Grey, do you have family you want to contact?" she asked.

"No." He said the word so fast Melody turned to him in surprise. He shrugged. "Well, of course I have family, but not that I wish to contact. They will have assumed me dead, mourned me, and moved on."

"But won't they want to know you're alive? I mean, I would." Melody watched his face as she spoke. "Won't your mother at least want to know?"

"My mother is dead. The witch who changed me into a wolf poisoned her." Melody felt the regret in his words. "My father and brother would be more troubled if I reappeared than if I stayed dead."

His eyes held hers and she knew he told the truth. She reached for his hand and her fingers curled into his.

"I understand. You have the opportunity to start over here," Nanna said.

Silence descended over the room. Where Grey's body brushed her seemed to chafe, she wanted more, not less, contact with him. This brushing of shoulders and thighs was not enough. His thumb stroked her wrist. She wanted to put her head on his shoulder, to feel safe and protected.

Would he love her even if she could never be perfect? Thoughts of their dreams made her remember how Grey shifted back and forth from human to wolf. Would he be able to do that now? If he could, she would be relieved. She would hate to be the reason he lost the wolf forever. She knew he loved to hunt and play as a wolf.

Without considering the consequences, she leaned over and put her head onto Grey's shoulder. He released her hand and put his arm around her. She should sit up, but she did not want to and Nanna smiled at her.

"Nanna, tell us a story," she asked, as she relaxed into Grey's embrace. Whatever happened later, right now she felt safe and loved.

"Of course, child. Which story would you like to hear?"

"Tell me about how you met Pop Pop, please." Melody requested. The smile that lit Nanna's face warmed Melody in a way no fire ever could.

"Of course."

Nanna leaned back into her chair. Her face calmed, her eyes closed and she began to speak. As soon as the story began, Melody's body relaxed further. She loved the way Grey's arm tightened around her, his heartbeat under her ear soothed, and the gentle stroke of his hand on her hair helped her forget the fears of the day.

Her mind drifted as she let the sound of the words and the caresses of his hand soothe her. She slipped into a peaceful sleep.

70

GREY

The clothes irritated his skin, rubbing, and binding. He hated clothes.

The house felt too small. He wanted the woods, the open space, and the sky.

The fire blazed too hot. He needed to feel the wind on his face, his shoulders, and his chest.

Red's body lay cradled against his. Everything was perfect.

This was what he wanted, needed so much over the past few months. Every time he followed her, listened to her voice, he longed for this moment. Well, maybe in his mind they wore fewer clothes.

She slept, relaxed. Her grandmother still spoke, her voice rough with age, yet still gentle, and her words carried a rhythm that made listening easy. She talked about a bear who was actually a prince cursed by an evil witch.

He was a man who became a wolf, who became a man again.

Now he missed being the wolf. Missed the freedom it gave him. Men had so many restrictions. Red was right. Their dreams gave them freedom to be themselves; in reality, as a man, he could not hold Red the way he did now.

He did not care. She belonged to him. They were made for each other, bound together, and if anyone tried to take her away from him he...he would kill them.

That knowledge should upset him, might have upset a man. He was a wolf; no one would take his mate. What if Red sent him away? What if she told him to leave? He had not been afraid for himself since he escaped the witch. Now he felt his heart pound in his chest and he breathed faster. His arms tightened around Red and she shifted, her hand slid up his chest.

Could that be what she tried to tell him earlier? Was she saying that she did not want him here in the real world? No, he did not accept that.

A few hours ago someone tried to rape her, she was upset. Despite that, she lay here in his arms, she trusted him enough to sleep against his chest. She might be frightened and nervous, but she remained his Red.

Memories of his brother's wife came to his mind. Minna wanted her house and her life clean and orderly. She expected people to behave the way they should and made sure you knew if you failed. Red never behaved the way she should. She fed hungry wolves, laughed when she should run, and fought for him even after he gave up on himself. She cried with a wolf forced to kill his pack mate, and learned to fight to defend her own pack. Red was brave, strong and good, perfect, nothing like his brother's wife.

Today she saved his life.

Red was unique and special. She was magic, and she was his, if she wanted him.

She did want him; she loved him. She had said so a hundred times in their dreams. They needed some time alone together to talk, but time did not seem like a luxury they would be granted soon. Unless...he looked down at her sleeping form and considered her dreams, their dreams.

"You love her, don't you?"

Grey looked up at Rose, startled. Her narration had halted at some point, Grey, so caught up in his own thoughts, did not notice until she addressed him directly.

"I have nothing to offer her. No home, no money, and no family."

"But you love her," the woman prompted.

"Yes, and I intend to have her." His gaze locked with Rose's in open challenge.

The old woman smiled. "In that case, I can help you."

71

MELODY

Melody opened her eyes and blinked. She felt warm and safe. Earlier today she felt weak and her chest ached when she breathed, now her breath came in an easy rhythm and, despite her bruises, she felt better. An arm rested on her shoulders, a warm solid body under her cheek. She could hear Nanna's light snores from the chair across the room.

Grey's hand stroked her arm. He was not asleep. Melody tried to sit up. His arm tightened.

"Let me up, Grey," she said, her voice husky from sleep.

"I like you where you are."

"I want to see your face. Let me up."

She heard his sigh, felt his chest rise and fall with the sound. His arm released her and she pushed herself up so she could see into his eyes.

"I've waited a very long time to touch you Red," he said. "I intend to have you."

Melody felt her face flush. What exactly did he mean? No, that was the wrong question. She knew what he meant. How could she respond to that? She chewed her lip, nervous. They needed to talk.

"Grey..." she began, but before another word could leave her mouth his head tilted, his eyes brightened.

"The hunting party is coming back."

Melody shook her head, confused. "How do you know?"

"I can hear them."

"Really, I can't hear anything."

He shrugged. "I can. Wolves have sharper senses than humans."

"Yes, but you're human now."

"I can still hear and smell like a wolf. According to Rose, the wolf is still part of me. It always will be."

Melody nodded. She stood and listened, but it took several minutes before she heard voices, the heavy fall of booted feet, and the occasional sound of metal hitting metal, as makeshift weapons wielded by the group clanged together. Melody moved to Nanna's side and gave her shoulder a gentle shake.

"Yes, yes, did I fall asleep? Oh, dear. Sorry, love."

"It's alright, Nanna, I slept, too. The townsfolk are back. I think Daddy will take me home now."

"Yes, of course. Grey will be staying here with me for a few nights. I'm going to give him the guest room." Nanna stood and moved to the front door of the cottage. She peered out the small front window, unlocked and opened the door.

Grey stood and stalked toward Melody. She watched the way his body moved. He did not walk the way other men did. His body was too fluid, his movements too intentional. He moved like an animal, like a wolf. He heard like a wolf, and as he held her pinned to the door in Nanna's bedroom, he smelled her.

No matter what Grey appeared to be on the outside, he remained a wolf. He said he intended to have her. What did it mean to the wolf to have her? She clenched her hands and bit her lower lip. He stood between her and the townspeople now.

Did he want to protect her or did he want to keep her for himself?

Did she care?

She wanted to be his. He was here, a man, and he definitely

noticed her.

Melody sighed and stepped around him. She did not care, but her father might. Her father moved into the cottage and took her hand. Grey frowned but took a step back.

"We didn't find him, Melody. We tried to track him, but after a while the trail vanished." Melody nodded. Her father wrapped an arm around her shoulders. "Let's get you home and safe, we can figure this out in the morning."

Melody allowed herself to be led to the door. Her father stopped and turned to Grey.

"Thank you again for protecting my daughter, Mr. Grey."

"Of course, her safety is important to me."

"If..." Her father paused and looked between her and Grey, "If you wish to call on my daughter, you have my permission."

"Thank you, sir. I will." The tone of his voice and the way he stared into her eyes as he spoke made Melody's heart beat faster. He made the words a promise to her, not a reply to her father.

Nanna draped the red cape over her shoulders and Melody allowed herself to be guided out into the gathering darkness. Her father led her through the front garden gate to the main path and road rather than onto the forest trail. She could not stop the shudder that ran down her back. She wished Grey walked with her. Her father put his arm around her.

They continued in silence for a while before he spoke.

"So, is this Mr. Grey the reason you decided you didn't want to marry Trevor? Or did you suspect his flawed character all along?"

Melody walked for a moment, trying to decide how to answer. She settled on honesty.

"It was Mr. Grey, Daddy. I never suspected anything. Trevor always behaved like a gentleman to me, until today. I knew he didn't love me, and I knew I didn't love him. You knew that, too, but I never thought..." Melody shrugged and her father nodded encouragement or agreement, she was not sure. "But, Grey-I mean, Mr. Grey-I love him. He's never said he loves me, but I think he might. He's certainly never spoken to me of marriage." She kept her voice low so only her father would hear.

He nodded and considered this. She did not think he planned to speak again, but after several moments, he did. "He seemed very interested in you tonight."

"Yes, something changed recently." Melody hesitated over her choice of words. How could she explain any of this to her father? "He's very... protective. He doesn't want to see me hurt in any way."

"That much was clear. Why didn't you speak to me about him before?"

"When would I have talked to you about him, Daddy? You're always at the mine. You come home long enough to allow callers to visit me. Not the best time to discuss another man. And, well, he hasn't said anything about loving me, only..." She could not finish the thought. What did it mean to a wolf to have her? Did he want to marry her, or simply sleep with her?

Her father remained silent for so long she thought the conversation was over.

"I'm sorry, Melody. After I lost your mother, the house seemed haunted with her. Every time I'm there, I miss her more. I've run from my own pain, but that made me run from you too. Today, when the dove arrived from Rose, there was a moment when I thought I'd lost you. I'm sorry I pushed you away. I'm going to try harder. I love you and, if you love this Mr. Grey, I'm eager to find out more about him."

Melody turned into her father's arms and for a time they simply held each other.

72

Grey

Grey lay naked on top of the quilt. Thank God, he no longer wore the clothes men forced on him. After a few short hours, his body felt too sensitive for the weight of the blanket. This house seemed too hot after so many nights spent outside. The mattress under him was too soft. Hard ground covered with pine needles and leaves gave more support. He held no hope of falling asleep tonight. He growled in frustration, he wanted to be with Red in her dreams.

Thoughts of Red made his body hot in an entirely different way. His memories of her were so vivid they seemed almost tangible. The soft warmth of her body pressed against his lingered on his skin. The idea that he lay here, human, and hours ago, his hands ran over her body still amazed him. He missed her and wished she rested next to him now.

The sound of her breathing and the warmth of her body would ease his tension and allow his body to relax. The ability to stroke her hair and kiss her would remind him why he became human. If she were here, he would be able to sleep, eventually. Ideas about how they would spend the time until 'eventually' danced behind his eyes.

A sound outside invaded the images, too quiet to reach a human ear, but loud enough for Grey to hear. He rolled off the bed and crept on all fours to the window. Crouching there, he stared out into the night. A shape moved around the back of the cottage, a large shape, bending over low, but human.

The woodcutter.

Every instinct Grey possessed screamed it. He growled, too low to be heard through the walls and the night, yet the man's head turned up. The shape of an axe defined itself on the man's shoulder and confirmed his identity as he stole through the darkness toward the door.

He could not know Grey hid inside, could not know the wolf became a man. Surprise remained Grey's strongest weapon. This man hurt Red, and he intended to cause her more pain by doing harm to her grandmother. Grey needed to protect his mate and his pack. Grey moved out of the room. He stayed on all fours and hid in the shadows as he inched along. He entered the bedroom where Rose slept and put his hand over her mouth.

She woke. His hand across her mouth stifled her scream. She focused on Grey and the fear in her eyes changed. He placed a finger over his lips and she nodded. He moved his hand from her mouth.

"You need to hide. The woodcutter's here," Grey whispered.

She nodded and her gaze flew around the room. Her eyes landed on the closed closet door and she indicated it with her chin. Grey nodded.

She stood and stumbled across the room to the closet. Holding the door open, she motioned for Grey. He shook his head. He would not run, not this time, not from this man. He heard her soft sigh and the quite click as the closet door closed. He searched the room and tried to determine the best strategy. The woodcutter was larger and heavier. Without his wolf's teeth and agility, he would be at a severe disadvantage.

He heard the sound as the front door opened. How? He had checked the lock himself. The faintest sound of human footsteps followed, too soft for such a large man.

He wished for his wolf's body. He needed the wolf.

Pain wrapped around his spine, rippled over his skin and flowed with his blood. Grey felt a wave of elation with the pain as he realized what it meant.

The transformation took several seconds. Grey panted as

muscles twisted and bones bent in a painful tumult to reshape his form. Knowing what was happening, Grey remained silent.

He could still be a wolf. He could continue to enjoy the freedom this form allowed him and tonight he would defend his mate and his pack. Satisfaction rippled under his skin with his newly shaped muscles.

Grey leapt into the old woman's bed as soon as the change passed. He stretched his body, head near her pillow and lay still, listening to the sound of the footsteps as they approached. This body felt so much more comfortable, with its claws, teeth, and grey vision.

He kept his gaze locked on the door and saw the shape of the woodcutter slide through the doorway and into the room.

The axe rose as he entered the room. He intended to kill the woman, a helpless old woman, to hurt Red. Rage swirled hot in Grey's belly, along with the need to protect. The man came closer. Grey could see an odd swirl around him. Like the magic of Red and Rose, but different, dark, and tainted. It moved differently too, not the calm gentle flow from Rose, or the colors he felt on Red. No, the woodcutter's magic was a swirling whirlwind that twisted and writhed like dark snakes around the man's body.

The woodcutter raised the axe higher, both arms extended over his head, only feet from Grey, still unaware that he had cornered the wrong prey.

Grey waited and allowed him to come closer. When the woodcutter edged close enough to swing the axe, Grey launched from the bed, jaws wide. His teeth tore into flesh, ripping into the man's unprotected stomach. The woodcutter screamed and dropped the axe onto the mattress.

The flavor of blood, hot and metallic filled his mouth. Like earlier, it tasted wrong, but worse, it burned Grey's mouth. It was so foul he gagged. He staggered away from the woodcutter to prepare for another attack. He moved past the man's body, positioning himself between the woodcutter and the closet door.

He growled past the urge to gag and allowed saliva to run from his jaw, hoping it would wash the blood from his mouth.

The woodcutter snarled a sound neither human nor animal. He tore his axe free from the mattress and turned toward Grey. Skin hung from his stomach, exposed muscles and tissue gleamed wet in the moonlight.

The man moved as if unaware of the wound. He seemed to feel no pain. He launched at Grey, axe held high. Grey dodged the blow. The axe slammed into the floor where he stood seconds before. Grey spun and sank his fangs deep into the man's shoulder while the woodcutter tried to dislodge his weapon. Grey ripped, ignoring the urge to choke out the taste of tainted blood. He kept his jaw closed and tore at the muscle. The man howled. Grey suspected the sound came more as a result of rage than pain based on his reaction to the gut wound.

Grey felt muscles flex as his prey released the axe. The prey spun and a fist slammed into Grey's head. His jaw released without him willing it. Grey fell against the floor and a foot slammed into his ribs.

Pain lanced through his body and it did not pass like the pain of the change moments ago. Grey staggered back to his feet. He snarled showing all his teeth. The man laughed.

"You can't win, wolf. You may have reached the old woman first, but the girl belongs to me. Your magic is too weak, your body too small. You can't hold her, she is meant to be mine. Her mind knows that already, soon her body will too."

Rage overtook pain. The room narrowed to a sharp focus. This man still wanted to touch Red. Grey growled deep in his chest, his body vibrating with threat. The man laughed and Grey sprang. He did not aim high. He hit the woodcutter's leg. Grey tore into his thigh. Letting go, he spun, using the momentum of his initial movement to carry him behind the big man and tearing at his calf muscle. The tainted taste of the woodcutter's blood was forgotten in his need to hurt and kill this enemy.

The man tried to hit him, reached to kick and lost his balance. He fell to his knees. Grey tried to move out of his reach but was not fast enough. The man's hand locked around his hind leg and he pulled hard.

Grey yelped at the sharp pain. He spun in the woodcutter's

grip, his teeth locking on the man's wrist, Grey tore. His fangs hit something important. Blood rushed out to fill his mouth. It covered his face and neck.

The man ripped his hand away and rose on shaking legs that dripped blood. Grey expected him to continue to fight, or to run. Instead, he stood very still. He covered his wrist with the other hand and spoke in a soft voice, words Grey did not recognize. The swirling mass of darkness around him slowed, stilled, enveloped him, and seemed to seep into his skin.

The bleeding slowed.

He was healing himself.

Grey used the moment's pause to assess his own injuries. Pain emanated from his head, his shoulder, and his back leg. The wound from earlier still ached and he felt weak. He suspected the blood he accidentally ingested now poisoned his body. Nothing fatal, yet Grey knew he could not defeat this man. The time had come for a change in strategy.

He needed to get the woodcutter to leave this place, now. Grey did not watch another second, did not wait to see if the man could heal all his injuries. He pushed himself across the room, launching from the ground as high as he could jump. Grey hit as hard as he could. He made no effort to bite. The woodcutter, distracted, did not anticipate the attack.

The woodcutter fell to the side and his head hit the ground with the thump. Grey ignored his first instinct, to try to drag his prey from the cottage. If he did that, his prey might realize the truth: that Rose still lived and Grey was merely the distraction.

All he needed to do was lead his prey away.

Grey moved past the prey, toward the door, leaving Rose, and the cottage. He paused outside, listened, smelled, heard a sound, a rasping breath, a movement, coming toward him. He moved further into the darkness, deeper into the night. He saw the woodcutter, moving out of the house, hunched over, holding one hand over the opposite wrist.

Grey growled loud and fierce knowing the prey would hear him. He launched himself, deliberately making it a glancing blow, meant more to anger than to harm. Another inhuman noise, a sound so dark his ruff bristled. The man lurched toward him and Grey ran.

If he turned back to make sure the woodcutter followed, the prey might suspect he was being led away. Grey did not look, but he listened and heard the sounds of the prey, the crash of the brush, the thump of footsteps, the inhuman snarls.

Grey ignored every stab of pain and every ache. He kept his pace even, weaving so that the man might catch glimpses of him without it seeming that he broke cover. He used only his ears and instinct to keep track of the prey. He led the man toward the town, toward Red.

It was a risk, but Rose remained alone. Red was safe with her father and the people in the town.

He did not run straight toward the town. Instead, he took his prey deeper into the woods toward the river, and then north toward the bridge he did not intend to cross.

At the road, he hid and listened to the woodcutter. As he came into view of the road, the man's eyes gleamed bright. Grey stayed still. The man did not move for a long time and Grey began to worry that he had miscalculated. What if the prey could sense him in some way? He felt a wave of relief as the prey crossed the narrow bridge into Red's hometown.

Grey moved, limping now, his muscles sore and aching. He went north to his old den, and passed it to the river. He climbed into the shallow, freezing, water and lay down. He let the water numb his body. Opening his mouth, Grey allowed the cold, clean taste of the water to flow through his teeth and over his tongue, to cleanse the foul taint of the woodcutter's blood from his mouth.

73

Melody

Melody closed her eyes, her knuckles whitened on the steaming mug. The idea of sleep terrified her. What if the void came when she closed her eyes? Grey would come, but how long would she have to wait for him? She could not fight. Not tonight. The void might devour her before Grey arrived.

"You're safe here, Melody," her father said from across the table.

She opened her eyes and watched him. He gave her a weak smile and ran a hand through his hair again. Melody tried to return the smile, but she could not help to notice how grey his hair had become in the past few months and the fine lines around his eyes that seemed so much deeper than this time last year. She wondered if he wanted to convince her or himself of their safety.

"I know. I'm not scared to be here." Despite her words, she shivered.

"I sent a dove to Briar Creek and the healer is going to come and see to your wounds tomorrow. I'll take you to Rose Cottage in the morning. She'll meet us there. That way she can check on Mr. Grey's wound as well. Perhaps you should stay with Rose for a while."

Her father delivered the information with an overbright smile, despite having told her the same thing twice already in the past half hour. Melody suspected he did not know what else to say. She wished she could help him. "Thank you, Daddy."

"Tell me what else I can do to make you comfortable. You still look so frightened."

"I'm not exactly scared. I feel wound up. Like there's too much energy in my body and I can't get rid of it. I know Trevor can't reach me here, can't hurt me, but my body doesn't want to rest yet." She wanted Grey, needed him. She wanted to talk to him, hear his voice, feel him hold her, but the idea of falling asleep and not finding him terrified her.

He raised an eyebrow and she smiled a little. "Really, Daddy."

"Well, I'm exhausted." He sounded encouraging, as if prompting might lead Melody to recognize her own need for sleep.

"Then you should go to sleep." She tried hard to mimic his parental tone. "I'll be fine. I'm in my own house, safe and sound." She assured him, turning the mug in circles in her hands.

He watched her for another minute and she took a sip of the chamomile tea she held and tried to act normal. She had let him make the tea because he wanted to do something to help, but she did not really want it. She suspected he felt some fraction of the nervous energy she combated. With a sigh, he nodded and stood, but before he left the room, he came around the table and kissed her head.

"I can't tell you how much I wish your mother could be with you to comfort you tonight. She would know what to do and say to help you. I'm here now, Melody. I know I haven't been, but I am now. If you want to talk, or cry..." He trailed off and Melody suspected he did not know what else to say.

"Thank you, Daddy. If I need you, I promise to come and get you. I can't sleep yet, that's all. I promise."

He left the room. Alone, Melody lost track of time. Her thoughts became disjointed. She replayed the scene with Trevor repeatedly in her mind and asked herself how she might have done things differently. Could she have done a better job protecting Grey? She wished a hundred times she had never allowed Trevor to court her.

How would things have been different if she had believed

Tara about Grey being like the swans? Perhaps Milo was right and all this was her own fault for not wearing long-sleeved shirts under her spring dresses.

Melody yawned and laid her head down on her folded arms. The bed would be more comfortable, but the idea of facing the void alone terrified her. Could Grey already be asleep? Would he be able to come to her dreams now that he had become human again or was it something only an animal could do? Within seconds, she started to drift into sleep. Gentle arms around her shoulders drew her eyes open, but her vision stayed clouded and blurry.

"Come, young one. Sleeping here will make you stiff and sore." The voice sounded familiar, and yet she had no idea who the woman was. How did she get into the house? She should be afraid, but she was not. She felt safe in the woman's arms and bed no longer seemed so terrifying.

"The dreams..." she protested as she allowed herself to be half led, half carried to her bed.

How or when she changed into her nightgown became a mystery, but as she felt the woman pull the covers over her, she yawned again. Lips brushed her forehead and a voice promised, "No dreams will trouble you tonight, my child."

74

Grey

Grey dragged himself through the night forest. His legs shook with each step and his body protested the effort. It took him far too long to get back to the cottage. He pulled himself from the river as soon as he felt clean and began the return journey. Rose was alone and unprotected. He should not have left her. Rose needed him. She was pack, but more than that, she looked at him with pride. No one had done that since his mother's illness.

No lights shone from the cottage windows and the door stood ajar as it had when Grey left. Should he go in, or wait outside?

He snuck around the house, staying in the cover of the thick bushes. He could not detect any movement inside. He crept around to study it from every angle. Nothing moved, and there was no sign of the fight that took place there mere hours ago. What if Rose lay hurt or bleeding and needed help? He could do nothing as a wolf. Frustration made him snarl.

His body was so battered that if it came to another fight with the woodcutter he would lose. If the man came back, though, Grey would fight him. He respected Rose and Red loved her. She was family, pack. For now, he did not dare leave the cover of the forest and go into the cottage.

He stayed alert, but unmoving over the course of the night,

lying in a position that let him see the entrance of the cottage.

An hour or so before dawn it started to snow. A breeze shifted and he caught a scent. His head snapped up and he scanned the surrounding area. The scent was new, fresh. A scent he recognized.

He let a low growl ripple through him and he stood. Limping, he followed the scent, but not far. The intruder stood downwind, a few feet from Grey. Grey was tired enough not to have heard the other wolf's approach.

He recognized the animal. This non-wolf had intruded on his territory before. Grey conjured a snarl from deep in his throat. This threat did not worry him the way the woodcutter did. A second smaller wolf that smelled of female emerged from the forest to stand near the male's shoulder. She growled a threat of her own. Grey hunched his shoulders low despite the pain and returned the challenge.

Then a third wolf broke cover. This one smelled like puppy. It did not growl or try to fight. It bolted straight toward Rose Cottage.

The female took off after the puppy. Grey lunged at the same moment. Ignoring every ache and stab of pain, Grey used his longer legs to outdistance both the female and the puppy. He beat both the other wolves to the open doorway as he stepped in front of the threshold. There he stood, legs spread and shoulders hunched ready to fight. He snarled and snapped his teeth at the new wolves. The puppy turned at the last second and dashed back toward the male. The two mature wolves stood and defied him as he guarded the doorway of the cottage. For a moment, they faced off.

To Grey's surprise the female sank back on her haunches and howled. The sound ran rich with frustration and anger. The male joined her and even the puppy started to howl. Grey did not move, only watched.

"It's alright, Grey." Rose's voice came from behind him in the cottage. "I've been expecting these wolves. I knew they would arrive in the next few days. They aren't the enemy."

Grey tried to process the words, but instinct told him he

needed to keep Rose safe. He turned and glanced over his shoulder at her. She stood wrapped in a blanket and her face appeared older than it had the night before. Still, she stood straight with one hand extended. In it, she held a piece of bread out to him. He glanced back at the three wolves and discovered a dozen more puppies of various sizes and shapes had joined them. He did not understand what was happening. However, Rose trusted him and he would return the gesture. He entered the cabin and took the bread from her hand.

Within moments, he became human.

75

Melody

Melody and her father left Varin the next morning as the sun came up. Once again, they traveled the longer, more established road rather than the forest path. As the mysterious voice promised, Melody slept untroubled by dreams, and yet Grey remained absent.

Could he not come to her now that he returned to human form? Did he regret what he lost like the youngest swan? Melody twisted her hands into her cape and pulled it closer around her body. Her father put his arm around her shoulder.

"It's alright, you're safe," he assured her, misunderstanding the reason for her nerves.

Even before she saw Rose cottage she heard the growl. It was not Grey; she knew his growl. Her body tensed.

"Grey." She pulled away from her father and started to run. She rounded the corner and stopped at the gate to watch the scene in Nanna's garden.

Grey, as a human, stood in the center of a group of wolf puppies. They jumped, pounced, and growled at him, but he never allowed them to touch him. He moved away, knocked aside, or otherwise averted all of their clumsy attempts to ambush him. Even Melody could tell the puppies were clumsy.

She could also tell they enjoyed the game. Tails wagged, ears perked forward, and mouths hung open in lupine smiles, all the body language she learned from their shared dreams spoke of fun and play. Even Grey seemed at ease. Did he wish he could be a wolf with them? More importantly, who were they? Where did they come from?

The colors! Thick and bright, they covered everything, like another world layered on top of the real world. So real, they almost frightened her. They clung to everything and everyone, moving in the air and through the earth.

The colors overwhelmed her for a moment. She could almost hear them whisper to her, feel them try to give her magic she was not sure how to use. She pushed the colors that murmured in her ear away and focused on Grey. His tones were earth brown and green, amber and grey. Threads of red, vivid green, violet, and blue weaved throughout his colors. Her colors, she swallowed hard, she had done that, weaved her colors into him.

The cottage door opened and a familiar voice called out, dragging her gaze away from Grey and the colors that not only surrounded him but also made him who he was.

"Make them come in and eat, Grey," said the young woman in exasperation. "Nanna Rose doesn't want them to chew on the furniture because they skipped breakfast."

"Tara."

Grey and Tara both spun to stare at her even though she whispered the word. She heard her father's sigh of relief as Tara turned toward them. Tara ran forward. Melody's eyes darted between her approaching cousin and Grey. A puppy nipped at his ankle and Grey glanced down at it and snarled. It sank down to the ground without further protest, understanding the game was over.

Tara reached her and Melody dragged her gaze away from Grey. Her cousin's eyes appeared different. They were gold, with hints of green in them. Colors, similar to Grey's, and yet still uniquely Tara answered the rest of her questions. She embraced her cousin. "You're a wolf?"

Tara nodded. "Nanna Rose told us what happened. Are you okay?"

"I am now," Melody said. "I'm so glad you're here. Will you stay with me?"

"Of course."

As they passed Grey, Melody, glanced up at him and tried to smile, but the gesture felt weak. She held her hand out behind her and felt his fingers brush hers as she moved past him into the cottage. She felt the pain move along her arm when he touched her.

"Are you hurt, Grey?" she asked over her shoulder.

"I'll survive." There was harshness in his reply she had not expected. Melody nervously bit her lip. Did she ask the wrong question?

Inside the atmosphere felt off. Andrew sat at the table. Children and puppies gathered around the fire. More could be heard toward the back of the house.

"What's going on, Rose?" Her father asked as he entered the house. Even he seemed to be aware of the wrongness in the cottage.

"Trevor came back here last night. He tried to kill me. His axe is still embedded in my floor, and my room is covered in his blood. I haven't felt up to cleaning it yet." She sighed and sounded so much older than she did a few hours ago. "Grey saved my life. He was injured again. It's good the healer will be here soon.

"Right around sunrise, because there hadn't been enough excitement for one night, Andrew and Tara showed up with this brood of ...children? I knew they would arrive soon and stay for a while. One good thing, this will make sneaking up on my house more of a challenge."

"Who are they all?" Melody asked.

"The orphans from my village," Andrew answered. "They are the sole survivors of a plague caused by dark magic, the only ones my mother could save." Melody did not have to see him to feel the bitterness of his gaze. "She's still tainted," he claimed.

"Like hell she is." Grey growled the words more than spoke them. Melody's head snapped up and she saw Grey snarling at Andrew. Worse, Andrew rose half out of his chair and growled back. Melody moved closer to Grey.

"Oh, yes, and then there's been this fun," interjected Tara. "Two alpha males in the same very small house; it's been a lovely morning." Tara waved a hand at Andrew and ordered. "Sit boy."

"The children have enjoyed them," Nanna said. Melody noticed the humor returned to her voice as she spoke.

"Children enjoy many dangerous things, especially these children. If we can get them all to survive to adulthood I'll be more than impressed," Tara retorted.

"So," Melody heard the slow patient tone in her father's voice; the tone he used while waiting for an errant child to admit their mistake. "We are standing in a house full of wolves?"

Melody looked from Grey to Andrew, who had sunk back into his chair.

Nanna answered the question. "Exactly, Timothy. All the people around us, even Tara, are dual-natured wolves."

A moment of silence passed. Melody watched her father to see how he would react to the news. He grinned and shook his head, good humor on his face and in his voice. "You always were disappointed Amber fell in love with such an average man, weren't you Rose?"

"Never. Not once, I saw the way you and Amber looked at each other. No two people could have loved each other more. The love is what matters, even if you are rather average, Timothy."

The remark was made with so much affection it could not be taken for anything but a compliment. Still, Melody was happy to see her father smile and move to hug Nanna. She did not want the two of *them* fighting.

Melody moved another step into the house, another step away from Grey.

"Well, you should be safe enough with a house full of wolves. How long have you been dual-natured, Tara?" her father asked.

"A few months. I changed because I decided to come with all the puppies to be pack mother. It's easier to be a wolf for the trip, and for dealing with the ones who don't change."

Melody felt overwhelmed. She moved toward the table and stumbled. She knew immediately whose arms caught her and whose hands held her upright. Her body felt too warm under his touch.

"Thank you, Mr. Grey," she mumbled.

"You can drop the Mr., Melody. If his name is Grey call him that," said her father. "Is this why you didn't mention him sooner? Because you thought it would bother me that he was a wolf?"

Melody flushed and nodded.

"Your grandfather turned into a bear. You thought I couldn't deal with a wolf?" he asked with a chuckle.

"Well, no one thought to tell me that my grandfather became a bear until after I mentioned I was in love with a wolf, did they, Daddy?" Melody snapped. She felt her cheeks flush red.

She sat in the chair opposite Andrew. The colors whirled around her, moving through the air, touching people and things, seeming to dance. Some of the colors she recognized; red, green, and orange. Others appeared as new; blends of gold and green, silver and blue, red and green. She reached out and touched a swirl of purple. It seemed to cling to her finger and follow the path she drew in the air. She waited for the pain that always came with using the colors in the real world. Nothing happened.

She dropped her hand and the purple faded away. Waving a hand in front of her face, she wiped the colors away then watched them refill the area she cleared. New mixes and swirls, silver and red, gold and purple, blue and sea green.

So many colors. She could see and feel them all, sense the way they would work on the world around her. The soft golden yellow could be baked into bread, it would help fill an empty stomach and make the eater strong and healthy. The deep green and solid brown could be mixed into the soil and make plants grow. The red and the orange, mixed with yellows and blues, could be woven into blankets and cloaks that would always keep a person warm no matter how cold the weather became.

How did she know all this? Why could she suddenly see all these colors? Overwhelmed, she closed her eyes only to find them dancing behind her eyelids. She forced herself to open her eyes and found herself staring at Andrew.

He sniffed the air and scowled.

"You're right. She isn't tainted anymore, but the scent lingers."

"Then don't smell her," Grey shot back. He stood behind her chair. She reached a hand back and his fingers touched hers.

"Boys, I told you not to fight in the house. It sets a bad example for the puppies," Rose scolded, but her voice sounded more teasing than threatening.

As if on cue, two small puppies ran, or more accurately stumbled, into the room. One hit the other with a growl and they both tumbled over. Melody tugged her hand free from Grey's, reached down and scooped up the smaller of the two puppies, the one who had been knocked down. She grabbed the other and lifted one in each hand. They were small; she would have guessed them to be a month or so old and wondered what that meant in human years.

She considered the bigger puppy for a moment. It met her gaze and growled, showing its tiny puppy teeth. "Is that so, little wolf? Well, you see him?" She lifted the bigger puppy so he could see Grey over her shoulder. The puppy's coat appeared to be a mix of grey, black, and white with golden eyes. "He doesn't frighten me one bit and his teeth are a lot bigger than yours. He bites, too, so you should rethink growling at me."

She heard Grey laugh behind her and she smiled.

The puppy tucked his tail and whimpered once in apology. "It's alright, but don't bite your sister in the kitchen. It's very bad manners. If you want to wrestle, go outside." The smaller puppy, who was solid black with a white tip on her tail and white tufts of hair on her ears licked at her face.

Melody brought them both close and hugged them, and then

she sat them on the ground. The male puppy dashed out the door but the female put her paws on Melody's dress and whined. Melody picked her back up and stroked her head. The puppy licked the tips of her fingers and then nipped them gently. Melody continued to pet her. She felt Grey rest a hand on her shoulder and leaned back into the touch.

"How did you know they were brother and sister?" Nanna asked, surprise in her voice.

"I don't know. I just knew." She did not say that the colors told her things, information she could not explain but simply knew. She saw the puppies and their colors told her they were brother and sister, and that the sister did not enjoy the game as much as the brother. "Maybe it's magic." She tried to keep her tone light, later she would tell Grey. He would believe her.

Tara snorted a laugh. Melody thought she was being made fun of until Tara spoke. "Can I have some of your magic, Melody? Mine is useless with these puppies. You got Jordon to recognize you as an authority within two minutes of meeting him. He listens to Andrew half the time, and he blatantly ignores me."

"My guess is he respects Grey, not me," Melody said.

"Well, yeah, the puppies all adore Grey. They have since the instant they saw him growling, bloody, and threatening Andrew in Nanna Rose's doorway. They're wolves. They recognize an alpha when they see one," Tara said.

"Melody's Grey's mate, she gets the same respect he does in the pack," explained Andrew.

Melody felt her face flush and she stiffened. Grey's hand tightened on her shoulder. Before either of them could respond, someone tapped on the door.

Rose went over to admit the healer. Melody went first into the guest room and the healer asked her lots of questions while she checked her scratches, her bruised face, and her back. She used a small amount of healing to help with the pain in her back and face and to close the scratches. Other than that, she declared Melody on her way to a full recovery.

Then it was Grey's turn.

76

Grey

Grey snarled at Rose for suggesting he enter the small room with the strange woman. He did not want her to look at him; much less touch him. Rose did not get upset. In fact, she smiled a little and suggested that Red accompany him into the room with the healer. The idea of Red staying with him, and the feel of her hand in his, calmed him.

In the room, he took off his shirt at the healer's request. He heard Red gasp. "Grey, what happened to you?"

"Your woodcutter came back." He could not halt the bitterness in his voice. His body hurt. Bruising covered his chest, abdomen and shoulders. The tainted blood made his stomach clench and burn. He had not tried to eat a full meal yet, afraid his body would not tolerate the food.

"He isn't my woodcutter." Her voice sounded harsh, but her eyes seemed so sad Grey regretted his choice of words. Her fingers opened and left his hand to brush up his arm to his shoulder. He felt cool clean magic flow over his skin where she touched him and relaxed, enjoying the feel of Red's power around him. No matter what the other wolf thought, Red was not tainted. She felt nothing like the woodcutter. No indication of pain marred her face today as she used magic. "Thank you, Red."

The healer touched the cut across his chest and shoulder.

"Nicely done. Effective," the healer said, as she watched Red work.

"Oh, sorry. I guess I shouldn't have..." Red opened her eyes and her fingers dropped off his skin.

"No, it's fine. Saved me some work. You did some very basic healing. Nothing major, but enough to alleviate some pain, or allow a person with a broken bone to travel to a healer. Your potential for improvement is strong. You could train as a healer if you wanted to." The woman redirected her attention to Grey. "Can you tell me what happened?"

"A man wants to kill Rose and hurt Red. He tried both yesterday." Grey snarled the words as the woman prodded at his sore rib cage. Red put her hand against his bare skin again, and more cool magic touched him.

The woman smiled at Red, and then her face took on a haunted look. "It sounds like you will need to be on guard for a while."

"Not long," Grey growled.

The woman nodded. Grey felt the pain dim, watched the wound on his shoulder fade from fiery red to a healthier pink as skin knit under his eyes. The pain in his stomach eased as both the healer and Red continued to ply him with magic.

A few dark bruises and faint scratches were all that remained after the healer finished her work. She left the bedroom with the door ajar. Grey pulled his shirt back on but left the buttons open, his stomach growled.

"I'm sorry, Grey. All this is my fault," Red said, her voice sad and her head low.

"Yes, of course. You forced me to fight the woodcutter last night. I could have run."

"That isn't what I meant." She looked up at him and he saw a spark of fire in her eyes.

"Then back off, Red, I'm not in the mood."

"My mistake. What exactly are you in the mood for?" She snapped the words and Grey took it as a challenge. He rose and took a step toward her. She did not back down, so he closed the distance between them to lean in and kiss her. His hands found her waist and pulled her against his body.

It was a rough, possessive kiss. His mouth opened on hers and as her lips parted, he took full advantage. She tasted good, clean, her mouth did more to erase the woodcutter's blood than the river or the bread from earlier. Her hands touched his chest where his shirt hung open. Her fingers caressed his skin. Much more of this and he was not going to stop. He forced himself to release her and step away.

He turned and left the room. He knew his actions might be rude but he did not care. In the last few hours, he'd gone from being a lone wolf, to living as a human, to having a family and now he found himself with a pack. Red stiffened when that male called her his mate. Did it upset her, or merely surprise her? Stupid male. He needed to talk to Red, alone. There were things they needed to work out.

A small reddish brown puppy bolted through the room, almost tripping Grey. It paused long enough to yip and wag its tail in apology before continuing. Grey rolled his eyes. He had acquired a pack full of puppies.

77

Melody

She sat alone in the house. One moment children, puppies and people filled the tiny cottage. Now all the puppies, and the children who became puppies, ran outside with Grey and Tara. Nanna collapsed into her rocking chair and fell fast asleep. Her father departed to escort the healer back to Briar Creek. Even the colors left, having slowly receded a while ago, growing fainter until they disappeared. She did not know where Andrew went, but she hoped he stayed away. Her mind still reeled and the break from the confusion that dominated the house came as a welcome change. She tried to calm her thoughts and digest the events of the past two days.

Her wish for solitude ended abruptly. The door opened and Andrew stalked into the room. Melody considered leaving, and then realized the unique opportunity she might not have again.

"What made me tainted, Andrew?" she asked before he could realize they were alone and escape from her inquiry.

He rolled his eyes, and asked, "Why do you care?"

"Well, for starters I would prefer to avoid any future taints," she snapped. Wolves respected strength. "Also, I want to understand what's happening around me."

She watched him, and now she understood why the feral look in his eyes seemed so familiar to her last time they met. Knowing about his dual nature made him far less intimidating. He grunted, shrugged, and then walked around the table to sit down across from her.

"What do you know about The Brotherhood?"

"The what?" She did not have to feign the confusion in her voice.

"That's what I expected," he sighed, but relaxed. Apparently, she provided the right answer. "Okay, let's start at the beginning. In the old world, over the Eastern Sea, the Ancients stayed more involved in human affairs than they have ever been on this continent. Over three thousand years ago, a group of humans formed a Brotherhood. By their own words, they sought power and eternal life without the aid of the Ancients.

"After about a century, they found the key to both. They found a way to feed their own spirits, or souls, whatever you choose to call the essence of who we are as people, from the negative emotions and suffering of those around them. They could not maintain a single human body indefinitely, although they could extend a human body's life and health for hundreds of years. However, human bodies eventually collapse and die. They can't live forever, not without a stronger magic than the Brothers found.

"They found a way to use magic and separate the essence from the flesh. So they took over another body, forcing out the previous soul in that body, essentially, killed the person, and gave themselves a new host for another several hundred years.

"At first, the Ancients were unconcerned with the Brotherhood. They dismissed them as a cult who found a way to extend their lives. The Brotherhood never grew; every time a member died they accepted a single new member. Of course, the 'new member' was the same soul in a new host. Since the group never grew, no one considered them a threat. No one figured out what they were doing.

"So the members of the Brotherhood continued to gain in strength. They used the deaths and suffering of those around them, becoming rulers of their own cities, and then kingdoms. They would torture and kill to feed themselves and maintain the power they amassed.

"After a time, one of them became bold. When his old form began to age he found an elf, and he did everything he could to take possession of that form, one with a life span that measured in the thousands of years. He failed and the soul, without a body died. The stories say that this is the act that convinced the Ancients to step in."

Melody nodded, her hands twisted in her lap under the table in her efforts to be patient. Hundreds of questions, not the least of which was 'what are the Ancients' threatened to spill out of her. Melody feared an interruption of any kind might cause Andrew to stop his story.

"Ancients, being immortal, have a different sense of time than humans, so they observed for a few decades. They watched how cruel, heartless and inhuman the Brotherhood had become. They decided that the cure to this much cruelty must be compassion. Therefore, they went out and found two hundred of the most compassionate human beings alive. This was the same number of the Brotherhood before they lost a member.

"It so happened that all of these people were mothers. So the Ancients brought these women together. Most, if not all, of them already possessed magic. The Ancients went further. They endowed them with almost unlimited power, and gave them the gift of their own immortality. They gave them the task of destroying the Brotherhood."

Melody knew her face reflected her confusion when Andrew stopped speaking. So she asked the question that troubled her most. "Why would they ask compassionate people to destroy?"

"It was a flawed plan, as they soon discovered. The women went to work in the towns, villages, cities, and kingdoms the Brotherhood ruled. They healed the illnesses, they rescued the tortured, and they soothed the negative emotions of entire towns. Several even found ways to enchant members of the Brotherhood. They forced them to see their crimes. Those Brothers renounced their allegiance, reclaimed their humanity, relinquished their stolen magic, and began to live as members of the communities they'd been feeding from, in an attempt to make amends. The Brotherhood hunted down these men and destroyed them if the Godmothers weren't careful to protect them.

"This wasn't what the Ancients intended. Within a matter of years, they grew frustrated and stepped in. They imprisoned the children of the women they made immortal. They trapped them in time; they couldn't grow, change, or live their lives. The Ancients told the women that until every member of the Brotherhood was dead their children would remain locked in time and trapped in their prison. The women were devastated. They all loved their children but none of them wanted to kill.

"So the women all met together and discussed the events and how they should deal with them. They decided that they could not and would not engage in open warfare with the Brotherhood. It wasn't who they wanted to be, but they felt that if they continued to undermine the efforts of the Brotherhood to feed the members would weaken and die of natural causes.

"This plan, however, meant losing their children, for centuries, maybe even millennia. They accepted this decision, believing their children were safe. So they decided that they would become

Godmothers to those in pain, those in need of magic, and those pursued or injured by the Brotherhood.

"That's what they did for hundreds of years. They undermined the base of the Brotherhood's hold by spreading love, joy, and hope. For close to a thousand years, a stalemate stood between the Godmothers and the Brothers, and the Ancients observed it all.

"During this period, the Brotherhood found that certain humans were born with deep magic, like many of the Godmothers. They found that if they could bond with a human with that type of power they could feed off them, draining the inborn power and using it to increase their own.

"Since the Brotherhood began as men they gravitated to males to replace their dying hosts, they generally sought women to bond with. They forced women with great magic to be their wives then drained them of magic. However, the woman's heart must be free. Love binds and if the woman was already bound then the Brotherhood couldn't force a bond into being.

"These bonded Brothers became immensely powerful and began to overpower the good the Godmothers did. After the Brotherhood grew strong they went to war. They attacked the Godmothers and the Ancients in an attempt to make the entire Eastern Continent their own.

"The Ancients and the Godmothers, along with many humans, elves, trolls, sylphs and other races, fought the Brotherhood. The war lasted two hundred years and left great casualties on both sides. Many of the Ancients were killed, or driven into the Earth. They still haven't emerged, but in the end all but a handful of the Brotherhood died as well, not the death they could come back from. They were truly dead.

"Those that remained were weak, drained and separated. Everyone who fought came away weary. Then the worst tragedy was revealed. The Ancient, who held the Godmothers' children, was destroyed in an act of cruelty by a surviving Brother. Nothing remained of his home or his prison. The Godmothers found the bodies of their children decaying in the rubble. After so many years of believing they would one day be reunited with their children, the women were torn apart by their loss.

"Once again they came together. They grieved together and they counseled each other and they debated what they could have done differently that might have saved their children and allowed them to hold on to their identity. Some of them went a little mad; they begged the others to kill them. A few went to one of the Ancients and begged for their mortality back.

"This Ancient, however, blamed the Godmothers for the war. They refused to give them mortality. Instead of allowing the women any freedom, the Ancient gave them more protections, and made it impossible for them to kill themselves or each other. The Ancient they pled their case to sent them out into the world again and told them to eliminate the Brotherhood before they could begin another war.

"A few, those so deep in grief and loss that they could no longer remember the compassion they used to cling to, went together and began hunting the Brothers who remained. They eliminated some before they themselves were killed. Another group decided that if they had to live they didn't have to do it awake. They put themselves into the deepest of sleeps in one of the caves abandoned by an Ancient. One story says that another of the Godmothers sealed and hid the entrance to lock them forever in the earth with their dreams of a better time and place.

"Those who remained decided to continue what they had been doing before. By that time someone had discovered this land. Several of the Brotherhood decided to escape the risk of the Godmothers by coming here. They hoped that the non-human races here, being less prepared, might be easier to overtake. Several of the Godmothers followed them across the sea, to this continent."

Andrew paused and spread his hands on the table in front of him. "I have heard a great many stories about individual Brothers and the Godmothers, but that is the early history as I heard the tale from an Ancient in my hometown, before a Brother came and destroyed it.

"What I smelled on you, the taint, was a Brother. Not just any taint, though. I smelled a Brother who was trying very hard to bond to you. His scent contaminated you, and you were either willing, or unaware. Given your relationship with Grey, I'm guessing unaware."

"Obviously." Melody rubbed a hand over her face. She hoped to cover her blush and give herself a moment to piece together the story she heard with her own life. "So a three thousand year old evil entity wants to create a bond with me?"

"Yes, most likely the man who tried to rape you."

"Trevor?" Melody stared at him in shock. She had had a crush on Trevor for years, until she fell in love with Grey. The idea of him as an ancient evil entity did not fit, except he had tried to rape her. That did not speak highly for his character.

Melody sighed and nodded. "Okay, so let's say Trevor *is* evil. He's lived in Varin for years and there's never been any mayhem, plague, death, barely even a lot of negative emotion. Not until the past year, since my mother died." Even as she said the words, she started to shiver and shake her head.

"Your mother's magic was luck. She couldn't manipulate anything, but by touching things her magic rubbed off. Right?"

"Yes, or even being there." Melody felt her hands shake and closed her eyes in denial against what she felt certain Andrew would tell her next.

"Why do you think she died right about the time that you were old enough to marry?"

Melody felt the blood drain out of her face. She sank her teeth so hard into her lower lip that she tasted blood.

Trevor killed her mother to get to her.

Fury, hot, red and black boiled inside her. She could feel the colors seep into the air around her, faint shadows of colors that grew brighter with each moment. Where did they go and why did they return? It did not matter. Her anger and hurt burned too hot. With her mind, she grabbed the colors. The fury she felt over her mother's murder fed them. Nothing existed but the colors as they thickened and roped into each other.

These colors could hurt. She could use them to kill. They boiled with strength, yet she held them, controlled them. The balance inside her shifted, the colors devoured her anger growing as they fed. They felt so powerful and heavy.

They begged to be set free. They pushed against her body and she wanted to let them go, to let them find Trevor, to kill and destroy. She refused to succumb to this desire to hunt Trevor. She would not become a murderer. She held the colors back with her will, kept them leashed in her body as they fought to be free.

Knowledge and desire warred inside her and for a time nothing around her made sense. She fought her own internal war, unsure which side of her would prevail.

A cool, wet nose touched her face. Grey infiltrated the black and red walls around her. The breach in the color allowed her to think, let her regain control.

Her eyes saw darkness, but she reached with her hand and touched Grey's head. More color invaded and the black and red lost their power over her. She grabbed at strands of green and purple, wrapping them around her grief and clinging to them the way her hand clung to Grey's fur. She let the touch and the colors soothe her.

The blackness lifted from her vision and she stared into the bright amber eyes of the wolf she had fallen in love with.

78

Grey

Red slid from her chair to her knees and wrapped her arms around his neck. She buried her face in his fur. Grey rested his head on her shoulder. How many times had they stood this way? Dozens, in their dreams, and even a few times in reality.

His eyes pinned the people who hovered behind the table, and he lifted his lip in a silent snarl. They let her sit there, alone and afraid. They felt the pain and fury flow from her but they refused to come close and help. Instead, they watched in fear as the emotion built to the point it almost took her over.

Even Rose stood in fear of Red's magic, afraid that Red would let herself lose control and lash out.

Red's fingers tightened in his fur. Grey turned his head and licked at her neck. He missed and mostly licked her hair. She giggled into his fur, and her body relaxed against his.

"Don't get doggy drool in my hair," she whispered.

He growled and she laughed again. "Sorry, wolf drool."

Relieved at her laughter he pulled away. He needed to see her face to assure himself she was alright. She gave him a weak, watery, smile and he could see the apology in her eyes. He licked her cheek, tasting her skin and the saltiness of her tears.

As Red stood, Grey trotted out of the room to the guest bedroom. There he found bread left out on a small plate. He gulped it down and felt the change sweep through his body. It hurt, of course, but the pain passed. He stood and pulled on the clothes that he left on the bed.

He emerged from the room to find Red sitting on the floor near the fire stroking the small black and white puppy she rescued from her brother earlier. Rose brought her a cup of tea. The old woman glanced at him and gave a small, almost guilty smile.

"It's not something I've ever seen before, Grey. You must give me a little grace here," Rose whispered.

He saw the confused look flash across Red's face, and heard the genuine regret in the old woman's voice. Seeing them so close together, he caught the resemblance the two shared. He nodded and Rose smiled a little more.

Red grinned up at him, a real smile. "I'm so pleased you can still be a wolf. I was scared you lost that. I know you like to hunt and play." She shrugged. "It makes me happy to see you can still change."

"Me too," he admitted, sinking down on the rug near her.

The puppy curled up against her leg and started to snore. Her grandmother left the room and, apart from the sleeping puppy, they were alone in this part of the house. They sat together in silence. Finally, Grey spoke. "Tell me."

"Trevor's evil. He killed my mother, he destroyed my father, he hurt the entire town, and he did it to get to me." Red shivered, and he put his arm around her. "I hate him, and I wanted to kill him. I think part of me still wants to kill him, but for a few minutes black and red angry magic was all that existed. I knew I could use it to hurt and kill, and I *wanted* to." Her voice sounded frightened.

"You've never used your magic to kill anyone, Red. You never would."

"How do you know? You have no idea how selfish I am, Grey." She turned to stare at him, her eyes wide and confused.

"No, Red, that isn't who you are. I do know you. I know you are far from selfish. Since the first time I met you, you've been fighting. Trying to protect the town, and even me, and beating yourself up when you couldn't."

It was the longest he had spoken since he became a wolf almost a year ago. He swallowed at the dryness of his throat and shifted his position so Red could rest against his shoulder.

"Andrew explained to me what Trevor is and why he wants me. I'm such a fool, Grey. For so long I've been given everything I could ever want or need. I started to expect that I would always have whatever I wanted, and I wanted everything. I wanted to be loved by the people of Varin, but I also wanted to be myself. I wanted Trevor to choose me over Jessica even after I knew I loved you. I wanted magic, but I never accepted the responsibility and power that came with it. What if Trevor chose me because deep in my heart I am flawed? What if really I am like him?"

Grey did not respond immediately. If he did, she would not believe him. Instead, he held her and considered her words, and his own. When he spoke, he did so with his cheek leaning against the top of her head.

"I think that inside we're all flawed, Red. I've never met a perfect person. Deep in our hearts, we all have things we wish we could change or do differently. Before I became a wolf, I allowed my family to convince me I was unreliable, weak, and untrustworthy. I refused to accept things about myself I knew to be true, and in the end that choice cost someone their life."

"Oh, Grey." Her hand reached up and stroked his cheek.

"Since the first time I met you, Red, you've grappled with the truth to figure out who you are and who you're supposed to be. Maybe the recognition and acceptance of our flaws is part of that process."

She nodded against his shoulder and her hand dropped back into her lap. For a long time they sat in silence.

"Grey..." She hesitated and he felt the slight shift in her body as she tensed and moved away from him a fraction. "When did you know I was magic?"

The way she spoke made his body tense. He did not understand the bleakness that clung to her.

"The first time I saw you walking. I could feel it on you."

She nodded but he felt the tension flowing through her body. She started to pull away in an attempt to stand up without waking the puppy. Something about his answer frightened her. He tightened his arm around her. "Gonna run, Red?"

She glared over at him and he saw the way her eyes snapped at the challenge. He grinned and could tell from how her eyes narrowed it was a wolf grin.

"You don't scare me, wolf."

"Liar. You're terrified." His voice low, he pulled her closer so his lips almost touched her ear as he spoke. "Tell me, Red."

She shook her head. He moved closer and pressed his lips to her neck. "Tell me why you're afraid of me." He whispered as his lips teased the skin under her ear down to her pulse. "You've never been afraid, not even the times you should have been."

"Grey, we can't do this right now."

"Fine." He put distance between them. If she wanted to run, he would let her, for now.

She stood, still careful not to wake the puppy. She watched for a long moment and he saw the uncertainty in her eyes.

"Nanna," she called as she turned away from him. He rose and followed her into the kitchen. Soon he would corner her and she would have to stop running.

79

Melody

What I want to know is why my powers are returning. Why they're coming back the way they are and what all this has to do with the Brotherhood and the Godmothers," concluded Melody once Andrew finished his story and she shared her new understanding of Trevor with everyone around the table.

"I think the best way to answer that would be to ask the Godmother who locked your powers away," said Nanna. "She had a reason for blocking them, but she never told anyone but your mother and your mother never shared the reason."

"How do I ask her? I don't even know her," Melody asked, with a note of desperation in her voice.

"I have a way to call her," Nanna sighed, "but I'm not certain she will come. Last time I spoke to her I told her never to return to my home."

"In the meantime we have more immediate needs to figure out," said Melody's father. He had returned as they all sat down to discuss the situation. "Rose, you cannot keep all these children here. There isn't space for them all, even with the extra room. Since Trevor has already attacked you once, I suggest you keep the men and boys here. Tara and the girls can come back to our house. We have room for them, but they can't be wolves in the town. No one's ready for that."

"But, Timothy, that's part of the problem. The youngest either cannot, or refuse, to change back from animal to human," explained Rose.

"Well, the puppies will be fine, as long as they don't shift back and forth. We can tell people we have some puppies for a while," her father said with a smile and a shrug. He seemed excited by the idea.

A grunt from Andrew made them all turn. "It's not as easy as you think, but sure, go ahead and take the girls. That's less that I have to worry about."

Seven girls, ten boys and her two cousins, Andrew and Anna, from a thriving village, they were the only survivors of an attack by a member of the Brotherhood. Melody shivered, wondering what would happen to Varin if Trevor chose to turn his full power against it. She looked at the puppies who slept on the floor in the next room and dreaded putting them through that again.

"Call the Godmother, Nanna. I don't want to go home until I understand what's happening and why. I don't want to give Trevor any reason to attack Varin. Beg her to come if you have to," Melody pleaded.

Nanna stood and disappeared into her bedroom. Melody clenched and unclenched her hands as she waited for something she could not possibly prepare for.

It took a few moments for Nanna to reappear and as she entered the room, Melody heard a light tap at the door.

"Oh, she must have been nearby." Nanna went and opened the door to the most beautiful woman Melody had ever seen. Her skin glowed a soft silvery white and long honey-blonde hair flowed down her back almost to her knees. It lay in thick, gently curling waves that Melody suspected never knotted or tangled. Her pale blue eyes seemed to shine in her smooth perfect skin. She did not so much as walk into the house as she glided.

"Greetings, old friend," she said, leaning in and kissing Nanna's cheek. All the weight that had settled on Nanna the previous night lifted from her and Red could see wisps of magic weave around Nanna. When the Godmother stepped back, Nanna looked better, healthier and lighter than she had moments ago.

"Greetings, Melea. Thank you for replying to my request, especially after our last encounter." Nanna whispered. "It's an honor to have you in my home again."

"Nonsense, Rose, the honor is, as always, mine. Of course I came, I would never leave you or Red in need." Her gaze swept the room and a tiny smile curved her perfect red lips. "Well, you do have an interesting mix of personalities in this house."

Her eyes came to rest on Melody and she felt a swirl of warm air around her and saw in her eyes and heard in her voice something she recognized and understood. The memory of the night before and the arms that tucked her into bed sifted into her mind. Melea had been in her house. Melea had kissed her forehead and now pain no longer troubled her when she used magic.

"Godmother." She could not take her eyes off the woman. Magic roped around the Godmother in thick braided layers. It radiated out of her skin, brilliant gold and silver that seemed to hold a rainbow glittering in the braided depths. There were so many questions she wanted to ask, and now as she gazed into the woman's eyes she did not have to. "I remember."

"Of course." The voice wafted like a cool breeze on a hot day, and not only did Melody remember, she understood.

"Oh, God, what did I do?" Melody cringed, trying to flinch away from herself. She could not escape the truth. It stretched out in front of her with no excuses or defense.

"Nothing," came the warm soft blanket on a cold snowy day. "You made the best choices you could with the limited knowledge you possessed, and in the end you made the right decision."

"But I came so close..."

"Close is different from arrival," replied the spring rain soaking into earth eager to grow.

"I was so close, how could I have let myself get so close..."

"Child." The blue gaze still held hers. "When someone is hurting they often hurt others in reaction to their own pain. Learning not to do that is part of life, part of maturity. You've learned something. You won't make the same mistake again."

Melody forced her trembling hands to unclench and she drew a deep breath, nodding. "Thank you, Melea, for everything."

80

The Brother

How could this have gone so wrong?

He arrived on time, even early. Her heart was not bound and her body remained free. He laid out a flawless plan: a tiny bit of magic to poison the mother to give the girl time to say her goodbyes and prepare for the loss.

He had been everything, forced himself to live a perfect life. He worked for his living, spent time with insipid people who bored him until he wanted to scream and kill. He even asked her father for his permission to court her. Once, at the peak of his strength, he ordered a woman to be his wife. She agreed or she died.

Melody, he wooed and he courted. She would have been different. She was different, even if she did not know it.

She would have been his queen.

He nurtured the anger and pain inside her, feeding from her as he fed her. They would have been perfect for each other.

No. She *would* be his queen. They *were* perfect together. Melody, with all her power and all her potential, would be his queen.

He spent years living a normal, powerless life. All for what? So she could decide at the last minute that she was too good for him? The wolf deceived her. His magic was weak, yet he managed to destroy the old woman. He was not really a wolf, of course, but one of the dual-natured, a sorcerer, perhaps, but a weak one. Still, he had been strong enough to damage a Brother.

The body would be easy to repair, simple magic, but it took time to regain strength. He stayed hidden in a secret room under his house in Varin. He fed on the negative feelings he had been encouraging in the town for years. He fed from Jessica's jealousy, her hatred for Melody. He devoured the townsmen's lust for Melody. He encouraged it and made her seem more lush and brazen than she was.

He sent out a tiny pulse of magic, and encouraged anger in a man who believed Melody deserved to be raped for teasing men with her body, only to deny them her attention. He found another man with similar thoughts and sent a tendril of power to him as well. The thoughts grew stronger and turned to words, anger increased. He ate and grew stronger.

He smiled. She would suffer for hurting him. After the pain, she would be his and she would understand that she was always meant to be his. He would not be harsh with her, not once she understood. He would be a good husband, treat her well, and perhaps even allow his body to give hers a child. Yes, a son. They would rule side by side and raise a son together. A boy who could grow into a strong man with magic of his own, a gift from his mother's blood. He could teach him to be a Brother and together the three of them would create an empire.

He would show her. She would understand that the only love she would ever get was the love he gave her.

81

MELODY

Melea was gone. She left as quickly and mysteriously as she arrived. Melody sat alone and frightened.

"Tell me," Grey said, as he came to stand behind her chair.

She turned and gazed up into his eyes. "Would you hold me?"

For a moment, he did not move and she felt certain he would say no. Grey lifted her off the chair to sit down and cradle her in his lap. She snaked her arm around his neck.

Maybe he wanted her magic, the way Trevor did, or maybe he wanted sex. It did not matter. Whatever he wanted, she would give him. She loved him. She wanted to be with him. To give him back a fraction of what he had given her. Through everything, he had been there for her, with her.

"Tell me, Red," he prompted again.

"As a very young child, I possessed magic; so much power. I knew how to use it, too. I made things grow and I made people strong and healthy with food I helped my mother make. I fixed things that were broken, but my magic was never like mother's or Nanna's. Mine I could use, theirs just exists. I was powerful, Grey. I did things that amazed people, and terrified them. One day a troll came. He took me away. I remember crying."

Grey growled and she felt his chest move against her. She

stroked his cheek, trailing her fingertips along his skin.

"He didn't hurt me. In fact, he treated me with kindness. He told me not to be afraid, that he planned to take good care of me and protect me. He promised to keep me safe. I believed him. My parents, of course, chased him with my grandfather. He was a bear. I mean, sometimes, like you're a wolf."

He nodded and her hands slid into his hair, feeling the soft strands on her fingers. She loved to touch him, to be held by him.

"Nanna called the Godmother and Melea found me. That part was all told to me by my aunt, but after that, things happened that no one else knew. The troll explained to Melea that their seers had a vision concerning me. Their vision showed me bonding to one of The Brotherhood, willingly giving him my magic, becoming his queen, his partner. It showed the Brother feeding from me and using my power to take over villages and towns. People died. We went to war with cities and kingdoms. Eventually we ruled, he and I. Blood and Death side by side; that is what I have the potential to be. Blood."

She trembled, the way she remembered shivering as a small girl in the troll's arms. Grey ran a hand over her hair and pressed her closer to his shoulder. She tried to absorb his warmth, tucking her head under his chin.

"I understood and I asked the Godmother and the troll to protect me, to not let that happen. I didn't want to be the cause of people's deaths and I didn't want to become an evil queen. Melea considered everything, and then she spoke to the troll. She told him that trolls tend to be pessimistic. Apparently, it's an acknowledged truth even among them. She said that it affected their visions of the future, visions they knew themselves were malleable. No vision of the future is set in stone; they are pictures of what may be. That was why they came to change the future, to keep me hidden from the Brother. I wasn't evil yet.

"She promised the troll that there was a way to keep me safe and to allow me to stay with my family. She told him that if I ever bonded to a Brother she would destroy me herself. She was that confident she could prevent the future they foresaw. The troll trusted her and gave me to her."

Melody sighed and moved her fingers further into Grey's hair. He kissed the top of her head and rubbed his cheek against her hair.

"She told me little girls should not have to worry about things like evil magic and members of the Brotherhood. She kissed my head and I forgot. Everything. The Brotherhood, the possibility of being an evil queen, that I ever possessed magic. Every trace of it vanished. Melea placed me into my mother's arms. She told my mother everything, and she told her there was always another path. The Godmother told my family that the best way to protect me was to keep my magic a secret from everyone, even me. She told them that for as long as my mother lived I needed to stay free from magic. She promised my mother that someday, if I made wise choices and found the right catalyst my magic would return."

"Catalyst?"

"Didn't you notice, Grey? I couldn't use magic until I fell in love with you. Even earlier today, the magic started to build as you approached the cottage. If I didn't love you, then my magic would never have come back. My love for you, my bond with you, is what released my magic. The stronger our bond grew the more my magic came back. In turn, it makes your magic stronger too. Last night, Melea came and kissed me, releasing the chains she placed on my magic all those years ago. Now my magic has returned completely."

She felt him stiffen, his hand stopped and his shoulder felt rigid under her cheek.

"I don't have magic." His voice sounded harsh.

"You do. The Godmother showed me. It allows you to see the truth of things and it let you hurt the Brother. It isn't like mine, or Nanna's or even Tara's, but you were born with it. Like I was, it probably feels like intuition most of the time."

He relaxed, but he did not stroke her the way he did before and she understood why. She said that their bond made his magic stronger, too. Implying they shared a bond, but he never said he loved her or wanted to be bonded. She bit her lower lip and tightened her fingers in his hair.

"Tonight, I would like to see you in my dreams," she said as she turned her head toward him and let her lips brush over his throat.

82

Melody

"I don't understand Grey sometimes," Melody said.

"Of course you don't. First off, he's male. Second off, he's more wolf than human," Tara replied.

Melody relaxed on her bed and stared up at the ceiling of her room. All the young ones were tucked in; humans in beds and puppies in piles of blankets on the floor. After a long, busy day, she and Tara finally had time to talk. "You have to understand Melody, being dual-natured is overwhelming."

"Do you hate it?" Melody asked. Grey did not seem to.

"No, not at all. The problem might be that I like it too much. It's hard to explain. There's an animal in me now and I like it. I love it. I want to be the animal more and more. It's hard to reconcile sometimes. For Grey, it's more difficult, I imagine."

"Why?"

"Well, I chose this. I knew what would happen and I planned to be a wolf so I could understand and help the children. I knew I could be human any time I wanted with a thought. Grey didn't. It was forced on him and he never guessed that he could become human again.

"He lived and survived as a wolf for close to a year, without any real human contact. Never even imagining he could be a human again. He's more wolf than I'll ever be, and trust me, I feel the wolf.

"I love to run, love the hunt, the kill, the instincts, and the senses. It calls me. How much more does the animal call to him than it does to me?" A deep wildness, almost a growl vibrated in Tara's voice as she spoke of the hunt. Melody never heard that inflection from her cousin before, but she recognized it from Grey.

"In a way it's a good thing. I mean, these children are a lot like him. Some stay wolf all the time and they've started thinking in wolf. I think Jordan and Jenna and some of the others have forgotten what it means to be human. Grey forgets sometimes, too, I think, when he's out running. He understands them better than the rest of us do, and they respect him more than they do Andrew or me. In a way, it's a huge relief that he's here."

For a long time the two remained silent. Melody tried to sort out in her mind what it meant to him to be more wolf than human. "I'm in love with him."

"Well, yeah, I kind of got that. The whole gazing at him longingly and touching him every chance you get gave it away."

Melody blushed. "He knows. I've told him about a hundred times in our dreams."

"Like the swan princess." Tara's voice sounded smug. "Told you so."

"Yeah, except being an idiot I didn't believe you. Even Nanna figured it out before I did. I asked him though, and he said he wasn't human."

"Remember, he didn't know he could be a man again."

"Yeah, yeah, so he said," Melody said. She turned her head so she could see her cousin, tucked into the bed of blankets she made on the floor. "Do you think he loves me?"

"Oh, there's a tough question. Yes, I think he loves you..." Tara paused and tilted her head.

"I sense a but," Melody prompted, her stomach twisting into a nervous knot.

"Well, there's no doubt that in Grey's mind you're his mate

and he loves you. Even the youngest ones in the pack recognize that, but wolves behave differently. I mean, they don't say I love you. They just take care of their mates. He certainly takes care of you, but you're human, not a wolf. You might want more. You might need more. You have to decide what you want and need, Melody, and you have to tell him. Wolves are even more clueless than human men."

Melody lay back and stared up at the ceiling lit by moonlight. Did she need more? There was no question that she wanted more. She wanted to be Grey's wife. She wanted to have his children and grow old with him. She loved him and she wanted everything. Earlier today, though, she told Grey she realized she could not have everything. Was she willing to settle for whatever Grey could give her? It was a long time before her eyes drifted shut and her mind let her sleep.

83

Red and Grey

The meadow shone bright and colors whirled, more colors than she ever imagined existed. Not only the colors of the rainbow, but every color the eye could see. They floated in the air and sank into the grass-covered ground. They melted into clouds and they swirled in ribbons around her as she twirled.

She laughed aloud as she spun, eyes closed, around and around. Hands caught her. She opened her eyes, startled. Grey smiled down at her. She grinned.

"Happy, Red?"

"So happy. No void invaded my dreams tonight, Grey. Only me and the colors. Look at them all!" She spun out of his hands. "It's gone. Trevor's gone. He was the void and I'm free from him now."

Grey saw the wisps of color cling to her and whirl with her. She looked so beautiful, her hair flared from her back as she spun and her liquid green eyes turned into emeralds. He had never wanted anything as much as he wanted her right now.

He caught her again. Reaching out, he pulled a ribbon of ivory from her hair and let it float away in a burgundy breeze before he kissed her. Her hands slid up his chest and into his hair and she pressed her body against him. He felt her breasts soft and curved against his chest. He slid his hands to her hips, pulled her against his body. She did not pull away, but pressed closer.

He pulled back a fraction. Her lips skimmed along his jaw and followed the line of his throat. "Red, you don't have to..."

"I know. You would never make me do anything I didn't want to, but, Grey, I want to give you this. I want to give you everything, anything you want from me is yours."

Something about the words bothered him, something about her voice sounded wrong. Then her lips caressed his chest and her clothes melted under his hands. The words were lost to sensations.

She pressed her mouth to his skin, flicked her tongue over it. He tasted golden and grey, perfect. She licked again and felt his fingers against her flesh. Cool hands caressed up her back, curled around her shoulder. She pressed closer and felt his heart beat under her lips. It pumped faster and she knew she caused that. It made her heart pound. He liked the way she touched him. It made her warm. Purple and gold air whispered over their skin.

She ran her hands further down his body, daring to touch. He growled and she found herself on the ground, soft cloudlike, green grass teased her skin. Grey leaned over her, his lips on hers. She wrapped her arms around him, weaving the purple and gold threads around them both, tying them together as she kissed him back.

He needed to touch her. His fingers ached; he wanted to feel her skin. He pushed himself off her body and ran a hand down her throat, over her chest to cup her breast. She gasped and he pulled back further to watch her face. Her eyes were wide as he rolled the rosy tip of one breast between his fingers.

Her back arched toward him and she whimpered his name. The sound rolled through him and his mouth found hers again, devouring.

She tried to match his kiss, tried to move in a way that would show him how eager she was. His hands slid down her sides, curved around her hips, lifting her. With a slow glide their bodies came together as one.

She gasped. He filled her every part. His hands held her still as he moved in her body. Her fingers dug into his shoulders and she heard herself begging for more. He rolled them over and moved her so she sat on his hips. His body pressed deeper into hers.

Her head fell back and she saw the colors dancing in the sky. Colors twirled and twisted, joining each other in an echo of the connection she made with Grey. She felt his hands run up her abdomen and then further. She moaned and leaned forward, her hips rocked against his and her heart raced under his hands. With closed eyes, his fingers explored her skin.

Grey knew that nothing had ever been this perfect. Then she moved, her body wrapped around his. He could feel the air, thick and heavy caressing his skin. He felt the colors woven around their bodies as they moved. Her body, hot and light, glided around his and her perfect breasts filled his hands.

The colors exploded around them as she cried out in pleasure and he came deep in her body.

Grey woke when Red's weight disappeared off his shoulder. He watched her stand, watched the colors follow her and enjoyed the site of her naked body until clothes poured over her. Her back faced him. There was something wrong with the set of her shoulders, the way she moved. She almost seemed sad.

She turned and saw him watching her, her face flushed pink. "Are you happy, Grey?"

Something in her words pulled his mind back to what she said earlier, anything *he* wanted. Anger grated inside him. "Is that what this was about? Making me happy?"

"Yes. No! I mean, I wanted it, too."

"Why? Because you think you owe me something? Because I didn't let some man rape you?"

"No, that's not it... I didn't mean--"

He cut her off, the anger rolled over his skin. "For your magic then? A special thank you, here in your dreams where it doesn't matter? Where it doesn't touch your actual body?"

"No, stop it."

The colors in the air solidified and shattered into a million tiny pieces. Color rained onto the ground. Not a single shard touched his body, but he saw them stain Red's skin and pin pricks of blood appeared where they touched her face and arms. "If you want me out there you can have me. Anything you want Grey, it's yours."

"Is that what you think I want, Red? No, thank you. I prefer not to be given sex in exchange for services rendered. What would that make me, what would it make you?"

The words hit with the physical force of a slap. She flinched away, almost feeling the imprint of his hand on her cheek. Why was he doing this? Anger roared to life inside her. Colors whipped around her and flowed out of her to fill the air with reds, oranges, and blacks, angry color.

"Stop it, you stupid wolf. I told you I love you weeks ago. Why else would I have sex with you, let you touch me? You're the one who doesn't love me. You're the one who said you would always come and then abandoned me. You made me fight the void alone. You didn't even give me a chance to explain. You didn't trust me to keep my word. I don't care if you saved my life, I just love you." Her hands clenched into fists at her side and she blew out a breath.

Grey stared at her for a long time; so long, that she felt the anger shift into fear. The colors changed. Her fear took on a sickly green hue that swirled into the red and black.

"I love you, Grey. That's why I want to make you happy. I know I won't always get what I want. You don't have to love me. You don't have to marry me. You can have anything you want, my body, my magic, my life, anything. If that isn't enough, then you can leave."

Red turned and he lunged. This time he would not let her run. He caught her around the waist and pulled her hard against his body, her back to his chest. "Running again, Red?"

The air around them grew thick and heavy with dark colors: orange, red, pale yellow, dark brown, and black. Fearful colors. Red was afraid. He spread his hand over her abdomen, pulling her close against his body.

"You think I don't love you?" he asked.

"You've never said..."

"If I could never be a wolf again, never run, never hunt, and never play, if I had to give it all up to be human, it would be worth it to hold you. I love you, Red."

Everything about her melted and relaxed, she stood so close to him he was sure they breathed the same air. The colors dissolved and changed blues and purples caressed their skin.

"I love you, too."

"I know." To his surprise, she tensed again. Orange and brown crept into the purple. She was still frightened.

"I told Trevor I wouldn't marry him, just like I said I would," Red whispered.

"I believe you."

"I tried to convince you to stay. I tried with my words and then with my body, Grey, but you left anyway."

"I'm a stupid wolf." He mimicked her words from moments ago. Her body slumped in his arms.

"I shouldn't have said that. I'm sorry, Grey. You aren't stupid." Red made a frustrated noise and closed her eyes, shaking her head. "After what the Godmother told me about not hurting because I hurt, please forgive me."

"I forgive you, Red."

"Why did you leave?"

"I told you, I'm a stupid wolf." He leaned down and kissed her shoulder. "I saw you with the woodcutter. He touched you, Red."

She heard the rueful tone in his voice as his hand caressed her abdomen. His body felt warm and solid against her back. Her head leaned back against his shoulder.

"I was hurt and jealous, so I hurt you. I left you alone even though I knew you couldn't fight the void alone. Forgive me." Grey sighed against her skin.

"Of course. I love you." Her voice sounded breathless to her own ears.

"I love you, too, Red. Exactly the way you are. You don't have to do or be anything to keep me. You're stuck with me forever."

She turned and gazed up into his face, relief flowed through her body. The colors in the air turned soft and warm: peach and purple, pink and violet.

He kissed her. She tasted of golden sunshine and purple air. To his surprise, she pulled away.

"You still owe me an apology," she frowned up at him. "What you said was mean. I didn't make love to you because–"

"I'm sorry," Grey cut her off he did not want to hear her call herself the words he had implied. "Forgive me?"

Her face flushed. "I forgive you, Grey." She laughed a little as he turned her back to him again and pulled her against his chest. He spread his hand over her stomach again.

"I wasn't finished," he muttered.

His lips trailed up her neck, and nibbled her ear. "I promise, Red, I can make you forget every mean thing I said before morning."

84

GREY

Grey rose and stretched forward onto his front legs and shook. His fur settled over his body. No one else appeared to be awake yet. As he picked his way across the wolf pile, one of the puppies stood and wagged its tail in hopes of a game. Grey growled at the puppy. The young one tucked his tail and dropped back down to the ground. To soften the blow, Grey licked his face. It was not the puppy's fault. He needed to see Red.

Now.

He needed to tell her here in reality what he expressed last night in their dreams. He left through the small flap in the door that carpenters built to accommodate a puppy's body. He did not care about the tight squeeze.

Red was right, he was a stupid wolf. No wonder she felt so frightened the day before. How could he have never said the words?

Humans needed words.

Red needed his words. Even he, more wolf than man, appreciated hearing the words from Red's lips.

No, that was not true. He adored hearing her say she loved him.

Last night he drew the phrase from her repeatedly while he touched her, kissed her and loved her. He grinned a wolf grin remembering the night before as he ran through the woods.

He wanted to touch her, with his human hands and say he loved her, and hear she loved him with human ears. He needed to tell her they would be married.

Ask her, he should ask her, but he already knew the answer.

He loped through the forest toward the river. He should have changed first, but he liked to move as the wolf. He could sneak into her village. It was early enough. He would change at her house, see her home for the first time, and tell her he loved her. Soon they would be married and he would wake up every morning to her face, her voice, her body next to his. Life would be perfect.

85

MELODY

Melody smiled and hummed as she cooked breakfast. Bread baked in the oven, eggs fried on the stove, and ham heated in the skillet. She cooked enough to feed a small army, because her home was filled with half a wolf pack. Nanna sent the food home with them the previous night. She smiled at Tara as she entered through the back door, wrapped in a huge blanket. Her cousin grabbed a pile of clothes and ducked into the washroom.

All morning she saw hints of colors from the corner of her eye. Thin strands that danced out of her view before she could reach them. The magic grew stronger every minute she spent with Grey.

"Good walk?" Melody asked as Tara emerged dressed.

"Yeah," Tara grinned.

Anna, and Sarah, a girl of about ten who changed between puppy and child as easy as breathing, entered the room, both human. They flopped in chairs and Melody sat plates in front of them. It felt good to cook for people, felt so good not to wake up alone. Within minutes, her father and two more young girls joined them. The puppies tumbled in after that, four of them, yipping and playing as they entered the kitchen.

Warmth from the stove and the bodies in the room seeped into Melody. She grinned and laughed as she served food. Once she piled everyone's plate full of food Melody sat down and puppy-Jenna jumped into her lap. She grinned as she took in the scene around the table. Her world made sense again.

"Good dreams?" Tara teased.

Melody flushed and dropped her gaze to the puppy in her lap. She fed her bits of egg and ham. Her family was together, except Grey, but he would be here soon. She could feel him getting closer, but maybe that was her imagination. Clothes lay folded on the chair near the back door for him.

She had puppies. The thought made her laugh a little. All the time she spent courting a wolf and now her house overflowed with puppies. She heard her father laugh at something Sarah said and she smiled at the puppy in her lap. Grey loved her. Everything would be all right.

A sharp knock at the front door drew everyone's attention. Tara rose and left the table to answer the door. Surprised male voices could be heard from the front of the house.

"We need to speak to Mr. Saltman and Miss Melody." Melody could make out the village elders voice to her surprise.

Melody rose and put the little puppy on the ground where it began to play with one of its friends. As they left the kitchen, her father took her hand and tucked it into his arm. He smiled down at her. Tara stood, filling the doorway to prevent anyone from seeing into the house. She glanced over her shoulder. "Cousin Melody, there are some *men* here to see you and your father."

Melody swallowed and straightened her shoulders. She attempted to interpret the message that Tara sent her and prepare herself for what waited on the other side of the door. Despite that, she was not prepared when Tara stepped aside and she and her father walked out onto the front porch together. Tara followed her out. A group of men waited for her there, including Trevor.

"You!" Her father dropped her hand and lunged forward only to be caught by two of the men. They held him back for a moment as the elder began to speak.

"Now, Timothy, wait for one moment. We'd like to take a few minutes to talk to you and your daughter in private. We want to work this out in a civilized way."

"Tara is my family, she can stay," Melody said. Her voice did not break and that surprised her.

"Well now, Miss Melody, some serious accusation have been made, both by you and against you and we need to work this situation out as best we can."

Her father strained against the men who held him. "He tried to rape my daughter, there's nothing to work out." Despite his words, he stopped struggling, pulling away from the men. Tara touched her hand and Melody stared at her cousin her eyes wide, she wondered if her face reflected the sick feeling in her stomach. Her father came to stand on her other side.

"Who has made accusations against my daughter?"

"Well, now," said the elder.

Melody wished he would stop saying that in his slow solemn voice. She suspected the words were meant to calm. Instead, they grated against her skin. She closed her eyes for the briefest moment and found only thin strands of colors nothing she could use. Grey was not close enough yet. He would come though, soon, she begged, please come soon.

"For a few months now there have been rumors about

Melody entertaining men, while you were living at the cabin, Timothy. It seems that some of these rumors might have been true."

"What?" Melody gasped the word out past the sheer horror that built in her chest. "I never–"

The elder raised his hand to cut off her protestation. "This man here is from Briar Creek and he says he spent time with you, Miss Melody, in the private sense."

"Get the healer," her father demanded. "They can confirm what Melody says."

Could they? Did dreams change a person's body? A tickle of fear crept along her back and added to the pressure in her chest. Still, she managed to keep her voice calm as she said with complete honesty. "I have no idea who that man is."

"Well now, we all know you have a history of not being the most modest woman in town, Miss Melody." For the first time she noticed that Milo stood among the group of men, her face flushed hot. "We've all seen that with our own eyes."

"Why are you doing this?" Melody asked. Tara's fingers wrapped around her hand and she felt stronger for the contact. The Godmother's words about pain echoed in her mind.

"Well now, it seems you accused Mr. Branch of trying to rape you. That is a serious accusation and the punishment is serious as well. He could be banned from Varin and Briar Creek. It's only fair to hear both sides of the story. Mr. Branch is a valuable and productive member of the community. He tells the story somewhat differently."

"I'm sure he does." Her father's voice sounded more like Grey's growl. "We have a witness who saw the events that took place. We have the healer's word that saw Melody and Mr. Grey yesterday and treated their wounds from the 'encounter' they had with him. What could you possibly have to argue with those things?"

"Where are these witnesses?" Trevor asked, his voice innocent, a tiny smile tugging at one side of his lips. How could she have found him handsome? How did she ever think she could be happy as his wife? "How could I have injured them if I myself am unharmed?"

"Mr. Grey is on his way here now. The healer will have to be fetched from Briar Creek. As for you, dark magic heals, Brother," Tara snarled the words and Melody saw the wolf in her cousin.

Trevor's eyes darkened from blue to almost black.

"Well now, I think we can settle this in a way that will please everyone without having to involve witnesses and holding a whole trial," said the elder, his voice strained now as he looked from Trevor to Melody. "Trevor has never been anything but a blessing to this community. He's done a great deal to help us."

"And Melody isn't?" Her father's voice made it more accusation than question. "Who has been feeding the community baked goods all winter? Who's given away clothing, books, furniture, blankets and anything else people needed since the fire?"

Melody looked at her father in surprise. She did not know he knew about all those things.

The elder ignored the words and went on as if her father never spoke, but the words meant the world to Melody.

"Melody, we all know you and love you from your childhood. I know things have been difficult since your mother died and it's natural for you to get a little wild..."

"She isn't wild, but I am," came Grey's growling voice.

Melody felt Tara stiffen beside her. She relaxed. He was here, she did not look over her shoulder, did not need to, he would come to her. "I'm the witness. I saw this man try to rape her. I saw her fight him, and tell him no. I saw him hit her and scratch her. I intervened and together we went to her grandmother's cottage and stayed there until her father arrived."

He came to stand behind her. One of his hands rested on her hip and she relaxed further. Colors lit the air around them with vivid beauty. She saw them and felt them at the same moment. Had they been sneaking up all along? She must have been too distracted to notice.

"I was provoked, she tempted me, always kissing and touching but never finishing what she started. It was not my fault." Trevor's mask slipped, his eyes too dark, but his voice remained confident. "A man has needs and limits. Look at her now, how she allows that stranger to put his hands all over her."

The elder held up his hand. "We aren't here to decide on punishment or fault. We want to offer a solution. Everyone knows that Trevor and Melody have been courting. I suggest we have them married by the town priestess this afternoon and then the problem will be solved. Trevor will have his needs met and Melody will not be so..."

"Over my dead body!" Her father stepped forward again. To Melody's surprise Grey dropped his hand from her and placed a restraining hand on her father's shoulder.

"That isn't necessary, Timothy," Grey said.

Her father turned and met his eye. She could almost see the communication that passed between her father and Grey. Her father stood a little straighter and nodded his head.

"Melody is already betrothed," her father said, as he turned back to the men. "She and Mr. Grey have plans to marry."

Melody's fingers tightened convulsively on Tara's hand. She looked at Grey and he met her gaze and raised an eyebrow. "Yes, we wanted to plan things a bit more but, if the village elder insists I suppose we could marry today," she said.

Grey nodded, his eyes bright and clear, and she felt the weight lift from her chest.

"Well now, I suppose that's not necessary." The elder glanced nervously at Trevor. Melody examined the colors around the men. So much red and black, she remembered how those colors overwhelmed her the day before. They took on a life of their own. The colors seemed to flow off Trevor and around the other men. She moved closer to Grey, pulling Tara with her. These men needed help, the way she needed Grey to help her yesterday except they did not realize it.

Grey stretched his arm and she slid into his embrace without hesitation. She fit against him; she belonged here. The anger around the men intensified.

"Mr. Grey, are you aware of the fact that Melody has entertained men in her home without proper supervision?" asked Milo.

With her mind, Melody reached out and pushed away the blacks and reds from the men as Milo spoke.

"Melody's past has little bearing on my decision to marry her," snarled Grey, his hand caressing her side. She almost laughed at the sound of her birth name coming from his mouth it sounded so wrong. Here at his side she did not even think of herself as Melody anymore, she was Red.

"So you're okay with accepting used goods?" asked the man she did not know.

She felt Grey growl against her side. She pushed harder at the black that resisted her. Was Trevor holding it here? A puppy appeared at her feet and growled at the men outside the door. Her father bent and scooped the puppy into his arms. It swiped its pink tongue over his cheek. Turning back to the door, the puppy snarled again.

The tension around her evaporated.

She smiled and as she did, the colors responded to her efforts and the black began to fade. Melody leaned into Grey a little more and his fingers caressed her side again.

"No one has ever *used* me," she said, while twisting blue into the air around the men on her porch. "Trevor, I told you that day at Rose Cottage that I don't love you. I cannot marry a man I don't love. I also told you, on that day, that you do not love me, even if you think you do. You cannot *force* love, Trevor."

The men began to relax. She pushed harder at the blacks and reds, sending them away. She pulled in blue, green, purple, and soft gentle yellow. The colors soothed not only the men but her father and cousin as well.

Grey's arm tightened around her. Could he see her magic, or feel it? She would have to ask him later. She dared a quick smile up into his eyes.

"So gentlemen, unless you plan to spend more time insulting my daughter, and personally I would suggest against that course of action, then I would ask you to leave," her father said, still holding the puppy in a restraining grip.

"Yes, I think that you're right. Miss Melody, we do apologize for any insult,"-Grey and her father made derisive noises together- "we might have caused you. I assure you we meant no harm, only to clear matters up between you and Mr. Branch," The village elder said in a consolatory voice.

"As to that," Grey spoke, dropping his arm from around Melody and taking a step forward. Several of the men, including Milo backed up. "I suggest you leave this town, Mr. Branch. If you and I meet again I will not be held responsible for my actions."

86

Grey

Grey fidgeted in the chair. He stayed human since he followed Tara's scent to Red's back door this morning. There, one of the young wolf girls let him in and fed him some bread and he found clothes waiting.

He needed to run. Humanity began to grate and he wanted to be outside. Red was the only thing worth this torture.

The group reformed at Rose Cottage, minus Red's father who returned to the mine. During the day Grey tried to steal a single moment alone with Red. He found the task impossible. When he stood by her side this morning and promised to marry her, he expected to earn some privacy privileges. If anything, the opposite proved true.

She had not avoided him.

In fact, several times she had tried to get alone with him but they had been interrupted by one thing or another. Everyone wanted to talk about the wedding, or who would live where and with whom.

He did not care where anyone else lived, as long as he woke up every day with Red.

He rose and walked to Red. "Come for a walk with me?"

She smiled up at him with relief on her face. "Yes."

He extended his hand and she entwined her fingers with his. Pulling her to her feet, he enjoyed the way her body moved. He ignored the giggles of two young girls who sat nearby.

Rose watched her granddaughter. "Please, be careful."

"Of course, Nanna," smiled Red. "I doubt Trevor's around anymore. Not after this morning."

"Don't underestimate the Brotherhood, Melody," said Andrew from the other side of the room.

"Nothing will hurt her," said Grey. He did not look at any of the other people in the room. He could only see Red, smiling, telling the entire room she trusted him to protect her after telling the entire town this morning that she would marry him, that day if they wanted. He wished the elder had pushed; he could have slept with her in his arms tonight.

"I'm sure it won't. See that nothing hurts you either, Grey," said Rose. The words warmed him. The older woman smiled at him as if his existence somehow pleased her. He felt more welcome in her home than he had ever been anywhere in his life.

Hand in hand, they left the cottage and Grey blew out a deep breath. He let the crisp early evening air wash over him. A breeze blew and Red shivered.

"Where's your cloak?"

"It was hot inside. I forgot to put it on."

He put his arm around her shoulder and she pressed herself against him. He smiled and led her through the garden and out onto the forest path. As they walked under the trees, he gazed at the shadows cast by the moonlight through the branches. Patterns of light and dark danced on the path around them. Even in this low light, he could still see the forest's colors, thanks to Red.

The path was familiar to them both so they walked with relaxed easy steps. How many times had he crept along as he watched Red walk this path?

"I love you."

Her words drew him out of his thoughts. "I know."

She gave a little bark of laughter and pulled away from him, gently punching his side. "That's not what you're supposed to say."

He caught her fist and pulled her hard against his chest. "Should I tell you you're beautiful? That I love the way you move, that you can seduce me from across a room just by looking at me."

He felt her arms twine around his waist and her head rested on his chest. "That's much better. Really, across a room?"

He chuckled. "Yes." He leaned down to kiss the top of her head. "Thank you."

"For what? You have saved my life, twice, rescued me from Trevor, what have I done for you?"

"You kept me human, you gave me colors, and you love me."

She laughed again. "You got it backwards, you gave me the colors, remember."

He pulled back enough that he could lean down and kiss her properly. "I love you, Red."

Nothing else existed anywhere but he and Red on the path in the woods. Her mouth felt soft and hot under his and he knew that a long engagement was out of the question.

She jerked back and glanced over her shoulder. "We have to get back to the cottage."

Terror ran through her voice. He felt the shift in power at the same time he heard the footstep. "Run, Red. I'll be behind you."

She took off and he backed into the brush, pulling his clothes off as fast as he could. Grey changed, feeling the pain race over his body like lightning and fade just as fast. He shot through the brush onto the trail.

A solid form collided with his side.

"You stupid fool." Trevor caught him in the ribs. The surprise knocked the breath from him, and for a moment, he lay defenseless. "Do you think you have enough magic to hold her, to keep me away? She is mine. I got to her first, and you cannot have her, wolf."

87

Melody

Melody turned at the same moment Trevor swung the axe over his head. She did not hesitate when Grey said to run. The knowledge that he did not follow occurred within a few steps and she turned to find him. Her eyes widened and her mouth opened in a silent protest. She forced her lungs to draw air despite the fear that gripped her chest.

"No!" she screamed, rushing back toward Grey. She threw her body over his. Searing pain hit her shoulder and burned down her arm and chest. The axe ripped through her body. She fell onto Grey. He shifted under her. If she stayed here, pinning him down, he would be an easy target. She pushed up on her left arm, her right hung uselessly at her side; pain rippled down the useless limb, but seemed to lessen. It retreated further from her with each heartbeat.

"Melody, you idiot. Look what you made me do!" Trevor knelt next to her. She saw the blood pool around the hand that held her off the ground, saw it soak into Grey's coat. Her blood? The pain vanished. A memory. She felt weak and tired. All that blood, so much blood, it could not be hers.

Trevor touched her. She should fight him, but she could not force herself to move. Grey squirmed out from under her and she collapsed face first onto the ground. She felt Trevor roll her over, heard Grey snarl.

"Shut up, wolf. This is your fault more than mine. She belonged to me first. You came and tried to take her away." He put a hand on her shoulder. She felt him fall away from her, heard flesh rip.

"Do you want her to die?" Trevor demanded.

She could not be dying. She did not even hurt. She tried to move, tried to lift her hand toward Grey to let him know she was all right. She could not feel her body's response. The colors, they could help her. She tried to find the colors she knew should be there if Grey was near her.

Nothing, like the nothingness in her dreams. It crept around her and enclosed her. It was getting hard to breathe.

"Grey," she gasped. He always made the void leave. Her body felt heavy. How could her body be heavy when she lay on her back? She drew another breath and her chest felt weighted, was something on top of her? She forced her body to pull in air.

It meant nothing. She did not need to be afraid. Grey loved her. He would come and save her.

She heard him whine, but the colors did not appear. She heard him howl, the sound long and low, she felt a hand on her chest, one on her back. Feeling faded, vision faded and she understood.

She was dying. That was why Grey could not force the void away. The void did not surround her. She fell into it.

88

Grey

Grey howled. They had not traveled far from the cottage and he knew the others would hear him. They would come. He hoped they would arrive in time.

The woodcutter abandoned his weapon, dropped it to the forest floor as he knelt beside Red's bleeding form. The first time he touched her, Grey had not been able to stop himself from attacking. He sank his teeth into the man's shoulder and threw his weight to pull him away from Red. However, the woodcutter said he would help her, and for some reason Grey believed him. Red's right arm hung almost severed by the woodcutters blow. Blood covered everything.

He watched helpless and guarded as the woodcutter put a hand on either side of Red's shoulder. He watched power flow out of his hands and into the gaping wound. She lay dying and her blood stained the forest floor around them. He could feel her magic fade with each new spurt of blood.

Throwing his head back, he howled again and heard the sound of feet in the distance. Humans and wolves burst through the forest around them and appeared onto the trail.

Rose stumbled as she comprehended the scene in front of her. "No!"

Grey shoved back the panic he felt at the woman's reaction.

Grey moved forward and watched more closely to what

Trevor was doing. He growled low in his throat. Everyone stopped around them.

"If you want her alive, back off, wolf." Trevor snarled the words without taking his eyes off Red's shoulder where his hands struggled to hold her flesh together.

Rose muttered something and moved toward them. "I can help her, too." She knelt and put her hands on Red, not pushing the woodcutter's hands away. Trevor glanced up at Rose in surprise, then back at Grey.

"You didn't kill her?" Trevor asked.

Grey growled again. His lip curled over his teeth.

"Of course, you saved her. How foolish of me. A hero." His voice dripped with disgust. "I save Melody's life and she's mine, wolf."

Grey snarled and fought back the urge to lunge at the man's throat. He might save Red, but he would never have her. Magic still flowed off the woodcutter, and now magic flowed from Rose to Red as well. It was not going to be enough. Blood still left her body too fast. At least he knew her heart still beat, but with each pump, more blood left her. Still he had seen enough animals die, killed enough to know that Rose and the woodcutter would not be able to save her.

He threw back his head and howled again. This time a sound filled with grief and pain.

As the sound faded, soft light filled the area reflecting off the trees and ground. At the edge of his sight, a swirl of magic began at the ground and took the shape of an oval tall enough for a human to step through. He heard Rose gasp and the wolves behind him began to shift and whimper.

The Godmother appeared through the magic swirl and it collapsed behind her.

"Godmother!" Rose cried out relief in her voice.

Grey gazed up at her. "*Can you save her? Please?*"

The godmother peered into his eyes and nodded her head. "Step back, please. Rose, I can save your granddaughter."

Rose hesitated a second, but stood, her hands dripping Red's blood. Trevor scowled and remained on his knees, his magic trying to seal the wound. "Why would you help me?"

"I don't intend to help you, Brother. I'm helping the girl, and the wolf. He said please."

The Godmother waved her hand and Trevor flew to the side, crashing into a tree. Grey glanced at the woodcutter and saw his eyes were closed. He turned back to watch Melea kneel and place her hand above the wound and it vanished completely. No more blood left Red's body. Still, Red's eyes did not open. Her chest hardly rose and fell, and her breath remained too shallow. She did not move and even in Grey's limited vision, she was far too pale.

"Is she alive?" Rose pleaded.

"She lives," Melea said, but her tone said more than her words.

Grey whined, "*Where is she?"*

"You said you could save her." Rose cried. Grey watched as Tara took the older woman in her arm and held her as she sobbed

Melea turned to her and said, "I'm sorry, Rose. She has gone to a place I can't reach. Her body is healed, but her spirit is too far to know it. She has to decide to come back."

"Can you send me to her?"

"If I do, you, Grey, might end up trapped there with her. You might not return."

Grey looked at Red and then back at the Godmother. "*She's worth it.*"

Melea nodded. "Lie down."

Grey lay on the ground, now soaked in Red's blood. He felt it seep through his coat and stick to his skin. He laid his head on Red's stomach and closed his eyes.

89

Red and Grey

He expected to be in the meadow, but instead he found himself alone on a vast beach. Sand stretched in every direction around him, except where the ocean washed against it. No seaweed littered the beach, no shells, and no crabs scurried in the sand. Nothing he would expect to find at the sea. In fact, there was no sign that anything lived here at all. The sky looked like it did in the last moments of light, when the sun passed the horizon, but its light still reached upward.

Grey could find nothing to mark his position. No rocks or driftwood, not even footprints on the sand. Light flowed pale and shallow around him, and the ocean lapped at the expanse of sand.

He could not find Red anywhere.

Finally, he saw a pale rainbow of color that seemed to come from within him. It flowed around him and away from him.

His eyes followed the colors as they snaked their way to the ocean. In the distance, down the beach, far away from the shore, he saw something. He ran. He needed more speed. Two legs moved too slowly. Never breaking stride he changed to his four-legged form and moved even faster. Color disappeared, but he could still see the magic. It seemed to fill the space between him and the spot in the water he sought. By the time he reached his destination, he could see the spot was just a tiny raft, hardly big enough to hold the curled up form of the woman who laid on it. Red.

The raft drifted further out into the ocean. If she disappeared on the water he would never find her. He plunged into the tepid water. He found it easier to swim in than he expected. There was no life here either, no seaweed to tangle his legs, nor fish moving past him. The magic grew thicker the closer he came to Red. It continued to flow between them, connecting them. He moved steadily toward the raft. It felt like forever before he reached it. When he did, he searched for a rope, a branch, anything he could grab with his teeth to pull her back to shore.

There was nothing. Her eyes stayed closed, and her body did not move. He swam beside the raft and knew there was nothing he could do in this form. If he were human, maybe, but as a wolf...

He willed himself to change, unlike in their dreams it hurt, the way it always did in reality. He slipped under the water as the pain hit him. He fought not to draw water into his lungs. Swimming as a human worked differently from swimming as a wolf and it took him time to find the surface. Breaking the surface, he drew a deep breath and searched for the raft. It drifted away from him and he swam to reach it. His fingers closed over the edge and he pulled it toward him.

The colors whirled and whipped around, they danced in the still air above their heads. He got the impression they were glad he found Red.

"Red, wake up. Open your eyes."

She did not move.

Grey pulled himself onto the tiny craft, water washed up around Red, covering her dress, and leaving it clinging to her body. The raft moved precariously under them, he was not sure it could hold them both. He reached out and touched her face. Her skin was warm and soft.

She responded to his touch, her eyes flying open. "Grey, what are you doing here? No, no, no, you can't be here, you can't be dead. I tried to save you." She shook her head back and forth, her eye wide with unshed tears.

"You did save me, Red. I'm not dead," Grey assured her.

"Then why are you here? How are you here? I died!"

"No, you didn't. The Godmother came. She healed you."

Melody searched his face and saw a hint of desperation in his eyes. She inspected the tiny raft they sat on, it barely held them afloat and water lapped at her ankles. She saw the colors flow between and around them, purple, and sickly yellow green. Passion and fear, his or hers, or both, she could not tell.

She shook her head, unable to believe his words. "It's too late," she said, as she surveyed the ocean around her. She could not see the land, what direction should she take to go back to the shore? "I'm lost. I can't get back."

"Then I'll go with you," Grey promised and his fingers touched her hand.

Her throat tightened, she looked into his eyes. "I love you, more than life itself. I would gladly die for you." The raft rocked and more water soaked into her clothes. "You shouldn't be here. I wanted you to live, don't you understand, Grey? I love you."

"Why do you think I came, Red?" He released her hand and reached over to stroke a finger down her cheek. "I've been in love with you since the first time you wrapped your arms around me in our dreams. I would gladly die for you, too. If you're taking this journey I'll take it with you. "

He leaned toward her, his lips were a breath away from hers and the raft tilted dangerously. He jerked away to compensate and the raft shifted again. They both held still, drenched in sea water as the waves settled under them.

"This raft can't carry us both," Grey admitted. "Not for any great distance."

Melody bit her lower lip and shook her head. "No, it isn't meant for both of us. I'm not even sure it's ready for me."

"Come home with me." Grey said, he took her fingers in his hand and lifted them to his lips. "We don't have to go anywhere, Red."

"I would love to have more time with you in the living

world." Melody reached out and touched his face. He turned into her touch and she closed her eyes. "But, Grey, how do we get back? I don't know where the shore is."

"Open your eyes," a familiar female voice encouraged her.

90

MELODY

Melody opened her eyes and sucked in a deep breath. She saw trees around her and felt the weight of Grey's head on her abdomen. She looked down as he opened his eyes.

"Grey," she croaked and tried to move, but her body felt too heavy. It held her down. She was not dead. Death had not felt like this. Grey was not dead either, his amber gaze bored into hers and she read love and relief in his eyes.

"Relax, child, you were healed, but very fast, it takes a great deal out of a body to be so grievously injured and healed so quickly. Not to mention the blood you lost. Your body has to replace that itself. It will take days for you to fully recover." The Godmother's voice flowed like a warm cloak, covering her and she relaxed back onto the ground. Pine needles and something sticky and wet clung to her neck.

She scanned the area and saw Nanna, supported by Tara. Tears streaked both their cheeks. She glanced the other way and saw a large reddish brown and black wolf surrounded by puppies of various sizes and colors, and knew that was Andrew. Her gaze fell on Trevor.

Meldoy gasped, but Grey had already seen the danger. Trevor was moving. She saw magic all around, felt the colors. Grey lunged for Trevor and she pushed him with a blue current of magic. He flew to where Trevor stood, his axe raised ready to throw.

As Grey's jaw locked around Trevor's arm, she sent fiery red into the skin with his teeth and heard Trevor's enraged howl of pain.

The axe fell onto the forest floor. Trevor swung his arm, dislodging Grey's teeth. He threw Grey off and she heard him hit the ground with a thud. Melody cried out.

The Godmother turned, and Melody once again watched enchanted by the rich, thick waves of golden power braided around her. All the color from everyone in this small part of the forest paled in comparison to her. She felt Nanna and Tara as they moved to her side. They lifted her into a sitting position, one supporting her on either side. Her head swam and her vision clouded. She would have fallen back to the ground except for their support.

Magic filled the woods. She could not see it but she felt it move around her. Her vision cleared and Trevor knelt before the Godmother, his hands behind his back bound by braids of gold and silver magic.

"You have proved to be an interesting man, Brother Trevor." The Godmother tilted her head. "You never wanted to hurt her. It's a small thing, but it is something."

She turned to Melody.

"What do you want to happen to him? If I were to place his life in your hands, what would you do with it?"

Melody stared at her. Could his life really be in her hands? This man killed her mother, tried to rape her, tried to kill Nanna and Grey. Yesterday, in the middle of her anger she wanted him dead, wanted to kill him herself. Did she still? "I want him to not hurt anyone again."

"Agreed. Should his life be forfeit?" The Godmother's voice sounded harder now, less like a gentle wash of water and more like a raging river. "He killed your mother. I can tell you that in his long life he performed many other acts of violence and destruction."

"I know." Melody licked her lips, watching where Trevor crouched in front of the Godmother. From the corner of her eye she could see Grey struggling to stand.

"Is Grey alright?" she asked, ignoring the question. She sent a strand of golden magic to Grey and watched as his muscles relaxed. The Godmother laughed, the musical sound filled the forest around them.

"Bruises, love. He'll be fine. Back to this, though." The Godmother nodded to Trevor.

Pain drove people to hurt others. What kind of pain had Trevor endured that made him hurt the people around him the way he did? Three thousand years was a long time to accumulate pain.

"Is there a way to let him live, but keep him from hurting anyone else?" Melody asked.

"There is *always* a way. Is that what you would choose? Would you give up vengeance in favor of justice and mercy?"

Would she? Grey moved toward her and she thought about what he said. She did have flaws, she could be selfish and self-centered, but she would not add hate to those. She would not become like Trevor, giving out pain and death because she hurt.

"Yes, let him live, but don't let him hurt anyone again."

The Godmother smiled and Trevor vanished. "That choice shows wisdom and compassion, something not common in one as young and as powerful as you." The woman knelt on the ground and everything around her seemed to freeze. The wolves stood like statues, she could feel Nanna's hands and Tara's as they supported her, but they held so very still. Grey stood next to her now, his body leaning against hers. She tried to lift her arm to his shoulder but it took too much effort. Instead, she wrapped her fingers around his leg, the only place she could reach.

"You have more power than anyone around you imagines. As much as any Godmother, but...no, you're not ready for that yet. In time you'll have to be." Melody shuddered and opened her mouth to argue but the Godmother laughed. "Don't worry child. I don't have the ability to make anyone a Godmother. Only *one* Ancient could do that. Besides, I would never condemn anyone to this life. "

She seemed so sad that Melody reached out and touched her hand. The Godmother smiled and shook her head. Then, despite the blood and dirt caked on her hand the woman took it in her own and kissed her palm. " *You* are one of *my* children now. Such irony. You can summon me whenever there is great need. Simply rub this place on your hand and say my name."

Grey thrust his nose against where the godmother held her hand and licked them both.

"Yes, Grey, you too are my child." She smiled at them, and her face took on a strange distant expression. Her voice became rough and her eyes lost focus. "There's a war coming. You both have a part to play. Keep each other safe. The war..."

Melody thought about how much Melea must have lost in the first war.

"You may win the war," whispered the Godmother at last, then her eyes focused.

Melody wondered if Melea knew what she had confessed. She began to rise and Melody tightened her hand around the Godmother's fingers.

"Wait, how do I contact you if there isn't a great need? What if I want to invite you to dinner? " The Godmother stared down at her startled. "I know what it feels like to be lonely."

The woman smiled and crouched, she placed a hand on Grey's head and one on Melody's. "Yes, Red, I suppose you do. Whisper my name to the wind and I'll come for a visit whenever you wish, if none of my other children are in peril."

Melody smiled and the Godmother rose. A portal of magic appeared in the woods and the woman stepped through and disappeared. Time began to move around them again.

91

Grey

Red lay tucked into her own bed. Grey had carried her home. No sooner did the Godmother vanish than he felt a change inside, a shift and adjustment that felt as much magical as physical. He heard her voice in his head. *One last gift for you, Grey.*

He understood, and with a thought, he became human. No pain, no effort, no need for food to trigger the change. He found his discarded clothes and carried Red home, both of them covered in her blood and debris from the forest floor. Her father met them halfway across the bridge. He never attempted to take her, but he hovered close and watched her as they walked. Grey never heard how he knew to come for them, perhaps the Godmother sent for him.

Red felt weak. Tara and her grandmother helped her bathe in the house's washroom. Grey scrubbed her blood off in bitter cold water from the river. He did not care. He wanted to be back with her, make sure she stayed where she was supposed to, and to do that he needed to be clean.

They were all gathered in the house, most of them, including the puppies, crowded into her bedroom. She looked pale and thin on the bed. The wound was healed, not a trace remained, but her skin appeared ashen, and her black hair seemed too dark against her skin.

He sat beside her and held her hand. Her thumb stroked the backs of his fingers occasionally.

"As soon as you're strong we can talk to the priestess. You can be married within the year. This can be your house and I'll move to the cabin." Her father talked so fast Grey struggled to keep up with his thoughts. Red yawned next to him. He did not think she was aware of her father words, but to his surprise, she spoke.

"Not so long," she muttered, after another yawn. "I want to marry soon."

"Tomorrow, then," Rose said. "The priestess can come and witness the handfasting tomorrow here at the house. This spring we will have a huge wedding feast for the entire family. I already sent word to Ellen to bring the purple dress. The one you wanted, love."

"Yes, after this morning, the entire village knows about your betrothal to Grey. The priestess will be happy to come tomorrow, if you feel up to it. Once you're handfasted, Grey can move in. Do you want to live here? I'll move to the cabin near the mine, maybe take a few of the puppies with me for company." Her father continued. Grey suspected the man's adrenaline still raced in response to the near loss of his daughter, again.

Red looked up at him, blinking in an effort to keep her eyes open.

"I think we can decide that later," said Grey, stroking her hand.

People began to leave; some of them took puppies to give Red a chance to rest. At last, only Rose and Timothy remained. Grey leaned over and kissed Red's forehead. The idea of another night away from her made him ache, he stood and her hand tightened on his.

"Don't leave me, Grey." Everyone paused. "Please," she whispered. "I don't want to be alone."

Grey turned from her pleading face to her father. He watched the older man shrug as he gazed down at his daughter's pale face and the way her hand clenched Grey's. "Become a wolf, and then you can stay here with her."

Rose made a noise in her throat. From the expression on her face, Grey suspected it was a laugh. Timothy did not know he could become human at will. Timothy left the room and Rose met his gaze with a hard stare. "Red is weak, she needs to sleep."

"Of course, Rose. I would never risk hurting her."

The old woman's face softened into a smile. "I know that. Red loves you, too."

"I know." Grey wondered if Rose realized she addressed her granddaughter by the name he gave her. "I won't touch her until she's strong." Not outside of their dreams anyway, he thought to himself.

Rose nodded and left the room. When he turned back to Red, her eyes were closed. He took his clothes off and changed, jumped onto the bed and stretched out next to her. She curved toward him and put her arm around his shoulder. Her fingers dug into his fur and she breathed out his name. He relaxed and closed his eyes, his body touching hers.

They slept.

92

THE BROTHER

"What have you done to me?" His voice sounded too deep; it contained an inhuman growl. His body felt too big. The Godmother stood in front of him, but he was too weak to touch her. Her magic pinned him down.

"All I did was to make what's on the outside match

what's inside." She spoke with utter calm. He roared and the sound echoed off the walls around him.

"This place, this castle, it's been placed out of time, as long as you stay within the castle walls the world will proceed around you without touching you."

"How dare you imprison me?!"

"I could have taken your life. Red granted you mercy."

Red?

No! That was wrong. The girls name was Melody. Not Red.

That girl was not Red.

The Godmother lied.

Fury washed over him. He struggled to stand, his body moved differently, it felt more awkward and he almost fell over his own legs. He glared down at his hands and saw the huge paws with curved almost talon-like claws. Long brown hair covered his hands and arms, thick black skin formed pads on his fingers and palm. Finally, he gained his legs and lunged forward. The magic released him but his own body betrayed him. His legs bent in an unfamiliar way and his weight was not distributed the way it used to be. Could he walk on two legs, or should he try moving on all four? He tripped over his own limbs and fell hard onto the grey stones at his feet. Cold seeped from the stones through his coat into his skin.

"You are not purely evil, Brother Trevor. I know you. I saw you save the child. I saw you withhold your hand from the old woman's family. I watched you try to keep Red alive. So, like her, I'm giving you a chance. Stay here and learn what it means to be human again, to have compassion and to care for someone other than yourself. Your needs will be met and time will wait for you. If you learn what you need to, then your human form will return and you can leave here and live the life of an average human. If you never learn...well, that's your choice, Brother Trevor. The castle can remain your home."

He roared again but she stepped back and vanished through a portal.

"I wish you luck, Brother." Her voice drifted back to him.

He let the fury take over. Trevor used his giant paws and

claws to rip at the stone floor below him. He left long gouges, marring the smooth floor. He roared and cursed, then roared again. Gaining his feet, he stalked around on his hind legs, using his front paws to destroy anything he could find. Through it, images flashed through his mind, pictures dulled by a thousand years. Red?

The Godmother must be lying.

Not Red, not *his* Red.

He pulled down thick purple drapes and shredded them. Pale sunlight filtered through a huge glass window.

"Godmothers lie!" he roared.

He used a wooden chair, thick with scroll work on the back and legs, to shatter the window. He ignored the shards of glass that pricked his feet as he tore the chair too pieces. His claws left nothing but splinters and scraps of fabric.

As he destroyed, some part of his brain recognized that he occupied a huge bedroom with a large four-posted bed, thick with soft linens and piled with pillows. He attacked this next, shredding the pillows. Feathers filled the air and fell thick on the floor. He shredded the blankets and sheets, then tore the mattress to pieces.

He raged for hours, leaving the floor a mess with thick piles of shredded fabric, shattered glass and splintered wood. His paws bled from a dozen different cuts.

At last, exhaustion took over. He collapsed onto his side on a pile of stuffing that had once been the mattress. Curling into a ball on his side, he slept.

About the Author

Christine Brant is a Seattle author who lives with her husband, three children, two cats, and Bob, the Ball Python. She won the Surrey International Storytellers Award in 2007 with her short story "A Decade of Scottsdale". In her spare time, when not herding cats and kids, she loves to read and gaze out her window at the Puget Sound. Visit her online at www.christinebrant.com.